THE 49TH MYSTIC

THE 49TH MYSTIC

TED DEKKER

THORNDIKE PRESS
A part of Gale, a Cengage Company

GALE
A Cengage Company

Farmington Hills, Mich • San Francisco • New York • Waterville, Maine
Meriden, Conn • Mason, Ohio • Chicago

Copyright © 2018 by Kiwone, Inc. f/s/o Ted Dekker.
Continuation of this copyright page can be found on pages 703–705.
Thorndike Press, a part of Gale, a Cengage Company.

Thorndike Press® Large Print Christian Fiction.
The text of this Large Print edition is unabridged.
Other aspects of the book may vary from the original edition.
Set in 16 pt. Plantin.

LIBRARY OF CONGRESS CIP DATA ON FILE.
CATALOGUING IN PUBLICATION FOR THIS BOOK
IS AVAILABLE FROM THE LIBRARY OF CONGRESS
ISBN-13: 978-1-4328-5154-5 (hardcover)

Published in 2018 by arrangement with Revell Books, a division of Baker Publishing Group

Printed in Mexico
1 2 3 4 5 6 7 22 21 20 19 18

Set me as a seal upon your heart, as a seal upon your arm.

Song of Songs 8:6 ESV

You are about to escape the old, limiting confines of your mind. The ride is wild and sometimes bumpy, so hold on tight. There is no greater thrill than finding freedom from the shackles of a common existence. The status quo is no life at all.

All of the neuroscience and psychology herein is firmly established. If in doubt, google it.

In addition, the nature of reality as demonstrated by Talya can be found in excerpts taken from his journal at the end of this novel. If in doubt, read it.

And so it begins . . .

PROLOGUE

I'm walking through a field of yellow daisies, wanting to love the way they sway in a gentle breeze, wanting to enjoy the scents of fresh earth and natural grasses, the bright blue sky, the sound of chirping birds in the trees just ahead of me. Wanting to love it all but not quite able to, because a voice deep in my mind tells me that it will change any minute now. Any second. And when it changes, I'll wish I was dead.

I run my hand through the tall grass, determined not to listen to that voice, because I'm smart enough to know that people get into trouble when they pay too much attention to the crazy voices that run through their minds. Not me. Not this time.

Still, the ancient memory of something off-color haunts me, so I stop thirty feet from the tall pine trees and look around, just to be sure.

Nothing. Nothing but tall swaying grass

and thousands of bright daisies. It's all slightly blurry to me because my eyesight isn't the best, but it's peaceful and full of wonder all the same. And not a sound except for the chirping birds.

See? It's okay. Nothing's wrong. Nothing to be afraid of.

So I start walking again.

I make it five steps before that distant dread finds me once more, insisting that something really is wrong. Terribly wrong.

My house is through the trees, maybe a hundred yards away, and I decide then that I have no business being out in the field. God only knows what could happen to a girl walking alone in a field. I walk faster, straight for the trees, and I begin to hum for comfort, for distraction from my thoughts.

The first three notes are sweet and high.

The fourth comes out low and guttural, snarling with static, and I pull up sharply, terrified to breathe. The sound had come from inside of me?

No, it comes from behind me, a loud, crackling roar that slams my heart into my throat. I spin toward the house and tear for safety with the threat at my back, gaining, gaining.

I sprint through the trees, running without

thought of the ground I'm covering. Praying I'll make it. Desperate.

Just before the roar reaches me, I crash through the front door and slam it shut. For the briefest moment, I think I am safe.

But now I hear a sound behind me. A soft chuckle. I jerk around with the door now at my back, and I see him. A tall man with slicked-back hair and penetrating red eyes.

Shadow Man.

I've seen him before, many times, and I know what he's going to say. What he's going to do. And although my lungs are frozen and my throat is tight, my mind is screaming.

"Hello, Rachelle," he says, drawing out each word through a slight grin. "Do you know what seven times seven is?"

I remember now. All of it. He's asked me the same question a thousand times and I know what he's going to do, but still I can't move.

"Forty-nine, the fullness of all that is," he says. "All the darkness and all the fear in the world, dumped into one worthless girl." He takes a step toward me, eyes gleaming with anticipation. "She must be punished for her failure. You know what that means, don't you, 49th?"

I am so terrified that my mind begins to

go numb. Waves of heat rush through my body. I want to run, to find my father, to hide. But my legs are lead.

"I'm going to blind you." Another step. "And when you see again, I'm going to blind you again. And again. And again, until even the thought of seeing makes you want to puke, because you know that I'm only going to blind you *again.*"

Another step. I'm trembling and I can smell his putrid breath. It's like dirty socks that have been deodorized with vanilla.

"Because of you, and through you, I'm going to blind the whole world. What happens to you happens to them all. It's all your fault, and they're going to hate you even more than they already do."

A weak plea manages to squeak past my throat. "Please . . ."

"This is only a fore-shadow."

In a flash he's on me, slamming me against the door, prying my eyes wide as I flail in a hopeless attempt to free myself from his iron grip. I know what he's doing. I think I would rather he kill me.

His mouth is spread wide, and in that last moment as my first screams fill the air, Shadow Man becomes himself, a shadow shaped like a cobra, spitting venom into both of my eyes.

12

Excruciating pain slices into my head and lights every nerve in my body on fire.

I bolt up in bed, screaming.

I didn't know I was asleep. I never do. But now I know I'm awake.

And that I'm blind.

1

It was the same nightmare I'd had every night for the past ten years, beginning at age six. The dream betrayed my deepest fears that nothing would ever change, but still, it was just a dream. I reminded myself every morning.

I couldn't have been more wrong.

My name is Rachelle Matthews, and I was born in a small mountain community well off the grid. The town was roughly ninety miles southeast of Salt Lake City, Utah — close enough to find help if the need arose, and far enough to be a world unto itself. When I say *off the grid* I mean completely self-sustaining in every way imaginable.

Eden, population 153 at last counting, sourced its own utilities and food, all generated and grown within the valley. We had our own law enforcement, our own hospital, our own government, and everything else required to sustain and protect life on an island.

Only we weren't on an island. We were in a deep mountain valley shaped like a bowl roughly two miles in diameter. Actually, most geologists would call the huge depression in the Rocky Mountains a sinkhole rather than a valley, but who wants to call their home a sinkhole? Certainly not Simon Moses, founder and incorporator of Eden, Utah. He envisioned a heaven on earth, a safe and peaceful environment, the polar opposite of the conflicted world we lived in.

But Eden was a sinkhole. My father, David, said the tall red cliffs that surrounded the valley made that much clear. And the only way in or out of the sinkhole was through a three-hundred-foot-long tunnel near the top of the western face.

My father once told me Eden looked like God had taken his walking stick and slammed it down into the middle of the mountains.

I was only seven at the time, and it was easy for me to picture a huge God standing over me with a stick, ready to hit me if I wandered off the proper path. That's what Simon Moses, whom we also called the Judge, preached. The last thing I wanted was to be squashed by that stick when God slammed it down.

"I don't like that image," I said. "And you don't really believe in God."

"Sure I do. Just not the way everyone else here does." My father believed God was more in our minds than he was a person in the sky with a big stick. "Either way, one day you'll be able to see the cliffs for yourself and you'll see just how beautiful they are," he said.

I couldn't see the cliffs the way my father did, because I'd been blind since I was a baby. Miranda said I probably had seen for the first five or six months, until the irregular formation of my red blood cells, a result of sickle cell anemia, caused all kinds of complications. Among them, very fair skin and damaged retinas.

My father was a psychotherapist, not a physician, but he'd made the healing of my blindness his life's sole ambition, and he knew more about how the brain and body work than most doctors. According to him, there was something more than sickle cell going on with me. Sickle cell was an inherited disease passed on by one or both parents who have the same trait. Neither my mother nor my father had this trait.

He sometimes wondered if my sickle cell anemia was linked to the complications and stress of my birth, which nearly killed me and did kill my mother, also named Rachelle. She'd given her life for mine, he once said. He'd never quite recovered from her death. Neither had I.

Still, I had learned to be practical about my situation in life, despite all the fears that haunted me. I had no mother, but I had a father who was sure I would see again if I followed his way. And I believed in a God who would ultimately save me if I was very careful and followed *his* way. I thought of my dad and God as two halves of a whole, both offering me hope.

In fact, I *did* have sight, just not the typical kind. Actually, I saw two different ways.

The first way was in my dreams. Not only did I dream in color, my dreams felt, smelled, and looked more real than anything in my waking blind life. Everything was still a little fuzzy and muted, but clear enough for me to experience it visually. For me, it was vivid seeing, because I had nothing else to compare it to.

Why I could see in color while dreaming was the subject of wild speculation. Maybe because I hadn't been blind for the first few months of my life, I knew what color looked like. But infants don't really see color well at that stage. And in my dreams I did.

The problem was, most of my dreams

were nightmares of Shadow Man always saying the same thing, always blinding me, mocking me, condemning me. Those nightmares weren't just kinda real, but so real that I dreaded falling asleep. I called it my nightmare sight.

From a psychological perspective, nightmares don't create new fears as much as they reflect deep hidden fears. The mind has to process these in some abstract way so it won't melt down.

What kinds of fears? For starters, the fear that I would always be blind, always suffer the same nightmares that had haunted me for the past ten years. Every time I closed my eyes to sleep I begged God to take away my nightmare sight.

But I had other more common fears as well. In fact, all negative emotions are rooted in fear, most commonly fear of loss, my father said. The fear of losing worthiness created jealousy, fear of losing honor created anger, fear of losing security created anxiety, and so it went. In the end, fear was the only challenge facing all humans, he believed.

The second kind of sight I experienced had nothing to do with sleep. While awake, I saw through echolocation, the same kind of "sight" that bats and dolphins use. I wasn't the first human to "see" in this way, but my father said I was probably among the best. Daniel Kish, perhaps the best-known blind man in the world and a hero to me, had his eyes removed in 1967 at thirteen months old due to retinal cancer. He mastered echolocation well enough to ride his bicycle through any park.

A specialist had come to the valley to examine me on two different occasions, and he'd been so impressed with my ability that he begged my father to allow further testing. So many blind people could benefit if we allowed him to study my brain, he insisted. The thought terrified me. My father refused.

While awake and using echolocation, I didn't see color. Or any definition, like features on a face. I only saw shapes. I saw them by clicking my tongue and almost immediately hearing the sound waves that returned to me after reflecting off objects. My brain took those very faint echoes and measured the distance, size, and shape of those objects around me, then sent the information to my visual cortex, where an image was created.

How can the brain learn to see shapes based on sound waves? One word: neuroplasticity. Not so long ago, science commonly held that the brain's neurons were essentially fixed at birth through genetic imprinting, but evidence to the contrary showed how the mind can create any number of new neurons and rewire old ones based on environmental input.

The first study to examine a human utilizing echolocation was in 2014, when researchers used fMRI to take high-resolution images of the brain while subjects who'd learned to echolocate clicked and "saw." Surprisingly, the visual cortex at the back of the brain, not the auditory centers of the brain, lit up, showing pronounced neural activity. The subjects really were "seeing" with the visual cortex. Their brains had rewired themselves to use sound and ears rather than light and eyes to perceive shapes, dimensions, and distances.

Echolocation didn't make me so special. I was only being human. We've known for some time the human brain can be rewired and reprogrammed. This is what my mind had done, but only because I, encouraged by my father, had developed the intention to rewire it.

I was much happier seeing through my clicks while awake than seeing in nightmares while asleep. I comforted myself with the thought that at least those nightmares never crossed over into my waking life in Eden.

And then one day they did and changed my life forever.

The date was Friday, June 8, 2018. The time was just after ten in the morning — I knew that because I had the news on, as undoubtedly most Americans did. Terrorists had executed a second wave of targeted cyber attacks against the power grid and thrown much of the East Coast into darkness.

My father was at the hospital that morning. I was standing over the stove, cooking eggs, my favorite food bar none. Eggs and ketchup.

I had one ear on the sizzle of the frying eggs and one on the voices coming over the television in the living room. Subtle shifts in the sound of the frying told me how well cooked the eggs were.

Most of my brain's processing power was occupied with the television. How a person said something spoke as loudly as their words, and in the absence of visual cues, I had learned to read inflections better than most.

The first cyber attack had hit the Northeast on Wednesday, two days earlier. It cut off power to over twenty million homes and businesses, including all of Manhattan, proving that the vulnerability of the power grid was one of America's greatest weaknesses. Not only because power plants and substations all ran on code that could be hacked, but because without electricity, everything stops.

And I mean everything.

At the moment, the voice on the NBC broadcast belonged to Cynthia Bellmont, a young woman in her thirties. Blonde hair and too much makeup, my father had said.

Makeup — something I didn't bother with, thanks to my limitations. My skin was pale and made my face look like a "ghost in a hood" because of my dark hair, if you listened to Sally, who was also sixteen. Today that ghost was dressed in jeans and a black T-shirt. I knew black made my skin look paler, but I wore only black so I could grab any shirt and know what I was wearing. Besides, although makeup would give my face color, any attempt to apply it myself would surely turn me into a clown.

"Someone has to be held accountable," Cynthia was saying. "The *Wall Street Journal,* among dozens of other respected publications, warned of precisely this vulnerability numerous times over the past five years and no one listened."

"Look, you're a news agency. Did NBC

listen?" That was Martin Seymore, grid expert. "Pointing fingers will come later. Restoring power should be our only focus, and that's looking more difficult by the hour."

Cynthia hesitated. "So how do we minimize the damage? Wall Street has been locked down for two days. There's a run on grocery stores and looting in some areas, based on reports we're receiving. Are there plans to send in the National Guard to restore order?"

"Send them from where? Governmental agencies like the National Guard are as dependent on power as Wall Street."

"Surely —"

"This morning's attack affected another forty-five power stations and nearly five thousand of the fifty-five-thousand substations on the East Coast. They've struck twice in three days, which means they could do more. Power stations farther west are reluctant to reroute energy to the east, concerned they might be next. If the president were to send assets like the National Guard to the east, it would leave the west vulnerable."

A pause.

"Things will get worse before they get better."

There was an edge to Seymore's voice that drew my stare. By *stare,* I mean turning my head so that both ears are equidistant from an object, thus allowing me to detect shapes and judge distances.

I clicked several times by habit, and the shapes of the room came into view. It was like turning on a small light for me. I could make out the objects in our small kitchen and living room, as familiar to me as the rest of the house, down to each edge and corner.

To my right: the electric stove with a range hood two feet over the burners. To the right of that: the refrigerator. Ahead of me a breakfast bar separated the tiny kitchen from the living room. There, two stuffed chairs and a couch were grouped around the television and a fireplace.

To my left, a hall led back to three bedrooms — one mine, another my father's, and the third a study that we shared.

My face was turned to the four-foot, flat-panel television as I imagined the looks on the faces of the worried talking heads. By the sound of Seymore's voice, the situation was worse than anyone was saying.

I forgot about my eggs as they continued to talk, now urging calm and suggesting steps that anyone in the west might take to prepare for the "unlikely" event the attacks cascaded to the Pacific coast.

How much worse could it get? The government always figured out a way to dig the country out of holes, right? Americans were inventive and resilient.

But I already knew how much worse it could get. Every person in Eden knew. "One day," Simon Moses often insisted, "the whole world will face catastrophic collapse. But we in Eden will prevail. We are and will always be a totally self-sufficient community protected by the walls God has given us for our safety."

I had always been more concerned about my personal fears than Eden's ability to survive nationwide catastrophes. My world of virtual darkness and nightmares kept me somewhat insulated from all the survival talk.

But what if it was actually happening?

Without electricity, cell phones and their networks go completely silent. Computers become hunks of plastic and metal. Commerce comes to a sudden stop. The first attack on Wednesday had already cost over a trillion dollars due to loss of trade, Cynthia Bellmont said.

But that was the least of it. Refrigeration ceases and food spoils in a matter of days.

Gas stations shut down. All flights are grounded. Sewage pumps fail and wastewater backs up. Water is cut off. Big cities become death traps with no way in or out except by foot. Survival instincts kick in and humans begin to do whatever is necessary to protect their own lives.

Chaos breaks out.

Maybe Simon Moses was as right about the world ending as he was about following God's law. Honestly, the thought of a nationwide collapse had a calming effect on me. It would prove Shadow Man wrong, right? He said *I* would bring blindness to the world, but here the failure of the grid was doing it without my help. Not that I believed my nightmares. They were only symbolic, like the numbers, seven times seven. Fullness. Of *course* I didn't really believe my nightmares.

But a tiny part of me did, and that part gnawed at me whenever they crossed my mind, which was far too often.

I turned my attention back to the eggs, heard that I'd let them go a little too long, and quickly scooped them onto the plate I'd placed on the counter, right next to the stove.

Now the ketchup. I stepped to the fridge, pulled the door open, and scanned the contents with a few quick clicks. Sonic waves reflected back to my ears and traveled to my visual cortex, where they were converted to shapes and sizes that showed me what was there. I knew them well. For my sake my father always bought the exact same items.

Mayonnaise, mustard, pickles, leftovers in a large Tupperware — that would be the sauerkraut and sausages from last night — milk jug. No ketchup? We always had . . .

Then I remembered. I'd taken the ketchup with some fries to my room last night. Must have left it on my desk. I closed the fridge and headed down the hall. Could have clicked, but I was so well spatially oriented in the house that I didn't need to. If I didn't feel like clicking, distances, angles, and slight variations in temperatures guided me in this familiar place.

I did click at the door, just to see that it was closed, before turning the knob and pushing it open. Three clicks and I saw the bottle of ketchup on my desk, right next to my computer.

The keys on my keyboard were raised with Braille, but I almost always used voice-recognition software that rendered the Braille mostly unnecessary.

I was reaching for the ketchup bottle when

the talking heads on the living room television went silent midsentence. But it was more than the silence that stopped me. It was the tiny popping sound that a television makes when it's turned off.

We'd lost power? But no . . . I could hear the hum of the refrigerator.

I turned toward the door. "Dad?"

I heard a slight creak, which would be him walking across the living room.

I grabbed at the ketchup and knocked it off the desk. Stooping, I clicked, saw the bottle, snatched it up, and headed for the bedroom door.

This time I called louder, "Dad?" fully expecting his gentle voice to echo down the hall. *Hi, honey* . . .

Instead, I got a soft but unmistakable chuckle that stopped me in my tracks. Someone was in our house. Someone who'd just chuckled under his breath. I knew the sound of that chuckle all too well.

But that was impossible, because I wasn't dreaming. And Shadow Man was a creation of my imagination.

Had I imagined him while awake? In my dreams, I seemed powerless to change my imagination, but awake I had full control over my perception of the world.

I was awake, right? What if . . . No, that

29

was impossible. I wasn't dreaming this. Or was I?

Ignoring the fear spiking down my back, I stepped forward, turned into the hall, and called out again, if for nothing else than to hear the sound of my voice echoing off the walls.

"Hello?" Then, "Dad?"

A voice began to hum the tune of a Sunday school song that had always filled me with terrible fear. *Oh be careful little eyes what you see . . .*

I flinched and dropped the ketchup bottle.

Oh be careful little eyes what you see . . .

Panic swarmed me even though I knew I was only imagining that tone, that pitch.

For the Father up above is looking down in love, so be careful little eyes what you see.

Shadow Man's voice. But that couldn't be! I was only remembering a song that had haunted me, a blind person. That was God and this was Shadow Man, and my mind was mixing them up.

"Hello, Rachelle," the voice said. "So good to finally see you in the flesh."

I remained frozen at the entrance to the kitchen with the living room on my left. Then my mind engaged properly and I let out a quick string of clicks so I could see him — see whoever was talking to me.

30

I saw nothing. I saw nothing because there was nothing to see and I already knew that. Something in my mind had short-circuited, and my dreams were crossing over to my waking life. After years of properly separating the reality I experienced in my dreams from my true reality here in Eden, I was mixing things up. Like a schizophrenic.

My mind told me all these things in rapid fire, and I took a tiny bit of comfort in them, but not much. Because my mind was also hearing the sound of his breathing now. Was he here or was it just my imagination? Which part of my mind was telling me the truth?

"Both," he said.

He could read my thoughts? Of course. He was in my head.

"You're not real," I said in a thin, wispy voice.

"No?" I could hear him cross the floor toward the kitchen and couldn't help but think of the knives there. "But I am. Just as real as you make anything else in this world."

A pause and a breath. I could almost hear him grinning.

"What do you say? Wanna see, baby? Really see?"

I couldn't stop fear, but while awake I had

31

learned to be aware of myself feeling it. I recognized my mind at work. It was only firing off certain neural connections associated with what it thought was danger. Like an internal guidance system, it was only ringing its warning bell based on what it perceived, whether the danger was real or not.

In this case the danger wasn't real. Couldn't be.

"Are you willing to bet your life on that?"

He was in the kitchen. I heard the scrape of a plate on the counter followed by the sound of something being eaten. My eggs.

But clicking, I saw no eggs floating. My plate was just where I'd left it, waiting for ketchup. Of course, that was just perception too. Maybe my mind was refusing to see what terrified it. I stood like a statue with a runaway pulse, begging my imagination to right itself.

"I'll make you a deal," Shadow Man said, speaking around the eggs I imagined to be in his mouth. "I'll trade my sight, which is perfect, for yours. Make this one exchange and you'll be able to see in this world, just like everyone else. I'll never bother you again. What do you say?"

My fingers were trembling. When I could see in my nightmares, he blinded me. Now

32

I was blind and he was offering to give me sight. I clicked again, just to be sure none of this was real. Nothing. It was all in my mind.

"The whole world is in your mind, pumpkin."

He was walking toward me. That's when I lost it.

I sprang from the hall, veered right, took two long steps to the edge of the counter, and after a bit of a mad fumble, snatched a knife from the butcher block. I spun, breathing heavily, knife extended to ward him off, even though I knew he couldn't be real. I was awake! I was awake and this wasn't happening.

"Come on," he said, close again. "My sight. For your sight. One way or the other, I'm going to get it."

"I'm blind!"

"Oh, but you can see, sweetheart. You're the 49th, the only one who can see. Let me see that world, and I'll let you see this world."

"You're not real," I said again, trying to convince myself.

"No, I suppose not." He spit something out. "No deal then? You're sure? That's your final answer?"

I was breathing too hard to respond. At

this point, all I wanted was for him to go away, because if he touched me . . . if he laid one finger on me . . . I would rather die.

He sighed. "Very well. But you must know that it took a lot of work to crawl inside your mind, and I'm just getting started."

He was so close now that I could feel the heat from his breath. I swung the knife about, stabbing at the air.

"See you in your dreams, my little dumpling."

And then he was gone, leaving me planted on the kitchen floor, gripping the knife, knuckles white.

The TV came back on. Familiar sounds filled my ears: a bird chirping in the large maple in our backyard, the hum of the refrigerator, a dog barking near the center of town, the clicking of the stove top cooling down. My pounding heart, the faint rush of blood in my ears.

My world was back in order.

The door between the garage and kitchen opened and I spun, knife extended again, clicking. My father took shape.

"Rachelle? You okay?" He closed the door behind him. "What's going on? You look like you've seen a ghost."

Now I felt a bit foolish. But this was my

father and I had never tried to appear any particular way to him. So I just stepped over to the counter, calmly set the knife down, and turned back to him.

My emotions caught up to me then, a huge surge that rose up my chest and came out in a single sob. Then another.

He reached me in one long step, strong arms around me, pulling me close, reminding me that I was his little girl and nothing would ever hurt me in his care.

"It's okay, honey." He rubbed my back. "It's okay."

"I saw Shadow Man," I said, pulling myself together. "While I was awake."

"It's okay. You're allowed to see whatever you see."

He didn't patronize me by telling me it was all in my head. We'd talked about this often. According to my father, our whole lives are in our heads. The separation between mind and body has been firmly debunked by neuroscience. The whole body is one big placebo effect. Our belief makes things so — even my blindness — which gave us both hope. Technically speaking, my brain could rewire itself to actually see through my eyes, not just through clicking.

He took my face in his big strong hands and tilted it up to his. "What do you see?"

I took a deep breath and clicked. "You," I said.

"That's right. And who am I?"

"You're the one who's going to keep me safe."

"That's right." He leaned down and kissed my forehead. "And I have some very good news for you."

"What news?"

He stepped back and breathed deeply. "CRISPR. It arrived by courier this morning."

I froze. CRISPR. Engineered segments of DNA that might fix my eyes. "It's here? So soon?"

"Simon bent over backward on this one." He was having difficulty containing his enthusiasm, which was something for my father, who was generally stoic. "Miranda's prepping for you now."

My heart was pounding again, but now with nervous anticipation. "Today?"

He stepped to the counter. "As soon as you finish the rest of your eggs."

I blinked. "Finish them? I haven't eaten any."

"Well, someone took a bite." He stepped over to the coffeepot. "You're not hungry?"

My mind was spinning. "Not really."

"Leave them. It's going to be a big day. I

can feel it in my bones."

He had no idea just how big that day would be.

2

David walked down the path with Rachelle, her delicate hand in his. They lived on the south side of the town, thus the common term for the small neighborhood that comprised thirteen homes, Southside.

"You really think this will work?" she asked.

David looked down at her. Dressed in her blue jeans and black shirt, as always. Her Converse tennis shoes were fraying, but she refused to wear any other pair. She was so fragile in so many ways. Short, just breaking five foot one. Thin, with small bones. But in so many other ways, she was the bravest person he knew.

And the smartest, even for her age. The only subject they rarely discussed was religion — he had no intention of compromising her faith, regardless of his own doubts.

"We'll go over everything again at the

hospital, but in short, yes. It's going to work."

Belief was half the battle, and the last thing he wanted was to reinforce any more fear in her. Between her blindness and the nightmares, she'd suffered far more than her fair share.

Everyone had fears, usually deeper and more pervasive than they realized. The mind simply suppressed them as part of its survival mechanism — a good thing in the short term. But that suppressed energy invariably resurfaced, usually through disease.

As a therapist, he was well aware of the dangers associated with suppressed fears, but the dangers of not suppressing them were even more debilitating in the short term. Panic attacks didn't serve daily life well. The only permanent solution was to root those fears out at their source — a tall task for anyone.

Rachelle was far more sensitive than most. It wasn't that she had greater fear than the average person; her mind just couldn't suppress the same fears that were hidden deep within everyone else. They lived with her 24/7.

No amount of encouragement or therapy had helped much. For some reason she'd developed a fear that if she did see, she would only be blinded again. The debilitating nightmares that had wormed their way deep into her subconscious were evidence of this. The numerology in those dreams — seven times seven equaling forty-nine, the number of finality before liberation, which was the number fifty according to numerologists — had become synonymous with her fear that she would always be stuck in blindness.

David wanted to cure his daughter's blindness, but relieving her of her fears was his greater ambition. If her eyes could be permanently healed, those fears would lose their grip. And CRISPR's genetic engineering was their best hope.

Unfortunately, like all procedures, CRISPR came with risks — in this case a rare but severe one.

Coma.

But after much deliberation they'd made their decision, and he chose to focus on the best possible outcome. Coma resulted only when genetic tags were miscalculated. He was sure they'd gotten it right.

"Feels surreal," Rachelle said. "Especially on a day like today."

"What, the end of the world as we know it? That's not gonna happen in Eden. Nor anywhere else. If there's an attack on the West Coast, then maybe. Let's hope not, because anyone who's even heard about Eden will be heading straight for us."

"I thought no one could get in."

"There's always a way in. Out's another matter. Let's just hope it doesn't come to that."

They turned onto Third Street and headed out of the neighborhood. The homes were uniformly placed on one-acre lots with small vegetable gardens and plenty of space for comfort. Most of the residents lived in Westside. All of the homes were built with the same basic materials — asphalt shingle roofs, fiberglass siding formed as boards and painted white, green, beige, or brown.

To the north: the warehouse and utilities. To the east: cultivated land that grew mostly potatoes, corn, high-yield wheat, and fruit trees. Vegetables came from personal gardens and were traded or sold at Saturday market or at the grocery store, all days except Sunday, the busiest day of the week despite being called the day of rest. All livestock, primarily cows and goats, were corporately owned and grazed on common land to the east.

"Morning, Doctor," a voice called from across the street. Betsy Williamson, wearing

41

a thin smile, was walking her white poodle, Puddle. Why Puddle, he had no idea. The sweet lady in her seventies suffered from recurring bouts of eczema. The rash on her arms and neck came and went with her stress.

"You need a patient?" she asked, crossing to them.

"Thank you for asking, but no, not today. I can see you tomorrow if you like."

"Actually, I was thinking of Robert." She glanced up and down the street. "Seems he's forgotten the proper courtship protocol."

Puddle had pulled Betsy closer, eager to sniff and nuzzle Rachelle's legs. His daughter bent down and petted the dog, whispering his name.

"Robert's making advances, is he? Sounds like a problem for Linda," he said, referring to the woman he technically reported to, one of four council members responsible for Eden's oversight.

"I wouldn't want to get him in trouble," Betsy said. "And to be truthful, I don't mind. It's just that I don't want him to get on the wrong side of things, if you get my meaning."

"Don't give it another thought."

She studied him. "Don't give him another

thought? Or don't give him getting in trouble another thought?"

"Think about Robert all you like, as long as it doesn't cause you stress." By the looks of the rash on her neck, she was stressed already. "I'm sure he'll go through proper channels if he wants to take things further."

She nodded but didn't seem convinced. Then he understood.

"So you *want* him to take it further."

She blushed. "I didn't say that. Heavens, I'm too old for all of that anyway."

"Well, if you decide you're not too old for all of that, I see no harm in offering him a smile and kindness. There's no law against showing love, Betsy."

She smiled. "I suppose not. That's why I like you, Doctor."

"I like you too, Betsy."

And then she was off, pulling away her feisty little poodle, which was clearly more interested in playing with Rachelle than following his master.

"Cute dog," Rachelle said.

"Cute dog."

The town square was empty other than Old Man Butterworth, who was skimming debris out of the large fountain, and three kids kicking a soccer ball back and forth on the lawn next to the church.

43

Various stores and places of business lined the four main streets that bordered the square — a hardware store, a clothing store, a café, and a small grocery store, among others — offering all the basics required to support a small town of 153.

Everyone was undoubtedly glued to their televisions or making what calls could get through to those they knew on the East Coast, getting the real scoop. Strange to think that in a world not so far away, millions of people were at their wits' end, facing grave threats that had them sweating bullets and scrambling for answers.

Electricity was like sight, he thought. You don't miss it until it's gone.

David led Rachelle past the square, continued up Third Street, then down Sixth and past a large sign at the edge of town: Eden Hospital. The sprawling white building rising from the middle of a wide green lawn was much larger than needed to service such a small population, but the Judge had spared no expense. Whatever equipment or supplies David or Miranda requested, they eventually received.

Like the delivery they'd received by courier today, which had not come cheap.

Only half of the hospital housed patient-care facilities. The other half was reserved

44

for research and labs, all utilizing the latest equipment. When the world collapsed, Simon wanted every advantage. He said this too was God's provision.

The equipment they used was mostly operated by one tech, Emerson Watkins, who loved the name they'd given him — RG, short for Resident Genius, which he was.

David and Rachelle entered through the main glass doors and headed past the reception desk, where Sue sat watching a television on the wall. She finally noticed them and stood up.

"Have you seen this?"

"Yes, I have. Hi, Sue."

"Hi, David. Sorry. Quiet day in here."

Wasn't it always? "That's a good thing."

"It is, thank God." She motioned down the hall. "Miranda said to tell you she's in 202. Hi, Rachelle."

"Good morning, Sue."

They headed down an empty tiled hallway. Room 202 was the second of five examination and outpatient rooms.

Miranda stood from a stool where she'd been hunkered over an array of tubes and needles on a stainless-steel tray. She'd pulled her blonde hair back into a ponytail as she always did "on duty."

Her soft brown eyes looked at him with expectation, sparkling under the fluorescent lights. She was an angel, he thought, not only because she cared for Rachelle as much as he did, but because . . . well . . . she cared for him. Selfish as that sounded, when he was with Miranda he was aware he'd hidden in his own isolated world with Rachelle for far too long.

Her eyes shifted to Rachelle. "Good morning, sweetie. I hear you're ready to tackle something brand new."

Rachelle hesitated. "That's what I hear too."

The door opened and RG barged in, always the nerd and proudly so, down to the black-rimmed glasses and white lab coat he often wore about town.

His eyes darted between them from under unkempt reddish curls. "So this is it?"

"This is it," Miranda said, approaching Rachelle. She nodded at David and took his daughter's hand. "Come sit on the table, Rachelle."

Rachelle hoisted herself up on the table, legs dangling, hands folded. For a long moment the others stood in silence, caught up in the gravity of the moment. David nodded at Miranda.

"Okay, sweetie, I know your father's told

46

you this, but just so you're clear, there are some risks, however small, that —"

"I know," Rachelle interrupted. "Coma. I understand. But that's a risk I'm willing to take." There was a light tremor in her fingers.

More silence. She was just being brave — they all knew that.

"I don't want to hear why it might not work," she said. "Just tell me why it is going to work."

RG looked at David, who nodded again. *The floor is yours.* RG slipped a hand into his pocket. "You know about epigenetics."

"It's the mind's way of making changes to our DNA," Rachelle said. "Like new code written by a software engineer to modify existing code. Change the code and the program does something different."

"Right. We're essentially very complicated computers — brain, body, and perception all working together as one organism. External factors like environment, as well as persistent beliefs and intentions, actually turn genes on or off, which changes the expression of those genes and thus our bodies. That's why we have pygmies in Africa and tall blond hunks in Norway, even though they all originated from one common ancestor. Science is only just learning

47

how it works, but there's no question that it does."

"We have the power to change our bodies through thought, we just aren't sure how yet," she said. "That's the point."

"Correct. Enter CRISPR, a more direct shortcut to changing our bodies. Rather than waiting for generational mutations to gradually change us, it's possible to switch specific genes in any DNA strand on or off, which then changes the expression of the cells that DNA controls."

"Using the Cas9 enzyme, which snips the desired DNA," Rachelle said, "and a guide RNA called CRISPR made to match the cut and replace it with a different gene."

Rehearsing the details had a calming effect on her, David thought. RG glanced at him, smiled, and continued. "That's right, professor. CRISPR has to be engineered for each specific gene. When we learn precisely which gene grows eyebrows, for example, a CRISPR could be designed to replace the gene that grows hair with one that grows bone. That's what all the fuss is about. In the wrong hands, it could radically change the human species. Even wipe it out. All of this has been known and verified for over a decade. What's new is how it's implemented."

He pushed his glasses up on his nose.

"Until recently, CRISPR was directly inserted into stem cells or embryos. Now they've figured out how to use it on the formation of new cells in a mature organism, simply by injecting it into the affected system."

"In my case, my blood."

"Your blood. More precisely, your red blood cells, which are deformed."

"The point is," David said, "we have a very carefully engineered strand of CRISPR designed to modify your bone marrow, which, as you know, produces new red blood cells."

Miranda lifted a bag of clear liquid from a silver icebox and carefully set it on the tray next to the table. She gently took Rachelle's hand and set in on the cool bag.

Over two years of research and calls to all corners of the globe came down to this moment. So simple. Yet not so simple at all. Years of research had gone into the engineering of the fluid in that bag. More accurately, the CRISPR Cas9 in that bag. Still, that changing a human genetic code could be so simple staggered David's mind.

"So this is it," Rachelle said, putting on a brave face.

"This is it," David said. "We inject

CRISPR into your bloodstream and it finds its way to the haemopoietic bone marrow, where stem cells will be repaired so they can produce healthy red blood cells to replace your sickle cells. It takes about four months for all the old red blood cells to die off and be replaced with new, healthy cells."

"So in four months I should be healthy."

"In four months your sickle cells should be gone. We can then repair your retinas using one of several available procedures without any concern that deformed sickle cells might destroy that repair. If all goes well, you'll be able to see with your eyes. Permanently."

Another long beat.

"Well, then," Rachelle said. "Hook me up."

The entire procedure took less than half an hour, all of it like a dream to David. It all seemed too simple, too easy, too quick. But they'd spent countless hours on the phone with doctors from Paris, carefully rehearsing details until there was nothing left to discuss. This was, amazingly enough, how it was done.

It was no wonder more and more laws were being written to control the use of CRISPR. What could heal could also deform, kill, or exterminate.

They had given Rachelle an oral sedative because the anemia constricted her veins and she was terrified of needles. They hadn't meant to put her out, only halfway there, but she fell asleep listening to RG's lengthy explanation of just how, in the near future, when science perfected gene editing in neural cells, the brain itself could be altered.

Miranda's careful intravenous insertion of the precious fluid took less than ten minutes.

And that was it. Miranda gave David's arm a squeeze for good luck, removed the IV, and dropped the needle, tube, and bag into a bin for safe disposal.

"Let's let her sleep," David said, watching his daughter.

"Should wear off soon."

He nodded. "Give me a moment with her, will you?"

"Of course." Miranda touched his shoulder. "I have a good feeling about this, David. I know it doesn't work on everyone, but she's strong. Have faith."

He put his hand on hers. "Thank you. I'll wait here until she wakes up."

He stood over Rachelle after they left, reviewing all that had preceded this moment. All the worrying, the endless nights

51

of fear she'd suffered. Such a brave soul.

He finally sighed and stroked her cheek, noting that her eyes were moving behind her eyelids. He wasn't a man of prayer, but he prayed in his own way that she was dreaming well.

She twitched and let out a faint whisper.

His mind drifted to his wife's death. She'd suffered nightmares during the last trimester of her pregnancy. She often woke in a panic, completely disoriented, memories jumbled. In the final week she'd become convinced that they were all part of an experiment in some elaborate conspiracy. Fearful of what she might do to herself and the baby, David had insisted the attending physicians give her sedatives.

She'd died in her sleep, here, in this hospital. Miranda managed to save baby Rachelle through an emergency C-section, but David had never forgiven himself for his role in her mother's death, regardless of the fact that sedatives had nothing to do with her passing.

Or had they?

The sound of the door gently closing behind him pulled him from his thoughts. He started to turn, expecting to see Miranda.

Instead he saw a tall man dressed in a

white jacket and dark slacks. Shiny leather shoes. Dark hair slicked back with oil, mouth grinning wide to show a perfectly formed set of too-white teeth. His eyes were a light brown, almost amber, gentle and piercing, inspiring warmth and confidence.

A stranger. What was a stranger doing in the hospital? Or in Eden, for that matter? A stranger wearing a single diamond stud in his left ear and two silver chains around his neck. David could smell his cologne at ten feet.

"Hello, David," the man said. "Name's Smith. Vlad Smith. I've come to bring sight to the blind." Smith shifted his gaze to Rachelle and stepped forward.

Alarmed, David moved to cut him off. "I'm afraid I'm going to have to ask you to leave."

Smith pulled up and stared at him. "You don't understand, David. The CRISPR you just injected into your daughter isn't going to work. I'm your only hope."

He knew about CRISPR?

"How did you get in? Simon —"

"Think of me as the one Simon reports to, although that isn't entirely true. Either way, I'm here to make a few small adjustments. There's something very wrong with this valley and I'm going to fix it. Your daughter's the key, so I need to fix her first."

David stood speechless.

"Are you going to yield to reasoning, or am I going to have to manhandle you?"

"Have you lost your mind?"

"Oh no, not me, David. But you have. You're as blind as your daughter. The good news is that blindness is merely a matter of bad programming and clogged memories."

Smith cocked his left eyebrow.

"Did you know there's a way to manipulate specific memories now? Erase old ones and overwrite them with new ones using neural lacing? Not my gig, but I can help people think clearly again. Once they see my power, they'll let me do what I need to do. The lives of everyone in Eden depend on it. So please, if you don't mind, step aside."

David shoved his finger at the door, heat flushing his face. "Get out!"

Smith stepped up, grabbed his shirt, and threw him against the wall like a rag doll. David's head crashed into the drywall and he dropped to his seat, dazed. He tried to get his feet under him, but they refused to respond in any helpful way.

"Stop!"

Smith was already moving, as if in slow motion from David's perspective. Bending

54

over Rachelle. Pricking her finger with something he'd withdrawn from his jacket . . . Then David didn't know what he did, because Smith's body blocked his view.

Smith shoved the object back into his breast pocket and touched Rachelle's eyes with his thumb and forefinger. "Welcome to the world of the seeing, pumpkin."

Rachelle suddenly sat up, eyes wide, screaming.

Startled, David finally clambered to his feet. Vlad Smith turned and walked toward the door.

Rachelle's scream faded, but her mouth and eyes were still stretched wide. And then, as if her plug had been pulled from the wall, her eyes and mouth snapped shut and she collapsed back onto the table.

David lurched toward the bed.

"Well done, David," Vlad Smith spoke softly behind him. He heard the door opening. "The world as you know it ends in six days."

David reached the bed, only one thought on his mind: to wake Rachelle from her sleep. He grabbed her arm and shook her. Her head wobbled, but she remained peaceful and oblivious.

He shook her harder. "Wake up. Wake up!"

She lay dead to the world. Which could

only mean that she wasn't merely sleeping.

Panic pushed reason from his mind. He slapped her face. "Wake up! Wake up, wake up, wake up!"

But she didn't.

He grabbed her wrist to check her pulse even though he could see that she was still breathing. But checking her pulse wasn't always easy due to her anemia. He released her wrist, dropped his ear to her chest, and heard her heart beating rapidly.

The pounding of feet outside was followed by the door swinging open and crashing into the doorstop.

"What happened?" Miranda asked. "I heard a scream and . . ."

"Wake up!" David shook Rachelle violently, lost in fear.

Miranda shoved him aside and grabbed Rachelle's wrist, instinctively checking for a pulse. "You're hurting her! Tell me what happened."

"I . . . A man came in and did something."

"Something? What are you talking about?" She snatched a small flashlight from the counter, clicked it on. "What man?"

David's mind couldn't find the appropriate words to explain.

Miranda opened Rachelle's eyes with one hand and shone the beam into each pupil.

"No dilation." She quickly pinched Rachelle's arm, then listened to her heart with a stethoscope.

When Miranda straightened, her face had paled.

"What's happening?"

"She's unconscious."

"I can see that! What else?" he demanded. "What's happening?"

"She . . ." Miranda hesitated. "I think she might be in a coma."

3

I remember falling asleep on the table, and even in that sleep I could feel the cool liquid flowing up my arm as Miranda administered CRISPR. After that I can't remember.

I can't remember because the deep pain that filled my eyes and slammed into my skull ripped all thoughts from my mind. I was screaming, I do remember that. My world had gone black.

I felt dis-membered from the reality I had known as Eden. Cut off from all dreaming, all thought, all reality. For a beat that lasted both forever and for only a split second, I didn't seem to exist. I was dead to life.

In the next moment I was re-membered. Meaning I was fully aware of my physical form, but in a different state of conscious-ness. In a dream, I thought.

In every other dream I'd had, I couldn't tell that I was in a dream. This time I could. A lucid dream.

I sat up, palms planted on the ground. On the sand. I was in a desert. I twisted and scanned the horizon. Everything was fuzzy. Real and clearly recognizable, but not sharply defined. Rolling dunes rose tall behind me and in front of me, boulders and shallow canyons maybe a hundred yards away.

Another nightmare. I knew it had to be because my hands were shaking, like I'd just come out of a horrible situation that I couldn't remember.

I was wearing filthy, torn pants and a thigh-length blouse — a white cotton tunic that looked as if it had been dipped in dirty water before drying. It was large and slipped off one shoulder. I had dusty bare feet with a cut on my right heel. My lips were dry and chapped and my throat felt like a gunnysack. And there was something off about my body. Something wrong. Something . . .

I looked down and saw it immediately. I was more developed. I wasn't mistaken, I was older. Maybe only a few years, but I definitely knew my body well enough to tell the difference. And my skin wasn't pale.

I pushed myself to my feet and looked around, feeling dread. My footprints were visible in the sand dune to my right. By the looks of it, I'd lost my way in this desert and collapsed.

Movement above caught my attention and I tilted my head up. Two flying creatures were high in the blue sky. Birds — huge, fluffy white birds that looked like flying squirrels, only much larger.

The creatures descended toward me.

I stood frozen on the sand, thinking I should run. But there was no way to outrun them, so I remained still, hoping they would leave me alone after satisfying their curiosity.

Instead, they circled once before floating down to the sand not twenty feet from where I stood. I took a step back. With wings folded, they looked more like huge plump bats or Ewoks, two feet tall with green eyes. They didn't look menacing, but when had that ever meant anything?

I'm not sure I was breathing at this point.

One of them, the slightly plumper one, was smiling, then waddling toward me with a pronounced limp. He tripped on a stone and flapped his wings to steady himself, and I saw that part of his right wing was missing.

I took another step back, glancing at the other one. The stern one with a fixed face.

"Greetings, daughter of Elyon," the plump

60

one said.

I blinked. They could talk?

"I am Gabil, mighty warrior of Elyon, and the serious one behind me is Michal, wise one. Not that I'm *not* wise." He paused. "You can see us?"

"Of course she can see you," Michal said, waddling forward. "Do you think she's just staring at the sand?"

"You can't blame me," Gabil said. The creature stared at her for a long moment, then stuck webbed fingers at the end of its wings into its ears. "Can you see what I'm doing now?"

"Please, Gabil . . ."

Gabil turned to his partner and quickly offered his defense. "Didn't I tell you she could see us?"

"Yes, you were right. Now stop with your antics or you will frighten her."

He faced me. "But you see what I am doing, yes?"

He waited for my response, so I finally gave him one. "I'm dreaming," I said.

"Dreaming? Then you didn't see what I did? Can you see all of me or just a part of me, like a white patch of fog?"

"Gabil . . ." The other one wobbled forward. "Please don't mind him. He's —"

"I just want to be sure," Gabil said. "Can

you see?"

Half my mind was telling me that talking to a fluffy white bat was impossible. "You . . . You stuck your fingers in your ears."

"Aha! I knew it!" He pumped his wounded wing, fist clenched.

I nearly smiled.

"We are Roush," Gabil said, bowing with one wing folded across his plump belly. "Servants of Elyon."

Michal looked up at me in all seriousness, ignoring his comrade. "And you, my dear. Who are you?"

"I'm Rachelle."

"Rachelle?" He glanced at my shoulder. "You're a long way from home, Rachelle. How did you get here?"

"And how can you see us?" Gabil piped in.

I looked at my bared shoulder and saw that I was marked by a tattoo — a pencil-thin line forming a black circle maybe three inches in diameter.

"I got here because I'm dreaming," I said. "In reality, I'm in a town called Eden, which is in Utah. And that's also why I can see you. This is a dream."

They exchanged glances, and I saw concern in their eyes.

"Dreaming?" Gabil said. "Don't be absurd. To dream, you would need to be asleep, yes? And yet I can see you as clearly as you can see me, and I will tell you without the slightest doubt that you are most definitely awake."

"Here I am. But there I'm sleeping on a table in a hospital. And there I'm blind. You're a little blurry, but the fact that I can see you at all is proof enough."

For a long beat both of them just stared at me.

"Then you're saying that I, Gabil, slayer of Shataiki and celebrated warrior despite several minor setbacks, am only a dream?" He spread his wings wide with all the grandiosity of a mighty ruler. "That I, who can protect the Albinos and vanquish Teeleh with a single swipe of my foot" — and here he executed a rather funny-looking kick — "do not even exist?"

Now I couldn't help but give him a smile, if only a hint of one.

"Not like this, Gabil," Michal chided. His eyes held mine. "Please forgive his enthusiasm. He refuses to accept his new limitations. A terrible battle only last year, you understand? If anything, he's more determined to prove his value."

"Do you know Thomas of Hunter?" Gabil

63

blurted, oblivious to Michal's prodding. "I taught him all he knows. He too once thought he was dreaming."

Michal snapped his right wing wide to silence his comrade, who settled back with a sheepish grin.

"What my friend means to say," Michal went on, "is that you are not the first to dream of the histories. It is well known that Thomas of Hunter also dreamed of them. Although I was under the assumption that gateway was permanently closed. Evidently I was misinformed."

"What histories?"

"This place you think you are from. Utah. There is no Utah now, but there once was, over two thousand years ago. It's written in the Books of History. Did you just wake up?"

My head spun. "No, I'm still sleeping."

"I mean here," he said, pointing at the sand. "Did you just wake up here?"

"Here? Yes. But not there. There I'm —"

"As I said, Utah is only a dream. If you ask the right questions in that dream, you'll see that it is all an illusion. You were dreaming of the histories while you were sleeping here. That is all. Just like Thomas of Hunter once did."

Was it possible? Logically, yes, I supposed.

But if so, why couldn't I remember this place?

"Who's Thomas of Hunter?" I asked.

Michal was taken aback.

Gabil started to lift his wing. "He's the one I taught . . ." He fell silent and lowered his wing when Michal held his up.

"You mean to say that you've never heard of Thomas of Hunter?"

"No."

"But of course you have. The whole world has. Most certainly all Albinos, of which you are one. And most certainly all Elyonites from the far side, of which you are one." Michal indicated the tattoo on my right shoulder. "A Mystic by your marking. So you see, you have heard of Thomas of Hunter, you just don't remember. What *do* you remember?"

I lifted a hand to my forehead and ran my fingers through my hair, trying to make sense of things.

"Nothing about this place," I said. "Other than waking up on the ground."

"The Horde must have forced her to eat the poison," Gabil said.

"But how did she get here? Elyonites have never crossed the pass to this side of the Divide." Michal waddled to my left, eyes fixed on me with even greater interest now.

65

They were utterly serious. I'd never had a dream remotely similar to this one.

"You remember nothing?"

"Nothing," I said.

"Then Gabil is correct. You've been given the poison that erases your memory." He paced quickly now, fingers on his chin. "In truth, you are from the far side of the Great Divide, where you must return. There, your memory will surely come back to you."

"What if she's the one?" Gabil asked.

"It's not for us to decipher," Michal said.

"What one?" I asked.

"Never mind," Michal said. "Now you should also find the rhambutan fruit. Consuming it will keep you from dreaming. If you stop dreaming, you won't dream of the histories. You can never trust such dreams. Some are true but many are —"

A gasp from Gabil cut him off. I quickly followed his stare to the dunes. A white horse plunged down the slope, leaving a trail of churned sand that covered my footprints. On this horse was a rider in a white robe that flowed as he leaned into the wind.

Both of the Roush dropped to their knees, heads bowed low, facing the onrushing rider.

I stood where I was. Two things kept me from running. First, the Roush were clearly

66

lovable creatures. I thought I could trust them. They did not cower but bowed to honor the visitor. But even more than the Roush, the very atmosphere seemed to have shifted. A palpable calm settled around me, as if the air itself revered this man.

The horse slowed to circle us. I turned with him before he stopped not ten feet away. The rider's eyes, like the Roush's, were green, and looking into them I was transfixed with assurance and wonder. His hair fell to strong, broad shoulders. On his feet, brown boots were laced up to his knees.

The man swung off his horse and walked up to me, watching me intently, smiling. He reached for my right hand and placed a kiss on my knuckles. A faint pulse of power rode up my arm, a warm vibration that might have startled me if not for the fact that it seemed entirely natural. Like an echo of something I already knew.

He dipped his head. "So good to see you, daughter."

I managed a slight nod.

"The poison they fed you has distorted your vision, yes? Would you like me to heal your eyes?"

"I . . ." I cleared my throat. "Can you?"

He winked at me, then lifted both hands and delicately touched my temples.

67

A flash brighter than any star blinded me and I recoiled. As quickly as it had come, the light vanished. And with it, my old view of the world, replaced by new sight.

My view of the man shifted into a clarity so vivid, so sharp, so real that I snatched my hands to my mouth and gasped. His eyes, only a moment ago green, were now such a bright green and so beautifully formed that I thought they might be a dream within my dream.

He was smiling. "Not a dream, my dear. You are merely seeing again the way you were made to do."

I stared at the dunes beyond him, the sky above, the two Roush still bowing on the sand. I could see every hair of their fur, every feather on their wings, every grain of sand. I'd never seen so clearly in any dream, definitely not when awake.

"It's a beautiful world, isn't it?" he said.

I looked back into his eyes, drawn into the mystery of them.

He glanced over my shoulder at the dunes. "We don't have much time, so I need you to listen carefully. Yes?"

Each word he spoke seemed to reach into me and touch my bones.

"Yes," I said. Then again, "Yes."

"Good." He lifted his hand and drew my

hair from my forehead, like a loving father. "All men, all women, all humans yet breathing live in fear in its many forms, even as they strive to find peace in this life. Though seeing, they do not see, just like you."

My eyes were wide. "But . . . I can see . . ."

"Can you? My dear, you don't even recognize yourself yet."

"I don't?"

"No. When you do, if you can, the world will change in the blink of an eye."

His words were gentle but true to the core, as if each syllable was a force. A knot filled my throat because he was describing my blindness in Eden, surely.

"It's no mistake that you've been allowed to feel the fear that resides in the hearts of all, fear both known and unknown. You, dear daughter, have been chosen to show them the way beyond fear in this life. Only when the shadow of death is vanquished can the lion lie down with the lamb."

His words rang so true that I accepted them.

"First, you will bring the world to a point of great crisis," he said. "Then you will show them the way out of fear. Do you understand?"

No. No, I didn't understand. But as he spoke it I didn't care that I didn't understand. I just took it for the truth.

"Yes," I said, voice thin.

"But to show them the way, you will need to resolve your own fear. The blind cannot lead the blind. To be set free from your own fears, you must rediscover the Five Seals of Truth before the appointed time. This is your quest now. Time is short. Follow the narrow way that few have found, a way unknown by flesh and blood. The seals will cost you everything and show you a power far greater than you can possibly imagine. Then you will truly see what is yet unseen."

His words swirled through me and stilled my breathing.

"Only if you succeed in finding the seals before the appointed time will you be able to complete your task and lead all who follow out of the suffering that enslaves. Do you understand?"

"Seals?" I didn't even know what to ask. "What are they made of?"

"Truths, not objects. You will see."

"This isn't a dream?"

"No more or less than the other," he said, removing his hand. "The seals are equally powerful in both."

My knees felt weak, and for a moment I thought I might fall. But that would not do, so I stood as firm as I could, considering the implications of his words.

He lowered himself to one knee, scooped up some sand, and cupped both hands around the grains. Gave it a squeeze. Then opened his fingers to show me a round lump of stone the size of a baseball.

"What do you see?"

I almost said sand, but it wasn't that anymore. "A stone."

"A stone. Everything you see with your eyes is like this stone. The world before you, the body you live in, the tasks you face." He placed the stone in my hand as he said it. "Everything."

I nodded.

"Is it heavy?"

"No."

"Who's holding it?"

"I am," I said.

"And who are you?"

The question confused me. I stared at my hand, my arm. *Who are you? Where are you from? Why are you here?* I wasn't sure.

As the questions whispered through my mind, the flesh of my hand and arm faded and became translucent. I could see through my skin. Through to the veins that ran down my arm. But those veins were not filled with blood.

Light, as bright as the sun, ran through

my veins.

I blinked to clear my sight. But the vision persisted. That was me? But more . . .

And then it changed. The light in my veins began to recede up my arm, replaced by dark blood as it withdrew. First at the wrist, then slowly up my forearm.

I was so taken by the sight that I didn't at first notice the weight of the stone in my hand. It was growing heavier. By the time blood had replaced the light past my elbow, the stone was unbearably heavy.

I almost dropped it but clung tight, thinking this was a test of some sort. But I didn't have the strength to keep my arm elevated. The massive weight pulled me to one knee and slammed my hand into the ground, overcome by the weight of that one stone.

The blood replaced the light up through my shoulder, like a creeping vine slithering through my veins. Then it was into my neck and brain, and darkness swallowed my sight.

Shadow Man's taunting filled my mind. *When you see, I will blind you again, and again . . .*

I began to panic and was about to scream for help when my vision returned, from the top down. I jerked my head to look at my shoulder and saw that the light was filling my veins again, replacing the blood as it moved down my arm once more. And as it did, my arm regained its strength.

Stunned, I lifted the stone off the sand as the last of my blood was replaced with light. As I stood, my arm and hand became opaque flesh once more. A normal body.

"Whenever you try to hold the stone in flesh and blood, it will overwhelm you," the man said. "Instead, look to the light. Don't be afraid of the shadow it creates. Remember who you are. Return to the truth of your origin and recognize yourself. For this, I will send you a helper. Do you understand?"

"I . . . Yes." But only in part.

He nodded. "Find the five seals for yourself, 49th. When you do, you will know your origin and you will recognize yourself. What happens to you will happen to all. You cannot lead the world out of darkness until you find the five seals for yourself."

I was the 49th? It's what Shadow Man called me. But if Shadow Man was darkness, the man before me was light. I blinked, filled with questions.

He took the stone from my hand, and I watched as it turned to sand and slipped through his fingers and fell to the ground.

"Who are you?" I asked, looking back into his green eyes.

"I am known by many names," he said with a whimsical wink. "But you can call me Justin."

"Justin? Just Justin?"

"It is enough."

And I knew it was.

He looked over my head to the dunes again. "They're here."

I twisted to see for myself. "Who . . ."

I saw who and caught my breath.

At least fifty mounted warriors lined the dune's crest. I could see their black leather armor, the swords strapped to the saddles, their long dreadlocks.

An odor reached me, carried down by a light breeze. The stench of something rotting. The Roush streaked for the sky.

I spun back, flooded with the familiar fear of my nightmares. "Who are . . . ?"

But Justin too was gone. Just . . . gone. I was alone again!

No, not alone. I twisted back and saw the first of the horses plunging down the dune. Terror crashed through my chest. They were coming for me!

My survival instincts swallowed me whole.

I sprinted breakneck toward the only refuge I could see.

4

David paced in the examination room, mind lost on the madness of all that had transpired in the last two hours. Nothing made sense to him. There had to be an explanation, a way to figure out what had happened, and once he made sense of that much, he'd be able to take steps to reverse it. His mind was caught in a loop, rehearsing the events as they'd unfolded.

They'd injected CRISPR, and Rachelle showed no adverse reactions at first. Then Smith arrived like a puppet master speaking in riddles.

He'd evidently pricked her finger. Nothing else that they could determine.

Rachelle lay on the bed breathing evenly, no sign of trauma, no indication of any nightmare. Miranda had taken all her vitals and started a simple saline IV to keep her hydrated. Other than being in a coma, there were no indications she had suffered any harm.

He took a deep breath and let it out slowly. *Easy, David. It's going to be fine.*

The door banged open and Miranda walked in. "Just got off the phone with Dr. Bouchard in Paris. Lucky to get through. Not much is getting across the Atlantic. It's a mess out there and I don't think it's going to get any —"

"What did he say?"

"He ran a test on the sample of the CRISPR they sent. Its coding is correct. They've never seen a reaction like this without tying it directly to the errors in the genetic coding. Neither have the Chinese, as far as he knows."

"What if Rachelle's different? Is there any chance a reaction like this could be traced back to CRISPR?"

"He doesn't think so. They have her blood work. You just have to give her time. Look at her."

Rachelle lay in peace. Miranda walked up to the bed and adjusted the blanket. "I really think . . ." She froze. "What's this?"

"What?" David stepped around her and looked at Rachelle's right shoulder. A black circle, roughly three inches in diameter, had been etched into her skin. "How did that get there?"

"Did . . . I don't remember it earlier." She drew her thumb over the skin. "I could swear it wasn't here an hour ago. Looks like one of those temporary tattoos."

Odd. As odd as Smith's sudden appearance.

"Hmmm . . ." Miranda pulled the blanket up around Rachelle's neck. "Truth be told, we're not even sure she is in a coma. If she hasn't woken up by morning —"

"Morning? No." He shoved a finger at the wall. "The world's falling apart out there! We have no idea what communications and transportation will be like tomorrow. If I'm going to take her to Salt Lake, I have to go today."

She stared at him. "You know that's impossible."

"I know that my daughter is in crisis!"

Rule number one in Eden: approved visitors and deliveries entered regularly, but Simon Moses permitted no member of the community to leave the valley unless their departure was to be permanent. No one ever had taken that option. Voluntary retention was one of Simon's greatest bragging rights.

Miranda rested her elbow in the crook of her arm and nervously bit at a fingernail.

"You do realize that even if you get out, you can't discuss CRISPR with anyone outside of Eden. What we did isn't exactly legal."

"I realize that. They don't have to know about CRISPR. You're saying her condition has nothing to do with it anyway." David headed for the door. "Keep an eye on her and call me if anything changes."

"Where are you going?"

He turned back. "Simon has to know. If nothing changes in the next hour, I'm taking her to Salt Lake."

It would take him five minutes at a jog to reach the administration offices. Attached to the north side of the church, the building was made of stone blocks fortified with enough steel to withstand a nuclear blast. Of course, if it ever actually came to that, the only people to survive would be those hunkered down in this building, and the supplies in the basement would eventually run out. There would be no surviving any nuclear blast, and they all knew that.

But it made a fine statement. And to say that Eden was prepared for any event short of a nuclear blast wasn't an understatement.

David and his wife, Rachelle, had been approved for residency by council vote seventeen years earlier. After seeing the idyllic setting, Rachelle insisted that Eden was the perfect place to raise a child. Even small towns need good therapists, she said. She'd been right. David had grown to love the town, even more after his wife's death.

He took the back way, in no mood to meet whoever was out and about. By the looks of it, business had resumed after the morning news rush. Cindy leaned against the wall at the entrance to Bill's Hardware, talking to John while she puffed away at an e-cig. E-cigs were allowed because although Barth Caldwell, council member and local enforcer, had kicked his nasty cigarette habit for the sake of the no-smoking law, he still needed his nicotine fix. So he'd replaced his cigarette habit with an e-cig habit and convinced Simon to allow the exception for the whole town.

Head down, hands in pockets, David ducked into the alleyway behind the administration building and hurried to the back entrance. He found it open and pushed in.

Hillary Moses, Simon's blonde wife, who looked a good ten years younger than her husband even though they were both in their early fifties, looked up from the copy machine. "Hi, David."

"Hello, Hillary. Simon in?"

She nodded. "Been a busy day. What do you make of it?"

79

"Make of what?"

She stared at him without answering.

"You mean the grid. Terrible. He's in the chambers?" David walked toward the hall, hardly eager for a prolonged discussion with Hillary, who rarely knew when or how to stop any discourse.

"Of course the grid. What else? They say it's spreading. Texas lost half its power an hour ago. The president's holding a press conference in twenty minutes. They say he's going to declare a national state of emergency. It'll be the first time since 9/11." She paused, then wagged her head at the hall. "He's in with Linda."

"Thank you."

David hurried down the hall before she could speak again. Texas? The revelation only increased his urgency. Under any other circumstance he might be glued to the television as well, but today terrorist attacks on the national power grid would have to wait.

Three raps on the door returned Simon's familiar low voice. "Come in."

David stepped in and shut the door behind him. The large council room consisted of the Judge's mahogany desk at one end and a conference table in the center surrounded by eight stuffed chairs. Cherrywood bookcases lined three of the walls — over a thousand books, each one with a story that Simon would gladly tell to anyone who asked. Half of them were collector's editions.

The Judge sat behind his desk, feet propped up on the surface, idly tapping his cheek with a pencil. A younger twin of Clint Eastwood with a full beard. His brown eyes were inviting.

"Good morning, Doctor. What's the good word?"

David looked at Linda Loving, seated in one of two high-backed leather chairs facing the desk. As the director of social well-being, Linda was responsible for all matters related to community interaction and health, which included the hospital. She was the youngest of the four council members and the only woman. Maybe forty-five, though David didn't track ages or birthdays closely.

Linda had blonde hair and a thin frame. Two children. Her husband, Evan, had fallen from their roof and landed on his head three years earlier. She hadn't remarried. The only single parent in town. Her entire life revolved around her children, which was appropriate for someone in her position.

"Hello, Judge. Linda." He walked up to the desk and sat heavily in the chair next to her.

"That bad?" Simon asked.

David was about to respond when the Judge dropped his legs to the floor and leaned forward, eyes bright. He stabbed the desk with his forefinger as he talked.

"I'm telling you, David. Every single hour we've spent preparing over these past twenty years, every dime, is going to pay off for us in the coming days, weeks, and months. How many times have I stood before the people and spoken the truth? Perilous times are coming, but our God will shelter us in times of trouble. Run for the hills, store up thy bounty. Some may say that our laws are harsh, but those same souls will find out just how lawlessness ends." He leaned back, satisfied. Not reveling in the destruction of others, but at peace with his provision of security for his people. "How many times, David?"

"Many."

Linda was smiling, a gentle and loving devotee.

Simon nodded. "Well, now it's time to reap what we have sown, and that, my friend, is good news for Eden."

"That bad, huh?" David echoed.

"The world will never be the same."

Hillary knocked once on the door and walked in, mug of steaming coffee in her hand. She crossed to her husband, set the cup down, and kissed the top of his head. "Two sugars, honey."

"Thank you, darling." He took her hand and returned a kiss to the back of her knuckles. They'd always been like this — he the gentle master, she the woman all too pleased to follow his lead and return love in every way she could. Rather sexist, David thought, but par for the course in Eden. At least their love was genuine.

Hillary slipped out and Simon continued.

"Whoever's behind these grid failures is no slouch. They aren't saying half of it in the media. Everything's much worse. Anyone with half a brain who's spent even an hour researching the vulnerabilities of our grid knows that."

He let the comment sit, creating as good an opportunity as any.

"We have a problem," David said.

"They do, but —"

"I'm talking about Rachelle."

Simon sat back and crossed one leg over the other. "The delivery came through as promised, which I might add is a good thing. We're closing the road this afternoon, assuming the council approves, which it will." He glanced at the clock on the wall. "We meet at noon. Half an hour."

"You're talking about CRISPR?" Linda asked.

Simon nodded. To David: "So what's the problem? When are you going to administer it?"

"That's just it. We already did."

Simon's brow arched. "That was quick. And?"

"And . . ." He hadn't planned to tell them everything, but it occurred to him now that he both wanted and needed their full support. Both were trustworthy and had good hearts, which was much more than he could say for the other two council members, Barth and Maxwell.

So he told them. Everything except for Vlad Smith's claim of authority over Simon and his claim that something was very wrong in Eden.

A shadow fell over Simon's expression. "What was his point? You're saying he physically attacked you?"

"Pushed me. He . . . I'm not sure what his point was. For all I know he's just some nutcase who found his way in. Says he wants to bring sight to the blind. But he's not the issue. Rachelle is."

The second hand on the wall clock clicked through time.

"Sight to the blind," Simon said. "Those were his words?"

"Something like that."

"Vlad Smith, you say. I'll let Barth know." He jotted down the name. "The last thing we need is an intruder. So how did our brave girl do?"

There was no graceful way to say it.

"Not good. She fell into a coma."

The Judge stared at him. "What do you mean, she fell into a coma?"

"I mean she had a reaction of some kind."

"To what this Smith did?"

"We have no idea what's happening. We reached out to Dr. Bouchard in Paris and verified the genetic coding."

"So it's not CRISPR then."

"If it is, it's a first. Either way, we have to deal with the coma now." A beat. "I think I need to take her to Salt Lake City. Today. I just need you to know that. We've exhausted our resources here."

Simon remained silent, eyes fixed on David.

"But she's safe?" Linda asked.

"No, Linda. She's in a coma!"

"I know, I just . . . I didn't mean . . . Forgive me, David. I don't mean to understate the seriousness of her situation. If we were talking about one of mine I'd be climbing the walls." She turned to Simon. "I think taking her to Salt Lake is a perfectly reasonable course of action."

"It's not that simple," the Judge said. "Our bylaws strictly prohibit it. Not to mention we're in a state of emergency here."

"My *daughter's* in a state of emergency," David bit off. "The situation is quite simple."

"No, it's not. Denver's next to go down, and that's if we're lucky. More likely, the power collapse is going to reach the West Coast sooner than anyone expects. When that happens, Salt Lake will be affected. Even if we made an exception, you might find Salt Lake without power."

"That's a risk I'm willing to take. Hospitals have generators."

"Not if the attack's an EMP."

"Like I said, I'll accept that risk."

The Judge studied him, frowning.

"I came because I respect and honor you and this valley," David said. "But if I don't see a change in Rachelle in the next two hours, I'll have no choice but to take her."

"Everyone has a choice," the Judge said. "You realize that if you do leave, you won't be able to return. I for one find Rachelle a blessing. And you're an indispensable member of our community. But I can't just bend the rules for the sake of one."

Heat flashed up David's neck, but he checked himself. "Please, Simon. Doesn't Eden exist for our children?"

"It does," Linda said, eyeing Simon. "It most certainly does. And with our restrictions on childbirth, each child is our highest priority. Rachelle may be blind, but she's more able-minded than any of her peers. I for one would support David's case for Salt Lake."

She was referring to a law that restricted the population of children under the age of sixteen never to exceed more than twenty percent of the general population. With such limited space, the growth of the community had to be engineered and contained. In any case, no more than two children were allowed for even the most loyal and God-fearing families.

Simon dipped his head. "Give us a few minutes, will you, David? I need a word with Linda."

"Now?"

He indicated the door. "Have a cup of coffee with Hillary. She likes talking to you."

"I don't need to stress how critical —"

"Just a few minutes, David. Please."
David hesitated, then stood. "Of course."

5

The thought that I was lying on an examination table in Eden, Utah, didn't even occur to me as I ran. Neither did the fact that I could see with stunning clarity for the first time in my life. Wherever I was, it was real, more real than any dream I'd ever had, and I could hear the thunder of hooves behind me. I kept my fists pumping and my feet churning. All I could think of was that narrow, twenty-foot-wide canyon directly ahead of me, jerking up and down in my view as I sprinted.

If I could just reach it, they could only follow me two or three at a time. That would slow them down. That's all I cared about. Never mind that I might be trapped inside.

I nearly made it to the gap when I saw a smaller opening to my right. How deep? No idea, but it was only wide enough for one horse, so I altered my course without breaking stride.

Someone with a deep, gruff voice was yelling. "Maco, to the back! See if there's a way out!"

And then I was there, through the narrow gap, sandwiched by vertical walls. The passage was maybe five feet wide, but it quickly opened up to twice that. Only then did it occur to me that I was in a fishbowl. If the bend ahead didn't offer me options, they would catch me right here.

None of this slowed me down. I rounded the bend in three breaths and saw that the canyon split into three smaller channels. I could hear the first horse snorting as it entered the gap behind me. But I was out of sight for the moment. I had to keep it that way.

I angled for the break to my left, because my move would be hidden from their view for a few strides more.

Of course, it didn't matter where I went because my feet were leaving marks in the sand, deep enough for even a blind person to follow. My only hope was to find an opening that was too narrow for not only their horses but them as well. I was skinny; they were hulking warriors.

A hoot and holler chased me. "No way out, Albino!"

The canyon I found myself in was as wide

as the one behind, but it too had several fissures. How deep did they go? What if these canyons ran only for a few hundred yards, like a giant rock that had been fractured over the years? They could just surround the whole thing and wait me out.

I pushed the thought away, tore into the narrowest of the fissures I could quickly identify, and raced forward.

Right into a huge sandy bowl, surrounded on all sides by sheer rising rock.

I slid to a stop, panting, frantically searching the walls and boulders for an escape, a place to hide, any option at all. They were still coming — I could hear them talking in low tones — but they'd slowed their horses to a walk.

They clearly knew something I didn't. One way or the other, they'd soon catch their prey.

If there was an exit or a place to hide in the bowl, I couldn't see it. Maybe I was supposed to encounter them as a way of facing my fear. Or maybe I was just in another nightmare . . .

A horizontal crack along the bottom of the wall to my left caught my eye. It was only ten feet away, and I reached it in three leaping strides.

I threw myself to the sand and rolled

under the cliff wall just as the first horse stepped into the opening.

A low chuckle. "She hides under the wall like a mouse."

The gap was only a foot high, and I scooted deeper on my back, then deeper. Into the darkness.

I stilled my breathing as best I could. To my left: blackness that could very well end in a few feet. Above me: a flat stone ceiling, inches from my nose. To my right: the thin gap under the cliff, glowing with light twenty feet away.

I could see the hooves of several horses in that gap. Then boots, as one of the warriors dropped from his mount with a soft thud. He settled to one knee, bent over, and peered in, staring directly at me. The man was mostly backlit, but the light revealed the side of his face when he turned. His skin was cracked, dark gray.

If I was an Albino Mystic, they were anything but. So then, these riders were what Gabil had called the Horde?

The warrior sniffed the air, then spat to one side and stood. I watched wide-eyed as four or five horses grouped around the first.

"How deep?" one of them asked.

"We'll need fire to see. But she can't be too deep, her stench is strong."

"Maco, strike a fire."

"Yes, sire."

I closed my eyes and tried to calm my frayed nerves. A panic attack now would get me killed. Only minutes earlier, I'd been stunned by new sight, but what good was that sight now?

Though seeing, you do not see . . .

But I did see. Right now I was trapped under a massive slab of granite. Or was I in Eden, lying on an examination table with CRISPR flowing through my veins?

Okay, calm down, Rachelle. Take a deep breath. Think.

My senses were far more acute than most humans'. Case in point: I already knew some things about the warriors that others would not.

Their leader was probably the one who'd asked how deep — the authority in his voice compared to the others said so. There were fifteen or twenty of them in the bowl now — I could tell by the sound of hooves, the creaking of their saddles, the small talk and coughs.

And in the dark . . . I could see in the dark where they would be blind, unless they too could use echolocation, which they couldn't, or they would have used it already.

Eyes still closed, I turned my head away

from the opening and clicked a few times. Sonic waves showed the form of my tomb, up to a point. It ran deep before fading. To a dead end? Could be. But I doubted it, because now at rest, I could feel a hint of air flowing over my skin from that direction.

Of course, this much air movement might come from a two-inch gap in the wall. That the air was flowing toward the horsemen meant they wouldn't have any success smoking me out.

Didn't matter. I was still trapped.

I grasped for ideas.

Two options came to me: I could wait here, hoping they would tire of waiting for me to emerge, or I could venture deeper in to find that source of air, hoping it was large enough to crawl through.

Neither felt very hopeful.

But then a third course opened in my mind. They already knew I was here, right? Why not talk to them? The thought terrified me, but by talking to them, I might learn more of my predicament. If nothing else, why they were chasing me.

A blazing torch filled the gap to my right. The warrior drew it back and forth, searching for me. I could see his eyes in the light, gray like his skin. In every other respect he looked like any other human.

I was evidently too far in for him to see. He withdrew the torch and started to stand.

"Hey," I said.

He bent down. Looked inside again. Then started to stand again.

"Hey!"

He jerked his head back down. "I can hear her!"

"I need to talk to your leader," I said, aware that my voice was shaking.

"She's talking to me!" the man said.

"You can see her?"

"No." He lifted his head and twisted back. "But she says she wants to talk to Jacob."

"To me? She knows my name?"

"No, she said leader."

"She wants to talk to the leader, then."

"Yes. That's what she said."

They went silent for a moment before the one I now knew to be Jacob spoke.

"And what did you tell her?"

"I didn't tell her anything."

"Why not?"

"Because she said she wanted to speak to the leader."

"Now you take orders from a runaway slave, Maco?"

"She's not a slave, sire. She's one of Ba'al's lab rats."

95

"That's hardly the point. She's an Albino. I, Jacob, son of Qurong, do not speak to Albinos. I will do my father's bidding, return this piece of meat to its proper place, and get back to the arms of the women who wait for me."

Someone farther away chuckled. "And how many women would that be?"

"More than you've had, Risin. Meaning at least one."

A soft chorus of laughter. They were clearly unconcerned about me escaping.

"Hey!" I yelled.

That shut them up.

"Jacob! Aren't you man enough to speak to a woman? Or do Albinos frighten you?"

A long pause.

"Tell her of course not," Jacob said.

Maco bent down and spoke loudly into the crack. "He says of course not."

"I know what he said. I can hear him."

"She says she can hear you," Maco told Jacob, turning back.

"Ask him how I ended up in the desert," I pressed. "Why I can't remember."

"She says she doesn't remember how she escaped."

"Of course she can't remember. Ba'al has cleansed her mind with his poison. Tell her that if she would just come out, we could all get back to our lives."

"She can hear you, sire. I don't think I need to —"

"Just tell her!"

So Maco did tell me. Some might think Jacob was dense, but I knew by his intonation that he was manipulating in his own way. His voice didn't carry cruelty.

"Remind Jacob that Ba'al will have his head on a platter if anything happens to me," I said loudly so Jacob could hear. My claim was pure fabrication, but I had nothing to lose. "Remind him that I am the 49th! Tell him that."

Maco started to relay my words, but Jacob cut him off.

"Ba'al said nothing of that."

"Perhaps Ba'al does not know."

"Perhaps she lies."

"I'm not lying!" I cried. "I *am* the 49th."

For a long moment, no one spoke. The 49th clearly meant something to them.

"Does she think tales of prophecies will save her? Tell her —"

"I'll bring the lion to lie down with the lamb," I said, remembering Justin's words and desperate for some advantage. "If it wasn't true, Justin wouldn't have said so."

Another long pause.

"Tell her that no harm will come to her if

she comes out. She has my word. In either case, she's trapped."

I had to buy myself some time, at least until nightfall. I could see in the dark; they could not.

"Tell her!"

Maco told me.

"I may have run out of space," I returned, "but I'm in too deep for you to smoke or dig out. Even if you did try to smoke me out, I might die from the smoke. So actually, I'm in charge of my surrender, not you. And I swear I'll lie here and starve to death before I come out without certain assurances."

He considered this.

"Ask her what assurances," Jacob said.

Maco waited for me to answer directly this time, clearly tired of Jacob's games. But I didn't answer, not right away, because the faint sound of hissing had diverted my attention. A snake . . . I despised snakes. But it wasn't close.

I turned my head back to the gap. "The first assurance is that I will ride with Jacob, on his horse."

Someone out there, several someones, thought that was funny. "At least she's a woman."

"An Albino," another said, then spat in disgust.

"Please, Brack. Don't tell me you've never —"

"Silence!" Jacob snapped. To Maco: "Ask her what else."

"I want some water in here," I answered without subjecting Maco to his absurd role.

"Tell her she won't need water in there because I'm going to grant her wish. She can come out now."

"Not now. I need to think about what other assurances I need. I need rest and water so I can clear my mind."

"Tell her no amount of thinking will help her. Her flight is over."

"It's not negotiable. If you want to return me to Ba'al alive, these are my terms."

"Your terms are more time to think of other terms?" Jacob asked.

"Yes."

"Fire!" a distant voice growled. "With arrows. Stick one in her leg, that will motivate her."

"Are you in command now, Risin?" Jacob said. "Tell me what happens if we wound her."

No response. Evidently I was to be returned unharmed. That gave me some hope.

"How much time?" he finally asked, speaking directly to me for the first time.

The more time the better. Darkness would be my only friend here.

"Till morning."

"What? Absurd!"

"No, that would be your high priest, for valuing me so highly. Otherwise you could just kill me and be done with it. After all, I'm just an Albino woman, right?"

Silence.

Except for that hiss again, now down past my feet. Suddenly I wasn't so eager to lie there and think.

"For the record," Jacob said, speaking in a low but adamant tone. I twisted my head to see that he'd dismounted and was now speaking into the crevasse. "I've never killed a woman, Albino or otherwise, nor will I."

I could see his face, smoother than the others' and covered with a gray powder or clay, which I thought might be the source of the flowery scent.

"We planned on camping here tonight at any rate," he said. "It's a full day's ride back." He slung in a leather pouch of water and it landed halfway between us. "You have your night. But in the morning, we go. I swear none of my men will touch you. Say yes."

That hissing was growing louder and I

began to panic. Because of my blindness, I'd never been claustrophobic, but snakes were the stuff of my nightmares.

"Yes," I said, mind racing. I had to move!

And I did. I started to shift up and away from the sound. But with the first flinch of my foot, something hard and sharp struck my heel.

Pain sliced up my calf, then my thigh. *I have to get out now! I have to surrender to Jacob so he can save me. I've been bitten by a snake!*

I started to scoot toward the opening, but I had moved all of three feet when the snake's venom reached my mind.

The world faded and then went black.

6

I could hear my breathing in and out through my nose as I took quick, shallow draws of air. I was safe, I thought. The bite hadn't killed me, just put me out for a little while.

I took a deep breath and opened my eyes, expecting to see only the blackness of the cave. But it wasn't black. It was white. White, marked by tiny holes. And two fluorescent lights.

I sat halfway up and twisted my head. I was in the examination room! Alone, with a blanket pulled up to my chest.

But of course I was. I had fallen asleep on the table and dreamed of another world. Earth, two thousand years in the future. I was . . .

It struck me then, like a bowling ball to the chest.

My eyes! I was seeing with my eyes! In Eden!

There, on the wall, was a calendar with a brown dog catching a small blue ball in its mouth. I assumed it was a June calendar, but I couldn't read — with my fingers, yes, but not with my eyes. The letters were clear enough, but they were completely foreign to me. Further proof that I could truly see. If my mind was making this up, it would probably ascribe some meaning to the words.

There, on the counter, was a silver tray with bandages and several drug vials. I picked up a large red syringe and recognized it by touch. Adrenaline — in the case of a sedative overdose, at my father's insistence. I'd held them before. This was the first time I'd actually seen one.

Stunned, I flung the blanket aside and slid off the table. Pain ripped up my arm and I saw I'd pulled an IV needle from my hand, leaving a small, bloody tear.

At the same time, pain flashed up my leg from my heel. The snakebite . . .

It seemed inconsequential to me now. I stood there beside the bed, staring around the room, overwhelmed with the sights, the colors, the shapes, the clarity of all that I saw.

I blinked. What if this *was* a dream?

The details of my experience spun through my mind, fixing me there on the floor for a few seconds. The white bats insisted I was only dreaming of Eden. Then Justin gave his charge to me: find the Five Seals of Truth.

Then the Horde and the cave and Jacob.

A dream.

But how, if Justin had given me sight in that dream? Maybe my mind had finally surrendered to all of my father's *you create your own reality* talk. Epigenetics in the now.

"Dad?"

My voice sounded hollow in the empty room. I hurried to the door, eager to show him. All the surfaces and objects that I'd known as dark shapes now lay before me in brilliant dimension and color, far more beautiful than I could have expected. The round silver doorknob, the smooth gray cabinets, the glass door . . . Just like in my dreams, only here and now.

I pulled up in front of that glass door and stared at my reflection. Blue jeans, black T-shirt, long black hair . . . So this is what a sixteen-year-old girl looked like. How I looked.

I turned to my right and saw a mirror on the wall above the sink, almost magically framing my image. I stepped up to it, amazed. Bright blue eyes above a small nose. Smooth, fair skin.

I was here and I could see. My father had to know!

The hall was empty when I stepped into it. I headed to the reception area, gazing at the dark green wallpaper and polished floor tiles, everything so amazing and clean.

My heel throbbed a little with each step, but the pain was already fading.

"Hi, Rachelle."

Sue sat behind the counter, watching the television. The president was talking — I'd never seen him but I knew his voice well. So this is what a television looked like. And this is what Sue looked like. Plump, with tangled blonde hair, totally different than I had pictured her.

"All done today? Your father left about an hour ago."

She knew nothing about CRISPR.

"I'm going to go find him," I said.

She glanced up. "You need any help?"

"Have I ever needed help?"

"Well, David's usually with you when you come . . ." She couldn't tell that my eyes were working. I supposed they looked the same to her as on any other day. I was under the cover of my own self. Incognito.

"It's okay, I got this, Sue." I headed for the front door, grinning. "By the way, I like your green dress."

"Well, thank you, dear."

"You're welcome."

I was halfway out the door when things clicked in Sue's head. "How did you . . ."

The rest was lost when the door swung shut behind me.

I looked at Eden for the first time. Bright green trees and manicured lawns. The buildings, the road, what might be a hawk in the blue sky. It was all new and stunning. I'd seen all these kinds of things before, in my dreams, but never here, in Eden, and never awake.

The sky . . . The sky was the only thing that looked different. Brighter and bluer than anything I had seen or imagined. Definitely bluer than the sky in the desert world.

Seeing really was like dying and going to heaven.

Running wasn't something that had ever come easily to me in my waking life. It's hard to run when you're clicking and seeing only shapes. As a consequence, I had spent most of my life walking — and carefully.

Now that I was able to see, my feet dared me to run and I couldn't resist. I bounded down the sidewalk, then turned down the street, headed for the center of town.

"Woo-hoo!" I cried, jumping in the air and

pumping my fist. I was like a superhero in this world, able to skip and jump and spin and shout at the top of my lungs if I wanted to, and I almost did.

Instead, I slowed to a walk, breathing in clean, cool air. No need to rush things. I should relish each step.

Seeing, you do not see . . . The phrase from my dream that obviously wasn't just a dream filled my mind. I might not be able to see whatever I was meant to see, but I was seeing for the first time in my life, and it was intoxicating.

I caught sight of my shoes and stopped on the sidewalk. My favorite white Converses. They were more tattered and stained than I'd realized. Maybe I should listen to my father and get a new pair.

It took me five minutes to reach the center of town, walking normally, glancing over as I passed several people. They just saw me as Rachelle, the blind girl they didn't quite know how to treat.

To me, on the other hand, they looked brand new. I had no clue who each of them was, because I knew people only by their voices and no one was talking. But I didn't want to stare and give myself away. Not before my father knew.

I walked down Third Street and past the

grocery store, which was busy enough —
two cars and three pickup trucks were
parked out front. I was tempted to walk in
and see what all the groceries looked like
but decided I had my whole life to discover
those things.

"Hi, Rachelle." The voice belonged to
Cindy Jarvis, who had just come out of
Bill's Hardware to my left. "You okay?"

I stopped and turned to her, unable to
hide my smile. "Yes."

"My, aren't we chipper today?" The
woman was prettier than I'd imagined.
Which might be why Bill Baxter, the owner
of the hardware store, had a thing for her in
secret, judging by the way he talked when
she was around.

"It's a beautiful day," I said. And then,
without thinking, "I've never seen such a
blue sky."

She took a puff on one of those electronic
vaporizers and glanced up. "It *is* a nice day."
She paused. Eyes back down, studying me.

That's right, I thought. *I can see! I can see
everything you can see. And seeing you, I can
see why your boss has a thing for you. Yup,
that's something I've already seen. So see, I
can see even better than you.*

The door opened and a boy my age
stepped out.

"You can see the sky?" Cindy asked.

But my eyes were on the boy. I didn't know who he was yet, but I could see how he looked. A foot taller than me with wavy brown hair. And blue eyes like mine, which looked amazing with his dark hair. Even more amazing with the blue shirt he was wearing, sleeves rolled up around strong muscles.

A part of me that didn't know any better fell in love with him at first sight. I was, after all, still a sixteen-year-old girl, and although boys had never really been a part of my life, I could see now why they should be.

He stared at me for a few seconds. "Who can see the sky?" he said.

Peter. This was Peter Moses, the son of Simon, the Judge. The same Peter who had never given me a second look that I knew of. The boy I had sometimes imagined being kissed by.

That was in my dreams. In real life, I didn't dare talk to him.

I could feel fear pulling me under like sinking sand as I stared at him. And the thought of falling back into fear terrified me more than the fear of talking to him.

So I impulsively stepped up to him, searched his face and eyes, and said, "The sky's as blue as your eyes, Peter Moses." I reached up and touched his cheek. "I never realized that you were so pretty."

He blinked but stood perfectly still.

"Rachelle?" a voice yelled. I spun to the sound of my father's voice. He was running down the street past the church.

"Don't touch her!" he yelled. To me: "What are you doing? How did . . ."

I ran to meet him, feeling like a goddess treading among mortals. And to me he looked like a god — beautiful and strong.

"I can see!"

Then I was in his arms, being swung around. He held me tight for just a moment, then set me down and held me at arm's length, staring at my eyes.

"What do you mean you can see?"

"I can see." I swept my arms wide, looking at the tall trees by the church and the blue sky with fluffy clouds up high. "Everything! I can see everything."

At least a dozen people within earshot of my announcement stopped what they were doing and looked at us. RG and Miranda were running down the street from the direction of the hospital. I was suddenly the center of attention. My life had just been made new.

"But honey, CRISPR doesn't work like

that," my father said, still stunned. "You . . . You blacked out. You . . . We thought you were in a coma." He remembered where he was and glanced around.

"She can really see?" Cindy asked behind me. A circle of sorts was forming around us. "What's CRISPR?"

Miranda and RG burst through the gathering crowd.

"It wasn't CRISPR," I said to my father. "I was healed in a dream. A man . . ." I stopped, realizing how absurd it would sound.

"What dream?" Cindy asked. "You can really see, Rachelle? Like normal?"

"I don't know what normal is," I said, "but I'm looking at the flowers on your shirt and they're green. Pretty flowers."

She glanced down as if to confirm what she obviously knew.

"What man?" Bill Baxter had joined us on the street and was looking me over.

"Vlad Smith," my father said, putting his arm around me as if to protect me. "A healer who visited the hospital today." He began to shepherd me away from them. "Please, give us some room."

With that he hurried me away, followed closely by RG and Miranda.

"It's true?" Miranda asked, hurrying to

catch us. "We should run some blood work." And then, when I didn't respond: "But how's that possible? Nothing we did could have caused such radical spontaneous remission."

When we were far enough away from the small crowd, all now talking excitedly, my father turned to me, eyes misted with tears. He cupped my cheek with his hand.

"You really can see? I mean, yes, but . . . You can see my face? My eyes?"

"For the first time." I smiled at him. "I always knew you were handsome, but didn't realize your eyes were so blue. Just like mine."

I don't think he'd believed this day would ever come. I know I hadn't, not really.

"Who's Vlad Smith?" I asked.

"No one, honey."

But Miranda didn't let it go. "You don't actually believe —"

"Of course I don't." He glanced at the chattering crowd. "Better for them to get lost in some harmless metaphysical psychobabble than ask more questions about CRISPR."

"You told them about CRISPR?"

"No. But I might have let the word slip."

"Who's Vlad Smith?" I asked again. "Tell me."

So he quickly told me how the man had come while I was sleeping and pricked my finger before reciting something about seeing.

A moment of confusion darkened my mood. There was Justin; there was Shadow Man. Who was Vlad? Shadow Man had insisted that he would blind me again, but I could see, really see.

"He said that?" I asked. "That he'd come to heal me and give Eden sight?"

"Something like that, yes."

"What else did he say?"

My father pointed me toward home. "He said that things aren't really what they seem. Like the wool's been pulled over our eyes. And he claims to know more than Simon."

"Do you believe him?"

"I don't know. No. I doubt it."

"But I can see. So maybe he did something good, right?"

He shook his head in wonder. "Yes, you can see." Kissed my forehead. "But I can't say he had anything to do with it. I think spontaneous remission —"

"Spontaneous remissions don't present in two hours," Miranda interrupted. "Not like this."

"We don't know when it started. Could've been keyed up for months now without our

113

knowledge. She can see, that's what's important."

"I should talk to him," I said.

"Not a chance," my father said. "I don't want you anywhere near him, not until we know more."

"David?"

We all turned toward the church, where Simon Moses stood, staring at me.

"She can see?"

My father took my hand. "Come on, honey." He led me toward the Judge. "Let's show them."

There were four of us and four of them seated at the table in the council chamber. I knew them all by their voices but was amazed by the difference between how they looked with echolocation sight and eyesight.

The four of us were me, my dad, Miranda, and RG.

The other four were Eden's governing council.

Simon Moses, the Judge, whom I had always thought of as God's authority on earth. I had a deep respect for him. He had soft but firm eyes, which suited him well. Simon had always been kind to me. Like a rock, but genuinely caring.

Linda Loving, who had a genuine heart

for the community's well-being, the children in particular. She kept looking at me and smiling.

Maxwell Emerson, who was in charge of all resources, meaning money, food, and energy. He wore a new blue suit that was too tight across his large belly. Bald, shiny head. I'd always heard a distant, uncaring quality in his voice, and seeing him now only deepened the impression. The flesh around his eyes drooped like big teardrops. I felt a little sorry for him.

Barth Caldwell, who was in charge of security. He reminded me of what I thought a bulldog looked like. Or a Rottweiler. A good-looking one who was as tall as he was thick. Black hair and bushy eyebrows. He made me nervous.

That was them, seated across from us with Simon at the head of the table. My father had just recounted all the details concerning the injection of CRISPR and the entrance of Vlad Smith. I should say, all the details except Smith's claims that something was wrong in Eden.

All four had listened with eager attention, and at times bewilderment. It isn't every day that blind people just start seeing.

"You're saying this Vlad Smith actually healed her?" Barth asked. "That this little

115

parlor trick of his somehow opened her eyes?"

"No, I'm not saying that. I'm just filling you in on what happened. Nothing more."

"God doesn't heal that way."

"You don't know that," Linda said. "Jesus healed the blind using mud."

He glared at my father, which surprised me. We'd come to give them the good news, but Barth looked like we'd just told him the hydroelectric plant had blown up. As I saw his reaction, fear began to creep back into my mind.

Barth scooted his chair back and walked to a liquor cabinet, illegal everywhere but in here, evidently. "The president's declared a national state of emergency, freeways are being closed along the East Coast to keep people from clogging them up, nothing's flying east of Denver. Salt Lake will be next. We need to shut down the road. Whoever Smith is, he's got to go before he causes any more trouble."

"Trouble?" Linda glared at him. "Have some decency! Rachelle can see, for crying out loud."

"You'll have to forgive his manners," Simon said, looking at me apologetically. "Tough times."

I smiled. "It's okay."

Barth lifted his glass toward me. "I'm happy for you." To Simon: "But this character's a problem."

Simon acknowledged him with a slight, nervous nod. He faced my father. "Who else knows about him?"

My father shrugged. "Everyone in the square. By tomorrow, everyone in town. You can't keep a lid on something like this."

The Judge slowly leaned back, face drawn. What struck me was how upset he was even without having heard the details my father left out. It made me wonder if the Judge really was hiding something.

I decided then that I didn't want to be in that room. The sooner we got out, the better.

"Where is he now?" Simon demanded.

"I don't know. He just walked out."

"Find him." He drilled Barth with a glare. "Find him now."

"Shouldn't be hard." The councilman drank the last of his liquor and set his shot glass down.

"Find him and bring him to me. Then seal up that tunnel. No one gets in without my express permission. You hear? Not a mouse."

"Why not just throw him out?"

"Because I want to know what he thinks he knows." Simon's eyes shifted to Linda.

"Call a town hall meeting for tomorrow night. I want every last soul there. The last thing we need right now is someone exerting authority based on a parlor trick."

His reaction had me thinking about my dreams again. It was something the Roush had said about how I could know this was a dream by asking the right questions.

Right there in those chambers, everything seemed real. But that's also how I'd felt when I was in the desert. What if *this* was the dream and I couldn't really see? I couldn't shake that feeling. The fear of that possibility pushed me over the top.

"Can I ask a question?" I said.

The Judge turned his head. "Of course."

"Do you think it's possible that something's wrong with Eden?" My voice was thin.

All eyes were on me. A shadow crossed my dad's face, and I regretted asking the question. But it was too late now.

"What do you mean, wrong?" the Judge asked.

"I mean . . . What if we're blind and don't know it?"

They just looked at me, including RG and Miranda.

Simon finally forced a polite grin. "What makes you ask that?"

"The man in my dreams."

"What man?"

"Actually, it was a fluffy white bat." I held out my hand to show size. "Two feet tall, called a Roush."

Silence.

I felt a little foolish. But I had only asked a question. Maybe I should have left out the part about the bats.

My father came to my rescue. "Metaphorically speaking, I think we all have our blind sides, even in Eden. You know that better than most, Rachelle."

"Blindness," the Judge said, "is the condition of the world. Not Eden."

I nodded. "Yeah, that's what I thought."

For a long moment that I thought might not end, Simon just stared at me. Then he abruptly stood and walked out.

"Meeting adjourned," Barth said, grinning.

My father was looking at my arm. I glanced down and saw that, seated the way I was, my T-shirt sleeve had ridden up my arm a bit, exposing a mark on my shoulder.

I reached over and pulled my sleeve all the way up. There, on my arm, was a circle about three inches in diameter. Like the one I had in my dreams. But how was that possible?

"What is it?" Linda asked.

I touched it with my finger, then rubbed it. A tattoo, not fresh but old, if I wasn't mistaken. My mind spun.

"Where did you get it?" my father wanted to know.

I quickly pulled my sleeve back down. "I'll explain later."

But I knew there was no way to explain it.

That day in Eden was without question the best day of my life. On one hand, everything was topsy-turvy because a part of me — the part with a tattoo from another world — couldn't stop wondering what was really happening. What was the 49th? Was it real like the tattoo on my arm? Was there really light in my veins? Of course not, so it all had to be in my mind. Symbolism, like my father insisted. If the 49th was real, that would mean Shadow Man was also real, right? I couldn't accept that thought.

On the other hand, being able to see filled me with wonder. And once I let go of my fear that I would fall back into fear, I couldn't wipe the grin off my face.

It faded a little when Miranda worried aloud that my sight might only be tempo-rary, a psychosomatic alteration prompted by dreams so vivid that they'd convinced my mind to manifest sight. Classic epigenetic spontaneous remission, she said. When people believe — really believe — then genes change and the body follows, regardless of religion, creed, or history. But when belief wanes, conditions revert.

My father scolded her. Considering my nightmares, she should know better than to voice the concern. She apologized.

My grin returned when my father took a sponge, dumped some soap on it, and vigorously scrubbed the tattoo on my arm, sure that he could get it off. He couldn't.

The pain in my foot was gone. I pulled off my shoe and found two small red spots on my heel, right next to a small cut from running through the desert.

Real.

So the dream I'd had wasn't a dream. Justin had healed my eyes, and the bite on my heel along with the tattoo on my arm proved it to me. As for Shadow Man, if he was real . . . Well, he was only a personification of my fear. Justin, on the other hand, had healed me. I refused to believe anything less. I could see.

And what I saw blew my mind.

I was the fascination of the town. After Miranda, RG, and my father had poked and prodded me and taken more of my blood to run even more tests, my father escorted me home. He didn't want me mobbed. Then he returned to the clinic.

I went out twice by myself that afternoon, in part to prove to myself that I had nothing to fear, in part just to see the town. Both times I was quickly surrounded by people I knew, though not by sight. And again that grin was stuck to my face.

"How many fingers am I holding up?" Randy Caldwell asked when he and four other kids hunted me down.

"That's too easy," his younger sister, Ashley, said. "What color is my bicycle?"

"Purple," I said. "With a white pinstripe."

"How many fingers am I holding up?" Randy asked again, holding his hands behind his back now.

"One. Your thumb. The rest aren't pointed up."

He did a double take. "You can see that?"

"No," I said. "It's how everyone holds their hands behind their backs."

Pretty Peter, the Judge's son, was leaning against the church, arms crossed, watching us.

"Excuse me." I left the group of younger kids and walked toward Peter, heart hammering in my chest.

He straightened and lowered his arms as I

approached. "Hi, Rachelle."

I could smell the lavender soap he used to bathe. "Hi." He was shy too, I thought.

"How did it happen?"

"Like my father said —"

"Yeah, I know. A healer. But what really happened? Because whatever it was, my father isn't too pleased. They can't find him."

"They can't find the Judge?"

"No, this Vlad Smith guy. He's gone."

I shrugged. "I don't know. I never did see him. To be honest, I'm not sure I gained my sight here."

"What do you mean, not here?" His gentle blue eyes were filled with genuine curiosity.

"Just between us? Because not even you will believe me."

"Just between us."

So I told him. Everything. Even the part about Vlad Smith saying there was something wrong with Eden. I told him because I wanted to tell someone, if only to hear myself speaking it. And I had to admit, hearing myself, I wondered once again if everything in my dreams was only the product of wild imagination, mirroring my own experience here in Eden.

I told him that as well.

"Then how do you explain the tattoo?" he asked.

I lifted my shirtsleeve and stared at it. "So, it must be real, right? Plus . . . I can see."

"Can I touch it?"

"Touch it?"

"First tattoo I've seen in real life."

"Me too." They were illegal in Eden thanks to a teaching that marking the body was ungodly. So was jewelry. And any clothing that revealed too much flesh. And unsanctioned courtship. "Go ahead."

He touched my skin with one finger first, drawing it over the thin circle, then with his hand, gentle and warm. I couldn't deny the way his touch stirred up butterflies in my belly.

Our eyes met. "Feels like normal skin," he said. But he let his hand linger a few seconds before lowering it.

My breathing had thickened a smidge. Could he hear it the same way I could? "Yup. Just normal skin." If people saw us standing here like this, they might get the wrong idea. "I have to run, okay?"

"Okay." His voice was strained.

"Okay." I started to leave but turned back. "Keep what I said between us, right?"

"I will."

I hurried straight home with my head

down, watching the road so no one would stop me. That smile returned to my face halfway there. I did believe I'd just had my first romantic encounter.

Yes, I knew from my father that such feelings were caused by a cocktail of hormones called limerence secreted by the pituitary gland to ensure the bonding and mating of the species. The "love" feelings associated with limerence lasted from six to twenty-four months before fading — just long enough for humans to relax their judgment of each other, couple, and bear children to keep the race alive. Beyond that, limerence had to be cultivated in the brain through intention. It was all hormones, you see?

Sure . . . So was the taste of a sweet peach. And I loved it.

By the time I kissed my father good night, I was thoroughly exhausted. I breathed a prayer of gratefulness to God. I was obviously doing something right, because I could see.

And when you see, I'm going to blind you. I'm going to blind you again and again . . .

Shadow Man's voice fell into my mind as I fell into bed, and with those words, fear darkened my world, as if the plug on my light had been pulled. I sat up in the darkness and turned on the nightlight. What if

125

the nightmare returned? What if Shadow Man really would come and blind me again? Now that I was able to see, the thought of losing my sight filled me with a new kind of terror.

I had to suppress the impulse to throw off the covers and rush to my father. But we both knew my fear was only in my head anyway. I'd faced fear my whole life. I could do it one more night.

I lay back down, intent on letting go of my fear. My experience in the desert, seeing the light being pushed from my veins until I was once more blind, gave me some comfort because it reminded me I was only blind to who I really was.

Was being blind to who you are better or worse than physical blindness?

One of my favorite stories of Jesus popped into my mind. It was about a young man born blind, kind of like me. Jesus healed him. When asked whether the boy's blindness was judgment for his father's sin or his own sin, Jesus said neither. The boy was born blind so that the work of God would be seen in him.

When I first heard the story in Sunday school many years ago, I could feel the rest of the class looking at me. What a cruel God, I had thought. What kind of father would subject his child to so much suffering just so the world could see God's light?

I'd rushed home and read the story over and over in Braille, feeling like a victim of some cruel joke, a pawn in a war for power. But then a new thought dropped into my mind and I gasped aloud, right there on my bed.

The boy hadn't been born blind so that the world would see the work of God. He'd been born blind so that he himself would one day see God's work in him! Which meant that even though I had been blind since I was a baby, maybe my blindness would one day allow me to see God's work in me. Blindness wasn't punishment, it was a gateway. An invitation.

Right then, the story became a favorite. I set it right next to my fear that I was being punished by God, unable to reconcile the two thoughts but finding hope anyway.

I clung to the story now as I lay in bed. More than two hours after climbing under the covers, I finally drifted to sleep. And when I fell asleep, I dreamed.

And when I dreamed, the whole world changed.

7

I knew I'd fallen asleep in my bed with a nightlight on, but when I awoke a moment later it was pitch-dark and my first thought was, *Oh no, Shadow Man was right! My blindness is back! I can't see!*

I jerked up in my bed and hit my forehead on something hard only inches above me. The blow knocked me back down, and my head landed on what I thought was my mattress.

I quickly glanced around, clicking to see. But I didn't need the clicks to see the dim outline of the gap twenty feet to my right. I was in the desert again!

Yes. I was in the desert at night, under the huge rock where I'd been bitten by a snake. I'd been dreaming of Eden.

This world was my true reality. It must be. The Horde had poisoned me and stolen my memory, so I dreamed I was blind in a place called Eden. Justin had healed that blindness, so when I dreamed of Eden again, I could see.

Here, in reality, I was trapped under a rock with my captors guarding against any escape. The only advantage I had was my echolocation.

And where did you learn to echolocate, Rachelle?

Then both worlds were real. And here, I was in terrible trouble.

Justin's words whispered through my mind once again. If I was to believe him, I would bring crises to both worlds and then show them the way to freedom. But I couldn't do that unless I resolved my own fear by finding the Five Seals of Truth. Discovering those seals was my personal journey, so I could help others find their way out of darkness.

My mind spun. One thing was clear: I hadn't resolved my fear.

I could hear soft snoring from the clearing outside. As promised, Jacob and his Horde warriors had camped for the night. My leg was stiff, but the snake's poison was wearing off. A good thing.

My situation was anything but good. The sun would eventually rise, and I would have no choice but to starve or surrender myself.

I clicked to my left and saw into the

deeper reaches of the crevasse. The gap narrowed in another twenty feet, too narrow to squeeze through. What about the other way, past my feet? But no, that was where the snakes lived. I turned my head back toward the Horde encampment. No glow from a fire. I'd rather take my chances with the warriors — at least I knew they were sleeping. Most of them anyway.

Taking a deep breath, I scooted right up to the gap itself. Two hulks slept on their sides ten feet from the opening, but I couldn't see beyond them.

Slowly, barely breathing, I stuck my head out and clicked. The rest of the camp came into dim view. At least thirty warriors slept in rings around a fire that had long burned out.

There had to be a wakeful guard stationed, but where? Maybe in the narrow passage that led from the bowl. It was too far off for me to make out that passage. I only knew that it was to the right, fifteen paces or so.

The sound of my pounding heart was far too loud, but it was unlikely their auditory senses were as developed as mine.

Using my hands as claws, I pulled myself into the open. None of them stirred, so I rose to a crouch. Still no movement. If I could get into the narrow passage, I would be able to see what they could not. At least that was the thought.

Stepping ever so gingerly, I eased along the wall. I dared not click here for fear of being heard. But when the wall began to fall away behind me, indicating I was at the passage, I had to click, just to see if there was a guard stationed inside.

Click, click.

The view from my clicking showed the guard who stood ten paces in, leaning against the wall. I heard the whinny of a horse.

For a long, terrible moment, I stood frozen as at least a dozen men bolted up from a dead sleep. I had to go now! I had to go now and I had to go clicking so that I could see.

Bent over in half, I bolted into the narrow passage, clicking wildly. The guard pushed off the wall, legs spread, ready to face the disturbance.

He might have seen me, I don't know, but he was pulling his sword when I dived to the sand at his feet and rolled between his legs. Then I was past and on my feet and lunging headlong down that dark passage, clicking to see the walls.

"Fire!" the guard roared. "Bring fire! She runs!"

I ran as fast as I could, knowing my head start would give me no more than half a minute as they quickly mounted and gave pursuit, using torches to guide them.

My challenge now was getting out of the labyrinth of towering rock the same way I had gotten in. Finding another hiding place would be pointless. Once the sun rose, I would have no advantage.

So I ran — down the first passage, then a second, hoping that my memory was serving me correctly.

The first guard was on foot, following the sounds of my scrambling feet, panting. I could hear his breathing bearing down from behind and ran faster.

So did he, surprising me with his quickness.

I had just burst from the canyon into the open desert when he reached me from behind. Something hit me at the back of the skull, like a mule's kick, and sent me sprawling facedown in the sand. Darkness crowded my mind as I fought to retain consciousness.

A grunt cut the night, and I thought he was going to impale me. A hand grabbed the back of my tunic, plucking me from the ground. I stumbled forward a few steps before the warrior hauled me onto the back of his mount.

Now at a full gallop, I twisted and tried to free myself, but his grip was like iron.

"Do you always try to escape those who free you?" the rider growled under his breath. "Stay!"

Only then did I consider the possibility that the warrior wasn't Horde. He certainly didn't smell like them.

"Who are you?"

"Not now."

The rider veered into a shallow draw and up a slope that led to the top of the canyon cliffs. He pulled up.

"Off! Quickly."

I slid off the horse, and he pulled his mount down until it rested on the ground. The stars shone brighter up here than in the canyon, and I could see that his skin was like my own.

Albino?

"Shh, Razor," he whispered in his horse's ear, smoothing its neck. Then he scrambled to the edge and peered at the desert floor below.

I crawled up next to him on my hands and knees. Far to our left, the Horde had spilled from the canyons on horseback, circling with lit torches, searching for sign of me. At their feet, one fallen warrior.

"You killed him?" I whispered.

"This way!" one of them roared. They had found our tracks.

My rescuer drew me back from the ledge. "They'll follow our tracks here but will lose them in the rocks." He stuck out his hand. "Samuel," he said. "Samuel of Hunter. You can thank me later."

I took his hand, looking at a strong, youthful face in the dim light. No more than twenty, I thought. By the sound of his voice I guessed that his gall knew no bounds. And I wondered if I'd been pulled out of the frying pan and into the fire.

"Hurry!"

8

Samuel of Hunter took the horse across the top of the canyon lands, sticking to the flat stone so as not to leave clear tracks. I sat behind him, one arm around his belly, the other gripping his leather chest plate.

I was riding behind a powerful warrior with long, dark wavy hair that whipped around my face unless I leaned in close. The scent of his skin was sweet and musky, like sweat-soaked lilacs. He rode the horse as if it were a part of his own body.

The Roush had mentioned Thomas of Hunter in the highest regard. Was Samuel related? Or maybe Hunter was a place.

When I tried to ask him, he hushed me. For twenty minutes we crossed the rocky plateau above the canyons before he pulled the horse into a pass that descended to the sand. He took the mount to a full run and headed into the open desert.

A gnawing wariness overrode my gratitude. Did he know who I was? Why had he saved me? Where was he taking me? Did I have anything to fear from him?

I tried to ask him again, after we'd long left behind the canyons and the rising dunes that surrounded them, but again he shut me down, urging his horse on. The night was dark, and I felt lost in the strange and desolate landscape.

"Excuse me, but —"

"No talking."

My frustration broke through. "Why no talking when we're so far out of earshot now?"

"Because it's my horse and I'm the one who rescued you. Or would you prefer to run back into their arms?"

"At least they told me who they are. You say nothing."

"And who are they?"

"Horde, riding with Jacob, son of Qurong."

He jerked his reins back and brought the mount to a stamping halt. "Son of Qurong, you say. You're sure?"

"Of course I'm sure. Why?"

Samuel stared into the night, face set. Then at me, as if considering his options.

"You're a fool if you think you can kill them on your own," I said, surprised by my

136

nerve. "They're over fifty, some of them twice your size."

"They would all be dead by now if not for you!" A deep bitterness laced his voice — the kind of hatred that is blind to all but darkness. "I've been tracking the Throaters for two days and could have blocked their way out of the canyon to pick them off one by one. I had them!" He spat to one side.

"Then you shouldn't have bothered with me," I bit off.

He took a deep breath and settled his temper. "No Horde is worth the life of another Albino. But why didn't you tell me the son of Qurong was their leader?"

"Because you refused to let me talk."

"And now he's slipped my grasp."

"I doubt he's going anywhere."

Samuel eyed me doubtfully. "You're only an Albino to them. Or have you forgotten that as well?"

"I'm not just a thing you call Albino. I actually have a name. It's Rachelle, and I'm an Elyonite from beyond the Great Divide, thank you for asking. Ba'al, the Horde's high priest, gave me a poison that took my memories. Jacob was sent to bring me back, and I doubt he's willing to accept failure. Please treat me with some respect."

He eyed me with fresh interest.

"Do you know who Thomas of Hunter is?" I asked.

"My father. You're saying that the Elyonites actually exist? How can you be sure, if the Horde poisoned your memory?"

"The Roush told me I was. And —"

"Roush? You've seen the Roush?"

"So they're real?"

"You ask? You just said they spoke to you."

"Yes, but for all I know I was hallucinating." Though I doubted that. "But yes, two white Ewok-looking creatures found me on the sands, one called Gabil, the other Michal."

"Ewok?"

You know, Star Wars, I nearly said. But then I remembered where I was. Or more correctly, where I wasn't.

"Just a word meaning a fuzzy little creature about two feet tall," I said.

His right brow arched. "No one has seen the Roush for decades. You probably imagined it based on the stories."

"No, that would be my dreams of another life. I didn't imagine the Horde, did I?"

"What other life?"

I hesitated. "A town called Eden. The Roush told me I was dreaming of ancient Earth."

Samuel studied me in the dark for a long

138

moment, then turned and nudged his horse into a trot.

"Can you at least tell me where you're taking me?" I asked.

"To a safe place where I can think." His tone had shifted. If nothing else I had managed to fill him with curiosity.

After a few minutes that curiosity got the better of him.

"My father, Thomas of Hunter, claims that half of what he knows came from dreams of ancient Earth," he began in a soft voice. Then he told me much more about his father, and I let him talk without interrupting.

He told me how Thomas had entered dreams of ancient Earth and saved humanity from a deadly virus called the Raison Strain, but at considerable cost. His actions changed the course of history, something Samuel couldn't quite fathom.

My mind spun. I, along with every living soul on Earth, knew of the Raison Strain, an airborne virus that would have killed most of the world's population if not for a man named Thomas Hunter. That Thomas Hunter was this Thomas of Hunter?

Samuel told me that, according to his father, every time he fell asleep in this world he woke up in ancient Earth, and vice versa.

Until a few years ago, the only way not to dream of the ancient history was to eat a fruit called the rhambutan, which kept him dreamless and sane, tethered to this world. But the gateway had been closed. The crossing between worlds was no longer possible — all of this according to Thomas.

Rhambutan. It was the fruit the Roush had mentioned. And Thomas was wrong, because I was crossing between worlds. Me, the 49th. Could it be? But I let Samuel go on, filling in many details of his father's dreams. He clearly wasn't convinced about any of it, but the more he talked the more I knew I had to speak to Thomas. He had experienced what I was experiencing. Maybe Thomas was the helper Justin had promised me.

"Where is your father now?" I asked.

He told me. They had all been Horde many years ago. But Justin had made a way for the scabbing disease to be healed. A Scab, meaning one of the Horde, had only to drown in one of the red lakes to emerge Albino, free of disease.

The Horde, who served their god, Teeleh, and his high priest, Ba'al, despised the red lakes and hunted all Albinos like dogs. They believed Albinos had been poisoned by the red lakes and lost their minds. From a

Scab's perspective, Albino was a disease. Qurong, ruler of all Horde, had vowed to exterminate all trace of them from the earth.

So Albinos had formed an alliance called the Circle, led by Thomas. They numbered roughly three thousand and were scattered among four nomadic tribes — nomadic because, as pacifists who were prohibited from defending or attacking, they could only run.

Samuel's biting tone showed his disdain for the nonviolence. There was clearly division in their ranks.

"You hate your own people," I said. "Do you also hate your father?"

He didn't answer right away. "We disagree," he said quietly. "The Horde killed my love, Anya. Two years ago, a week before our wedding, I found her body butchered and strapped to a pole on a cliff. My father speaks of forgiveness, and I tried." Samuel spat. "If he knew how deep my anger runs, he would probably confine me to quarters."

"Maybe he does know."

"Perhaps. But there's more than the death of Anya. My father's wife, Chelise, was once Horde, daughter of Qurong. Whenever I see her now, my stomach turns."

"So you hate your mother as well? I can't imagine —"

"She is *not* my mother. I was born to Thomas's first wife, who also was killed by the Horde, many years ago. So you see, there is too much for me to forgive."

I felt only compassion for Samuel in that moment.

"I'm sorry for your loss," I said. "I lost my mother as well, but I can't imagine the pain of finding someone you love like that."

The horse snorted and plowed on.

"What was your mother's name?" he asked.

"Rachelle. My father named me after her. My father in my dream world, that is. Here . . . I don't know."

He twisted back. "Rachelle, you say."

"Yes. Why?"

He faced the dunes again. "My mother's name was also Rachelle."

I didn't know what to make of that coincidence. By his silence, I guessed he didn't either.

"How many Horde are there?" I asked after several long moments.

"Too many to count. Millions among seven forests. Surely this comes back to you now with my recounting."

I thought about it. "No."

After a gentle grunt he told me more. The Albinos were like dogs trapped in canyons, waiting for Justin to return and save them before they were slaughtered. In the meantime, they were lost in a wasteland of darkness, fearing the Horde.

Slaves to fear, he said. And they were, I thought. Saved in a world to come, but slaves to the fears of this world, just as Justin had said.

"So then, what's the advantage of drowning and becoming Albino?" I asked him.

"Because one day the Horde will be slaughtered by Elyon while we enter paradise."

The story was familiar to me. Not here, but in Eden.

"I think that might be true," I said.

He shrugged and looked up at the starry sky. "I've seen no evidence of this paradise for many years. Children will believe anything, but there comes a time to grow up."

"But it's coming, right? I think that's the point. One day you'll be saved. Simon . . ." I stopped, realizing details from the other world would only confuse him.

"Simon?"

"Someone from my dreams. Never mind."

"Your dreams. Yes, of course. Well, whatever you do, don't bring anyone back with you. Terrible people have crossed over before, if I'm to believe the stories."

"Maybe you should. I'm living proof."

"Yes, well, as I said, my father says the gate between worlds is closed, regardless."

"Are you deaf? You think I'm just making this all up? I've been there. I *am* there!"

We rode in silence for a full minute as he chewed on my claim.

"Then tell me, Rachelle. Tell me how it's possible that you live in the histories and that I, flesh and blood, am only a part of your dream."

"You're not just part of my dream. You're real, like me. But don't ask me how it works because I don't understand it myself."

He grunted. "Then at least amuse me with your knowledge of the histories."

So I told him. I pretended that I was in Eden only dreaming, and I explained to him the whole world as I knew it. He went along with it, asking me questions with more than a touch of skepticism.

How did planes fly?

How could power travel through metal string and a grid that powered contraptions a long way off?

How could voices be heard on a phone object when it wasn't connected to these wires?

What was the internet?

What was an atomic weapon?

I offered simple explanations and left out details that would only raise additional questions.

The sun rose in the east as we talked, Samuel lost in my story of an impossible world, I lost in this one. But I couldn't dismiss the powerful horse beneath me, nor Samuel's body, which I clung to. The heat of the desert as the sun climbed the horizon, the musky scent of his sweat, the creak of the saddle and tackle, the beating of my heart and his — all real.

I can't say he believed much of anything I said, only that with each passing mile his tone grew warmer and his questions less confrontational. I decided Samuel was a child at heart, full of bravado and more questions than answers.

The sun was directly above us when we reached a small grove of trees near a watering hole hidden in canyons.

"How far is your tribe?" I asked as he brought his horse to a stop.

"Another day's ride north and east." He slipped off, dropped to the sand, and offered me a hand. "But we spend the night here. I need to think."

"Think about what?"

He lowered his arm. His bright green eyes captivated me — I couldn't say why. Maybe because we were about the same age and our time together on the horse had been the first time in any world that I'd been in such close proximity to a man for so long. Maybe because he had saved me from certain death and I saw him as a kind of savior.

"Think about you," he said. "There's no denying you're the greatest mystery ever to have fallen into my lap."

I looked back the way we had come. "How can you be sure they won't find us here?"

"If they do, my father might excuse me for cutting them down to protect a dreamer like him."

"They're fifty. You're one."

"True. But they won't come. It'll take them a day to find our tracks if they're lucky. The wind has been at our backs, so they haven't been able to follow our scent."

"I don't know . . . They seemed pretty good —"

"Have no fear!" he said, effortlessly withdrawing one of two long knives strapped to his thighs, twirling the blade in his fingers like a drumstick. "Unlike my father, I live by the sword. The old ways of the Forest Guard still live in me and those I lead. I swear to you, not a hair on your beautiful head will be harmed as long as Samuel of

Hunter watches over you."

He winked at me, dropped the knife back into its sheath, and extended his hand again. I tried not to smile, but my mouth wasn't paying attention to my mind.

I took his hand, swung from Razor, and dropped down next to him.

"The water's safe to drink?" I asked, watching the horse amble toward the pool ten paces ahead.

No response.

I turned to face him and saw that his eyes were fixed on my shoulder. My circle tattoo.

"Where did you get that?" he asked.

"I don't know. The Roush said it marks me as an Elyonite. A Mystic."

He slowly reached for my shoulder and traced the thin line with his finger. "A Mystic? Could it be true?"

"Everything I told you is true," I said, aware of his flesh on mine.

His eyes were full of wonder. "No one has ever seen an Elyonite, much less a Mystic — a race of Albinos marked by a single circle who supposedly live beyond the Great Divide. It is said Mystics can wield the sword like no other."

How could I respond to that?

"I don't know about wielding a sword, the

Roush only said I'm a Mystic. The 49th."

I might as well have dropped a bomb.

"The 49th Mystic?"

"Yes, evidently."

"And the prophecy," he said, hand still on my shoulder. "The Roush said that was true as well?"

"What prophecy?"

" 'A child will be born among us, the 49th Mystic,' " he quickly recited. " 'And she will divide to expose the shadow of death. Then the lion will lie down with the lamb.' "

"That's what Justin said!"

His hand fell from my shoulder. "Justin?"

"That's who he said he was. Justin."

"You're saying you've *seen* Justin? That he talked to you? When?"

"Just before the Horde came."

"Why didn't you tell me this?"

"I . . . Didn't I? You weren't exactly listening to —"

"What did he say?" he demanded.

I nearly told him about the five seals, but then I remembered that they were my personal journey. And that I had to find them before the appointed time. But what was the appointed time?

"He said I would bring the world to a point of great crisis. I've been . . ." I hesitated, thinking my charge sounded

148

absurd, then said it anyway. "I've been chosen to lead the way out of darkness and fear in this life. Assuming I can find that way before the appointed time myself."

"He said that to you?" He paced, lost in thought. "Then he speaks of my people. Albinos, clean on the outside but mastered by fear still . . ."

"But I don't see how —"

" 'The lion will lie down with the lamb' can only mean that the Horde will be crushed," he said, turning back. "What else did he say?"

I hesitated, thinking. My memory of the words was like a dream fogged by time.

"That my journey would cost me everything."

"Not with me by your side. No harm will come to you under my charge, I swear it. What else?"

"That he would send me a helper."

"And here I am. What else? Anything about the Books of History?"

"No. What books?"

"Ancient volumes that record all truth as experienced in all of history. My father claims they allowed others to cross between realities before the gateway was closed."

"I thought you didn't believe in —"

"That was before. How can I deny what

my eyes show me? The gateway has been opened by you, the 49th. Only you. It must be!"

"The books are the gateway?" I asked. "But I don't have a book."

"Blood makes them a gateway, my father says. It's also rumored that whatever's written in them by a believing soul manifests in reality. The gateway is supposed to be closed, but it would make sense that you, the 49th, might open that gateway. You're from ancient Earth, right? So it must be."

"If this is true, why now?" I asked, speaking as much to myself as to him. "And why am I younger there and older here?"

"You are?"

"Yes."

He shrugged, undeterred. "These are mysteries to be discovered. After all, you are a Mystic, yes?"

I wasn't sure what to make of it all.

Samuel, on the other hand, had suddenly become a true believer. He grabbed my hand and tugged me toward several large boulders in the shade. "Tell me more."

"I've already told you everything."

He released my hand, rushed over to the horse, and quickly untied a leather bag of water and a satchel of food affixed to the saddle.

"Tell me again," he said, hurrying back. "That circle on your arm" — he motioned to my arm with his chin — "is the first real evidence that speaks to more than we know. If the Elyonites do exist, then there are more than a few thousand Albinos alive to form an army against the Horde. I, Samuel of Hunter, will know what you know. All of it."

9

There wasn't much more to tell Samuel, but this time he hung on my every word, so it felt like I was telling him for the first time. I told him every detail from the moment I first woke up in the desert, again leaving out the part about the five seals. Somehow that felt private to me, like a treasure I was to seek for myself. And then I told him again as we chewed on strips of dried jerky and ate stale cabush bread harvested from a desert grain. We washed it all down with sweet water from the oasis. And still again as he paced, hands running through his hair.

As the hours passed, the doubter in him yielded to a deep seed of hope that had taken root and sprung up.

He told me wild tales of a time not so long ago when his father was a young man, when all evil had been contained in a forbidden forest. All humans had lived innocently, without the knowledge of either good or evil, because everything was wildly perfect. They lived in a village near a lake at the base of a colored waterfall. The powerful waters filled all who drank with intoxicating wonder.

But then Tanis, firstborn among them, was seduced by Teeleh and crossed into the forbidden forest. Tanis ate Teeleh's fruit, thereby opening the way for evil to flood the land.

The Shataiki, Teeleh's creatures, infected all with the scabbing disease. It was said that Teeleh himself, like his queens, was much larger than those vile beings, but even one of them could tear through twelve men and leave them in shreds.

Justin drowned to create a way to be free of the disease, but fear ruled the hearts of men nonetheless.

I couldn't help but see how this world's history mirrored the history of my dream world. Ancient Earth. The world of Eden, Utah. But by Samuel's recounting, the entire history from Tanis until now transpired in less than forty years. I found it fascinating.

"If the Shataiki can kill, why haven't they just killed all humans?" I asked, thinking of the wounds suffered by the plump Roush Gabil.

"Who would they inflict their fear upon? Who would they rule? They keep the Horde as their prize." He paused. "Or perhaps they can only influence. Or, more likely, they don't exist anymore."

Influence. I couldn't help thinking of Shadow Man. According to him, my nightmares were only a fore-shadow, which is why I called him Shadow Man. A deep dread spread through my bones. And yet, what if he could only influence? What if he couldn't take life himself? He hadn't killed me — maybe his only influence was fear through his accusations and threats.

What was I thinking? Of course he couldn't kill me! He was only part of my nightmares.

"You've never seen these Shataiki?" I asked. "Not even as a child?"

"Perhaps." He frowned. "I can't remember. All memory of those times is like a fog to me. But I do suppose they once existed. No one has seen the Shataiki since then." He eyed me curiously. "Have you?"

"No."

"And yet you've seen Roush."

"So you believe me."

He was seated on a boulder under the shade of a large palm, one foot planted on the sand. His eyes were daring, and everything in his tone told me that he did believe. But I wanted to hear him say it, if only to support my belief.

"Of course I believe you," Samuel said, rising. He walked toward Razor, his horse, who was feeding on soft reeds on the pool's bank. "I believe in the woman named after my own mother who has come to me out of a dream." He turned, walking backward with arms spread now. "For all I know, this is *my* dream, and you're the maiden I've called to rescue me from myself."

He flashed a grin and let his statement stand for a moment. Then he turned to the horse, jerked two swords from their scabbards on either side of the saddle, and faced me, blades hanging from each hand.

He walked toward me. "And if the rumors of Elyonites really are true, then *all* of them must be true, wouldn't you say?"

"Not necessarily."

"Including the rumor that among Elyonites, the Mystics are second to none in the fighting arts. Also called the *Roush* arts." He stopped ten feet away. "Show me."

With that, Samuel of Hunter tossed the blade in his left hand toward me.

But I wasn't a warrior. I had no idea what to do with a sword. So I simply watched the blade sail past me, clatter against a large boulder, and land in the sand at my feet.

I looked over at him. "I told you, I have no clue how to hold that thing, much less swing it."

"No, of course you don't. You've lost your memory. And without memory of who you are, you can't *be* who you are. This much is obvious even to a child. But that doesn't mean you can't recover the memory of who you are."

Justin's words came to me. *Re-member who you are. Recognize yourself.*

"Maybe, but I can tell you —"

"You didn't even reach for it! How do you know you can't wield it?"

I heard a rustle in the tree and glanced up. There, perched on a limb, was the plump Roush. Gabil, the one with a limp.

"What is it?" Samuel had followed my stare and was looking directly at the Roush. "The southern breeze. It still carries our scent north, away from the Horde, who are still far south. Trust me when I say we Albinos know how to remain hidden."

Gabil fluttered down and landed on a boulder just behind Samuel. He was grinning in a sneaky way, as if having played some great joke.

I stared, trying not to look too astonished at what Samuel couldn't see.

"It is I and I alone," Gabil said to me. "And I must remain at a distance. I'm not to meddle. Do you think this counts as meddling?"

"Humor me," Samuel was saying, focused on me again.

"Humor him," Gabil said, hopping down to the sand, where he nearly stumbled before righting himself. "Show him the move I showed you before Justin came."

Gabil was real. Yes, of course he was and always had been, I knew that. I also knew that I couldn't speak to him without appearing foolish to Samuel.

"Don't look so shocked," Samuel said, approaching. "My logic is sound. If you really are one of these Mystics and have just lost your memory, then I want to see if I can help you recover the most important part. Which is the memory of wielding a sword."

He reached for my hand and I gave it to him without thinking. Before I realized his intention, he'd pulled me up, spun me around so that he was at my back, and had his arm around me, sword extended in front of me.

"Take it," he whispered in my ear. "I'll guide you."

"Let him guide you," Gabil said, behind me now. "This is Samuel, son of Thomas, as worthy a companion as any. And he does know the arts, I must say. I don't think I'm meddling when I say 'take the blade,' do you?"

Only a part of my mind was engaged with Samuel — his one arm snug around my waist, the other extended before me holding the sword. His breath on my ear and the pounding of his heart against my back. These were all things my senses, heightened by years of blindness, registered in full.

But most of my mind was racing with questions for Gabil. The seals, my identity, my quest, the dreams — surely he would have insight.

Samuel reached all the way around me with his free arm, gently lifted my hand alongside the blade, then folded my fingers around the hilt.

"You see?" he said. "Just like this. You remember the feel of the well-heeled leather hilt in your hand, begging you to join in. Albinos may not use the blade to kill Horde these days, but even children are trained in the arts. Think of your relationship with the sword as you would a courtship ritual. And remember that, as an Elyonite, you are among the best skilled in these arts."

I only half heard his words, because Gabil was hopping around us and now faced me again, just there, ten feet in front of me, grinning with delight.

"It's true," he said. "As a Mystic from beyond the pass, you must have been very skillful in all the arts. Go on, play with him."

Play? It was all a big game to these two. To make it certain, Gabil leaped in the air, executed two slicing swipes with his feet, and landed in a pile. He quickly righted himself. "Sorry. Maneuvering on the ground isn't exactly my forte. But it is yours."

Oblivious to the Roush, Samuel slowly removed his hand from mine and stepped around me, eyes bright. In doing so, his leg passed through Gabil's wing as if it wasn't there at all. Still, the Roush quickly got out of the way.

"Go on," Samuel said, scooping up the sword he'd thrown past me moments earlier. "Like this." He slowly weaved the blade side to side. "Remember?" He effortlessly twirled it through a full circle once, then twice, without removing his eyes from mine. "Let it come back to you. Show me that the young maiden from the other side of the world is as skillful as she is beautiful."

"Show him!" Gabil cried, swaying and bobbing his head.

Wearing half a smile and feeling silly, I moved my arm, felt the weight of the heavy sword, still utterly clueless. "Like this?"

Samuel's smile softened. "No, not like that."

The late afternoon air grew still. Without warning, he sprang forward, spun once in the air, and brought his blade about in a wide, slashing arc directed at my chest.

I can't say how what happened next did, because I wasn't thinking. I only reacted, dropping to a crouch and jerking my own blade up to intersect the path of his. The clash of metal on metal rang out in the canyon.

"Like that," Samuel said.

He was over me, his blade pressing against mine as if frozen in time. For a moment we just stared at each other, he as shocked as I.

"You could have killed me!"

His eyes flashed. "I would have pulled short."

"I knew it!" Gabil cried, flipping through the air, swiping his wings like blades. "I knew it! All Elyonites are . . ."

I lost the rest of what he said, because Samuel was moving again, swinging his blade through a reverse arc. I easily blocked this blow as well. And the next, a round-house kick with his right leg. And then the knife he palmed from his thigh and sent my way with enough force to cut through any

160

breastbone.

The last I slapped away with the back of my hand, but not without feeling the sharp pain in my knuckles.

"Stop it!" I cried, dropping my blade and running back a few steps. "What do you think you're doing?"

He stood up straight, confused. "Sparring."

"With real blades? What if I'd missed that knife?"

"It was headed past your right shoulder. I would never actually harm you."

"I don't know what I'm doing!" But I did know. I was blocking his blows without any conscious control, and that frightened me.

Samuel looked at me, dejected. "Forgive me. I wanted to shock it out of you. You know, force your instincts to kick in." He shrugged. "It worked. Which means you have me hilt, blade, and scabbard. You're far more skilled than I could have hoped, and we've only just begun!" He dipped his head. "I will follow you to the ends of the earth."

"Because I can fight?"

"Heavens no. But it *is* a part of who you are. Like your beauty. And like the mark on your arm. Is there any doubt that I was summoned to your side?"

I noticed the odor of burning acid then. Just a hint on the breeze, but enough for me to spin around and scan the canyons. Nothing.

"What is it?" Samuel asked.

This was different from the scent of Horde, I thought. Then it was gone.

A flurry of wings behind me spun me back. Gabil was making for the sky in haste. No meddling.

"What are you looking at?" Samuel asked, gazing about.

"I thought I smelled something."

He tested the air. "Nothing. I told you we were safe here. Yes, Jacob is rumored to be good, but no Horde is that good." He stepped up to the blade I'd dropped and scooped it up. "No more knives, I promise. Just swords. Maybe you can teach *me* a thing or two."

The stench returned, this time full force, as if a blanket of it had been dropped over us. I jerked my eyes up and saw them, thousands of them, settling on the cliffs above us. Large black creatures with glowing red eyes. Like hooded serpents with wings.

I froze, breathless. These had to be Shataiki. We were surrounded by them!

Samuel was by my side, staring up unseeing, but my reaction had his full attention now.

"What do you see?"

"Shataiki," I whispered. But I was thinking, *Shadow Man.*

He slowly turned, face white, searching the cliffs. "How many?"

"Thousands. We have to leave!"

"You're sure they're real? It's not just a figment —"

"They're as real as you, trust me." I was trembling. "We have to run!"

"Calm down," he said, but his voice was tight with fear. "I'm positive they can't hurt us."

"I'm not."

"They can only make you afraid."

"I don't care, we still have to leave. We're trapped in this canyon! Why would they be here? You're sure you can't see them?"

Samuel set his jaw and looked me over. "You. They must know who you are." He nodded once. "Okay, we leave." He grabbed my arm and guided me toward the horse, casting furtive glances at the darkening sky. "I have to get you to my father."

The Shataiki were perched high a hundred yards from us. Even at that distance I felt their power reaching down to smother me. Fear. The kind that works its way deep into a mind and blinds a person to anything but survival. The kind I had felt a thousand times through a thousand nightmares.

Even as I thought it, one of them leaped from the cliff, followed by two others. They circled down toward us, floating on wide black wings tattered from abuse. The air filled with distant hissing and clicking, the sound of swarming locusts.

I hurried, passing Samuel. But the nearest of the three approaching Shataiki veered and settled to the ground between us and the horse. I pulled up. The Shataiki had a long snout with bared fangs, a snapping tail, and beady, pupil-less eyes. He was like a rabid fruit bat. Or a cobra. The wings, its hood.

"What?"

"There, on the ground," I whispered. "Between us and the horse."

Samuel stepped up next to me. "Razor doesn't notice."

"I do."

The creature sprang into the air, flapped for us, and landed on Samuel's shoulder, red eyes fixed on me.

"It's on you!" I cried, jumping away.

"What's on me?" Samuel faced me, frowning. He swiped at his shoulders, but his hand went through the creature. "You're saying a Shataiki is on me? I don't feel a thing."

The Shataiki's jaw opened, hissing. Its fangs locked onto Samuel's head and a long pink tongue snaked into his ear. All the way in . . .

Fear washed through me like acid. "Don't move," I rasped. My heart was hammering and my palms were sweating.

"What do you mean, don't move?" He batted at the air. "Enough with this! We ride! We ri—"

He went still. The Shataiki took flight with a clicking hiss that cut to my heart. Samuel stood frozen for a moment, then dropped to all fours and pressed his ear against the sand. And as he did, I heard the pounding hooves beyond the hissing of the Shataiki.

"Horde," he growled, standing. A dark glare drenched with bitterness transformed Samuel's face.

The hosts perched on the cliffs above us rose like a blanket of flies from a carcass. They swooped to the canyon's entrance, where they hovered over rising dust from the desert.

"Follow!" Samuel sprinted for his horse, which was now stamping and snorting.

I followed. He reached back, hoisted me by the waist, and threw me onto the horse.

Snatching the reins, he swung under the mount's neck like a tetherball and landed on the saddle in front of me. He shoved a sword into my hand and tugged a bow from its sling behind me.

"We go straight for them," he said, kicking the mount. "Remember, you know how to use that sword. Use it!"

Then we were galloping for the wide canyon mouth, straight toward a line of thundering Horde mounts now in clear sight. I didn't understand why we weren't taking the escape route he'd told me about. It was behind us, past the pool at the back of the canyon.

"Why this way? We don't stand a chance! Why not —"

"They'll only follow! We don't have the speed, both on one horse. We need one of theirs. If you see him, tell me which is Jacob."

I understood his logic concerning the horses. But I didn't understand his reckless- ness in also taking a swipe at Jacob while the opportunity presented itself. Our lives were at stake. *My* life was at stake!

They came in a wide line, at least thirty abreast. And we, just one horse with both of us bent forward, blazing for certain disaster.

"Samuel!" I was lost to panic. "We can't

do this!"

"We *are* doing this. I take the left, you the right. Go for the head."

Still they came. Still my heart pounded. Still my mind screamed its warning of imminent death. The Shataiki hovered above the warriors, a wall of black against the graying sky. I forced my eyes back to the Horde.

"Like a Shataiki out of hell, Razor," Samuel said. Then he released the reins, strung his bow with an arrow from the quiver at his knees, pulled the string back at a full gallop, and let the arrow fly. I watched its trajectory: rising at a thirty-degree angle, sailing through a lazy arc, heading back down toward the line of horses.

We were closing fast, fewer than a hundred paces now, and yet Samuel's arrow reached one of the warriors at precisely the right point. The Scab grabbed at his neck and tumbled backward off his mount.

"You see him?"

"Who?"

"Jacob. We have to kill Jacob!"

"We have to escape!"

He'd lost his mind, I thought. The Shataiki had poisoned him with its tongue. How could anyone be so headstrong? Or he knew something I didn't about their ways. I prayed it was the latter.

Samuel shot another arrow. Took the warrior next to his first victim from his mount. Then a third. My scattered thoughts finally made sense of what he was doing when he veered for the narrow gap he'd created.

"Take the one on the right!"

The calculating frontal lobe of my brain shut down when we were ten strides from them. Panic gave way to raw survival instinct. I wasn't aware of what I was doing. I just did it.

Gripping Samuel's leather breastplate with my left hand, I hung down to my right, sword nearly dragging on the ground, light in my hand.

Then we were on top of the Horde warrior. I didn't see his face. His blade swung for Samuel at the same time mine cut deep into the mount's foreleg.

Samuel easily ducked the slicing blade. The Scab's horse had no such opportunity. It snorted in pain and collapsed full stride in our wake.

"That's my girl." Samuel continued in a full gallop, pulling Razor to the right in pursuit of one of the riderless stallions. "You see him?"

I didn't bother answering.

We drew abreast of the horse as the warriors behind us doubled back.

"Take Razor. If we get separated, he'll take you to Thomas. There are four knives strapped to the saddle. One more pass, and if you see Jacob, gut him!"

Then he was off and straddling a terrified black mount, which he struggled to control.

I, on the other hand, had no such problem with Razor. My body knew what to do. I shifted forward, grabbed the reins with my left hand, and dug my feet into the stirrups, close on Samuel's heels.

It took only a dozen strides for the Horde stallion to know he had a new master. Samuel reined him high and abruptly pulled him around. Our eyes met and held for a moment. Then he dipped his head with respect, spurred his horse, and tore back the way we had come.

We'd covered half the distance to the Horde when I realized that they were waiting for us. They had no desire to repeat the first pass. Did they know about the passage out the back? No. Jacob intended to trap us in the canyon if we got past them this time.

It occurred to me that the knives were far more useful to me than the sword. Why? Because I was better with the smaller blades.

I quickly shoved the sword into its scabbard and palmed two of the four knives strapped to Razor's shoulders. One went between my teeth, the other in my right hand.

Samuel had already taken down two of the Horde with arrows before I threw my first knife. I watched it fly true, end over end, before slamming home in a warrior's chest. Heavier than an arrow, the blade sliced cleanly through his leather armor. He was likely dead before he hit the ground.

I was low and ready to hurl the second knife when one of the warriors to my left veered toward me. "No harm to the woman!" he thundered. "Let them pass!"

It was Jacob. I knew his voice.

He'd seen my skill with a knife and surely knew that I would make him my next target, yet this didn't seem to bother him. Why?

If you see Jacob, gut him!

How could I kill this man I had spoken to, negotiated with? It wasn't in me. And yet, this was my course, wasn't it?

I snatched the knife from my mouth, drew back, and sent it with all of my strength. But before the hilt left my hand, I flinched. The blade flew true, but my *true* was now a foot to Jacob's right.

It didn't matter. He snatched the blade from the air with a gloved hand as if it were a feather, and I knew then why Jacob had been chosen to hunt me down. This was no ordinary warrior.

Our eyes met as I raced by and broke through the gap Samuel had made. There was curiosity in those eyes, not malice or anger. Even if I could have killed him, I was glad I hadn't tried.

"That was him?" Samuel yelled over his shoulder.

"I missed."

He cursed, but Samuel was no fool. We now had two fast horses and an escape route the Horde knew nothing about.

The Shataiki were screeching above us, but I was bent low over Razor's neck and refused to look up. Samuel led us at a full gallop past the pool and the trees nestled around it. I followed him wordlessly as he angled for one of two narrow passages at the end of the canyon.

We entered before the Horde rounded the trees, but they would still be able to follow our tracks while there was light. This fact was worrying me when Samuel abruptly turned and took his mount up a steep, rocky incline. Razor followed, struggling for footing. I saw why Samuel had been so reluctant to try with two on the horse's back.

And yet the Horde would know we'd cut up the incline.

We quickly reached the rocky canyon lip. "This way." Samuel took us a hundred yards on flat stone, then guided his mount down a narrow chasm that led back to the canyon floor. To my reckoning, we were headed back in the same direction we had come. Madness.

But I'd learned not to second-guess Samuel.

He stopped at the end of the passageway, looked around its edge, then led us back into the same oasis we'd come from. This time we headed for the second of the two passages that led out the back.

The Horde would eventually figure out what we'd done, but by then we'd be long gone on two fast horses.

I pulled up next to him and saw his wide grin. "Never doubt Samuel of Hunter," he said. "Can you go without sleep?"

"If I have to." The night was suddenly and eerily quiet. I glanced at the sky. The Shataiki were gone. Why?

We passed the trees surrounding the oasis at a steady trot. "Then we'll join Thomas and my tribe by sunrise."

The Horde was behind us, headed in the wrong direction. The Shataiki had left us alone. But something else in the gathering night had my attention. The air seemed to be charged. I could feel it at the nape of my neck.

Samuel saw him first, just as we rounded the pool, and he reined his mount to a halt. A lone rider sat on a pale stallion, calmly watching us. He was dressed in a light robe and wore sandals rather than boots. His hair was white and his beard was long. Two braids held his hair off his face and swept back over his ears.

Next to him stood a second riderless mount — a black mare.

"Albino," Samuel said, staring.

"Is he alone?"

"I don't know." He nudged his horse forward and I followed.

The rider showed no concern. Where had he come from?

Samuel pulled up five paces from him and studied his horse, his robe, his face. "Are you alone?" he asked.

"There are two others here," the man said in a strong, gentle voice.

Samuel scanned the perimeter.

"They sit on horses before me," the man said. He was speaking of us.

"I see," Samuel said. "And who are you?"

"Do you ask for my identity or what they call me?"

"Let's start with what they call you."

"They call me Talya. A Mystic from beyond the Great Divide." His eyes shifted to me. "And I've come to take the one you call the lamb back."

"The lamb?"

"Rachelle. The meaning of the word is 'lamb.' "

Samuel eyed him carefully. "Take her back where?"

The man called Talya hesitated. "Home," he said.

"Don't be absurd," Samuel snapped. "I take her to Thomas. Any Albino in this desert is under his jurisdiction. Rachelle now belongs to us."

"Her name is not Rachelle, and she belongs to no one on this plane. She was raised by Mystics, who were pushed out by other Elyonites. Three months ago she was taken by the Horde and delivered to Ba'al's dungeons."

This Talya was the helper Justin had promised me? I wanted to know more, much more.

"Mystic, you say." Samuel wasn't eager to buy into Talya's claims. "I know what Horde are, who Rachelle is. Who are you to call yourself a Mystic that I should even consider trusting you?"

"A Mystic is only one who believes that

Elyon is infinite, not subject to polarity."

"Polarity? What is this nonsense? Of course Elyon is infinite. All Albinos know this. Does it make us all Mystics then?"

"How little you know, Samuel of Hunter," Talya said gently. "I will take the 49th, as is my charge."

Samuel sat on his horse, face blank. But before he could speak, a beast came out of the boulders behind him. A lion. As surprised as I was to see a full-grown lion slinking up to us, I felt no fear.

Samuel uttered a grunt and jerked back.

"This is my lion," the old man said. "He is called Judah. You have nothing to fear from him."

The lion settled down on his belly and yawned wide. Talya's mount stepped forward as if guided by the man's thought.

"You will not follow us, you will not harm Jacob, you will not gather an army, you will not cross the Divide, you will do absolutely nothing but stay alive as long as you can. Do you understand?"

"I . . ." Samuel glanced at me. "No, that can't be right. I only . . ."

"I know you're taken with her. I don't blame you. But a great crisis approaches like a dark storm. If the 49th succeeds, and if both of you survive what is to come, you can try to woo her all you like, though I assure you she has a mind of her own. Until then, we have far more pressing matters to consider."

It was from Talya the Shataiki had fled, I thought. He was the one who would help me on the quest. My journey would cost me everything, Justin had said. I wondered briefly what that could mean. A chill washed down my neck.

"I should at least come with you," Samuel said. "You do know that I saved her from certain death."

"Go home, Samuel." Talya's voice rumbled with an authority that seemed to reach into my chest and squeeze my heart. The air felt electric again. What power Talya possessed, I didn't know, but I did know I had to follow him.

"Doesn't she get a say in this?" Samuel demanded, face dark. "Or is she just a pawn?"

Talya studied me, then slowly dipped his head. "As your servant I would be remiss if I didn't inform you that should you go with Samuel now, your body will die young. Jacob is no fool. If you come with me, your passing from this plane may be delayed. You might complete the tasks of your role. The choice is yours."

I liked the way he talked — the tone of his voice, his odd choice of words. There was a truth in them that seemed to quicken an ancient knowing in my bones.

"I'll go with you."

"A wise choice." Talya dipped his head again. "Jacob has found your tracks and is doubling back. We have to leave now." As if it could understand, the lion stood, yawned once more, then looked east, ears perked.

"And you, my dear, must dream. Look for the words that point you to the First Seal."

"The First Seal? You know about my dreams of the other world?"

"We won't be stopping tonight; you'll have to sleep on your horse," he said, ignoring my question.

I hadn't slept for nearly a day, but I doubted I could sleep anytime soon, not now. Certainly not on a horse.

Samuel was watching me like a lost boy hidden behind a strong jaw and flowing mane. He might think of himself as a fierce warrior, but I saw a gentle and lonely man in desperate search of himself. Not unlike me.

Until that moment, I hadn't realized how fond I'd become of him in such a short time. The sentiment surprised me.

I guided my horse over to his and reached

177

for his hand.

"I have to go with him, you must know that. Whatever's happening is beyond both of us. But I'll never forget you, Samuel of Hunter. We will meet again."

"I will find you," he whispered.

"They are coming," Talya said.

He'd maneuvered his mount beside my own and I turned, thinking I would mount Talya's second horse and leave Razor for Samuel. But I never made it that far.

Talya was there and his hand was there, at my chin, then over my eyes.

"Dream," he whispered. The word echoed through me and carried me away. I felt myself slumping toward him as my consciousness faded.

And then I was dreaming.

10

I dreamed a dream that wasn't a dream, and in that reality I guessed that I was sleeping on a horse, somehow secured so I wouldn't fall, riding due east behind Talya, an older man who had the stamina of the lion that trotted ahead of us.

And then I was waking up to the sound of birds chirping outside my window. The same birds I always heard when I woke up, usually between seven and eight in the morning, just as the town began to come alive.

I was back in Eden.

I opened my eyes and slowly looked at my room: the drawn curtains glowing blue in direct sunlight, the Apple computer on my desk, the white ceiling and its orange-peel texture — one of the few surfaces in the house I hadn't touched. But now I didn't need to touch to see. Or click.

I could see because a man named Vlad

Smith had come into town yesterday and sent me into a coma, where Justin had healed me.

I was living in two realities that were somehow connected and directly affected each other. And by all accounts I would throw both worlds into crisis.

I lifted my hand and looked at my right forefinger. The tiny pinprick Vlad Smith had administered was still there. Slowly, like a descending fog, dread settled over me.

I sat up in bed and stared around the room. Something was going to cost me everything. Yesterday had been the best day of my life. Today . . . I was afraid today would be different.

I threw the covers off, slid out of bed, and stood up, dressed in yellow pajamas printed with little white bunnies. It all felt . . . off. Wrong. Very wrong.

"Dad?"

His voice came back from the front of the house. "In here, honey. Just fixing us some eggs."

I had to tell him.

It only took me a minute to strip out of the ridiculous pajamas and throw on a pair of jeans. Pulling open my closet, I was greeted with the sight of a dozen shirts. All black. Might have to change that, but in that moment they could have been a dozen different colors and I would have grabbed the closest without caring.

Bacon and eggs were sizzling by the time I'd brushed my teeth and hurried out into the kitchen.

"Morning, sweetheart." My dad grinned. He kissed my hair and stepped back. Spread his hands. "Well?"

"Well what?"

"You . . . I mean . . . You're not clicking."

My sight. I was no longer as taken with my sight as he was, but then I'd just spent a full day seeing in my dreams. Then again, if Justin was right, the whole world was blind. Including me.

"Still good," I said. "Don't worry, my sight's not going to revert."

"No, of course it won't." He stepped over to the frying pan and scooped the eggs and bacon onto two green plates. The scent and sight reminded me of my hunger — I'd eaten nothing but strips of jerky and stale bread . . .

No. That was in another world.

"But there is something else I need to talk to you about," I said.

"Sure. Have a seat." He set the plates on the breakfast bar and crossed to the coffeepot. "Big day today. Something's going down on the West Coast. No one's saying what it is, but all the major networks are offline, and the internet is down."

I glanced at the muted television, grayed out with static. Words scrolled across the screen, but of course I hadn't learned to read with my eyes yet. Something about a loss of signal, I guessed.

"Cell phones still work, but I tried to connect with my sister in Seattle and couldn't get through. Probably on her end. Coffee?"

"Sure." I walked over to the breakfast bar and scooted my stool out. "None of that upsets you?"

He brought two cups of coffee to the bar, mine with a little puppy on a big white mug. "How could I be upset? My daughter can see. We live in a protected environment with all the power and food we need. I have all I need right here." He stroked my hair.

"Until they start rappelling over the cliffs with automatic weapons," I said.

"Well . . . it's not going to come to that. And if it does, we're prepared, aren't we?"

He meant the weapons the council had stockpiled. But his willingness to even consider using them was news to me. I let it go.

"I suppose we are."

"Sit."

I sat.

"Eat."

I picked up a piece of bacon and bit into it.

"So, what's on your mind?" he asked, lifting his coffee. "More bad dreams?"

"Not exactly. Not bad, I mean. Depending on how you look at it. But it might sound a bit . . . crazy."

"Tell me. Nothing sounds crazy to me anymore."

So I told him everything. Beginning with my waking in the desert and meeting Justin before the Horde came. Samuel's rescue of me, our encounter with Jacob at the oasis, and being taken by Talya.

Everything except the bit about me bringing a great crisis. And the five seals.

He asked me polite questions as I rushed through tales of white bats called Roush and black ones with red eyes called Shataiki, and Horde and Albinos, and I knew he was thinking it was all in my mind, a fear of losing my sight. But I just wanted to get it all out.

"And that's it?" he asked when I was done.

"That's it."

He set down his empty cup and faced me. "Speaking as a psychologist? I think it's a good sign."

"A sign?"

"Think about it! These are the first lucid dreams you've had, right? The first time you've been aware that you're dreaming while dreaming. And you have some control in those dreams."

"Yes, but —"

"Rather than being a victim of nightmares in which you have no clue you're in a dream, you're now lucid in those dreams. This is fantastic! Whatever happened in your mind to correct your blindness also might have shifted your dreaming patterns. Naturally you're still contending with the fear of blindness, but these dreams could very well signal the end of your nightmares."

"I think you might be missing the point. What about Thomas Hunter?"

"What about him? The whole world knows about his role in stopping the Raison Strain ten years ago. You know it too, and now it's entered your dreams. Perfectly understandable."

I shook my head. "No. It's more than that. We don't even know how I regained my sight! Something else is happening. Tell me again what Vlad Smith said in my room at the hospital."

My father shrugged, but his eyes were fixed on the wall. "Sight to the blind, religious nonsense."

But not nonsense to me.

"And?"

"I suspect he's somehow connected to Simon, who isn't telling us everything." Eyes on me. "But it's got nothing to do with you."

"Okay . . . What else? He knew all about me, so what else did he say? About me?"

"That he needed to earn our trust by doing what he did with you."

"And?"

"That's it. That you were the key."

"He said that? Like the key to a door?" An idea struck me. "Or a gateway?"

"I took it as the key to getting the town behind him in correcting whatever he thinks is wrong. As far as what part he played in your spontaneous remission, it's impossible to say without knowing more. The mind is a powerful thing. And completely reprogrammable."

"It is indeed." The voice came from behind us, and we both twisted in our seats.

A tall man dressed in black slacks and a white jacket stood in our doorway. Hair slicked back, thumbs hooked in his pockets. My father hadn't breathed a word of what Vlad Smith looked like, but I knew I was looking at him. And the moment I saw him, a chill rode up my spine.

"Forgive me, but the door was open," he said. Without looking, he shoved the door closed with his heel. It slammed shut.

"Smith," he said, eyeing me. "Vlad Smith. So happy to finally be seen by you, Rachelle. Glad to have been of help."

My father was on his feet. Smith's eyes cut to my soul, and I suppressed the urge to run. I can't say I recognized him as Shadow Man, because things are different in nightmares than in real life, but he gave me the same feeling.

Then again, this was the man who'd somehow facilitated my waking in another world. Why? Samuel suggested that I, as the 49th, had opened a gateway to that world. If so, did Vlad Smith intend to use me? To what end?

Vlad interlaced his fingers, cracked his knuckles, and stepped to the center of the kitchen. "You have to forgive me for being so . . . direct with you yesterday, David. But as I'm sure you can now appreciate, Rachelle needed me. Fair enough?"

My father looked uncertain.

"I know this has all been a bit of a shock to both of you, so I've come to set the record straight before I illuminate the rest of the town. You want to know how I did it, right?"

My father found his voice. "That would be helpful, yes."

"Maybe we could begin with a thank you," Vlad said, still fixated on me.

My father hesitated. "Thank you."

"You are so welcome, my dear." But I wasn't the one who'd thanked him.

He pressed his hands together and bowed his head, as if praying to me. "I must say, your mind's an enviable work of wonder. To think, all that tissue up there, folded in on itself, packed with neurons and energy . . . It can do so much with the right programming. Amazing. I like to call the human organism a tissue-top." He pointed at his head. "It's just tissue in there. Algorithms. In fact, all organism is algorithm. You have to go beyond tissue to find more."

The more he talked, the less I liked him.

"So how did you do it?" my father asked.

"Yes, of course." He spread his arms wide. "How on earth did I manage to give Rachelle her sight back?"

"Yes, how?" I asked, daring to be heard.

He flipped his jacket back and shoved a hand into his pants pocket. "It's quite simple, really, when you understand polarity. You do understand polarity, David?"

"Of course."

"Plus and minus, what goes up must come down, electrons and protons, good and evil, angels and demons, all of it. Every action creates an equal and opposite reaction. The world of expression we all love and hate so much. All romance, all war, all religion, all life, all existence . . ." He swept his free hand wide. "The entire universe is built upon and depends on polarity. Fair statement?"

"Fair enough."

"True statement?"

My father nodded once. "True."

"Cause and effect. In both scientific and religious terms we call it the law." He stopped, as if he'd given us a complete answer for my sight, though it was no answer at all.

He took a deep breath and shifted his eyes over my head, looking into the distance. When he spoke again, his voice was softer.

"But what if there was a way *beyond* polarity? What if you could escape the matrix of cause and effect that holds us all hostage? Anything would be possible, right? In God-talk, we call it *grace*. The law says that if you step out of a boat at sea, you'll sink. But grace says you're not bound by those laws and you can actually walk on

188

water. Yes?"

We both stared at him, unsure what he was getting at. I'd never heard anyone describe the workings of the world in those terms.

"You're saying Rachelle's recovery was miraculous?" my father said. "That's your explanation?"

Vlad wagged a finger. "Too much baggage, David. Let's not use words smothered in centuries of muddy dogma. Let's just stick with escaping polarity. All it takes is opening your mind to the belief in something other than polarity. Belief! Like a placebo, which is a very weak version of the kind of belief I'm talking about. If you truly, truly, truly believe that something has happened, it manifests. Whatever you ask, believing it has been done, it will be done, isn't that what he taught?"

"Who?" my father asked.

"Jesus," I said.

"That's right, Rachelle. Bravo. As a man of God myself, it comforts me to know that even two thousand years ago, someone got it right. Of course, he was rather special."

But Smith wasn't a man of God, I thought. He was a viper in God's clothing.

"The point is, the power of belief is far greater than what science has yet confirmed.

They're getting closer with all of their dabbling in quantum physics — entanglement, superposition, all of that basic stuff. But science still lags behind what the mystics have known for millennia. Either way, you'll eventually figure out how consciousness works to change the physical world."

My ears burned at his mention of mystics.

"So enlighten us," my father said.

"I'm trying, David. Give me a minute. The world is changing through thought and belief alone. This whole valley, for instance, exists as it does only because you believe it is the way it is." He tapped his temple with a long finger. "Tissue-tops."

In some ways, my father had already taught me much of this using completely different terms. The body manifests what the mind believes to be true. Quantum physics went further, demonstrating that our consciousness directly affects all material manifestation, including the world around us. It was a law that somehow governed the entire universe, though no scientist knew why or how, only that it did.

"Drop the God-talk and it will make more sense," my father said.

"But it makes sense to Rachelle, doesn't it, 49th?"

It's him! This is Shadow Man, come in the

flesh. The moment I thought it, the faint scent of dirty socks masked by vanilla seeped into my awareness, and I swallowed, fighting back a terrible fear.

He was using his God-talk as a form of manipulation to gain my confidence, speaking truth, although I doubted he was any part of it himself.

He paced, stroking his chin. "What if I could give you a demonstration, right here? Prove the power of belief right in front of your eyes."

Quicker than I could follow, Vlad took one step toward the counter, grabbed something I couldn't see, spun around, and threw it at me.

Everything in the room seemed to stall for a moment. I saw the object in flight as if we were in a movie and someone had hit the slow-motion button. And then the apple reached me, an inch from my mouth.

It stopped there because my hand was already around it. I had reacted without thinking.

My father took a step back, stunned. "How . . . What was that?"

"That was your daughter knowing that she can do what cannot be done," Vlad said. "Go on, take a bite."

Fingers trembling, I set the apple on the

counter.

Vlad looked at me, supremely satisfied. "I'll get to the story of how your wife was a victim of the law in just a moment, David. But —"

"My wife? What do you know about her?"

Vlad lifted a finger. "But first, indulge me for just one more minute."

He pulled out a very old-looking book with a brittle leather cover and held it between his fingers. At first sight of that book, I felt my heart crash into my throat. A Book of History?

"Now, let's pretend that this book has magical power. I mean, really, really pretend. For just a few minutes let's become like little children and really believe."

He stepped around the breakfast bar so he was facing us. "May I?" Without waiting for a response, he gingerly placed the book down in front of me.

"Now, as children we will treat this book with reverence." His voice was laced with gravity. "Very few people have ever laid eyes on, much less written in, such a book. The truth is, whatever you pen in this book actually happens."

His words pulled at me. Did he know that I knew what the book was? I doubted it.

Vlad pulled a long black pen from his

pocket and laid it down on the counter. "Let's pretend that, by placing Rachelle's blood in this book," he said, pulling the cover open to a blank page, "I opened a gateway that allowed her to enter a dream world where she could see. A dream so powerful that it was real to her. With that power of belief, her mind self-corrected, and when she woke up here, she could see."

We didn't need to pretend! That was exactly what had happened. Why he'd pricked my finger. He had a Book of History from the other world, but only my blood could activate it.

Had activated it.

"Today let's try something new." Vlad was speaking the words as if too much force would shatter them. "Today you will take the pen and write me into that same world. In our story, only you can do it, because only you have entered that gate. Do this, and we'll see what happens."

Yes, that would be a good thing. If I don't he's going to blind me. I lifted my eyes and stared into his — pools of urgent mystery that drew me in a way I could not explain.

He slid the open book closer to me. "Give it a try. I gave you my sight, now you give me yours."

I blinked.

It took some effort to shift my eyes away from his and back down to the page, and the moment I did, my intention to write anything about him in the book collapsed.

But I was still afraid, and I had to know if I had the kind of power everyone in the other world was saying I had. So I placed my hand on the page. A vibration like a current rode up my arm, and I jerked my hand away.

"You okay, honey?" my father asked. He reached over and touched the book. Flipped the corners of a few pages with his thumb. "Seems harmless enough."

As the pages flipped, a dark smudge on one of them caught my eye.

"Harmless," I said in a thin voice. But my fingers were shaking.

Vlad had picked up the pen and was holding it out to me. "Go ahead. Use your own words. Just write me into that dream world. Who knows, maybe I'll vanish right in front of your eyes."

My father cleared his throat. He wasn't buying any of it.

I peeled back the pages to the one with the marking. There at the top of the page was a smear of blood. My blood. I was right . . . He'd used my blood with the book to open the gate for me. I could now use it to send others through.

But my eyes were immediately drawn to the thin, four-inch circle in the middle of the page — a circle like the one on my arm. Inside of that circle was a white band about a half inch wide.

In the center of the circle were written these words: *What begins as White that man has made Black?* I was reading with my eyes. How was that possible?

My heart skipped a beat. "It's a riddle," I whispered, thinking of Talya's instruction to look for words that pointed to the First Seal.

"A riddle? It looks like blood," my father said. He looked at Vlad. "Rachelle's blood?"

Vlad ignored him. His breathing had thickened. "A riddle, you say? You see words?"

Neither of them could see the circle or the words.

What begins as White that man has made Black? This was it. A riddle that would lead me to the First Seal of Truth. I knew it in my bones.

I touched the page, then ran my hand over the words, feeling for the slight indentation all writing made. All but this writing. The page was perfectly smooth.

"I don't think I will write in the book," I said, removing my hand and looking up.

"But can I keep it?"

A momentary rage, blacker than midnight on a starless night, gripped Vlad's face and was gone so quickly I wondered if I'd imagined it.

He picked up the book and put it back into the inner pocket of his jacket. "It came from the mountains of Moldavia. A sentimental affair."

"I think you've made your point," my father said.

"No." Vlad walked around the bar and faced us from the center of the kitchen. He showed no sign he'd hit a wall with me. "Not yet, I'm afraid. But I had to give the easy path a try. Sooner or later I'll work the truth into your thick skulls. For your sakes, I vote for sooner. This is only a foreshadow." He headed for the door.

If there was any doubt lingering in me, his last words sealed the truth of his identity. He probably knew more about the 49th than I did. And he needed me to write him into the book. To what end, I didn't know. And why I was the 49th, I didn't know either. In fact, most of what I knew right then was that I was terrified of being blinded again, subject to his ravaging nightmares.

"And my wife?" my father asked.

Vlad turned back, hand on the knob.

"Your wife, David, was murdered because she, like the daughter she birthed, was special. Her mind wasn't fit to cope with the laws of Eden. But I would walk very carefully with that fact. Barth isn't one to mess around with."

And then Vlad Smith opened the door, stepped outside, straightened his jacket, and walked away, leaving the door wide open.

11

Jacob, son of Qurong, supreme ruler of all Horde, stood in the Thrall overlooking Qurongi City, so named by his father when he crushed the Albinos who lived in this forest. The Horde had drained the red lake and cleared the trees to make room for the thousands of homes now spread out before them. On his right stood his father, Qurong. To his left, Ba'al, whom Jacob despised.

His mother, Patricia, ever the fussing worrier, had suggested they ignore the high priest's call for an immediate audience upon his return less than two hours earlier.

"You know he will tear you apart with all his foul words!" she'd cried. "Does he rule here? Is the city named after him?"

She paced in a long, flowing lavender robe. Her light gray skin was smoothed with morst, a perfumed paste the wealthy wore to ease the annoying pain of the cracking skin common to all Horde. Strange how the

Albinos called them Scabs. To think the vision of beauty before him could be called a Scab was preposterous. Like the moon draped in regal linens, she floated over the polished stone floor.

"No, Mother," he said, slightly amused by her fear of Ba'al. "But I do have charge of the Throaters. Our charge is to Ba'al, no matter how absurd his antics. What kind of man would I be to cower from my duty?"

"Refusing to go is not to cower. It's to let that scoundrel know whose son you are."

"Which is why I will always go when Ba'al calls me. To let him know who I am."

She scowled. "If you would stop this ridiculous nonsense of chasing down phantoms who present no threat and spend more time accepting the advances of women, you too would have a son."

"Is that what you think of me? A warrior concerned only with Albinos? Do you forget my songs, my dancing late into the night with women hoping to be swept away by the son of Qurong?"

"Then take one!" she cried, slapping the tabletop next to her. An apple toppled from the bowl, rolled off the table, and landed on the ground. So the truth of her fussing about had finally surfaced. As it always did.

"Must you steer every conversation into this?"

"Is it wrong for a queen to long for a grandson to love?" she demanded.

He wondered if he would ever find a woman as spirited as she.

"Never fear, Mother," he said, finishing his meal and wiping his hands. He rose and kissed her on the cheek. "I only wait for one who knows true love. Until then, I will play my role as the finest warrior in all the land."

He started for the door, then turned back. "This Albino we seek . . . Ba'al sent me after her because she bears a mark on her shoulder. A mark never seen on any other Albino in his dungeons."

"And what should this mark mean to me?"

"Did you know she claims to be the 49th Mystic?"

His mother's face froze like porcelain. "Nonsense," she finally said. "Absurd."

"I don't know. I found myself oddly affected by her."

"In what way? She casts spells?"

"Nothing so superstitious. I just . . . She believes it. Somehow I do as well."

He watched her eyes as his conviction slowly overtook her doubts. She crossed to him, robes swishing. When she spoke, a terrible fear laced her every word. "Then you must go now! Your father must know!"

"He doesn't?"

"If he did, I would know. You do know the prophecy . . ."

"I've never paid much attention to fear-mongering."

"Fearmongering?" she scolded. "And what if it is true? If the 49th succeeds, all Horde will be forced to drown and become Albino! Our way of life will be destroyed and your father reduced to nothing!"

"It's only legend, Mother. More of Ba'al's ranting."

She grabbed his arm. "You must tell them. Tell Qurong. They must know!"

Jacob left then, disturbed by his mother's response to the 49th. There was something refreshing about the Albino he'd had in his grasp. Something innocent in her way of speaking that haunted him.

Overlooking the city with Ba'al and Qurong, Jacob pushed his mother's fear from his mind.

"Look at it all," Ba'al said. "All that you have built and called home. How many have died among the Horde for you to possess what you do?"

His father frowned. "Not so many. Our enemy would rather run and hide than face us like men." He turned to Ba'al. "Why do you suggest so many have died?"

"Because I know what will happen to the Horde if we fail. Not a house you see will be left standing. The streets will be lined with the dead, bloating under the hot sun. Qurong will be known among those who survive as the one who failed to heed Teeleh's warning and bowed to the lamb."

"Enough!" Qurong turned from the overlook and strode into the inner sanctum.

Jacob suppressed a smile and followed. He didn't relish facing off with Ba'al, but his father leveraged his authority with pleasure. Jacob hadn't mentioned the 49th. Perhaps Qurong's demeanor would change when he learned the truth, assuming the girl really was this 49th Mystic they all feared.

The high priest's feet slapped the stone behind them. Ba'al might be the scrawniest Horde still living, but his power could not be doubted. His magic spells and rituals had left hundreds dead in the last year alone.

Herein rested the precarious but effective balance of powers. On the one hand: his father, a good and kind man who ruled with authority. On the other: the priest of Teeleh, who'd spurred them to defeat their enemy many times and would surely do so again.

Teeleh's graven image glared at them at the head of the altar, a large winged serpent coiled like a dark, hooded cobra with red eyes, ready to strike.

Qurong turned back at the altar used by Ba'al to slaughter his goats. Blood. It was all about blood for the high priest and his Shataiki. Jacob hated the altar almost as much as he hated Ba'al.

"You will speak to me plainly," Qurong said. "No embellishments. Your grand statements may work for your priests, but I am not a priest."

Ba'al eyed Jacob with accusing eyes. At times Jacob wondered if the reason the high priest was so pale was because his own blood had been drained by those he served.

"As you say." The old goat picked up one of the long, jeweled daggers they used to do their business. He held the knife in his spindly fingers. "Who holds this blade?"

Qurong's brow arched. "This is what you call plain speech?"

"I do," Ba'al said. He flipped his wrist with surprising speed and sent the dagger toward Jacob, who watched it fly, alarmed. He caught it in the air, inches from his throat.

"And who holds it now?" Ba'al asked.

"I do," Jacob said. "Would you like it back

the same way?"

"Few Albinos wield the blade. Only we, as Horde. We have the advantage and we have the army. But soon, very soon, that will change. We won't be the only ones wielding the sword."

"You speak of Albinos as if they are something to fear," Qurong said. "These weaklings you capture to study and dissect like insects in your dungeons. Even if they do take up arms, they're only a few thousand. Flies for our horses to swat off their backs. Gathered as one, my army would number over five hundred thousand."

"Thomas of Hunter's Albinos number only a few thousand. But they are not the only Albinos."

The Elyonites, Jacob thought. From the far side where the young woman had come from. He'd known that Ba'al's summons was about his failure to bring her back, but watching the priest now, Jacob realized he might have underestimated the weightiness of the matter.

Had Ba'al known she was the 49th?

"The Elyonites have never crossed the Divide," Qurong said. "They have no interest in our world."

"Not today, but if she reaches them, that will change."

"Who?" Jacob interjected. "The Albino who escaped you? The one who claims to be the 49th?"

Ba'al glared at Jacob. Qurong had gone still.

"You let the 49th Mystic out of your grasp?" his father demanded of Ba'al.

"You think I knew?" the priest snapped. "I only just learned the truth myself!"

So Ba'al had spoken to one of Jacob's men already.

"And how can you be sure?" Qurong asked.

"Because I stole her memory, and yet she now makes a claim that can only come from powers beyond this world." He paced, hands gripped tight. "She is the one, I now know this in my bones."

"How could you allow this?" Qurong thundered.

"Are you deaf? I did not know!"

"Then what good are you to us? A prophet with no power to know the greatest threat when it arises? You should have killed her while she was in your dungeons instead of subjecting her to all of these nonsensical tests and dissections you perform on Albinos!"

"No. Not kill. The 49th must be taken alive. If we kill any 49th, another will only rise in their place. No, she must be made to betray her kind, this much is certain. In either this world or the other. It is the only way to be done with the threat forever."

"The other?" Qurong eyed him with disdain. Ba'al had occasionally spoken of other worlds, but neither Jacob nor his father gave such talk any mind. They were the mad ramblings of a religious fool.

"I realize you don't care about other dimensions," Ba'al said. "But you will. Indeed, her defeat in that other world will facilitate her defeat here, and vice versa. She must betray herself, either here or there. To this end, Teeleh long ago dispatched a Leedhan to the other world to wait for her. If the 49th doesn't betray herself, all Horde are doomed."

The prophecy. *Then the lion will lie down with the lamb.* Meaning the lion, all Horde, would bow to the lamb and become Albino. Ba'al insisted that he knew this from Teeleh.

This, Jacob could grasp. But Ba'al's speaking of other worlds confused the matter. How could such a thing be possible?

Qurong's jaw flexed. "If there is this other world, and if Teeleh dispatched a Leedhan to deal with the 49th long ago, why is there still a problem? This is the typical posturing your kind always —"

"Because the 49th only becomes the 49th at the fullness of age," Ba'al interrupted. "Three sevens. This clearly occurred only recently. Rather than question what is known, I would set my mind on correcting the failings of your son."

Jacob refused to cower. "There is no failing," he said. "Only a delay."

"I have talked to the men," Ba'al said, biting off each word. "Twice she was in your grasp! Twice she slipped through! How does a frail Albino without any memory escape the clutches of Jacob, son of Qurong?"

It was a good question, one Jacob had been asking himself. Short of magic, he couldn't fathom how she'd managed to escape them in the darkness.

The second encounter was less of a mystery. She'd proven herself to be adept with knives. He could still see her eyes as she bore down on him, blade clenched between her teeth. But her weapon flew wide. Intentionally so. Why, after killing his other men so readily? Something in her eyes intrigued him.

"She went east," Ba'al said. "East, where the Elyonites live. They would use her to crush us."

"Now you speak sacrilege." Qurong glared at the priest. "No Albino army can crush the Horde."

"None but one led by the 49th. Or do you now doubt the words of Teeleh?"

Qurong remained silent.

"I do not question your armies, my lord." Ba'al dipped his head. "They are far superior to any other. But we cannot pretend to know more than Teeleh. The 49th must be taken before she falls into the hands of our enemies, or they will rise in a holy terror to enslave all Horde."

"Let them try." But Jacob heard concern in his father's voice.

"She's far more powerful than you realize," Ba'al said.

"I won't let her reach the Great Divide," Jacob said, eager to move beyond the talk of superstitions.

"You won't." Ba'al walked up to Jacob and plucked away the dagger he'd thrown. "Because I will send Campous."

Campous, a cutthroat whose hatred for all things Albino made up for his lesser skill with a blade.

"Nonsense," Jacob said. "My men are already saddled on fresh horses, waiting for me at the northern gate. Did you think I came back for wine and women?" He suppressed his anger. "This is the reason for your urgent summons? To cut me down in front of my father?"

Qurong was lost to his own thoughts, staring out the far window. "Take additional horses," he said, facing Jacob. "She has only six or seven hours on you and she'll need to rest — the Divide is a full five days' ride even at the best pace. She must not be allowed to reach the Elyonites. Do you understand? 49th or not, we can take no chances. She must be stopped. If you must, kill her."

"Alive!" Ba'al snapped. "It's the only way to defeat the prophecy and forever bind this world to Teeleh."

"What makes you think you can force her to betray her own?" Qurong demanded. "You've already failed to deal with her."

Ba'al ignored the slight, jaw firm. "He will force her hand."

"He?" Qurong searched the priest's eyes. "The one sent by Teeleh into this other world you speak of?"

"Yes. Together, we cannot fail. She will betray her own, but not if she slips our grasp."

"Fine. Take her alive. But if you can't, kill her before the Elyonites take her. Am I clear?"

"They won't reach the Divide," Jacob said, walking for the door.

"They?" Ba'al turned. "There is more

than one?"

Jacob turned back. "Didn't my men tell you? We found the tracks of a third Albino at the oasis. She rides east with him."

This seemed to puzzle Ba'al, but he brushed his concern away. "You must take her," he said.

Jacob stared him down for a moment, then headed out. "Of course. Alive, and subdued for your sharp little daggers."

12

It was amazing how only a few short words could completely change a person's perspective, David thought. How just one strand of code could alter a program, how switching one gene on or off could modify an entire organism's expression. Vlad Smith was right about one thing: all organism was algorithm.

But those weren't the words that had short-circuited David's brain. Vlad's other statement had done that trick.

Your wife was murdered.

He didn't believe the man, naturally. Not fully and completely. He'd made that much clear to Rachelle after trying and failing to track down Vlad only minutes after he'd left.

David didn't believe . . . but he did. At the very least, that something about his wife's death didn't make sense. For years he'd blamed himself for her death, but now a door had been kicked open to another possibility, one that was much darker than

211

any he could have imagined.

He knew this was just how the mind got people into trouble, but that didn't stop *his* mind from trying to get *him* into trouble. The mere suggestion of something afoul was enough to set gears in motion, and once they were churning, their momentum took on a life of its own. Years of guilt, anger, and self-condemnation had created new neural pathways in his brain. As they said, neurons that fire together, wire together. Those well-worn ruts in his frontal lobe had accepted and embraced the new content Vlad had supplied. Namely, that his wife had been murdered because she was special. Like their daughter. Which David knew to be true. The man might be onto something.

He'd also been onto something in implying that this information wasn't something David could just throw in Simon's face, true or not. Regardless of whether Simon knew anything, he would immediately pull Barth in. And Barth wasn't the kind of man you could question or cross without consequence.

David let it all stew, knowing he was feeding his own fear and anger without being able to set the accusations aside. He would have dismissed the matter altogether, but he didn't have that kind of control over his mind. Truth was, Rachelle was more practiced in the disciplines of dealing with fear.

There was more to consider, of course. For starters, how Rachelle had managed to catch the apple Smith had thrown at her with enough speed to strike out most ballplayers. Without the slightest warning.

Then there was the book Smith had pulled out.

Rachelle was concerned about how her mother may have died, but she feared something far more ominous was happening, and right now, not just back then. She tried to explain that her dreams were more than just her way of working through her blindness.

Even if she was right, which he doubted, it all stemmed from his wife's death.

After an hour, David told Rachelle to stay put — he was going to the hospital to clear his mind. Maybe Miranda would have some ideas.

"Ideas about what?" Rachelle asked.

"A clinical perspective. If your mother was murdered, we should be able to find evidence."

"What evidence? That was sixteen years ago."

"We never did an autopsy. Maybe exhume her body."

"No. Not that. Even if you find some evidence, Simon will have an explanation."

She had a point.

"Let it go, Dad. At least for the next five days."

"Why five?"

"Because Vlad told you six days, which now leaves five."

He'd forgotten about Smith's claim that the world as they knew it would end in six days. That was yesterday.

He looked at his daughter pacing, biting on a fingernail. The young girl who'd bounced around the town only yesterday, proclaiming her sight to the world, had been stolen and replaced by a young woman who believed the fate of the world rested on her shoulders.

He had no desire to feed her paranoia. She was already obsessed. He had his own obsession to deal with.

He caught himself. No, that wasn't true.

"Okay, I'll let it go," he said. "But I'm going to talk to Miranda. Promise me you'll stay put. If Smith wanted to harm either of us, he's had plenty of opportunity, but I don't want you taking any chances."

"Chances? Like accusing Barth of murder?" she said.

He nodded. "Yes, chances like that. I got it."

But he hadn't really gotten it, because his mind was screaming past its hopeless attempt at denial. Even knowing this, he felt powerless against it. He turned his back and headed for the door.

"Dad?"

"Yeah?"

"What begins as White that man has made Black?"

He thought a moment. A riddle. "I have no idea. But I do know what's black and white and red all over."

"What's that?"

"A skunk in a blender."

Rachelle nodded, but he doubted she'd even heard him.

"If I'm not here, I'll be at the pasture," she said. "I need some air."

"Okay, but nowhere else."

He found Miranda at the hospital with RG, but it took him a while to work through how to tell them what Smith had done and said. He finally just laid it out for them exactly as he understood it himself.

"Well? What do you think?" he asked.

"Sounds like someone wants to stir up

215

trouble so he can sell his snake oil," RG said.

"I don't know." Miranda was more reluctant. "There could be some truth to it. The mind's more powerful than we know."

"Exactly!" David stood and crossed to the window. "The question is why? What was so threatening about my wife?"

"No, not the part about your wife," Miranda said. "I agree with RG. Smith's just stirring up trouble. Ignore it."

That put him back.

"Then exactly which part makes sense to you? The part about my daughter dreaming of white bats or the part where she has to save the world?"

"Those are just dreams. But even snake oil can work if the salesman does his job and gets a susceptible customer to believe."

"She was out when he pricked her finger!"

"True," RG said. "But our subconscious mind hears and registers everything around us while we're sleeping."

David knew that.

He also knew that they weren't going to bite. Miranda had hopes of replacing his wife and wanted nothing to do with an investigation into how she'd died. She definitely wouldn't jump at the idea of exhuming her body. And RG . . . Well, RG was too logical to think past what was right in front of him.

It was nearly four o'clock in the afternoon before David made the decision that he would talk to Simon. He simply had to, if not for his own sake, then out of respect for his wife. He wouldn't go in hurling accusations, which would endanger them all. Instead, he'd speak to Simon without even mentioning his wife. He'd win the Judge's confidence by dutifully reporting the danger that Smith presented in throwing out wild suggestions that the residents of Eden were somehow being manipulated.

He would watch the man like a hawk. Simon had balked when Rachelle asked if something was wrong with Eden. How would he react to more pointed insinuations?

But he wouldn't mention his wife. Not yet.

David told Miranda and RG that he had to check in on Rachelle, then he slipped out a side door, in no mood to talk to Sue at the front. He walked quickly, head down, hands in pockets, straight for the council chambers, hoping Simon would be there monitoring outside news on the ham radio, assuming the satellite feed wasn't back online.

Funny, he'd hardly thought about the grid crisis all day. The world was in a nosedive out there and he hardly cared. There would be plenty of time for that later.

It only took him a few minutes to reach the back entrance to the administration office. He climbed the four wooden steps to the porch and put his hand on the knob. Then hesitated.

He released the handle and ran his fingers through his hair, rehearsing his act one more time. Maybe he should just come out with it. Only way to really know. Maybe Simon would agree not to share any details with Barth. Or maybe he —

"David?"

He spun around. Hillary Moses stood on the gravel walkway holding the hand of her youngest, Carina.

"You need something?"

David hesitated. "Well . . . I just wanted to talk to Simon for a second."

"You haven't heard?"

"Heard what?"

"Terrorists detonated EMPs over Los Angeles, Phoenix, and Salt Lake City. Isis, they say."

He stood still, dumbstruck. "Electromagnetic pulse blasts?"

"Large enough to shut down the West

Coast and disable all electronic devices in a hundred-mile radius around each city."

"When?"

"Simon just heard it on the ham radio half an hour ago."

"Mommy, can we go?" Carina was tugging on Hillary's arm.

"Just a moment, sweetie." Hillary smoothed the blonde curls of the seven-year-old. She looked back up. "Sorry, we were on the way to get some ice cream. I don't think any of this should affect the children."

"No," he heard himself say. "No, of course not."

"Simon's off the grid." She caught her own pun and grinned. "So to speak. Says he needs to get his ducks in a row for the meeting tonight."

The town hall meeting. He'd forgotten.

"What time again?"

She glanced at her watch. "Two hours. Six o'clock. I thought you knew."

"Yeah. Sorry, I'm . . . Wow. An EMP, huh?"

"Three of them. But Jesus will protect us. This is going to change things around here, David. I've never seen Simon so focused. It's really happening."

Simon Moses stood at the tunnel's inner gate, fumbling with keys. Barth had locked the massive barred entrance yesterday, effectively cutting off Eden from the outside world. But Simon had to be sure that all was in order. He had to know because he knew what none of them possibly could. All except for Smith. Smith might know.

And if Smith knew . . .

He found the key and glanced at his watch. Five oh three. An hour. He had to hurry.

With a quick twist of the key, the titanium lock fell open. Two steps to the control panel. The gates rumbled when he hit the large red button with his palm.

Power was still on. That was good. He hurried back to his Dodge Ram, climbed in, shoved the stick into drive, and took the truck through the opening gate and into the dark tunnel.

It had taken them a month to blast the seventy yards through this cursed cliff. Another seven months to lay the two-lane road that snaked its way into the valley behind him. Even without gates, Eden was secured from the outside world by its isolation alone.

A long line of yellow lights along the ceiling cast an amber glow on the asphalt road.

He'd always known that a day might come when the whole thing came down. That was part of the deal. But the speed of the developments over the last few days had taken him by surprise.

Worse was the sudden appearance of a man who didn't fit into the equation. Vlad Smith was either working with the benefactors or against them. There was no way his insertion into Eden was a matter of coincidence.

Following the girl's question yesterday whether something was wrong with Eden, Simon had broken protocol and made an attempt to reach the benefactors from his bunker. No answer. This in itself wasn't necessarily a problem — the scheduled call was always on Saturday, today. But when he'd been unable to establish contact at nine o'clock this morning, his concern gave way to fear. For the first time in almost two decades, Eden was completely out of contact with the outside world.

He exited the tunnel, eyes on the valley thick with trees beyond Eden. The road rounded a bend and ran through the main control building a hundred yards farther.

Anyone entering or leaving the valley had to pass through the large structure and its heavy steel doors, operated by a switch in its control room. Like the rest of Eden, the gatehouse was powered by the hydroelectric plant with two backups at the north end of the valley. Loss of electricity would never be their problem.

Beyond the gatehouse, the rest of the world. Deep inside the gatehouse, a control room known only to him. A fail-safe with redundant communication lines to the outside world.

He slid the stick into park, stepped out, and approached the gatehouse. Using a key, he opened the door that led into the control center. Entered and flipped on the overhead lights. Scanned the room.

At first glance the panel looked in order. It had four lights, red or green, two of which were now green. Open. That would be the tunnel gates he'd just passed through. The third was red — the large steel doors. The last light was for the titanium door to his right, which led into the second control room, which only he had access to.

Simon crossed to the door and quickly entered his nine-digit code into the panel that operated the locks, expecting the familiar *clunk* when the internal latch disengaged.

Only there was no *clunk*.

He drew his sleeve over his forehead to clear the sweat, focused, and tried again. Same result. Had the benefactors reset the code? Or had a surge fried it? Couldn't be a surge, the circuits operated on a protected loop.

He tried a third time, deliberately entering each number as he spoke them aloud. The lock remained engaged.

A chill washed down his back. How was this possible? Without access to the chambers behind this door . . . Had they cut him off? The questions boomed through his mind like a cluster bomb. Above them all, one thought.

Vlad Smith.

A soft, barely audible chirp from behind him cut through the stillness. He spun. Silence.

But he'd heard that chirp. Or had he?

Sweat now coursing down his face, he glanced at his watch again. Five fourteen. He had to get back, collect his thoughts, and lead them as he always had. Far too much depended on the role he played in Eden. Without him, the town would collapse, with or without the grid failure.

Simon slapped the door, grunting. He was halfway across the room when the chirp came again. He froze. The sound had come from down low. Under the metal tabletop that housed the control panel.

Two strides and he was there, dropping to one knee and peering under the tabletop.

One look and he saw the small black box with the tiny red light winking at him. His heart thudded into his gut. A handwritten note on yellow notepad paper was taped to the concrete wall.

Open the main gate and the whole thing blows.
Enter the chambers and the whole thing blows bigger.
Cut or remove any wire and the whole thing blows like a neutron star.

VS

Blood drained from Simon's face. The entrance was booby-trapped. From the inside.

VS. Vlad Smith.

But was he working with the benefactors or had he entered the valley on his own? It had to be the former. How else could he know so much? Either way, there was a new player in town, and Simon's lifeline to the outside had been cut off. A test? Or the result of a failure? Like the grid failure. Problem was, Simon didn't know whether he should kiss Smith's feet or blow his head off.

He stood. Closed his hand to steady his fingers.

Dear God.

13

I stared at the words Peter had scrawled in the dirt at our feet. *What begins as White that man has made Black?* With a stick I scratched a circle into the soil surrounding them.

Somehow my reading of the words in Vlad's Book of History had opened my mind to the meaning of words and letters, not only in that book, but everywhere. I could only guess that I could read in my dream world too.

Peter had learned from my father where I was and sought me out. I'd decided then that I would share the seals with him and him alone, for now. Why him, why now? Maybe because after my encounter with Vlad, I wanted someone in Eden to believe me.

We'd spent the last few hours under the large maple tree at the pasture's south side. The four horses feeding on tufts of grass thirty feet away had no concern other than filling their bellies.

I, however, did have other concerns. Like filling my mind with the right thoughts. And it wasn't going so well.

"Maybe you're right," Peter said, leaning back on one elbow, absently chewing on a soft reed.

"You think the answer is Eden?"

He shrugged. "That Smith guy said there was something wrong with Eden. My father's dream has always been a kind of utopia here. That's white. And now Smith intends to destroy his vision. That's black."

I frowned. "Maybe. I just keep thinking that the image I saw in the Book of History *was* the seal."

He was looking at me with those inquisitive eyes of his, topped by long lashes. His dark brown hair was unkempt, but the daisy I'd slid over his ear was still in place.

There was a lot about Peter Moses I wouldn't have guessed. Like the fact that he would believe my stories of dreaming in two worlds. Of course, his judgment might be affected by his interest in me, but I didn't mind that either. It felt good to be liked.

"Then you already found it. But nothing happened."

"I know, so I obviously didn't find anything, other than a riddle. Which makes sense. Justin called them Seals of Truth. So then maybe they aren't physical objects but . . . well . . . truths."

"So then what? You solve this riddle and, poof, you have the seal? That doesn't sound right."

"I know."

"And you have to find five of them before some random appointed time or you fail?"

"Something like that."

"Actually, the seals kinda sound like the treasure in the field."

"The parable?" I said. "The one about the man who sold all he had to buy the field the treasure was in? It cost him everything." Simon taught that the treasure was both a place like Eden and the truth, which was the law.

"Exactly."

"The kingdom is within you," I said.

"What do you mean?"

"That's what the Gospels say. Maybe the treasure is in me."

"Does finding the seals affect this world, or is that just part of your dream world?" Peter asked. "In Other Earth." We'd started calling it Other Earth to simplify matters.

"Both, but maybe not in the same way." I just couldn't understand how I, a girl who'd essentially been born blind in a town in Utah, could possibly play any role in vanquishing the shadow of death in Eden, much less the rest of the world. Or in Other Earth.

He sighed. "Or maybe the riddle really is only about the grid failure, like we said. White is power and black is loss of power."

"Maybe." But I didn't really believe that either. "Maybe they're all just symbols or mirrors of the same thing."

I dropped to my back and spread my arms, facing the dimming sky. Dark clouds were rolling in from the west, but half of the sky was still blue. A brilliant blue. Bluer than the desert world's sky. Less atmosphere up here at six thousand feet in elevation. The desert was probably at sea level.

I hadn't told Peter about my catching of the apple, or the fighting skills I evidently had in Other Earth. I wanted to. Who wouldn't want to say they just woke up and discovered they were from another reality and had mad ninja skills?

But I couldn't bring myself to tell him, because those skills, like the tattoo on my arm, made me feel distant from him. Like I was an alien and he was a human. Telling him about the five seals had stretched him enough. I hadn't told him about Talya and his lion either. Or Samuel's affection for me.

And how did I feel about Samuel?

"I'm a Mystic," I whispered, watching dark clouds beyond the swaying leaves.

"I can live with that," Peter said. "The whole world's wrapped in mystery. Sometimes I think my father's only goal in life is to strip it all away and become his own god."

See, that was an insight I wouldn't have expected from Peter. I turned my head and saw that, leaning back on one elbow, he was above me now.

"A Mystic is someone who believes that God is infinite," I said.

"Really? Doesn't everyone believe that?"

"Evidently not."

My stomach was in knots. The dread I'd felt this morning had eased a bit when Peter found me, then returned after hours of talking through seals and Roush and Shataiki and Vlad Smith without making any more sense of it.

I didn't want to be anyone special. I certainly didn't want anyone's future to depend on me. I just wanted to be a normal girl who could see like everyone else and could now discover the beauty of a whole new world in a whole new way.

I shifted my head to a more natural position. "Tell me about your father. Not the Judge, but who he is as a dad."

He stared off at the cliffs. "My father's always been sure of himself. Never seen anyone more focused or, in some ways, so demanding. But he's also fair. Never laid a finger on me, 'cept when I deserved it."

"He's beaten you?"

"Sure. But I learned long ago not to cross the line. I haven't seen that side of him for a while. You just follow his rules and all is smooth. There's the law, and he's the Judge. I can't even remember the last time I broke his rules."

I gazed into his bright eyes. "What about now?"

Looking into someone's eyes was the most breathtaking part of being able to see, I thought. Like staring into another galaxy. Part of me wanted to crawl inside of them.

"Being here with you?" He was blushing. "I'm not exactly courting you, am I? Now, if I did this" — he traced my palm with his finger — "an argument could be made that I was." Lifted his finger. "But I'm not."

"Well, maybe you should," I said, then immediately regretted opening my mouth. Before he could respond I withdrew my hand and rested my head on it, eyes turned back to the sky. "Or maybe you shouldn't."

"I guess I would need approval from the council. But I'm not sure my father would —"

"The council meeting!" I cried, sitting up. "What time is it?"

He straightened. Grabbed the iPhone from his pocket. Pushed the home button. "Crap . . ." He was all arms and legs, struggling to his feet. "Crap, crap, crap, he's gonna kill me!"

Enough said. We were both on our feet and running down the path.

"I'm sorry, this is my fault," I said.

"No . . . No, it's mine. I just . . . Don't worry about it, just run."

We ran. I knew that the meeting was mandatory. I also knew that failing to meet any mandatory requirement could not go unpunished. At the very least, isolation for twenty-four hours for some soul searching. Worst case, corporal punishment, but that was rare. I was aware of only three instances of public beatings. What happened behind closed doors was another matter.

Peter had gone from sweet, flirting teenager to terrified child in the space of three breaths. My fault.

It took us less than ten minutes at a fast jog to reach the center of town. No people in the square. Not even a dog or cat. Only cars and trucks, lots of them, lining the streets. Dusk had settled quickly, graying the sky with each passing minute as we ran.

"What time is it?" I asked, panting hard.

"Six twenty." His voice was thin and his face was pale. We were twenty minutes late.

Thoughts of seals and Smith and Talya and Justin had been pushed clean out of my mind by the time we hurried up the steps and slipped into the foyer of the church.

There were three doors leading into the back of the auditorium, one that opened to the center aisle, two that opened to either side. Peter veered to his right and motioned for me to split to the far side. Of course. We couldn't be seen entering together.

I watched him run up to the door and, quiet as a feather, slip into the sanctuary. But I held back. Entering through two doors at the same time would look as bad as walking in the same one together. Worse, like we were trying to hide the fact we'd been together.

So I hung back and paced, listening to the muted sounds of Simon's booming voice over the PA inside.

"It's the only way to protect what we've built here," Simon was saying. There was a desperate edge to his tone. "I know this may sound extreme to some of you, but Jesus

233

was very clear when he told us to take up the sword. He came to divide, not unite, and we are that division, my friends, separated from the world. He said run to the hills, we ran to the hills. He said to prepare for the worst, we've done that and more. And now we heed his call to take up arms and protect ourselves."

I could imagine them now, a hundred and fifty faithful seated with rapt attention, trusting the one who'd created their secure world here in Eden. The council would be seated on the platform — Linda Loving, Maxwell Emerson, and Barth Caldwell. Their families, along with Simon's, would be on the front row, nodding respectfully. Then the other founding residents, and behind them, those who'd come into the valley after it was established. Like my father, who always sat with Miranda on the last row, for my sake more than his own.

Peter would have had to walk all the way to the front. Visions of him being beaten flashed through my mind. Surely Simon wouldn't go that far with his own son.

I paced and wiped the sweat from my brow as someone, Cindy Jarvis by the sound of her faint voice, expressed some concern. "Forgive me for asking and I'm sure it's just me, but do you really see them coming over the cliffs? I mean . . . we really need snipers?"

A short pause and then Simon's response, dripping with condescension. "Why yes, Cindy, I do, or I wouldn't have said as much. Do you not understand what an EMP can do to a society?" I could hear him walking on the platform, imagine him drilling her with a stare.

"Today's attacks over Los Angeles, Phoenix, and Salt Lake City are only the beginning. Whoever's behind this began with limited attacks in the Northeast — just enough to compromise our government's emergency responders. Then they deployed EMPs over several strategic western cities. Suffice it to say, the United States is crippled in a way few could have imagined. Even if there are no more attacks, life as all Americans have known it is now officially finished. It'll take them years to recover. But not us. God has given us all a valley of refuge."

Silence gripped his audience.

"Tell me, wouldn't you protect what God has given you with the same ferocity he would?"

No answer was required.

The Judge continued. "They will come! In one day, one week, or one month, they will come. And when they do, we will be ready. The first leg over the lip of those cliffs gets a bullet in it. By Utah law, and I do abide by that law, we are fully in our rights to defend against any trespasser."

After a short pause, someone asked about cell phones, but Simon shut him down quickly. The cell tower that serviced the valley was offline. All communications in and out of the valley were offline, including all satellite transmissions. Eden was completely and, until further notice, irrevocably cut off from the outside world. Which was our only saving grace.

"Think of yourselves as in the world but not of it," he said. "Any attempt to leave or communicate with that world will be met with the harshest consequence."

It was worse than I'd realized. The whole country was falling apart around this little paradise of ours. But something was wrong in this paradise, and I was sure that Simon knew it. He was speaking boldly, but his tone was soaked in insecurity.

Slowly, my hard breathing settled. There was no way to get in without being seen. No way to pretend my tardiness and Peter's weren't somehow connected. No way I would lie if they questioned me. Better to just slip in beside my father and be done with it.

I grasped the handle, took one last deep breath, and opened the door to the center aisle. I'd intended to keep my head down and walk straight to my father, who was seated in the last pew. But I looked up as I entered, and what I saw stopped me.

It was the first time I'd actually seen the sanctuary with my eyes. I knew every nook and cranny through echolocation sight, yes, but actually seeing the platform from this viewpoint and in full color took my breath away.

Simon, dressed in a black judge's robe trimmed in gold, stood at the podium built into a judge's bench. The other three council members were seated behind him in high-backed chairs upholstered with deep red fabric.

On either side of the long judge's bench, two sculpted marble pillars reached to a domed ceiling. The sides of the platform were framed by long purple velvet drapes. Simplicity and plain living were things Eden prided itself on, but not in this sanctuary. It was both beautiful and intimidating.

But that's not what stopped me.

It was the large, round, backlit image of God etched into stained glass on the wall behind them. A stern, bearded man held the scales of justice. He wasn't wearing a blindfold, like the lady in the traditional images, and he was staring directly at me. Justice might be blind, but God was not.

With his free hand, God was pointing a long finger down to a Bible that had been fixed to a pedestal on the wall below the stained glass. I shifted my eyes back up to the image of God and shivered as a thousand fears surfaced.

My father had once told me that you could get that big black book to say anything if you tortured it long enough. And I supposed he was right, but I'd always chosen to believe what Simon insisted it said.

"Anyone who does not comply with even the most benign law in Eden will be sequestered." Simon was staring at me as he spoke, and others turned their heads to see who he was looking at, including Peter, who'd taken his place next to his sister, Carina, on the front row.

I had taken one step toward my father when the lights went out. All of them. There were no windows. The room was pitch-dark.

Eden had just lost its power.

Cries of alarm filled the room. Simon was urging calm and Barth was shouting them all down. "Everyone remain seated! Do not move!"

My hearing quickly picked up my father's

voice. "Rachelle?"

I stood fixed to the carpet, clicking and seeing the shapes of at least a dozen people standing, including my father, ten paces ahead on the last pew.

"Let there be light!" a voice boomed from the stage.

The lights suddenly popped on, illuminating the auditorium. With the coming of that light, a hush. And in that hush stood Vlad Smith. Dressed in the same white jacket, legs spread wide, hands in his pockets.

Every eye turned to look at the man who stood on the right side of the stage. His were directed at me. No one moved.

"I have come to bring sight to the blind and set the captives free."

Barth Caldwell palmed a gun from his waist and leveled it at the man.

Vlad slowly turned his head toward the security man. "Really, Barth? You really want to go there?"

Barth looked like he did.

Simon looked like he'd been gut-punched. He slowly lifted a hand to his second in command, but Barth kept his weapon trained on Vlad Smith.

The lights went out again. Black.

A momentary flash and crack from a gunshot punctuated the darkness. I instinctively ducked. Barth fired his weapon two more times in rapid succession.

Then nothing but darkness. No one was yelling — they were too shocked, I thought. First the power failure, now gunshots. Two firsts in the hallowed sanctuary.

With a loud snap, light once again filled the room. Half the residents were now on their feet. Vlad hadn't moved except to raise one hand and snap his fingers. He was still staring directly at me, like a viper, unblinking.

"You see?" he said. "I give and I take, and in the world of polarity, that which is given *must* be taken. What you will quickly realize, every single last one of you, is that, for all practical purposes, I am now your god. So if you want any power in Eden, I strongly suggest you take a deep breath and put the weapon down before I cram it down your throat."

"Put it away," Simon said, voice thin. This time Barth complied.

"Attaboy." Vlad's gaze swept the auditorium. "As I'm sure you've all heard by now, yesterday I brought sight to blind eyes — a sign so you would know my power. Today I show you I can just as easily take sight away."

He withdrew his other hand from his

pocket and held up a small gray device between his thumb and forefinger. "Do you know what this is? Hmmm?"

He showed it to both sides of the room.

"No? It's a transmitter with two buttons. One of them cuts off the power from the hydro. The other blows it up. I have four more just like it. And in the event someone gets the bright idea to off me so they can take possession of my little toys, the whole town goes up in smoke. Take my word for it."

Someone to my right dropped a hymnal. No one seemed to notice.

"I'm glad we have that out of the way," Vlad said, sliding the device back into his pocket. He turned to the council members, who were all on their feet. "Leave my stage." Each glanced at Simon, who hesitated, then nodded. They filed off the platform, lastly Barth, who glared at Vlad all the way.

To the rest of us: "Sit."

I was still there at the back of the sanctuary, frozen in place. Part of my brain was telling me to run. But the reasoning part told me running would end badly. I had taken two steps toward my father when Vlad's voice stopped me.

"Not you. You stay exactly where you are. I want them all to understand how and why this is all your doing."

My father was back on his feet.

"Sit!" Vlad's tone carried a crushing authority. Then it softened. "Please, David. Let me do my job. You and I have work to do, but your wife's body isn't going anywhere just yet. Sit."

My father looked confused, but he slowly sat back down.

Everyone had taken a seat, leaving Vlad Smith alone on the stage and me alone in the aisle.

"Good." Vlad walked to the center of the stage, measuring his audience with steady eyes. "Very good." He picked up a wooden gavel from the podium and slammed it down. "Court is in session." He tossed it back onto the bench. "In short order, you, not I, will deliver a verdict based upon all the evidence I intend to present to you. You are the jury and I am your judge. We know that this God you think you understand is the final judge, and I'm not him. But as of now, I will do the speaking for him. Can I get an amen?"

No one spoke. Like me, they probably couldn't have if they wanted to.

"Please, just one. So I know you're listening."

"Amen," Cindy said. A soft chorus of

242

amens quickly followed.

"Excellent, the jury has spoken. The next time all of you, please."

It's hard to explain how I felt in that moment. Inside, I was shaking all over, terrified of being alone and vulnerable in that aisle while Shadow Man strutted across the platform, weaving his spell over them all. But part of me was remembering Justin and Talya and my other self from Other Earth. Those voices told me to stand there and let him say whatever he wanted to say. Those voices were asking, *What begins as White that man has made Black?* Over and over, like a skipping record.

Vlad folded his arms, leaned back on the judge's bench, and crossed his legs. "First, some background, which, however philosophical, is crucial for all tissue-tops. We must break through those thick skulls that protect that mush in there. You've all been brainwashed, every single one of you. That much will be plain soon enough. But I'm going to give you a head start today. It's time to set the record straight."

His lips were flat and his eyes deadpan.

"There are those among the human race called mystics who know that God is infinite."

The familiar words crashed through my skull.

"These mystics say that God is infinitely powerful, infinitely complete, infinitely knowing, infinitely present, and infinitely loving. And what is infinite cannot be compromised by what is finite. Does the jury agree?"

A few amens were quickly joined by many more.

Vlad lowered his arms and stood tall.

"They ask, if a finite little pit bull like Barth here was to come upon a being who was infinitely more powerful than that little ferocious thing" — he pointed to the gun at Barth's waist — "would the infinite being cower in fear? Of course not, the mystics say, because no finite pit bull, regardless of how ferocious he *thinks* he is, can threaten a being that is infinite. Correct?"

A ripple of tentative agreements, though most were undoubtedly balking at his reference to Barth.

"These mystics say that this infinite God of theirs created all that exists, including time and space. And that, as the Creator of time and space, he's not bound by it. He knows everything that has happened and ever will happen. Nothing can surprise such an infinite being. He doesn't wake up one morning and say, 'Crap, I didn't see that coming. I am so disappointed!' "

And I was a Mystic in Other Earth, I thought. Here as well, but one who was standing there dressed in jeans with my arms hanging limp at my sides, feeling as vulnerable as a sheared lamb.

Vlad shoved a hand back into his pocket and walked slowly to his left.

"Follow me here, because it's important. Would such an infinite being ever fear *anything*? No. Does he ever feel insecure or upset? Does he worry that something might go wrong with his plans? No, because there is no finite power that can possibly undermine or compromise his intentions in any way, ever. The pit bull might have his free will, but no will of any finite creature can cause a problem for an infinite being who cannot be compromised."

His voice rang out across the auditorium. A few more amens piped up, but he continued over them.

"God is infinitely secure, the mystics say. Would such a being ever need to *defend* himself against an enemy that poses no threat to his invulnerability? Any defense would only recognize and honor the pit bull's nonexistent power to threaten him. These mystics say that humans have problems but God does not. Having problems, most humans, regardless of their religion, can't fathom the true, infinite nature of God because they've made God in their own image. A God with problems like theirs. Can I get a true, full-blooded amen?"

"Amen." But there were only a few, just following Vlad's orders. This wasn't the God Simon had taught us about. I'd always assumed God had problems. Big ones. But hearing Vlad, I wondered if he was speaking truth about what mystics believed, even though it went against everything I had ever learned.

"That's what the mystics believe." Vlad drilled me with his gaze. "But the mystics are wrong."

He was saying all this for my sake more than the others'. Determined to get under my skin. And it was working. I was suddenly fearing myself — my beliefs and my identity — as much as I was fearing Vlad.

"We, my friends, know if *that* kind of God existed, the mystics would be right — God would have no problems. But we're smart enough to know that God has many very big problems, and he's upset about those problems, just like you and I are. Therefore, God cannot be infinite."

I stood perfectly still, gripped by fear. He

was now describing the God I had always believed in even though I said he was infinite. Could I have been wrong this whole time? Or were the *mystics* wrong?

Something gentle and warm settled over me the moment that thought crossed my mind, like a breath offering me comfort.

"For starters, God lives in fear that he might lose you, his precious children. Something has indeed gone terribly wrong with his plan, and he now depends on you to accept his fix or all hell will break out for you. Literally. In fact, it already has. If you threaten one of his children, he will scream with rage. If you curse his name, he will slap you silly. If you pluck out the eye of one of his offspring, he will allow the devil to pluck out your eye. If you run away, he will wring his hands in worry, hoping you won't be stolen by his enemy, because if you are, only you can save yourself by believing the right thing. He's a God of law, and that law says the fate of his creation, including you, is in your hands now."

My mind was racing. His last statement about our responsibility in life triggered my memory of Justin's words. *Find the five seals for yourself, 49th. When you do, you will know your origin and you will recognize yourself.*

"This is the God of Eden." Vlad pointed

at the council, drawing his finger down the row. "This is the God of law you all worship. The law, my friends, is the sword that you live and die by. It is your accuser and keeps your path straight. You need the law like you need the air to breathe. God fears and so must you, because your terror of God only mirrors his fear of losing you. If the source from which you come fears loss, how much more should you? We have no choice but to protect ourselves from the pit bull, because it's strong enough to threaten God."

Betsy Williamson, who often saw my father for stress due to a surplus of fears stemming from an abandoned childhood, was on her feet, waving a Bible in her old hand. "That's right! You tell it straight, preacher." Her arm was covered in a red rash. So was her neck.

John Baxter shouted his endorsement, then many others followed suit. This was Simon's gospel.

A part of me joined in with them, because this was what I had grown up learning. I stood there, fractured.

But another part of me was feeling that breath that flowed over me like a breeze now, calming my mind. Something was going to happen, I could feel it. Something was already happening.

What begins as White that man has made Black? Find the seals . . . When you do, you will know your origin and yourself.

"The jury has spoken. I must say, you've been programmed so well." Vlad touched his tongue and marked the air with his finger. "Score one for the tissue-tops. Amen?"

"Amen."

The warm breeze was stronger now, caressing my hair. Something was happening, but only I seemed to notice it. The rest were oblivious to the flow of power that was sweeping over me.

"All your life you've followed what Simon says. Simon says, and you believe, and that's what protects you. I hope you now all understand why it's so important for you to follow the laws that Simon says and why you will forgive Barth for enforcing those laws. The whole world is falling apart out there, and Eden will suffer the same fate unless you follow every single jot and tittle."

Vlad shoved his hands into his pockets and walked back to the center of the stage. "Unfortunately for Simon, I now control much more than the grid in this valley. What used to be Simon Says is now Vlad Smith Says. Otherwise, every single last one of you will perish."

His words reached me as if spoken from a distant hole.

What begins as White that man has made Black? When you find the seals, you will have found your origin.

"As the new judge in Eden, I wish to put my flock to a simple test, just to see if you understand the consequences of breaking God's laws, which are now my laws."

The seal is a truth . . .

"That test will be asked of one girl, who is far more powerful than any of you can possibly understand. You know her as Rachelle." He reached his hand toward me, palm up. "The girl to whom I gave sight yesterday."

They were looking at me, I knew that, but I was somewhere else. It could have been in my mind's eye, but I was back in the desert, facing Justin, who had just given me a stone to hold. The hot sun warmed my skin. His bright green eyes smiled at me, then turned down to my arm. I saw that my veins were filled with light. That light was my fabric. My source. Without it, the stone in my hand would grow too heavy to bear.

Look to the light, I heard Justin say. *Don't be afraid of the shadow it creates. Remember. Return to the truth of your origin and*

250

recognize yourself.

With those words, I knew what the First Seal was. Like a tsunami the truth crashed over me, and immediately tears filled my eyes and slipped down my cheeks as I stood there, caught up in another world.

All my life I had lived in the regret of believing I disappointed my Father, God, the one who made me. All my life I had lived in fear of the consequences for my failure.

But I had been blind. Blind to his infinite power. Blind to his unthreatened love.

A knot filled my throat and I could hardly breathe as my tears flowed there in the desert in front of Justin. But I knew now. I knew the First Seal and I opened my eyes, expecting to see him and tell him I had found it. Then I would throw my arms around him.

Instead, I found myself staring at the platform. I blinked to clear my sight.

Vlad was holding up the same Book of History he'd shown my father and me that morning. Behind him, that stained glass with the god of law made in man's image loomed over us like an idol.

And the Bible below Vlad's god? It could not, in the end, point to anything but an infinite God who could not fear any loss or be threatened in any way.

Vlad looked slightly amused by my show of emotion, but he continued whatever he'd been saying.

". . . and she refused. Just a few words in a harmless old book. You would think a girl who owes me her life would be thrilled to show her gratitude."

My feet were moving already. I walked without fear, one foot in front of the other, drawn by the Book of History. Drawn because I knew it had something to show me.

My uninvited approach stalled Vlad for a second, but he took it in stride.

"So now I will make myself clearer. If the one I healed refuses to write what I've asked her to write in this book, then I will throw you all into darkness. If she still refuses, then there will be harsher consequences. This I have spoken. This is now the law."

Voices peppered the auditorium as I walked, urging me to write. Vlad had said his piece. Everyone thought they knew the stakes, but they couldn't possibly know what I did.

My father whispered a warning as I passed him, but I walked by without looking. Vlad Smith let me come, but I didn't pay him any mind either.

I had to get to that book.

A hush fell over the room when I reached the steps. I could hear Vlad's steady breathing when I set my foot on the platform. I could feel his stare as I walked up to him, refusing to look him in the eyes.

Look to the light. Don't be afraid of the shadow it creates. Re-member. Return to the truth of your origin.

"The book," I said, holding out my hand.

He hesitated, then set the book on the podium, and next to it, a pen. I now knew his purpose here. He needed me, the 49th, to write him into Other Earth. Which was a very bad idea.

I had no intention of writing what he wanted me to write. I was thinking about the page I'd seen earlier, the one with the white circle. The emblem that neither Vlad nor my father could see.

As if in a dream, I reached out. Touched the book. Felt the ripple of power flowing up my arm like the light I'd felt in my veins. The room behind me went dead silent.

I slowly opened the cover and peeled back four pages to the one that had been smeared with blood. My blood. And there, below the blood, the emblem. A pencil-thin line encircling a wide band of white. In the center, the same words I'd been repeating to myself all day.

What begins as White that man has made Black?

I knew, didn't I? It was plain to me. God. White wasn't a color, but the light! Black wasn't a color, but darkness. The answer to the riddle was God. We had made God — the Creator, our Origin — like us, subject to the knowledge of good and evil. Peace and disruption. Love and hate. Mercy and revenge.

But that wasn't who he was. God wasn't white or black. He was infinite.

Look to the light. Don't be afraid of the shadow it creates. Vlad, the shadow, had unwittingly played a role in leading me to the light.

Return to the truth of your origin.

Vlad's hot breath was in my ear, smelling of dirty socks. "One way or the other, you will write me into your dreams so I can finish what I was made to do, you sick little puke. The only question is how many bodies I'm going to have to step over."

Though I walk through the valley of the shadow of death, I will fear no evil. Vlad was that shadow, *only* a shadow. But suddenly I was afraid. What if I was wrong?

Trembling, I reached for the pen with my left hand. But at the same time, I moved my right hand over the emblem. Then slowly lowered my palm to the circle.

"Origin," I breathed. "Origin is Infinite."

At first nothing happened, and I thought I'd been wrong. But I knew, deeper than my bones, that even if I had the words wrong, I was right.

The white circle under my hand began to glow. Bright, like the sun. I could see it between my spread fingers!

The glowing circle winked out, and a rush of power surged up my arm, then into my mind, where it exploded like a star.

I gasped. My whole body shook, too frail to contain the staggering power flowing through me, even though that power was only a thimbleful in an endless ocean made of light.

I knew that like I knew my Source, my God, my Father, my Origin, was infinite — uncompromised, unthreatened by anything ever.

This was my Father. I had never upset him.

My knowing of him in that way flooded me with a raw love for him that erupted from every cell in my body, defying all I had known of him up until that point. I could not breathe.

The book was pulled out from under my

hand and the light vanished, leaving me standing with my back to the audience and Vlad towering over me. The residents of Eden couldn't possibly know what had just happened, or if *anything* had happened.

But I was swimming in an infinite ocean of light, aware of my origin for the first time in my life. To me, *everything* had just happened.

"So, then," Vlad was saying, gently closing the book. "The battle begins."

I looked up and met his eyes. They weren't filled with anger or bitterness. They were completely expressionless, like a dead man's eyes, which was worse. I knew he hadn't seen the glowing circle, but they'd all heard my gasp and seen me shake as the power rushed through me.

Vlad faced his confused audience.

"What sight I gave to her, I now take from you," he said. "Your fate is now entirely in Rachelle's hands."

The lights went out on cue. Cries of alarm filled the room. Shadow Man was casting his darkness over Eden, and that shadow was pitch-black.

I moved then, spinning and clicking to find my way. People were shouting in the darkness, groping along the pews. I had to reach my father before they blocked the aisles and I lost sight of his form.

"Rachelle?" It was him, calling in a panic.

I sprinted down the center aisle, dodging three people, and got to my father just as he was stepping into the aisle, pulling Miranda with him.

"Hurry!" I cried, grabbing his hand. "We have to get out."

I led him out the back, easily navigating my way through the door, across the foyer, and out into the moonless night. We hesitated at the top steps.

Eden was dark. Not a light could be seen. Heavy clouds covered most of the sky, leaving only a few pinprick stars to the east.

"We have to get you to safety," my father said. "I don't know exactly what happened in there, but I don't think you won any friends."

I looked to my right and could just see the images of my father and Miranda beside me. It wasn't the starlight that gave me that sight, or any clicking.

It was the slight glow from my arm.

I reached across with my left hand and pulled up my sleeve. A wide white ring had appeared on my right shoulder, just inside the black circle. Not a flat white ring on my skin, but one that had depth, set deep into my flesh, more like a brand than a tattoo.

My heart was slamming against my rib cage. I touched the ring. Perfectly smooth. Other Earth was real. All of it. I had to sleep so that I could dream! Talya would know what I should do now. I had to show Talya!

"What in the world is that?" Miranda asked.

I quickly lowered my sleeve.

"The First Seal," I breathed, then hurried down the stairs, clicking for good measure.

"Slow down," my father said. But of course, they could hardly see. "Where are you going?"

"Home," I said. "I have to dream."

14

The first seal was on my arm and Vlad Smith had just made me enemy number one. Until I wrote him into the Book of History, Eden would be without the electrical power they treasured.

By not writing in the book, I was causing a crisis, just as Justin had said. But he'd said it as if that crisis would extend far beyond Eden. I had to find out what to do. From Talya. Which meant I had to dream.

Even with the seal on my arm, it had taken me an hour to convince my father and Miranda to give me a mild sedative so I could sleep and return to those dreams. And then another hour, lying on my bed in the darkness while listening to their quiet, urgent voices in the living room, waiting for the sedative to calm me.

The last time I knew, it was just after nine thirty p.m. in Eden.

And then I was waking on horseback,

slumped over, staring at the sand. The horse had come to a stop. Birds chirped above me. My cheek rested on the mare's mane.

I jerked up, but leather tethers tied to my wrists prevented me from sitting straight.

"Easy now." The distinctive low rumble behind me was Talya. "You'll forgive me for securing you so you wouldn't fall off and crack your skull open on a rock. Just slip your wrists out."

I did so and looked around. We were at the edge of a small, clear lake with a forest to our rear, the first I'd seen since waking in the desert two days earlier. Mountains rose beyond the lake. Shafts of sunlight glanced off the mirrored surface. I had been sleeping all night and half the day?

"What time is it?" I asked.

"Time?" Talya slipped from his saddle and rubbed his stallion's neck. "It is time to begin your training, I would say." He looked up at me, eyes glinting with a mischievous light. "Wouldn't you?"

Had he slept? I couldn't see how. He looked exactly as I'd last seen him, long white hair held off his face with two braids tied at the back. Bushy eyebrows and smooth skin — no sign of fatigue. And no sign of his lion, Judah.

He winked at me. "Suffice it to say that I

require less sleep than you. But yes . . ." He smoothed his beard. "I do sleep and I do eat, and right now I could use a good bath, but that will have to wait."

His comment made me think of where I was from, not only here in this world, but in my dreams.

"I'm dreaming each night that I live in a place called Eden," I said.

"Yes, you are."

My pulse surged. He knew! A dozen questions bombarded me, but he spoke before I could form the first.

"You've entered a gateway that bridges two worlds through the Books of History, which have been activated by your blood. Whatever you willingly write in it now will manifest."

"Vlad's book."

His brow arched. "He calls himself Vlad there?"

"Vlad Smith. Who is he?"

"He's from this world, sent to the other to wait for you, the 49th Mystic. The gateway in the Books of History was closed and can only be opened by the blood of the 49th. He expects you to make a way."

"So I shouldn't write him in."

"Inadvisable."

"Why didn't he show himself sooner? He's

been stalking my dreams for a long time."

"Because you only became the 49th when you turned twenty-one, just three days ago."

"I'm only sixteen in my dreams."

"Regardless, twenty-one here. Three sevens. His efforts begin now."

"What efforts?"

"As the 49th in fullness, now twenty-one years of age, you are chosen to represent all humanity in fullness. As such, you will once more bring the sword that divides fear from love in every human heart. If you succeed in awakening to love by finding the Five Seals of Truth, the lion will lie down with the lamb in a return to innocence."

He grinned and grunted softly.

"Ironically, the Horde believes that if the lion lies down with the lamb, they will be forced to become Albino. Most Albinos believe it means they'll be enslaved by the Horde. Thus, you are enemy to both. Please, step down, it's time to begin."

"What about Vlad?"

"If the shadow of death can thwart you in either reality, you will fail in both realities. What happens to you in one reality — death, say — also happens in the other. Vlad is the one sent by Teeleh to foil you in the other reality, thus vastly improving his chances of stopping you here. But he isn't permitted to kill you by his own hand. His goal is to keep you from finding all five seals before the appointed time."

"What appointed time? When?"

"Soon. Very soon. You will see."

He paused as my head spun.

"You must understand, dear daughter: the seals are truth in both worlds. If you fail to find all five before that time, the prophecy of the 49th is vacated, and this world will be forever locked in blindness. Vlad will stop at nothing to keep you from finding all five seals. But your greatest antagonist is your own mind. My role is to help you. Only when you know all five seals can you possibly prevail in your mission to lead all from fear. Then and only then will the lion lie down with the lamb."

A beat.

"Please, step down from your horse."

Hearing my mission so clearly laid out once again, I felt completely overwhelmed. I dismounted, muscles stiff, heart in my throat.

"So the fate of all depends on me?"

"You represent every human bound in polarity. We are one, symbolized by you, the 49th. The journey you take now will be the journey of all, sooner or later."

Polarity. Vlad had used the same term.

"Yes, polarity," Talya said, as if hearing my thoughts. "Like the poles, north and south. Opposites." He picked up a pebble, walked to the edge of the lake, and casually flicked the stone with his thumb. It plopped into the water and vanished beneath the surface. "The world of plus and minus, up and down, good and evil, love and fear. The laws that govern all you think you know. If you toss a stone in the water, it will sink. Gravity and such. Yes?"

I stood beside my horse watching him, ten paces away. "Yes."

"The dimension of polarity." He clasped his hands behind his back and faced me. "And it is in this dimension that you journey to re-cognize yourself beyond all those laws once more. *Re,* meaning 'once again,' and *cognize,* meaning 'to know.' To know once more. To align or to awaken. This is the summary of the Five Seals of Truth. Believe me, awakening is an experience far too wondrous for the human mind to comprehend. It's the journey of all. You will lead them."

My head swam with his words. They seemed to carry a power beyond their form.

His eyes were on my shoulder. "I see that you have encountered the First Seal," he said softly. "The light."

I glanced at my right arm. The bright white ring had joined the tattoo in this reality as well as in Eden. Wonder flooded me. The First Seal was now a part of me.

"The light," I heard myself say. "We think there is some darkness in the light, but we're wrong. Origin is Infinite."

With my uttering of those words, a great peace settled over me. The birds were still chirping above me, but as if in another dimension. A perfect stillness alive with its own energy shut down all of my senses for a few seconds.

Then I blinked and the world around me came back into its familiar form. But even then, the air seemed to have changed.

I slowly faced Talya, who was staring directly at me. A tear slipped down his cheek.

"You see how powerful the truth is, daughter of Elyon?" he said. "All fear is rooted in a failure to know Elyon as infinitely complete, experiencing no fear, only love, because there is no fear in love."[1]

"Beyond polarity," I said.

"In it, but not of it." He dipped his head. "Well done. You will need the first three seals to save Eden. The fourth and fifth lead all beyond polarity. Against the Fifth Seal there is no defense. Until you have all five, you are vulnerable to being blinded once more."

His mention of blindness might have unnerved me, but I had the white seal on my arm and felt no fear in that moment.

Talya stooped, plucked up another pebble, and tossed it into the lake.

"I still remember the day long ago when you drowned and emerged, healed of the scabbing disease. A red pool, much smaller than this lake. Justin's red waters saved you in the same way they save all who drown. Thus you were Albino, like all Albinos in the order of Justin."

He took a deep breath and let it out slowly.

"But Albinos, unlike Justin, still have a problem. And so we come to the crux of the matter, dear 49th. Our problems here in polarity."

I walked down the narrow shore and stared out at the water beside him, trying to remember my drowning.

"Do you know what a water walker is?" he asked.

"Should I?"

"In Mystic-speak, a water walker is one who can overcome the laws that bind us to the world of polarity, both metaphorically — as in stepping beyond fear and walking on the troubled seas of this life — and at a higher level, materially. Overcoming the physical laws of polarity." He wagged his chin at the lake. "Do you think it's possible?"

"Stepping beyond fear or actually walking on water?" I stared at the lake's surface, perfectly calm.

"In the end they are the same. Is it possible?"

"I don't see how."

"The idea that you can't is only a story you've been led to believe, no more real than any other tall tale you've bound yourself to, thus making it so in your experience. Try it."

"Walk on the water? It's water."

"And so you are mastered by this story you believe about yourself — that you will be a victim of the water. All live in one story or another, a victim of this or that." He looked down at me. "We can also change our story. Try it."

"But I . . ."

Talya stepped off the shore and walked into the lake. But then I saw that his feet weren't in the water. They were *on* it, as if the surface was made of soft glass. I blinked and looked closer, stunned by the slight bending of the water under his sandals.

He turned, faced me with a mischievous

glint in his eyes, and spread his arms. "This . . . is the story I believe."

I gawked at him. "How?"

"Through a shift in perception, our entire lives change. It's the basis for all that is miraculous — the shifting of our perception of the material world beyond time and space. When you look at what's beneath me, what do you see?"

"Water," I said.

"And can you walk on it?"

I looked at the shimmering water under his feet. "No."

"And so you are bound by that belief. Instead, look with new eyes. Change your cognitive perception, your thinking. Yeshua called this practice *metanoia* as written in ancient Greek. *Meta,* which means 'change' or 'beyond,' and *noia,* meaning 'thinking' or 'knowing.' Metanoia."[2]

He made it sound so simple, but nothing about him standing there in that impossible place seemed simple to me. "Just rewire my mind?"

"Don't conform to the patterns of the world you see. Step off the shore of your old mind and into a new mind. Walk on water."

"I don't see how I can do that."

"Try it and you will see how."

I stared at the water, feeling silly and way out of my depth. But he said walk.

Heart hammering, I gingerly stepped forward. Cool water swallowed my feet and ankles. Then, with another step, my calves. But of course. I already knew I couldn't walk on water.

"Or not," Talya said, right brow arched over a slight grin. "Have no fear, we only just begin."

He walked past me, stepped onto the shore, and strode toward his horse. "You see, 49th? It's as difficult for Albinos to overcome the polarity of love and fear as it is for them to escape the polarity of gravity. They're still stuck in an old story about who they are and what the world is and so remain victims of that story." He grabbed his reins and swung into his saddle, eyes on me. "But one day, if you pay attention, you might believe a new story and walk on the troubled seas of this life." He paused. "We ride."

I sloshed out of the lake and hurried for my mount, mind buzzing. He was comparing overcoming fear with overcoming gravity, which I got. But how he could actually do it was beyond me.

I mounted and drew my horse next to his as he took us into the trees. Still no sign of his lion, Judah.

"The problem of polarity," he boomed, spreading both arms wide to the world around us. "This . . . is the crux of the matter. Yes, 49th?"

My mind was churning through wild possibilities.

"Light and darkness, up and down, love and fear. And the greatest miracle is rising above the seas of fear rather than being pulled into them. This is the true power of a water walker. Yes?"

"Yes," I breathed, caught up in his passion.

He lifted a finger. "All fear springs from an aversion to being threatened or wronged on some level. And yet it is written that true love holds no record of wrong.[3] Love does not take wrong into account. There is no fear in love. No polarity. This is Elyon's love, which sees no threat against itself because it is whole and cannot be disturbed or upset by any finite threat."

My mind spun.

"It is further written that all confessions of faith, all knowledge, and all belief are nothing without a love that holds no record of wrong. Furthermore, those who follow the way will be known for such love. Do you know those who hold no record of wrong, 49th?"[4]

"No." Then softly, "They would be like water walkers."

"And thus, the problem with Albinos. Though saved in the next life, they cling to judgment, holding records of wrong and thus subjecting themselves to what they believe threatens them. Without love that holds no record of wrong, they are as powerless as the Horde. Your journey is to find the vine of true love beyond judgment, then abide in it. In the end, this is the meaning of all five seals."[5]

A low hum of anxiety replaced my wonder. "You're saying I should see no threat in Vlad? It's impossible to hold no record of wrong. Even for a short time."

"And for that short time you will find yourself a victim of fear and conflict, professing your beliefs but compromised by grievance. Your beliefs are powerless to save you from worry and fear when you hold any record of wrong. True love holds no record of wrong. It's the only way you can walk on water."

His words frustrated me because he was talking in esoteric terms, nothing concrete that I could wrap my brain around.

"It still doesn't make sense to me. You're saying no one knows how to love?"

271

He turned his head and drilled me with a penetrating stare. "Origin," he said with absolute authority, "is Infinite."

I stopped my horse, taken aback. "My Father does."

"Elyon," he said, voice now soft. "Does he not love you with the same love he asks you to love others with? If he were to hold a record of wrong for even one billionth of a second, then for that billionth of a second he would be compromised. A victim threatened by what is finite. Do you think so little of him?"

He might have hit me with a sledgehammer and I would have felt less of an impact, not because of the truth of his statement, but because I felt small for having so recently felt that overwhelming love in Eden only to have already argued against it.

"You must simply learn to see what he sees. To see with the eyes of love. To see with the eyes of Justin. This we call faith in Justin, the evidencing or manifestation of things unseen by the old mind. In this you can move mountains. In this you are a water walker."

I let his words settle, imagining a world in which no one held records of wrong. There would be no arguments, no division, no hard feelings of any kind. It would be . . .

heaven on earth. A true garden of Eden.

"What about the law?" I asked. "Like in the Scriptures. It holds record of wrong, right?"

"The law is an old wineskin," he said. "Weak and useless — fear based. A decent teacher at first, but that harsh schoolmaster can only lead you to true love by its failure to save you from fear. The more you try to follow the law, the more it fails. Indeed, the fulfillment of that old law is the new law called grace. Grace is found only in faith that surrenders to a love that holds no record of wrong. So we never condemn this world of polarity and law. We honor it for the lessons it brings us as we move beyond it."[6]

With that one statement, a dozen confusing teachings from Eden shifted and came into focus. I was clearly mastered by the law, which caused all of my fear.

"Any assessment of what's been written that doesn't lead to true love is simply a misunderstanding," he said. "Powerless."

"Because it takes you back into law," I whispered. "And so you sink."

He nodded and we started the horses forward again.

"No need to condemn yourself, daughter. Your Father doesn't accuse you. Your faith in the law is your accuser, as written."[7]

My Father didn't accuse me, and this had been written? "Written where?"

Talya turned his horse to face me and looked me in the eye. "My dear, everything I say has been written in the ancient texts, with which you are quite familiar. You mentioned the Scriptures yourself. Everything I teach you is from the teachings of Yeshua, Johnin, and Paulus."

Simon had never taught them like this.

He took a deep breath and his horse resumed its walk.

"The love that frees you from fear begins with knowing Origin is Infinite, not subject to fear. Few Albinos truly know Elyon as infinite, beyond threat, much less who they are as the sons and daughters of Elyon. They look only to the life to come, while blind in this one."

"Seeing, they do not see," I said. "Those were Justin's words."

He nodded once. "He too came with a sword to divide the old mind from the new. Grace and truth always cause havoc in the face of the laws of polarity."[8]

I recalled the rest of Justin's words. I would bring crisis . . . But I didn't want to be someone who caused conflict. Nor did I feel remotely qualified to lead anyone anywhere. I couldn't even lead myself. If they expected me to hold no record of wrong . . . Maybe God could do that, but me?

My familiar friend anxiety drummed softly in the back of my mind.

"Know that there's only one way to find true peace in this life. It is this forgotten way that Justin invites you into."

I remained silent as I considered his words. The five seals were that forgotten way. I wasn't sure I wanted to pursue it.

"Who am I?" I asked. "My mother and father. The Mystics."

He looked up at a blue jay fluttering between branches above us. "There have been many Mystics, but most have been killed. You'll meet those who still live in this world soon enough. Elyonite authorities found your mother and father guilty of heresy and banished them to the wastelands when you were three years old. When you were found by our tribe, both had passed. The Mystics raised you as their own. You were taken captive and traded to the Horde. Ba'al, servant of Teeleh, poisoned your mind and erased your memory as part of his customary practice."

"You told Samuel that my name isn't Rachelle."

"Because it isn't and it is. A person's true name is their identity beyond their earthen vessel. The earthen vessel is only a mask they wear, though they believe it to be their identity. As you know who you truly are, you'll see that your name, your true identity, is *Inchristi*. Daughter of Elyon. The label of your earthen vessel is Rachelle. On occasion I will call you by that label, but it's not who you are."

"So my real name is Inchristi? Like Christy? But my earthen vessel is called Rachelle. This isn't clear to me at all. Why not just call me Christy if that's my name?"

"Inchristi," he corrected. "This will become clear as well."

"What if it doesn't? You said many Mystics have been killed. What if I am?"

"Then there will be another 49th." He looked at me and winked. "But I rather like this 49th. She is full of fear, just like the rest of the world. And yet doing so well. To this end, I serve you for a while before I leave you."

"What do you mean leave me? You just found me."

"It will take us five more days to reach the Great Divide. Time enough for you to begin seeing with new eyes."

It was all too much, too quickly, like trying to drink from a fire hose.

"We plunge into rivers of living water, my dear, not a little drinking fountain."

We'd come to the edge of the forest and faced another desert that butted up against the low mountain range I'd seen earlier. Talya's lion, Judah, rested on a low hill, watching us with lazy eyes. I assumed if there was any trouble nearby, he would be the first to warn us.

"I presume Jacob stopped in the city for fresh horses and is already tracking us, so we travel with haste while we can. We train as we ride." Talya faced the desert. "For the next six hours, you will follow close behind me in silence and observe. Your faith is currently in this world, as we both saw back at the lake. Now see with new eyes beyond the laws that limit you. To this end, I give you an ancient promise."

He whistled and Judah rose, trotting east.

"What promise?"

"Patience, 49th." He studied the wasteland before us. "It is said that in this desert, yellow flowers bloom every spring. The Roush harvest them to feed their young. Look now, do you see that harvest?"

I saw only light brown sand and rock with a few tufts of grass and the occasional small shrub. "No."

"The promise I offer you is found in one of the most powerful teachings in all of history. In summary: 'You say four months until the harvest, but I say' " — he lifted a finger, tapped his temple, and swept his hand across the desert vista — " 'Lift your eyes — change your perception — and in that perception you will see a realm beyond time in which the harvest is already ripe, now, not in four months.' He called this realm the kingdom of heaven. Also called eternal life. It's the experience of life not bound by the laws of time and fear, up and down, cause and effect. It is now, not in some future, as many suppose."[9]

He turned bright eyes to me. "Do you know who taught this?"

I shook my head.

"Yeshua — Jesus — who taught obsessively about perception. It was he who also taught that the eye, perception, determines our bodily experience in this life. With clear perception, you see only light, unbound from the polarity of light and darkness. But if your perception isn't clear, you will see darkness. Fear. So remove the plank of judgment that blinds you. Pluck out your eye if you must. It's better to be physically blind and perceive the kingdom beyond polarity than to have two eyes and be in darkness."[10]

Oh be careful little eyes what you see . . .
The song from Sunday school. I swallowed.

"An unfortunate distortion," he said. "Yeshua's teachings on perception are a staggering invitation to see beauty instead of darkness. A shift in cognitive perception. Water walking. Metanoia, remember? Say it for me."

"Metanoia," I said.

"Good. There are two worlds to see in this plane of existence. In any given moment you place your faith in one or the other and are bound to it. Step beyond the polarity of time and space, and see what cannot be seen with earthly eyes. Practice. Six hours, not a word."

He glanced at the trees behind us, patted the rump of his stallion, and took it into the desert.

Leaves rustled, and I watched as Gabil glided down through the canopy. He landed on the back of Talya's horse, hopped around, and faced me.

"That goes for you as well, Gabil," Talya said as the Roush found his grip on the blanket behind the saddle. "Not a word."

Gabil grinned at me like a child who'd been caught with his hand in the cookie jar. "Hello, daughter of Elyon."

"Gabil . . ." Talya warned. Then to me:

"Forgive my new friend. It's been a long time since any Albino has seen him. He's quite excited about it all."

Gabil made a little salute with his wing and contented himself with clinging rather precariously to the mount while keeping his big green eyes fixed on me. I found it hard to tear my stare away from his perpetual smile.

But this wasn't the sight Talya wanted me to focus on. I had learned how to see without using my eyes, right? Having lived blind had its advantages.

What if we were all born blind and didn't know it?

I nudged my mount and followed ten or fifteen paces behind Talya, and I tried to practice what Talya called metanoia.

I tried. For two hours I tried to see another world by changing my perspective through the shift of the mind Talya called metanoia. Problem was, I didn't really know how to "lift my eyes" and see that the harvest was already ripe. What was I supposed to do? Stare at the sand until my vision blurred? Close my eyes? Focus my thoughts on what was behind an object? In an object? The essence of the object?

Polarity was the world of space and time

governed by laws of physics, and quantum physics had proven over and over that there was an accessible reality beyond space and time — the realm of the miraculous, beyond the law that most humans clung to. In the same way, polarity was also the realm of liking and not liking, threat and no threat, anger and judgment. Love, on the other hand, held no record of wrong.

That was fine for God, who created all that was, and for Talya, who was clearly far greater than me. But I was trapped in polarity.

This got me thinking about the Eden in my dreams of ancient Earth, where I was sleeping at this very moment while my father and Miranda were pacing and fretting over what might come next. I had to figure that out as well.

Gabil calmed my nerves somewhat. His adorable stare was terribly distracting. And when he jumped off Talya's stallion and landed on the head of my mare, thoughts of anything but him were virtually impossible.

The horse couldn't feel or see him, naturally. But I could and I did, touching his wing and then his head. Talya made no attempt to discourage him. I began to wonder if he was part of the test. He touched my hand with spindly fingers, then jumped behind me and rode with his wings wrapped around my belly.

It had to be part of Talya's lesson, so I forced myself to focus once more on my surroundings.

For two more hours I tried. Then for two more, before finally concluding that changing the perception of the brain could not be done using the brain itself. Hadn't my father taught me that? What was it Einstein had once said? *A problem cannot be solved on the same level of consciousness that created it,* or something similar.

If metanoia constituted a change in perception, then I needed more than a change in my brain's thinking pattern. I needed a whole new operating system. Clearly, I wasn't understanding his teaching because I was using a mind wired with old programming, and that frustrated me. Maybe that was his intention — to frustrate my old patterns of logic so I would let go of them.

These were my thoughts when Talya finally stopped us to make camp on a high stone ledge that overlooked the vast desert we'd been crossing. The sun was on the western horizon, shifting from a blazing white ball to a fiery orange sphere.

"I'm begging your pardon, but I must be leaving now," Gabil said, jumping back on the horse's head to face me. He gave me a respectful bow. "It has been my greatest pleasure to ride with you, daughter of Elyon."

I resisted the urge to give the furry Roush a hug. "The pleasure was mine. Once I got past the distraction, that is."

"I distracted you?"

"Well, you are far too cute."

"Cuteness! And you are beautiful. But I have to fly back to my side of the woods now or Michal might scold me." He sprang from the mount, spread his wings, swooped low to catch some speed, and soared into the dusky sky.

"What did you see?" Talya asked as I watched Gabil quickly gain altitude, headed west.

I faced him. "I saw that seeing the way you want me to see will require a whole new operating system."

He gave no sign that he didn't understand what an operating system was. For all I knew, he did. The Utah of my dreams existed two thousand years ago, and everything that had happened there would have been recorded in the Books of History.

"So then," he said, "you saw only polarity."

"I guess so."

"And your failure to understand frustrates you?"

"Yes."

"Good."

"Good?"

"An excellent first step, especially for those who depend on their own logic."

Talya dropped to the ground and quickly untied the straps on one of his saddlebags. His comment frustrated me even more. Didn't we all depend on our own logic?

"Why can't you just tell me what I need to know in terms I can understand?"

"Patience, 49th. Can a student write before they know the alphabet? In time you *will* understand."

"You speak in half riddles. Why can't you just tell me how to find the seals?"

"Half riddles?" he said, brow raised. "You mean like the half riddles Yeshua used to hide his meaning from those who didn't have ears to hear?"[11]

Parables. And it was true, they were like riddles, hard to understand.

"When the student is ready, the teaching appears," he said, turning back to his mount. "Seek and you will find. The treasure is hidden for you to seek, not for me to give you. Only in that quest will you finally relinquish all that you think defines you to possess the staggering power of that which does define you, as Yeshua taught."[12]

He withdrew a bundle from the saddlebag. "Now if you'll excuse me for a moment, I would enter ceremony. If you don't mind, find us a few sticks of wood to burn."

I watched as Talya hurried to the edge of the ledge, flapped open a thick wool blanket, swept his robe back, and sat cross-legged. A few shrubs scattered about provided all the wood we would need, and I ambled about, gathering dried-out branches. But my eyes kept shifting to Talya.

He gingerly unwrapped the bundle and withdrew what appeared to be one of several old books, which he laid on the ground before him. His back was to me so I couldn't see the book, but I was sure it was a Book of History.

Pulse spiking, I dropped the wood and started toward him. But I'd taken only two steps before he lifted his hand to stop me. This without looking back at me, as if he had eyes in the back of his head.

I hesitated, then collected the wood I'd spilled, all the while watching him. Judah sauntered back to our camp, took up a position close to me, yawned wide, and watched his master with me.

Talya began to sway gently as he read

aloud from the book spread out before him. I could barely hear his mumbling, only enough to know he wasn't speaking English.

After ten minutes he lifted his arms to the desert now cast in an orange sunset and cried out in a deep voice that seemed to shake the very air I was breathing.

"Inchristi is all; Inchristi is in all." Then again, louder. "Inchristi is all; Inchristi is in all! This . . . is the forgotten way!"

I saw that Judah's ears perked up and his jaw closed. When I looked back at Talya, he was on his feet, swaying and dancing in that long robe of his. Doubling over and throwing his arms up, chanting with delight. The sight mesmerized me. He was like a grown child, oblivious to this world.

Finally, he faced the desert, pressed his hands together as if to pray, and dipped his head to the vista before him as if bowing to an unseen master. Then he gathered up his book, returned it to the bundle with the others, carefully tied them back up in the protective leather wrapping, and strode back to me. He looked like a child who'd just experienced his first exhilarating ride on a roller coaster.

"Gather the sticks into a pile, daughter of Elyon!" he cried. "Tonight we feast by the fire!"

286

Caught up in his joy, I quickly formed a pile, though I had no idea how to make a fire.

"Good enough," he said, spreading his blanket out on one side, then a second on the other side for me. He squatted on his heels, facing the wood.

I folded my legs under me so I was seated across from him. "You spoke of Inchristi," I dared to say. "Inchristi is all. What do you mean?"

Without any spark that I could see, the wood burst into flame. Firelight shone in Talya's eyes.

He winked at me. "They are only ancient words that will be meaningless to you until you know them yourself."

"I don't know the words now?"

He tossed something at me over the fire and I caught it. A hairy red fruit of some kind, the size of a golf ball.

"Do you know the fruit?" he asked.

I turned it in my hands, trying to recall something, but nothing came. "No."

"Then let me tell you about it. It's called a rhambutan. The skin is bitter. The flesh inside is translucent and sweet, wrapped around a large seed only good for planting. If you eat the sweet flesh you won't dream. Which means as long as you eat this fruit, you won't awaken in the Eden of ancient Earth. You could go a whole year, eating the fruit each night, and not once dream. For all practical purposes, that ancient world would cease to exist for you."

Both the Roush and Samuel had mentioned this fruit, the one Thomas of Hunter used to stop dreaming.

"Now . . ." Talya stared over the flames as he squatted. "Do you know this fruit?"

I nodded. "Yes."

"But you are wrong. You don't *know* this fruit. You only know *about* it. To know is to have intimate experience with, as a woman knows a man to produce the fruit of a child. You may know *about* Elyon and commit your life to the infinite Origin of all that is, but that doesn't mean you *know* Elyon. When you *know* Elyon, you will experience that realm called eternal life in this very moment, as Yeshua taught. Then you will produce the fruit of love that holds no record of wrong. This is your path."[13]

I thought about my experience in Eden, finding that First Seal. I had been *knowing* the truth of my Father, experiencing the infinite intimately. Wonder washed through me as I understood at least this much.

"Now, once more, dear daughter. Do you *know* this fruit?"

"No."

"Good. In the same way, you can know *about* the seals, even their meaning, but until you *know* them, until you yourself experience their truth, they will remain powerless. Do you understand?"

"Yes."

"Tonight you will taste this fruit. You will *know* it so that you don't dream. As you will the next night, and the next." He stared into the fire. "You must find the treasure in the field of this life through your own experience. Only then will you pay the price that costs you everything to gain peace and true love in this life."

His eyes met mine.

"And you will need that power, because when you next wake in ancient Earth, you will find yourself in a great darkness."

15

"You think it's possible that she's right?" Miranda asked.

David sat on the couch, tapping his right foot, a nervous tic he'd developed after his wife died. Or was murdered. Which was it? He glanced at the clock on the wall. Just past midnight. Thankfully, it was battery powered — he didn't own a wristwatch. Without power, his iPhone would soon die.

Candlelight from three small flames cast the room in a dim orange light. Rachelle had been asleep for over two hours and didn't appear to be having nightmares. At least that much was good.

"You mean the dreams? We've been over this."

Miranda stood from her chair and crossed to the kitchen. "Yes, but maybe we're thinking too small." She put her hand on the pitcher of water and stopped. "What if Rachelle is somehow connecting with the fabric of reality, not as we know it, but beyond our understanding?"

"You mean spiritual reality?" he said doubtfully.

"I mean all reality. Like an oracle who's going to the beyond and bringing back the keys to truth. We could be sitting on one of the most extraordinary events in all of human history."

"I think that's the job of science, not dreamers."

Miranda turned back. "I don't think you're keeping an open mind, which surprises me. All of these years teaching Rachelle to believe in the impossible, but now you're unable to practice your own dogma."

"Me? No open mind? You seriously expect me to believe a person can travel in their dreams? Because that's essentially what she says is happening."

She poured herself a cup of water. "Before seeing what happened in the sanctuary, I wouldn't have dreamed it was possible either."

"So you actually believe her now? An hour ago you flatly dismissed it."

Miranda leaned back against the counter, cup in hand, staring absently over his head. "I'm not necessarily saying I believe her, but I do believe that she believes herself.

And I do know what I saw."

"An hour ago you were adamant —"

"No, an hour ago, *you* were adamant and I was agreeing." She set the cup down without taking a drink and walked to the breakfast bar. "Have you ever known anyone with a mind as reasonable as Rachelle's?"

He thought about that. She was only sixteen. A child still. One who'd suffered more than anyone else he knew in Eden. The black sheep in this paradise of theirs. Reasonable, yes. But still . . . so young.

"Listen to me, David. I know it's hard to see your own daughter as more than a little girl who's struggling to be typical, but trust me, she's far more than that."

"Maybe, but I'll settle for typical."

"Vlad Smith clearly has her on a pedestal. Why?"

"Vlad Smith is a predator who sees Eden as an opportunity ripe for the picking. Rachelle is only an object of convenience for him." David heard himself saying it, but only part of him believed those words. "This is all about control for him. He's using her to make a point. Write in the freaking book already. It's a test!"

"But he has the same book she dreamed about."

He shook his head. "Her dreams are

fabrications — personifications — of her hopes and fears. Like I said, Smith is testing us by using her."

"If it's a test, I've never seen anyone as brave. She walked right up to him, took the book, and then refused him. But there has to be more to it."

"There is no more. What more?" Why was he reacting so strongly? But he knew . . . If there was any validity to Rachelle's claims of this other world she was living in, everything he knew about reality was upside down. He couldn't accept that. And he was surprised that Miranda was now doing an about-face.

"The point is," she said, walking around the breakfast bar, "her reaction to the book. Something happened to her, you can't deny that. It might as well have been an electric socket she plugged her hand into."

"Psychosomatic," he shot back. "The body does as the brain does because the body is part of the brain. What she believed manifested in her body. What do you think we've been slaving over all these years?"

"I know. Epigenetics. Placebo. But so dramatically?"

"You know the studies. Convince someone with an allergy to poison ivy that the cream in your hand is filled with poison ivy, and their arm breaks into a rash when it's applied, even though that cream is only hand lotion. You call that less dramatic than what happened to her?"

"She was blind!" Miranda sat down, leaning forward. "Blind, David. You know as well as I do that CRISPR didn't repair her sight. Nor did a placebo, not all of her blood cells that quickly."

"I don't know. Rapid spontaneous healing isn't unheard of. So-called miracles happen more frequently than we realize. We're only just beginning to comprehend the power of the brain."

"Granted, and if it was only her healing, I would be inclined to agree."

"It's all related, Miranda. It's all about her dreams, I'll give you that, but it's her belief in those dreams that are affecting her. She's been tormented by them for years. Somewhere along the line they became an expansion of her reality. She no longer knows what's real and what's the dream."

David stood, paced to the window, and peered through the drawn curtains. Not a light to be seen. The room felt muggy without air-conditioning, but he was reluctant to open a window. Not muggy enough for him to sweat — that was just nerves.

He released the curtain and drew the back

of his hand over his forehead. "Either way, her dreams are now the least of our problems. It's only a matter of time before they try to force her hand. We need to buy ourselves some time! If Barth was behind . . ."

David caught himself. Miranda had already pointed out that his preoccupation with his wife's death was distorting his perception, and she was right. Best not go there now.

"Maybe we should just take her now," he said. "Get her up in the woods where at least she'll be safe. Or out of the valley altogether."

"We've been over this. The tunnel is sealed. We run and they come after us with a posse, shoot on sight, remember?"

They were grasping for straws, the same straws they'd already drawn and discarded.

"Then we take her straight to Simon first thing in the morning and settle this business once and for all. He's a reasonable man."

"You mean settle the real business, which is confronting Barth about your wife's death."

"I mean that *all* of this ties back to something Simon and Barth are keeping from us, and it's tied directly to why my wife was murdered and why Rachelle was born blind!"

There, he'd just come out and said it.

"Maybe," Miranda said, leaning back and crossing her arms. She'd clearly forgotten about her cup of water. "But we can't let them force Rachelle's hand. We have no idea what will happen if she writes in that book."

He closed his eyes and drew a deep breath.

"You really think it's all in her mind?" she continued. "That everything we've seen is just her body reacting to new neural connections in her brain? That we can't even consider the possibility she's not writing in the book because it really will have consequences?"

He wanted to say yes — the alternative was far more difficult to explain or accept.

Miranda stood, grabbed his hand, and pulled him off his seat. "Come here."

"Where?"

"Just come with me."

She picked up one of the half-burned tapered candles from the table and led him down the hall to Rachelle's room. Touching a finger to her lips for quiet, she opened the door and walked up to the bed.

Rachelle lay on her side, head on one pillow and right leg thrown over a second. She'd pulled her long hair into a ponytail to keep it from her face while she slept. Cheeks amber in the candlelight, smooth as silk. A life lived mostly indoors had protected her from sun damage.

To think something was actually happening to her at this very moment that would affect life here was incomprehensible, if not absurd.

Miranda reached out and gently lifted her T-shirt sleeve. The white ring on her arm glowed faintly. The perfect circle seemed, by some optical illusion, to have depth. Impossible, but so was the tattoo itself.

"Is this just the result of her beliefs too?" Miranda whispered.

If a poison ivy rash could manifest through belief, why not other discolorations on the skin? But David knew he didn't believe that either. Rachelle had called it a seal. The First Seal.

"She got this from touching the book," Miranda said quietly. "Until you can come up with another explanation, I'm going to believe her."

A loud bang on the door to the kitchen shook the house.

Miranda gasped and spun around, and David instinctively moved to put her behind him. The bang came again.

"Wait here!" he whispered.

He was halfway down the hall before he realized that she'd closed the door to Rachelle's room and was following. But his mind was on the banging, now accompanied by a voice, demanding they open the door.

Barth Caldwell. David had feared this scenario, but the fact that the man had the gall to demand an entrance in the middle of the night also infuriated him.

"David!" Miranda was warning him, but he held up a hand, setting aside caution. They were defenseless here, better face-to-face than in hiding now.

He flipped the dead bolt, turned the handle, and pulled open the door. Light blinded him and he jerked his hand up to shield his eyes. The light shifted and David saw who'd come.

Barth stood on the gravel, holding a military-grade flashlight. But he wasn't alone. Six of his joint forces, as he called them, stood by his side. The Glocks on their hips were holstered, but three of them also carried assault rifles.

Barth glared from the shadows, in his element.

"What do you think this is?" David demanded. "Raid on Entebbe? It's the middle of the night, for heaven's sake!"

"Wrong, David," Barth said. "It's the

middle of a crisis. Or hadn't you realized? The council requires your daughter. Now."

He could sense Miranda behind him, and a part of him wanted to shove her back, slam the door, and take their chances. But the part that knew Barth had something to do with his wife's death resisted any move that could be seen as cowardice.

"So a terrorist strolls into church and holds this town hostage, and you're going to give in to his demands, is that it?" David shot back.

"Wrong again, David. I'm giving in to my own demands, and my demands are that I take control of a situation that undermines the very foundation of this town. Electricity is the lifeblood of this valley. My first order of business is to restore that power at any cost. Then I'll deal with Smith. Basic strategy. Anyone who stands in my way is in direct violation of Eden's laws. I, not Smith, enforce those laws. And I will enforce them vigorously. Now, unless you want a bullet in your head, stand aside."

A male voice yelled from the direction of the town square. Something was off here. But Barth was fixed. Once he had his jaws clamped down, nothing was going to dislodge him. David had seen the man break Claire Davis's jaw two years earlier when she'd been found stashing liquor in her house.

"Take it easy. I'm sure we can work something out, but I want this in front of the full council. You hear me?"

"Oh, I hear you all too well." Barth's right eye twitched. He slowly withdrew his gun and leveled it at David's forehead. "The question is, did you hear me?"

"Easy . . ."

"I don't think you understand our situation here. The country's infrastructure is collapsing. Millions are going to die out there. A few might die in here. Smith is our terrorist and we'll deal with him. But to do that, I need leverage. Your daughter is that leverage. I don't give a tick's whiskers if you live or die tonight because, frankly, the survival of Eden has nothing to do with you. It does, however, depend on me. So I'm going to tell you one more time. We need the girl. Now."

"Stop this!" Miranda brushed past David. "Who do you think you are, storming in here to take a young —"

Barth's gun bucked in his palm. The night air exploded with the sound of its discharge, cutting off Miranda's voice. Her head snapped back and she dropped to the ground in a heap.

300

It happened so quickly, so unreasonably, that David wasn't sure it had happened. Barth had shot Miranda? His mind refused to accept what he'd just seen.

"Extreme times, David," Barth said, gun trained on him again. "Extreme measures. You can either move or join her."

"Barth!" Someone was running toward them. "Barth!"

David stepped back, eyes on Miranda's body. Blood was soaking into the gravel from the gaping wound on her head. Simon had come, he knew that. Barth had acted alone, he knew that as well.

But he still couldn't get his mind working to process what any of it meant. When he lifted his head he saw Simon staring down at the crumpled body.

Simon's face flushed. "Have you gone mad? You have no right! You can't just go around killing innocent people!"

Barth returned his stare, undisturbed. "I have the right to do as the council orders."

"This," Simon snapped, stabbing his finger at Miranda's dead body, "was *not* what we discussed."

"Actually it was, you just weren't a part of that discussion. You gave up that right when you let Smith take the stand without opposition. Seeing as how you don't have the balls to stand up to Smith, Max and I agreed that task falls to me. I'll do whatever's necessary to end this threat. It's not the first dead body on our watch."

Simon backhanded Barth full in the face. "How dare you!" The Judge was taller by four inches, but Barth was a bull with twice his muscle. Despite the loud crack, his head didn't budge.

"You have no idea what's really happening here!" the Judge roared. "No idea! This is exactly what he wants. Don't you see that?"

Barth stood still, as if for the first time considering he might have misjudged the situation. But David was no longer misjudging. The full horror of what had just happened crashed over him, and he felt his legs go weak.

"You're playing right into his hands." Simon stabbed at Barth's chest. "I will deal with Smith! Me, not you! Now get rid of her body. No one can know about this."

"And if someone heard the shot?"

"Tell them you killed a coyote." To David: "I'm sorry about this, David, I really am. I'm closing the hospital as of now and ordering martial law. No one leaves their house without authorization. And I mean no one. We have to get this under control."

"What about the girl?" David heard Barth ask.

"The girl stays where she is until I speak to Smith. Now clean this up!"

16

Vlad Smith. This is what they called him because this was the label he'd chosen as of late. His true name could not be put into words, but they all knew it. Intimately. And he would see to it that they soon knew it as their own.

Vlad stood on the roof of their church as a graying dawn edged into the far horizon like the coming of an ominous tide. Overhead, their sky was clogged with dark clouds. A light breeze tickled his skin, a sensation he relished. From this vantage point, he could see all of Eden, and beyond it, the trees and fields that butted up against the great cliffs that encircled the massive sinkhole. And beyond the cliffs, the rest of the world, blinded by crisis — he could see that as well, though not with his eyes.

Not a single volt of juice flowed through Eden, not a glimpse of light, not a hint of power. Darkness and darkness alone. If the tissue-tops now soundly asleep only knew what was happening here in their little paradise . . . A rush of satisfaction flowed down Vlad's body, and he allowed himself to tremble with that sentiment. Human juice. Such a wonderful thing.

Organism was only an algorithm — this much could not be disputed. He'd watched with curiosity as Barth, the pit bull among them, had yielded to his programming. Rachelle was a threat the man could deal with, so he would, if only to protect his security. Common sense. He'd gone after the girl earlier than Vlad expected. Then killed the other tissue-top, something else Vlad hadn't seen coming so soon.

He may have underestimated Barth. Caution might be warranted — he couldn't allow the man to kill Rachelle.

Following Miranda's early expiration, David had reacted as might be expected of any tissue-top. He'd rushed to wake Rachelle but then decided to leave her in peace, though he could find none for himself. He'd spent most of the night on his face in the living room, weeping into the carpet before settling into his armchair, blinding himself with bitterness.

Blind. Blind as worms, all of them, just

like the rest of the world. Most of them anyway.

Truly, the only one who was even beginning to see in Eden was the girl, and this concerned him more than he'd anticipated. What happened to the others wasn't his concern — it was Rachelle he needed. Only Rachelle.

How many years had he waited for the coming of the 49th after being dispatched to this world with the book? Too many to count. The plan had been simple: prevent the 49th from finding all five seals before the appointed time by undermining her in this reality, not only in the other, thus ensuring her failure. To that end, this world had no clue what it was in for, not only here in Eden but far beyond.

He'd known that she was the 49th the moment she'd been born in the other reality — the shift in his consciousness could not be denied, though he had to wait five more years for her to be born here.

Blind. The irony was brilliant. This was his doing, naturally, first by tormenting her mother. Even more ironic was the fact that Rachelle had been born here, in a bubble called Eden, of all places.

Some said there was no irony or coincidence. That the light only used the darkness to reveal its brilliance. The thought brought a shudder to his bones.

He would prove them wrong.

Curious, he'd tested her to see if she might write him into the book before understanding her power. As expected, this simple tack had failed. As had his second approach in the sanctuary. Now that she'd discovered the First Seal and tasted the power of Origin, one might think he'd suffered a blow. Not so. She would eventually use her power to save what she valued. There was still time. More than enough.

As long as he found his way into the book before Rachelle found the first three seals, his purpose would remain intact.

Vlad blew out a long breath, smoothed his greasy hair back with both hands, and pressed them lightly together, as if in prayer to the great cliffs before him.

All organism was algorithm. It was time to change up the programming a bit.

He spun around, strode for the access ladder, and quickly descended. The streets were dead at this early hour, and they would remain empty — the Judge's martial law would see to that.

He headed down the dotted lines on Third Street, dead center. He'd left his white jacket in the hospital's basement room, where he'd taken up residence. Other than his skin, he was now all black. Reconsidering the decision, he wondered if it might have been more interesting to wear the white jacket and sing at the top of his lungs for all to hear. Let them see their god in all his glory.

It took Vlad less than three minutes to reach the Moses residence. Simon would be holed up in his safe room, hoping against hope that his battery-powered ham radio would allow him to make contact with the outside world. It would not.

Either way, the Judge was a concern only in that he was in the way. The situation required a few tweaks.

The front door was locked. Vlad gripped it with a firm hand, twisted hard, and heard the tumblers in the locking mechanism snap. He stepped in and closed the door behind him.

Silence smothered the house. He made no attempt to walk with caution — the time for subtleties had passed. Truth be told, he enjoyed the sound of his shoes walking on the wooden floors.

He entered the hall and tried the first door. A boy's room. Peter, sound asleep under his blanket, oblivious to the fact that he likely had less than a few days of life left on this earth. So sad.

The next door opened to the young daughter's bedroom. She might survive, he hadn't decided yet. All of the children might survive, lucky little brats. Or maybe not.

Knowing now that the last door had to be the master bedroom, Vlad entered, closed the door behind him, and walked up to the king-size bed without so much as glancing to see if Hillary was still asleep.

She lay under the covers, snoring softly. He'd chosen her for two reasons, the first being that she was Simon's wife. The second being that he required a particularly malleable brain for his purpose. All tissue-tops — excepting the Mystics, who knew their true identity — were compliant, of course, but some, like Hillary, were more easily reprogrammed than others.

Vlad leaned over the bed and slapped the top of her head with enough force to startle the dead. The woman grunted and jerked up, eyes wide.

"Hello, Hillary. So nice to see you this fine morning. I see that your husband has abandoned you again."

She gaped at him, clinging to her covers, and she was about to scream, so he clamped his hand over her mouth and shoved her back down into the pillow.

"Hush, hush." He touched his forefinger to his lips and held her firm as she struggled. "Shh, shh . . . It's Vlad. Vlad Smith. You remember me, right? I'm the new god in town. God will only hurt you if you don't listen to him and accept his gifts. So I need you to shut up and listen."

Eyes like saucers, she quieted. The fear-of-god talk was over the top, but with her kind, it sometimes actually worked.

"I'll let go of your mouth if you promise me you'll listen quietly. Nod if you agree."

She faltered for only a moment, then complied.

"Good." He lifted his hand from her mouth and nodded his appreciation when she remained silent. "Are you listening?"

Her head bobbed once more.

"Even better. Now . . ." He sat down on the bed next to her. "I'm tempted to seduce you, Hillary. I really am. Just for the fun of it." He cocked his head and looked at her. "Do you think I'd succeed?"

She was still in too much shock to respond with more than a tiny squeaking sound, so he helped her out.

"Of course I would. Few women manage to resist my gentle charm and surprising understanding of their deepest longing to be heard and loved." He let his words sink in. "I'm not sure you even know what it's like to be truly loved. Not the way Simon loves you, with all his conditions. Be this, do that, don't do that or else . . . That's not love, sweetheart. That's called conditional manipulation. Nearly all marriages are based on it. Is yours?"

She blinked.

"Never mind. Actually, I don't know how to love unconditionally either. I'm bound by polarity, just like you. So I'm going to cut to the chase. Fair enough?"

She was still staring. He slapped her on the cheek, just hard enough to get her attention.

"Say yes."

"Y-y-yes."

"You see how easily the fear of punishment manipulates?"

Hillary still wasn't getting the hang of things, so he slapped her again.

"Answer me when I ask a question."

"Yes," she said.

Vlad felt a stab of pity for the poor thing. She'd been lied to her whole life. The thing about humans that few of them realized — they were powerful beyond imagination. Law just blinded them to it.

The thought of that power bothered him and he made a quick decision, no longer

311

desiring to play his game with her. Not here. Not this way.

"Close your eyes, sweetheart. Do as I say."

She looked unsure.

"Go on. Just close your eyes."

Her eyes fluttered shut.

Vlad slugged her right temple with enough force to knock her out cold. She slumped back, at peace. His small gift to her.

He grabbed her nightshirt and dragged her body from the bed, across the floor, and to the door. There, he scooped her up with one arm, hiked her over his shoulder, and walked from the house the way he'd come in.

"I'll have you back in a couple hours," he muttered. "Just before curfew."

Plenty of time to flip some switches.

17

While Shadow Man's darkness was blinding minds in Utah, I was crossing deserts and mountains with Talya, my teacher in another world. Earth, two thousand years in the future.

For five more days we traveled, and each night I knew the rhambutan fruit, which silenced my mind so I wouldn't dream. On each of those days, Talya asked only one thing of me: "Watch. Look. Lift up your eyes. Change your cognitive perception, or, as it was written in ancient Greek, practice metanoia. Reclaim your innocence. Become like an infant, a little child who hasn't yet learned not to believe the impossible, because, in truth, nothing is impossible."[1]

I tried. And when I tried too hard, Talya told me to try by not trying. That didn't help me either. So I must confess, for those first five days I mostly learned that I could not see whatever he was seeing.

This didn't seem to disturb Talya in the least. He would offer me a slight grin and wink. "When the student is ready, the teaching will appear. You aren't ready yet, dear daughter. You have more lies to unlearn."

Each day, he would find a suitable spot to practice ceremony, which was only a formal form of metanoia, he said. Each day he would casually bend the world in some small way that left me awestruck, whether it be lighting a fire without a spark, or calling a bird to sit on his shoulder, or finding water where there was no spring. All so I would know it was possible.

I learned about many things those first five days.

Was he a magician? Elyon forbid, he said. Magic was done in polarity by attributing special power to special words. Religions used words this way. It worked on occasion, but even when it did, it was belief in the power behind the words, not the words themselves, that carried weight.

"Take the name of God," Talya said. "There are many ways to say *God* in different languages. Which word has power? Many tribal Christians in ancient Earth call God *Allah Nogoba,* meaning 'God our Father.' Do the words *Allah Nogoba* have less power than *Elyon our Father* or *God our*

Father or *Origin* or *Source?* None have power in themselves. These are just labels that represent God. Only identification with the essence beyond the label can shift polarity. Attachment to specific words is an attachment to magic. We don't use magic."

I learned why some sacred teachings seemed to be lies but were not. For example, *Whatever you ask in my name will be done,* Yeshua taught.[2] There was no exception to this, Talya said. Ever. *In his name* meant "in his identity," but few ever asked in that identity because they didn't know themselves in that identity. They didn't recognize themselves in that identity. They didn't ask *in* his identity. Instead, they asked in their earthen vessel identity, using the word *Yeshua* or *Jesus* or *Justin* like a magical incantation with little to no effect.

Faith in that identity rather than the earthen vessel self, he said, was the actual evidence of the unseen — the very substance of it. But few had true faith in the unseen. Their faith was in the seen, the world of polarity, which thus mastered them.

"How can I awaken to my identity Inchristi?" I asked.

He winked at me. "You will see."

I learned that the Horde were still giving chase, less than a day behind us now. Jacob, son of Qurong, wasn't one to be denied.

I learned that my body had retained the muscle memory of the ancient Roush arts in a way that surprised even Talya. The movements, taught by certain elite Roush who were highly skilled in aerial combat with Shataiki, were like a dance to him. They came back to me quickly as he demonstrated around the fire each night. If I couldn't change my perception, at least I could spar with him. I had impeccable reflexes. But of course, Talya said. I had thousands of hours of practice growing up in the desert with the Mystics.

I learned that Judah, his lion, liked me. Enough to let me pet him and use his belly as a pillow. I quickly fell in love with Judah.

I learned that the Albinos who lived beyond the Great Divide were vast, over a million strong, compared to the Albinos led by Thomas of Hunter, who numbered only a few thousand. Albinos who'd followed Justin by drowning in the red lakes comprised four basic religious sects: the Elyonites, the Gnostics, the Mystics, and the Circle under Thomas.

The Elyonites were by far the largest sect. They had developed many doctrines of what was right and what was wrong based on ancient writings once canonized as Holy

Scriptures. But they missed the point of these writings, Talya said. They clung to the world of flesh and bone and thus were bound to the world of polarity as much as the Horde. They, like the Horde, used the sword if they believed it suited Elyon's purpose as interpreted by them. They believed Elyon would one day rid the world of all Horde and all heretics who refused to embrace their holy doctrines.

The Gnostics were a splinter group who argued that all flesh was either evil or of no consequence. They claimed Justin could not have existed in the flesh because flesh was evil. In cursing the material world, they made the material world their enemy and thus were enslaved to struggle.

The Circle under Thomas of Hunter were deeply loving Albinos who longed to be Mystics without yet knowing it.

Then there were the Mystics. Forty-nine including me. Seen as the worst kind of heretic by Elyonites and Horde alike. I would soon know what a Mystic was, Talya said. And by know, he meant *know,* as in experience. I wasn't sure I wanted to experience being a heretic among people who lived by the sword.

I learned that it was Paulus, Paul the apostle, who'd coined the term *Inchristi.*

He'd used the term more than any other designation in his speaking and writing. Without it, nothing made sense, Talya said.

It was also Paulus who insisted that experiencing Inchristi was done by fixing our spiritual sight on what was unseen — that is, the eternal self — not on what was seen — that is, the identity of our earthen vessels.

"If you lose your eyes, are you less than a person with good working eyes?" Talya asked me once.

"Of course not."

"And what if you lose the function of part of your brain?"

I shook my head, thinking of those born with disabilities. "No."

"How about all of your brain?"

I thought about it but didn't respond. Who would I be without all of my brain?

"Before you were in the womb, Elyon knew you. When you know yourself as Elyon knew you before you were born, then you will know your truest self. This is the unseen — not your earthen vessel, which is seen."[3]

This was the task I was trying and failing to do.

So, as I said, I did learn *about* many things, but I still couldn't see the way he saw. In fact, if I knew any lesson in those five long days of travel toward the Great Divide, it was how little I could see. I felt rather helpless, even knowing that this was Talya's intention.

With each passing day my frustration at not being able to see the unseen grew. It spread like a dark fog, which in turn drew me even deeper into frustration to the point where trying to "fix my eyes on the unseen" began to feel like a cruel joke.

I finally caved in on the sixth night. We were in the heavily wooded slopes that led up the final mountain range before the Great Divide pass, which we would reach early the next morning. The Horde were gaining, Talya said. We had to hurry.

"What will happen when we reach the pass?" I asked. "You keep talking about the Great Divide, and I'm beginning to wonder if it's some kind of metaphorical divide in my mind. Where are we going beyond it?"

"Not we, daughter. You."

"Without you?" The thought terrified me.

"You will see."

He'd given the same answer to a hundred different questions, but when he said it then, my resolve to be a good, diligent student failed me completely.

"No," I said, half under my breath. "I don't think I *am* going to see."

319

He was leading me by five paces, following Judah. They both stopped at the sound of my words. Judah turned his big head and looked back at me. Talya did not. His mount snorted once, then continued up the pathless route where Judah led us.

His ignoring me only sent more blood up my neck.

"It's been six *days* and I'm not seeing anything."

He continued on as if I hadn't spoken, much less snapped at him.

My mare ambled forward, following his. "Have you ever stopped to consider my predicament for a second? Let me see if I have this right. My parents were killed when I was three years old and I was raised by heretics, none of whom I know, who live in the high desert somewhere."

With every word, the injustice of my predicament deepened.

"I don't even know who I am, because I was kidnapped and poisoned by the Horde. I'm totally lost here and you just want me to see what can't be seen? How?"

"Inchristi is all; Inchristi is in all."

"Inchristi is all? You might as well say the moon is the sun. It sounds like some New Age nonsense Simon warned us about."

"That ancient philosophy you call New

Age was just another label, and it, like all religion, was mostly bound in attachment to earthen vessels. Heavens no. We don't deal in magic but fix our eyes on the unseen, beyond labels and the judgments of earthen vessels."

I let the rush of emotion take me away. "Have you stopped to listen to yourself? How can you fix your *eyes* on anything that by definition can't be seen?"

"It is the only way to know truth, blind one."

"Do you know what I *do* know to be true? At this very moment I'm asleep in a bed in Eden, Utah. The world's falling apart around me there. Vlad Smith wants to kill me!"

"No, he wants to bind this world to lasting darkness by getting you to betray who you really are," he corrected. He was goading me, I knew that, but I was so fixated on presenting evidence for the injustices in my life that I plowed forward.

"Did I ask for any of this? Did I ask to be born blind? Did I ask for my mother to die during childbirth? Did I ask to be a Mystic? Did I ask to be chosen?"

"Feeling a little lost, are we?" he asked, totally unconcerned.

"Stop it!" I pulled my mount to a halt.

"Just stop all of this!"

"If we stop now, we only give Jacob an advantage. You have a mission. For that mission you will need to find all five seals before the appointed time, the most important being the fifth." He continued up the path, slouched in his saddle as if on a lazy Sunday afternoon ride through the woods. "Your mission is far too critical."

He said more, but I lost his words to my thoughts. I felt like I was in a nightmare again. He still hadn't told me when the appointed time was. In the darkness that swallowed me, I was only the young blind girl being crushed by Shadow Man's threats. And now Talya would be leaving me?

"Please . . ." My anger fell away, replaced by desperation. Tears blurred my vision. "Talya, please . . ."

He stopped his mount, then slowly turned his horse back and studied me. "Now you're getting somewhere," he said.

I wanted to tell him that he was wrong, but a boulder was lodged in my throat.

"Getting lost is part of the journey. When you have lost something, such as your identity, it is still yours, only misplaced and forgotten. Such is the state of all. The question now is, how long do you want to stay lost, my dear little prodigal?"

Getting lost is part of the journey. Justin had said that my life of pervasive fear was part of my journey.

I cleared my throat. "I don't want to be lost."

"What would you give to find the forgotten way?"

"Everything."

Thunder rumbled in the distance.

Talya dipped his head. Then scanned the forest around us. "Tell me what you see here."

I looked around, hoping to see more than trees, but I was blind to all but the darkening of the sky, now billowing with ominous clouds.

"Do you see the valley to our right?" he asked.

A snicker sounded from the trees there and I twisted in my saddle. I could hardly mistake the sound of Shataiki.

"No. Did you hear that?"

"Do you see the cliff directly ahead of us?" he asked.

We were headed for a cliff? "No." The sky above the canopy flashed with light.

"Remember this: in every moment, you manifest what you believe. You place your faith in one system or the other, not both. Will you be blind and see darkness, or will you see and know light?"

"Blind?" Fear gripped me. "Why do you say that? Of course I don't want to be blind."

Talya turned his mount away from me. "We shall see." He clicked and the stallion took off in a fast trot, then a gallop, weaving between trees as Talya's cloak flowed behind. "Hurry, daughter. Ignore them! The time is closing in. Follow me!"

The air filled with the clicking and hissing of a dozen Shataiki. Red eyes blinked to life in the treetops on either side. Wind gusted through the canopy.

"Talya!"

"Ride! Ride like you've never ridden before. Straight ahead! Whatever you do, don't stop when you see the cliff. Over it, daughter. Over it!"

He was pulling away from me, hard on the heels of Judah. Then they vanished into the trees, out of sight.

All I could see were Shataiki, hundreds now, streaking for me with claws extended and fangs gaping, and I was sure they were coming for my eyes.

I dug my heels into my mare's flank and took off, straight ahead. "Talya!" Gale-force winds roared. No rain.

The first Shataiki to reach me nipped my

head and I screamed, desperate to keep them from my eyes, swatting wildly as my horse tore through the trees. But then they were on me like a swarm of flies.

"Talya!"

I could just hear the cry of his voice far ahead, but I couldn't make out his words above the winds.

I rode faster, head down. Then faster, slapping the mare's rump as she dodged trees at breakneck speed. Another Shataiki made contact with me, this one with its wing, nearly knocking me from my mount. I hugged her neck and held on.

A break in the trees revealed a long valley to my right. Dark clouds boiled overhead, but it was the movement below that shut down my breathing. The trees were moving with thousands of the black beasts, surging to join those now diving at me.

A talon grazed my cheek, and I screamed again. I was a girl accustomed to nightmares, but the thought of losing the sight I had just gained filled me with fresh terror. I threw my left arm over my eyes.

Still the Shataiki screeched, deafening me to all but those cries cutting deeply into my nerves.

Still the storm roared about me, winds and black sky without rain.

Still I raced on, screaming with them, wildly swinging one arm as I clung to the mare's neck with the other.

The large black bats nipped at me, pulled at my tunic, smacked into my arm, threatened to gouge out my eyes.

I suddenly broke from the trees and saw past my arm. I could see the mountain peak in the distance, a few hours' ride. The Great Divide. I lowered my gaze. Talya had pulled up on a flat outcropping a hundred yards ahead, hair and robe streaming in the wind. Relief flooded me.

Then I saw the wide gap between us, fifty paces ahead. The cliff!

Panic abruptly dismissed my relief. I had two choices. The first and only reasonable course was to pull up while I still had time and take my chances with the Shataiki. The second was to do as Talya had said. But I didn't see how my horse could cross such a wide gap!

I went anyway, beyond reason now, desperate to be free from the threat of blindness.

My fear fell from me like shattered shackles ten paces from the cliff, at the point of no return when I accepted certain death. I simply closed my eyes and let my mount leap. Then soar. Twenty feet, five seconds, but to me it felt like an eternity. And in that eternity, I was a bird who had no fear of falling to the ground.

The mare landed on the far side, clambered up the incline, and came to a jarring halt on the ledge next to Talya's stallion. I could hear the hissing and clicking of the Shataiki above the wind and rain. They'd stayed in the trees.

Talya was already on the ground, snatching his bundle of books from the saddlebag.

"Hurry!" he urged, striding toward the ledge that overlooked the valley.

Buzzing with exhilaration, I dropped to the ground and ran after him. In that moment, I felt that if I jumped off the ledge on which he stood, I would discover I had wings and could fly.

Breathing hard, I gazed over the vista of rolling wooded lands that gave way to desert. Beyond the desert I could see the lower mountain range we had crossed two days earlier — all of it capped by a black lid of a sky. Millions of Shataiki teemed over the canopy — a living carpet of death. I stared, dumbfounded.

The shadow of death.

Talya faced me, wind tugging at his flapping robe. "Are you ready?"

"For what?"

"To understand why, though Albino, you are powerless in this life like so many. Why seeing, they do not see, as Justin said."

I stared, wide-eyed. "Yes."

"Blind, you see in fear, yes?"

"Yes."

"But as you rise up the mountain, your view of all that is below can change. So it is with the world of the spirit. At the lower consciousness of polarity, you feel fear. But at the higher consciousness of love, what once caused you fear falls away. There *is* no fear in love. Only as you experience that love can you know it rather than know about it. Do you see it?"

I stared at the valley. "I see them . . . the darkness."

"And it masters you! There are two systems at work in this plane of existence: the system of fear and control, and the system of love and freedom. These two realities cohabitate at all times, though most experience only one. There is the realm of polarity — the law — in which all living things must forcefully protect against what they fear, trading and fighting, back and forth, up and down, winning and losing. And the realm of love. A grace that is beyond polarity, in which there is no battle, no fear, only love. No darkness, only light — because it is finished! The lamb has overcome."[4]

He looked out over the vista.

"Can you see the light?"

Did I? I almost thought I could. I certainly understood the teaching.

"Two systems," he rushed on, lifting his fingers to the air. "As it is written. One kingdom is a dimension seen with earthly eyes, the other realm is unseen by earthly eyes. In the first you struggle with fear. In the other you're already complete, risen Inchristi and beyond harm. In the first you live in a temporary earthen vessel, desperate to avoid the shadow of death. In the other you are an eternal being, beyond death. You can align yourself with only one of these masters in any given moment."[5]

"Earthen vessel," I breathed.

He gestured to my body. "Earthen vessel. Jar of clay. Costume. The mask you believe yourself to be. Show me your hand."

I held it out.

"Is this beautiful flesh you? Are you these fingernails so that when you cut them you fall to the ground? Are you your hair, your cells, dying by the millions every moment? Are you your clothes, your sweat, your fingers?"

"No."

"Are you your memories, snatched from

you so easily by poison or a blow to the head? Never! Are you your emotions and thoughts? Never. These are all part of your earthen vessel, a beautiful gift that is here today and gone tomorrow. Protecting yourself from death is only a temporary and utterly futile war you wage in polarity until your earthen vessel finally dies and you discover death always was only a shadow. There is no death. There is no darkness in light. It is finished. Inchristi is all; Inchristi is in all!"[6]

I didn't really understand it all, but my heart and mind soared with his words.

"And the Roush?" I asked, mesmerized.

"The Roush and the Shataiki are all a part of polarity, bound in the knowledge of good and evil, like all Albino, all Horde, all humans, all the world bound by time and space."

Talya clapped his hands and snatched his fingers into two fists held out before him.

"Two systems. Two selves, one that is temporal and bound in polarity, and one that is eternal and Inchristi, only temporarily experiencing life in this earthen vessel, a blink in the scope of eternity. One in blood, one in light, just as Justin showed you when he gave you the stone. Do you understand?"

My breathing was thick. I felt like I was

leaping into a whole new world, yet unseen by me.

"I think so."

"Do you, with Yeshua, want to sleep in peace as the troubles rise like a storm to crush you? Do you want to see beyond this storm that causes fear? Really see?"[7]

"Yes." My voice was unsteady.

"Will you see what is unseen, daughter? Past the illusion of fear. Will you fix your attention on what is unseen, not on what is seen by the eyes in your head?"

He sank to one knee and withdrew one of the books from his bundle. I knelt beside him and stared at it for the first time. On its ancient leather cover were etched these words:

The Writings of Johnin and Paulus
A Book of History

"Put your hand on the cover," he whispered. "Let the scales fall from your eyes."

A hot breeze swept in from the distant desert and blew my hair off my shoulders. I lowered my hand and gently placed it on the cover.

The moment my fingers made contact with the leather, my mind was blown open and I saw. I saw because I was suddenly above my body, staring down at myself kneeling there on the outcropping next to Talya.

I was staring at me. I was the "I" who was staring down at "me," which was just my temporary earthen vessel. Like a costume I lived in for a short time.

The atoms and cells that made up the bodies below me were held in place by swirling energies, like clay or dust gathered by a force field.

A hot wind hit me full in the face, carrying on it the distant sound of children giggling. Other sounds filled my ears. Birdsong, and falling water, like a distant downpour. Faint music. High-pitched strings.

The tones grew, as if angels were singing in long unbroken notes that vibrated through my body. My bones resonated in perfect alignment, like a tuning fork that vibrated in perfect pitch.

A nearly irresistible urge to join in that song pulled at me like an ancient memory.

I lifted my eyes and saw the valley below us. A moment ago it had been filled with terrible winds and darkness and Shataiki.

Now it brimmed with forests and green meadows sprinkled with brilliant patches of red and yellow and blue flowers. A village lay nestled in a shallow valley at the center, maybe thirty homes in all. A tall Thrall hugged the far side of the village.

All of this I saw in a single glance. But it was the color of the houses and the trees that held my focus. They were colored — many brown trunks, yes, but also blue and red and gold. It was a colored forest, enchanted with wonder and beauty the likes of which I had never seen. At least not that I could remember.

My eyes were drawn to a large waterfall on a far cliff, cascading down the sheer rock face like oil that shone in colored hues as the light reflected off its surface. At the bottom of that waterfall was a lake with a sandy white shore. This was the world Samuel had told me about, the one before evil had come.

And then I knew — I had been in those waters. I had come from this valley. This was my home!

"The scales fall from your eyes and now you see," I heard Talya cry out.[8] "The valley of the shadow of death and the valley of Justin's kingdom are both here, thus the same valley. Within. Your perception is the lamp that reveals to you one or the other. In any given moment, you will see love and innocence, or you will see fear and grievance, not both. There is no fear in love;

there is no darkness in light."

I was seeing. And in that seeing, the power of love flooded my body, a love in which there was no fear or darkness. From Elyon's perspective, there was no problem. There never had been one. *Origin is Infinite.* Problems were experienced only in polarity, where the me below was making them. Identifying with them. Clinging to them. Empowering them through my faith in them. I had made them my god.

Hello, dear daughter.

The voice spoke tenderly to the Rachelle on the ground, and I couldn't tell if it was male or female, only that it filled Rachelle with wonder and deep longing. What if it was my mother?

Do you want to know who you are? The voice washed through Rachelle, and I saw that she was sobbing.

"Yes," the me who still had her hand on the book said.

It spoke again, and Rachelle trembled with each word. *I will show you that I am in you, and you are in me. Joined as one, dear one.*

Inchristi is all; Inchristi is in all. Joined as one in spirit, not in flesh.[9]

But I already knew this, I realized. I, meaning the me who was looking down at Rachelle. Only Rachelle didn't know. She'd been born blind to that realization.

The voice was tender like a mother's, comforting Rachelle so that she could know her unseen self. The unseen me who was joined with her Creator.

I looked to my right, half expecting to see my mother looking down at Rachelle, but I only saw the shimmering air. And I doubted the voice actually belonged to a mother.

What is known that cannot be named?

I blinked. It came again, fading.

What is known that cannot be named, daughter?

The world I saw vanished and I gasped. I was back in my body, kneeling over the Book of History. Talya had pulled my hand free.

I frantically looked around, searching for any sign of the dimension I'd just glimpsed. The valley I saw instead was once more dark, dim, a shadow of its true state. The storm was gone, as were the Shataiki.

"You saw," Talya said.

I lifted my hand and stared at it. Five fingers. But this wasn't really me, was it? This was my temporal earthen vessel. A jar of clay. I nodded slowly, wondering why I could no longer see it as plainly as I had only a moment ago.

Now we see through a glass dimly. Polarity

did that.

"Yes," I managed.

"And you heard?"

I looked up at Talya as fresh, silent tears slipped down my cheeks. "I thought it was my mother at first."

"Neither male nor female. You say you heard it as a woman?"

"I couldn't tell, just a voice."

"Your helper and comforter." He stared deep into my eyes. "In your Old Testament, the Holy Spirit is always feminine. In many languages, like Greek, there is no feminine word for Spirit, so most humans translate the Holy Spirit as an *it* or *he*. Labels. In truth, the Infinite has no gender, nor is there any separation between the aspects of Elyon. We identify with three aspects — Father, Spirit, and Son — but they are one, so that if you see one, you see them all."

"No male or female . . ."

"These are metaphors. There is no male or female Inchristi. Elyon is One. Revealing your union with Elyon is the Spirit's primary purpose now, as Yeshua first taught."[10]

"Can I call the voice my mother?"

"He's infinite. You'll hear in terms that are personal to you and draw you into intimate awareness of who you are as the light. It isn't the place of any human to

336

condemn your union with Elyon." He paused. "The important thing to remember is this: the self-righteousness of the earthen vessel is like filthy rags, used up and worthless, like the law. But that is not who you are in union with Elyon. You are the light, yes?"

"Yes." I was swimming in wonder.

"To deny your identity as the light, one with Elyon, is to blaspheme the Spirit, who reveals your union with the divine light. In that state of denial you will find yourself unforgiven, not by Elyon but by yourself. Thus they call it the unforgivable sin. Unforgiven by you. Elyon will not override your free will. You will see yourself either as light or in darkness. In truth, you *are* the light, as Yeshua taught. When you feel lost, know that it is always because you are covering up your identity as the light with your denial of it. Like hiding your light under a basket."[11]

"A basket . . . my earthen vessel."

He dipped his head. "Life in polarity occurs in cycles of remembering and forgetting, often many times in a day. Re-member who you are. It's the only way to find the peace of God in this life."

I looked back at the valley, now smothered in shadows as the sun set. No Shataiki, just trees and cliffs. "I saw a colored forest. A village and a lake."

His eyes were bright and he smiled. "You saw your home, not so far from here beyond the Great Divide. The Realm of Mystics. You will see them soon."

"The Realm of Mystics," I said, liking the sound. My home.

"And now I can tell you, it's this very realm that both Horde and Albino will attempt to destroy in the coming war. If you don't find the Five Seals of Truth before that appointed time, all will be lost. You must find all five before the Realm of Mystics is crushed."

I couldn't understand why anyone would want to destroy the Mystics, nor how I could find all five seals in time, but in that moment of wonder, none of it concerned me, even though I knew it should. Maybe that's why he'd waited to tell me.

"Do you understand?" he asked, searching my eyes.

"Yes."

Talya slipped the book back into the leather cloth and we stood, he as a man on a mission, I unsteady, lost in thoughts of that valley I'd seen.

"I . . . I have the second riddle," I said.

"Riddle? You mean the finger."

"Finger? No, a riddle. A clue."

"We call it a finger. It points the way, like a finger that points to the sun. It isn't the sun, it only points to it. Like Scriptures. They aren't the Word; the Word is Justin. The Scriptures only point to the Word. Remember, set your eyes on what is unseen, not on the finger itself. If you focus all of your attention on the finger, it will block your sight of that to which it points. In this way the letter — that is, Scripture — kills, but the Spirit gives life, as written."[12]

I was sure I had read that once, the last part anyway. "Then I have the second finger."

"Good. The Second Seal will come to you when you're ready, not before."

"I *am* ready."

"Are you?" He glanced over his shoulder. "Jacob is close behind. As is the other one."

"Which other?"

"Samuel. As I suspected, he could not resist hunting the enemy who hunts his newfound Mystic."

The revelation surprised me. Samuel was coming after me? On the one hand, I loved him for it. On the other, I couldn't imagine what was in store for him.

"We go to the high pass before we sleep," Talya was saying. "You will not eat the rhambutan fruit tonight. You must dream and do what you must do. And when you wake in this world tomorrow, you will face a deeper darkness."

Our eyes met.

"You will face it without me," he said. "It is time for me to find Thomas of Hunter."

18

I woke slowly, with visions of light and color swimming through my mind. I had seen, and my skin still tingled from it all. Was it possible?

I opened my eyes and the white ceiling came into focus. I was back in Eden. A knot formed in my throat and my eyes misted with tears. Was it the same here as there?

Having been blind most of my life, I knew the workings of the human eye and the optical processing center of the brain better than most. Right now my eyes were receiving data and transmitting it to the back of my brain, where sight actually occurred based on neural programming. Change the program and you change what is seen. Red could become blue, and round could become square. Science had proven this much.

The primary challenge to changing the way we see is that a full third of the brain is dedicated to sight, the most complex of the senses. Thus, the mind is heavily invested in the perception of what it has learned to see. I would have to let go of my attachment to one system of sight to see with another.

Just like the perception of realities. Being so heavily invested in one interpretation of truth, a person couldn't see another. Seeing, they could not see. True sight required metanoia. The transformation of the mind. Awakening.

So what was I "seeing" right now? Not what was necessarily there, only what I had learned to see through countless years of genetic imprinting. But in my dream I had seen more. Much more.

Could I see the same way here?

I closed my eyes and breathed deeply. The soft, tender voice of Spirit hung in the back of my mind, a distant memory now, and yet still present.

I opened my eyes.

What is known that cannot be named?

I sat up in my bed as my situation crystalized. Leaving the overlook, Talya had led me up the mountain to a wide ridge above the tree line. The Great Divide. In daylight, the largest of all Elyonite cities could be seen far below, he said. I'd fallen asleep next to a fire without eating the rhambutan fruit.

The events of the previous night in Eden

dropped into my awareness like a hammer from the sky. I yanked up my sleeve and saw that the tattoo was still there. White, like a pure white ivory ring set into my shoulder.

Vlad had turned the town against me. But if both worlds were linked and if I was that link, then what Talya said was true there was also true here. When he spoke of polarity, he also meant Eden, the town — I was sure of it.

The audio clock beside my bed was silent. The backup batteries must have gone dead during the night. So what time was it? No sound from the house. My father was already gone — it had to be late.

I quickly dressed, gave my teeth a once-over, pulled my hair free of the ponytail, and ran into the living room.

The drapes were still drawn, no sign my father had made any breakfast. The sound of gentle breathing first alerted me that I wasn't alone.

Spinning to my right, I half expected to see Shadow Man watching me from the corner of the living room. Instead, I saw that my father had passed out on the couch. No sign of Miranda.

"Dad?"

He shot off the couch and faced me, appearing dazed but otherwise fully awake.

"Sorry, I didn't mean to —"

"What time is it?" His voice was frantic. He answered himself as he glanced at the wall clock. "After ten?"

I didn't know why he'd slept so late, but that didn't really concern me right now. I was focused on what I knew I had to do.

My father leaped to the window, jerked the curtain open, and peered outside, as if expecting to see something that shouldn't be there. He turned back, face drawn, eyes fixed on mine.

"They killed Miranda last night," he said.

"Miranda? What do you mean?"

He told me what he meant in one long rush. My pulse joined the pace of his words. For five full minutes I stood there listening, sinking into fear and alarm.

It was only the beginning, I thought. Just like the terrorists who took down the grid beyond this valley, Vlad would only increase the intensity of his assault. And I was the only one standing in his way.

A voice in my mind told me I was to blame for Miranda's death. Vlad had come here for me. If not for me . . . I shoved the thought out. I had seen darkness in my dreams and risen above it. Strange how I didn't feel that same way here, but I had to try. My father was clearly possessed with that darkness.

Those gentle words echoed across time. *What is known that cannot be named?*

And Talya's voice.

See what is unseen, daughter. See past the illusion of fear. You are not merely your earthen vessel or its memories. Fix your attention on what is unseen, not on what is seen by the eyes in your head.

The power of that sight still lingered in my mind like a distant hum.

I crossed to my father and gently put my arms around him. He immediately dropped his head on my shoulder and began to sob.

"I know how much Miranda meant to you," I said. Eden had now taken two women from him. He was breaking under the weight of it all. "It's okay."

"It's not okay," he said, shaking his head.

"I know. But it will be. You'll see. It's going to be okay."

He began to settle, then stepped away. But the worry would not leave him and he started to pace again, running his hands through his hair.

"Dad?"

But it was pointless. He crossed to the window and peered out again, and as soon as he did, he began to talk in that quick manner of his, expressing his disbelief at what was happening and laying out a strategy of revenge that sounded less like him and more like Barth.

"I have to go," I said when he came up for air.

He was talking about guns and continued without pause. "The problem is getting *into* the armory. I can't believe they all agree with him. If I can just turn one of his enforcers, maybe Russell or Francis, and a few of the others. If Cindy knew . . . heck, if Hillary knew —"

"Did you hear me, Dad? I have to leave."

"What do you mean, leave? You can't leave."

But I was no longer the sixteen-year-old I'd known only yesterday, was I? I was the daughter of Elyon, a twenty-one-year-old Mystic from another realm.

Right?

"Can you sit down for a second?" I asked. The resolve in my voice gave him pause.

"The only way to keep you safe is to arm ourselves," he said. "Both of us, I'll grant you —"

"Father!" I pointed to the sofa. "Sit down for just one second and listen to me."

His jaw clenched, but he finally nodded. "Okay." He sat. "I'm listening."

I eased into the chair opposite him and took a deep breath.

"I know that I'm your daughter, and I love you more than I know how to love anything else. But I have some things I have to do, regardless of what you think. The truth is, Vlad needs me alive. He came to this valley for one reason and one reason alone. Me. I know that like I know I have a white tattoo on my shoulder. That's why I have to go. And I have to go now."

"Go where? It's way too dangerous!" His heel was bouncing.

The jittery man before me was hardly the same father I'd turned to for comfort only two days ago. Fear and rage were compromising his frontal lobe — brain-speak for reasoning faculties.

"There's no way a sixteen-year-old girl can face off with that monster and hope to survive." He was shaking his head. "No way."

"I'm not going to Vlad. Or Barth. I'm going to Simon. He knows more than he's saying, and I think I have a way to get to him."

"Even Simon," he protested, standing now, stepping over to the window to peer out again. "You know what happens if you break his law. And it's martial law now."

I was getting nowhere. So I stood and

walked to the door.

"Where are you going?" he demanded.

"I told you."

He looked dumbfounded. "Didn't you *hear* me?"

"I heard everything. No one in the streets, new law. Barth has a taste for blood and would love to start with yours. You give him the least excuse and he will come after you with swords drawn." Swords? I went on without bothering to correct myself. "Which is why you can't leave this house. If something happens to you, who'll be around to take care of me?"

My words caught him flat-footed.

"I, on the other hand, have great value to both Barth and Simon. Alive, not dead. Which is why I'm going. Give me two hours."

I opened the door.

"Two hours? I can't wait here for two hours!"

"Two hours," I said, and I shut the door behind me. I would apologize later.

Except for Spotty, the Franklins' Dalmatian, who'd gotten off his leash, Eden was a ghost town.

I felt no fear as I walked down the sidewalk in my tattered Converses. No fear as I strode right into the center of the town

348

square, a solitary sixteen-year-old girl. No fear as I stepped into the church.

The first stab of fear hit me when I entered the sanctuary. Soft light from the stained glass didn't take the edge off the stern-faced image of God pointing down at the Bible. Memories of a hundred Sunday school lessons flooded my mind. I knew that Simon was well meaning, but the concept of God he taught and the one I'd encountered when I found the First Seal were hardly the same.

What if everything Talya was teaching me was wrong?

But I refused to believe that. Or at least I tried to.

I walked through the auditorium into the administration offices, right up to Simon's door, part of me hoping he'd be there, part of me not wanting to face him, because he represented that old view of God that had caused me so much fear. And there was no fear in love.

The office was dark when I pushed the door open — which was why I could see the line of light at the bottom of another door behind the desk.

I stepped up to the door, heart pounding. Cracked it wider, peering in.

Simon stood in the light of a lantern with his back to me. He was holding a black book up to the light, drawing his finger along a page. I could read the header at the top.

Experimental Protocols
Emergency Override

I pulled the door open. "Judge?"

Simon spun, face white. "Rachelle!" He jerked a drawer wide, dropped the book inside, and slammed it shut. "What are you doing here?"

I knew then my father was right. Simon was hiding something. But I was there for another reason.

"The door was open . . ."

He crossed to me, shoved me out, and slammed the door shut behind us. A dead bolt automatically engaged, sealing the door seamlessly into the bookshelf.

For a second, he stood there in the dark office as if unsure what to do. Then he grabbed my hand and led me to a side door that opened into the sanctuary. "As far as you're concerned, that room doesn't exist. It's just a place I escape to when I need to clear my head. Please keep it to yourself."

"Okay."

"You have no business being here," he said, leading me to the steps that descended from the platform. I was so used to dutifully following his guidance that for a moment I forgot why I'd come.

I stopped by the altar and looked up at him, then drew a breath and steadied my resolve.

"I've come to help you," I said.

He stared at me with blank eyes, lost in concerns I knew nothing of. He stepped to the side and sat heavily in the chair behind the bench. Stared off at the far wall.

"I've always liked you, Rachelle. In all of this you've been so . . . unique. Gracious, despite all your challenges. But what's happening here . . ." He turned to me. "It's beyond both you and me. Between us, I want you to know I never meant you or anyone else any harm."

My heart broke for him. "Do you mind if I share some thoughts with you?" I asked. "Do you ever wonder if everything you believe about something critical is . . . well, just not so?"

He stared at me. Answered slowly. "Such as?"

"God, for starters. You saw what happened to me last night. It wasn't in my mind. Something else happened. Something real."

"Maybe. I'm more of a hard-facts guy. Theology, science, what's written and proven. The rest is hard to swallow."

"Everything is hard to swallow unless you've been trained to believe it," I said. "Take away all your memories of what should be, and suddenly the world opens up to all kinds of new possibilities."

He eyed me carefully. "There is no bending God's laws," he said slowly.

"True. But what *are* God's laws? An eye for an eye? Or is his law called grace now? Didn't he give both? So then maybe both are true: one to experience this world of ups and downs, and one if you want to experience God beyond polarity. And we're all bound by whatever system we serve."

"What are you suggesting? The law holds this town together."

"True, but what if that law is weak and useless, like Paulus wrote?"

"Paulus?"

"Paul, I mean. Ultimately, only the law of grace is effective." I cleared my throat. "What if God isn't disappointed in us?"

For a moment I saw deep hunger in his eyes, and I thought he might break down. It was almost as if he wanted to tell me something, or believe something, but just couldn't bring himself to.

Simon looked off again. "Like I said, there is no bending God's laws. It would all fall apart."

"Maybe the law has to fall apart for us to see what's beyond it."

Eyes back on me. "Where did you get all of this?"

"From my dreams, which started with Vlad Smith's book."

He frowned. "I don't believe in magic."

"Let me tell you what I believe. I believe that Vlad Smith only wants one thing, and that's for me to write him into the book. But I can't. I won't. Tell me why you think Vlad came to Eden. To take over a small town so that he could be the boss? You've heard him speak. A man with his charisma and intelligence could take charge of far more than a small town that offers him nothing."

"We have power," he said with no conviction. "A way to survive."

"And if he wanted that, he would've already taken it. You'd be dead and this would be over. But he wants something else, so he's using what we value most to manipulate us into giving him that."

"And you think that's you."

"Me. And to get to me, he needs you against me. The whole town against me."

"Even if this book business was true, there would be easier ways to force your hand. And write in a book? Do you realize how absurd that sounds?"

"There are no easier ways to get to me because he knows that I have to write willingly, believing what I write. It can't be forced, trust me. Even if he tried, what would holding a gun to a sixteen-year-old girl look like to the rest of the town? Barth's one thing. The town trusts him, you've seen to that. But a stranger? They're not that fickle. He's creating the environment to make me do what he wants. In the process, you're going to lose everything you built here."

He was listening now.

"And you propose what, exactly?"

"Three things. First, that you do what you're doing to keep everyone locked down. No one moves. If no one moves, no one talks, and if no one talks, no one gets bent out of shape."

He frowned. "Go on . . ."

"Second, that you and I stand together. We present a united front without backing down. You publicly denounce Vlad and gather the town with us."

"He controls the electricity."

"So let him have it. We can survive long enough as long as no one panics. Take the town and the power off the table. Force him to find another way."

"And if that way includes violence?"

"Then the town will despise him. Mob him. Destroy him."

"I don't know . . . He seems pretty powerful to me. He healed you."

"No, he didn't. Justin did that." Hearing how that sounded, I adjusted. "Meaning something real lies beyond polarity."

He stared. "Beyond polarity?"

"As in cause and effect, up and down, the natural world."

"I see. And the third thing?"

"Rein in Barth. He's a bomb and he's already going off."

He was still thinking, that was good. But there was a desperation about him that made me wonder again what he was hiding from the town. Still, I didn't want to go there. I needed him as an ally.

"All this over a book," he said. He nervously rubbed the back of his neck. "That's an awful lot to swallow."

"Truth that conflicts with what you hold sacred is always hard to swallow at first."

He went still, mind lost in another world.

The backstage door banged open, and a moment later Barth walked onto the platform, hauling Peter in by his ear. Barth wore the same white dress shirt he'd worn yesterday, now smudged and unbuttoned halfway down his hairy chest. In his right hand, a billy club. He scowled when he saw me.

"Let me go!" Peter struggled free from the large man's grip, face red. He shoved a finger at the councilman. "He's gone nuts! I wasn't doing anything!"

"You were in the streets. We're under martial law." Barth was speaking to Peter, but his eyes were on me. "What's she doing here?"

"I was only looking for you," Peter cried, imploring his father, who'd pushed himself out of his chair.

"Mind your tongue," Simon snapped. "Looking for me, why?"

Peter glanced at me and answered his father. "I can't find Mother, sir."

"She's in the house."

"No, sir, I checked everywhere. The bed's unmade and she's gone."

Barth was still eyeing me like an eagle. Fear, the kind I knew I didn't have to give in to, seeped into my bones.

"I said, what's she doing here?"

"Have you seen her?" Simon demanded of Barth.

"I'm staring at her right now."

"Not her, you idiot! My wife! Hillary."

"No. But this one doesn't belong here." Barth adjusted his grip on the billy club and moved toward me like a bull.

A voice spoke from the back of the auditorium. "You lay one hand on her and I swear . . ." I spun to see that my father stood at the back door, ragged and crazed, holding a baseball bat at his side. "I'll rip your head off your shoulders."

Barth stopped at the edge of the platform. "Is that a fact?"

"You killed my wife. You killed Miranda. I'm not going to let you kill my daughter."

Silence.

And then Barth was moving — jumping off the platform, striding down the aisle, gunning for my father.

My feet refused to move.

19

I had insisted that my father wait two hours, and if he'd listened, none of it would have happened. But Shadow Man had worked his way into his mind and convinced him that stories of other worlds were nonsense. More, he had an obligation to defend the honor of his wife. Justice had to be served — that was the only story he was listening to here.

I didn't blame him. My father was dutifully following what hundreds of years of social conditioning, bound in polarity, had taught him.

I stood frozen, smothered by fear.

"Father?" It was Peter talking, but Simon wasn't listening to his son. "Father!"

Barth reached my father then, just as Peter's last warning echoed through the sanctuary. My father met him halfway, rushing forward with his bat cocked. Then swinging.

But to a man who made defense his life, a baseball bat might as well be a twig. With catlike quickness, Barth sidestepped the bat, took one step, and slugged my father in the face while he was off balance.

"No!" My feet found themselves. I moved without conscious calculation, only one thought in mind: Barth was going to kill my father.

Three strides down the center aisle, I decided the long way around wouldn't do. I leaped to the backs of the pews and flew across them, two at a time, eyes focused on the bull who was just now turning back.

Five more long strides and I was there. But Barth was far faster than any man his size should be, even caught off guard by the sight of a sixteen-year-old girl sprinting toward him on the backs of pews.

He scooped up my father's fallen bat and swung at me as I launched off the last seat. I was already in flight, and if not for his swing, my heels would have struck his head.

But there was that swing. A vicious strike at the end of two powerful arms that would have broken my body in two.

I threw my head forward and shifted my weight to execute an aerial flip up and over the bat. Air buffeted the back of my head as I rolled forward. I twisted midflight and landed light on both feet, facing his unprotected back.

But Barth was fast. Blindingly fast, bringing the bat around as he turned, putting his full weight into his second swing. A low swing aimed at the skinny young girl who'd somehow gotten behind him.

I could have stepped into his arms and brought my palm up under his chin, but I went high, leaping up, two feet above the bat. Then shoving my heel forward, toward his thick head.

The rubber sole of my right Converse slammed into his face. I heard a crack and knew I'd broken his nose. Then I was on both feet again, bouncing back to create space, and for the first time thinking rather than simply reacting.

On my left, my father was trying to get his feet under him, grabbing for the dropped billy club.

In front of me, blood was pouring from Barth's broken nose.

On the platform, Peter stood beside his father, gawking at me as two of Barth's men rushed into the auditorium.

Inside of me, a voice whispered caution. They had guns. Killing wasn't in me. But it was in Barth, and he didn't even seem to notice the blood flowing down his chin. He was coming again, more calculating this time.

"Stay down!" I snapped at my father. The authority in my voice more than the soundness of my advice gave him pause. He withdrew his hand from the billy club and stayed on one knee, one arm draped over the back of the last pew.

No, killing wasn't in me, but protecting myself was. Barth could swing all he wanted; I was too fast for him.

Barth pulled up five feet from me. Eyed me curiously for a second. Then dropped the bat, palmed the gun on his hip, brought it up quick as a blink, and pulled the trigger.

I saw the muzzle flash before I heard the detonation. Everything was moving slow, far too slow. And by everything I mean everything, including me.

I was already throwing myself to my left as he pulled the trigger. But then the bullet was tearing through the skin on my right shoulder.

"Stop!" Simon's voice thundered.

Barth fired again.

I was off balance and falling, and I was powerless to avoid that second bullet, which tore into my right thigh and shattered my femur.

I collapsed in a heap and immediately tried to push myself back up. My right shoulder burned; pain throbbed up my leg and hip.

"Enough! For the love of God!" Simon stormed down the aisle, face white.

But it wasn't over yet, because my father had just seen his daughter shot down. He was back on his feet, running at Barth in a blind rage.

Barth turned, hit him on the side of his head, and dropped him. This time he was out.

Simon walked up to Barth, snatched away his gun, and tossed it on the floor. "Enough. You want to kill everyone in this town?"

Barth's jaw remained firm.

The Judge pulled out a handkerchief and flung it at the man. "Clean yourself up, you look like a butchered rooster."

Barth snagged the rag and wiped it across his mouth, stared at the cloth, then tossed it away. His face was still smeared with a mask of blood.

I watched it all from the ground, helpless. Horrified. Trembling now. The older me in another world might have known a better way to deal with the situation, but I wasn't her right now.

I was just me. My father had been hit in

the head twice, hard, and my leg had a bullet in it. This was why Talya had wanted me to dream?

Simon was pacing, fuming. He turned to Barth's men, who were working their way down the aisle. "Get David out of here."

One of them looked at Barth for direction. "The cellar?"

"No," Simon shot back. "Lock him in the shed. I don't want him anywhere near her."

They grabbed my father by the collar and hauled him to his feet. Hoisting his arms over their shoulders, they dragged him out the back door.

"Don't you dare hurt him!" I snapped.

Simon's eyes traced my body and stopped at the hole in my jeans, now soaked in blood.

He squinted. "Where'd you learn that?"

Barth was quiet. I'd gained some respect from him. He was looking at my right shoulder and I followed his stare. My arm was hot with pain. The bullet had torn through my T-shirt sleeve, now soaked in blood. The bottom arc of the circle tattoo was visible below the hem.

Simon saw it as well. "Where'd you get that?" He stepped up to me and pulled my sleeve up. Blood glistened on my skin where the bullet had sliced through the flesh. But that was it.

He drew a finger through the blood. There was no wound now.

"How . . ." He rubbed his fingers together. "Blood but no wound? How's that possible?"

"The book," I said. "Do you believe me now?"

He stood up, frowning. Nudged my leg with his foot.

Pain flashed up my thigh and I grunted. Whatever had happened to the wound on my tattoo wasn't happening to my leg.

Peter stood behind his father, still looking stunned by what he'd seen. "Her leg's broken. She needs a doctor."

"A man's gotta do what a man's gotta do," Barth said. "Question is, what do you want me to do with her now? I strongly recommend encouraging her to write in that stupid book."

"No. Under no condition. Do I make myself clear?"

Barth hesitated, then shrugged.

Simon gave me one last glance and turned back up the aisle. "Put her in the cellar."

"Father . . ."

Simon turned and walked away.

The cellar, as it turned out, was nothing

less than a full-security prison two stories under the sanctuary, complete with barred cells. I doubted anyone but the council and a few members of security even knew it existed. But I did. I was in it.

The guards hauled me down. One had my armpits, the other my legs. I don't remember the whole trip because I was only half conscious, fighting throbbing pain. But I knew it was two stories because I heard one of them say so.

Barth led the way with a flashlight. A key opened the door at the end of a hall, and another the barred gate to my cell. If the bullet hadn't broken all of my thigh bone, the rest of it cracked when they dropped me on the concrete slab.

I cried out, but Barth wasn't in a compassionate mood.

"The next time the bullet goes through your head. Dodge that."

Then the bars were secured and the light from their flashlights faded down the hall, leaving me in pitch darkness.

I clicked a few times as they left, but echolocation would do me no favors now.

For thirty seconds I just lay there, trying to focus on anything but the pain. A gentle examination of my leg only confirmed what I already knew. I could feel the entry hole, no exit wound. My jeans were sopping wet with blood.

I drew my arms up to my chest and hugged my body. Then I began to sob. Softly at first, because every movement hurt. But I couldn't hold it back. The weight of so many things gone wrong crushed me.

I tried not to cry, I really did.

Then I only wanted to sleep. To sleep and to dream. But the pain in my leg wouldn't let me.

What is known that cannot be named?

Known. As in experienced. Named. As in words? Identity? Label? I let my mind work through the possibilities, trying my best to ignore the pain shooting up my side, but my mind was of no use to me in that state.

"Mother?" My thin voice echoed softly in the cell. There was no response. Memory of the gentle voice that had spoken to me on the cliff seemed so distant as I lay there in the dark. I closed my eyes, desperate for her voice. "Mother . . ." Sorrow rolled up my chest and I began to cry again. "Please . . ."

All I could hear was my own breathing, my own voice. All I could see was darkness.

I don't know how long it was before sleep finally shut down that world. Maybe twelve hours. Maybe more.

20

Jacob, son of Qurong, commander of all Throaters in service to Ba'al, sat upon his steed in the moonlight, studying the plateau. No more than an hour's ride across it, ominous cliffs rose to meet the Great Divide. Next to him: Maco, his right hand. Behind them: a hundred men, all mounted, waiting in silence. Darkness had fallen four hours earlier — morning light would gray the eastern sky in four more.

The horse sign was unmistakable. The woman and her mysterious guide had stopped here in the last few hours before continuing up the pass.

"He should be back by now," Maco said. "It's been two hours."

"Risin takes care, my friend," Jacob replied, voice low.

He'd dispatched the scout with strict orders to pick his own way to the Divide and return with the lay of the land. They were in uncharted country under control of the Elyonite Albinos, rumored to wield the sword as few others could.

A horse snorted softly behind them, impatient with so much standing. But they would not dismount in such treacherous lands without knowing more. With any luck, this priestess Ba'al was so desperate to control had bedded down at the pass. He had no desire to extend their mission beyond the Great Divide.

"Permission to speak freely, sire."

"Speak as you will."

"I don't like it. The air feels wrong to me."

"The air *is* wrong for you. It's thinner up here."

"Beg your pardon, sire, but the thin air doesn't reach to the base of the gut, which speaks its own story."

"Then tell me your story, Maco. Bend this tired ear."

"My story tells me a noose awaits. I have no desire to walk into a trap."

"Set by whom? Two Mystics?"

"The Elyonites."

"Which is why I sent Risin to report on any sign of them."

Maco's mount shifted under him. Under any other circumstances, the warrior would be the one urging them up the mountain, come what may. But the last six days of relentless pursuit had unnerved them all.

No matter how hard they pushed, their prey seemed to match their pace, staying just out of reach. For the last two days, they'd eased to save the horses, only to learn from the age of the sign that the girl and her companion had eased as well.

They'd closed the distance somewhat today. But it appeared Jacob wasn't the only one who couldn't shake the feeling that they were being toyed with.

"I don't like it any more than you do, Maco. Which is why we must take them tonight. Risin will tell us what we need to know."

"Of course, sire. It's just . . ." The man hesitated.

Jacob looked at him. "Something else?"

"Melina," Maco said.

But of course. Maco's bride, Melina, was to give birth to their first child soon. Jacob had forgotten. Most Throaters took a vow of celibacy under pressure from Ba'al, who insisted that women only compromised men headed into battle. It was an absurd restriction, Jacob thought, but one that might have served a man as passionate as Maco.

"Don't worry, Maco. In one week's time you will be holding your newborn son in your arms."

His man looked sheepish. "She wants me to leave Ba'al's service," he said. "I told her I didn't serve Ba'al, only you."

"Leave the Throaters and serve how?"

"As a builder, actually. I would serve the army when called upon, of course. But the prospect of having a child has done strange things to my thoughts."

Jacob suppressed a grin. Maco's admission took courage, even if Jacob was the only one to hear it. If there was a man he might call brother, it was Maco. They'd served together for three years, often depending on each other like hand and glove.

"Then you must become a builder, my friend. Leave the fighting to men like me who still have reason to impress young maidens with impossible tales of bravery. I didn't know you were handy with a hammer and saw."

"My father taught me a few things when I was —"

Jacob snatched his hand up for silence. A horse had rounded the boulders ahead. Risin had returned.

"If you wouldn't mind . . ."

"Don't worry, Maco," Jacob said, kneeing his stallion. "Your secret's safe with me."

"Thank you, sire."

They rode out to meet the scout halfway. "Speak."

Risin reined in his horse, still skittish from the descent over steep terrain. "They sleep in a small gulch to the north of the pass, sire. The woman and an older man."

"Older?"

"Ancient by the look of his beard. Finding them wasn't easy, they are well hidden."

"Any sign of others?"

"None that I found. If there are warriors on this mountain, they are ghosts."

Jacob studied that dark mountain behind Risin. He still couldn't shake the thought that all was not what it seemed, but the girl was there, asleep with only an old man and her own blade to protect her.

"The way up?"

"To the north, off the path, through the trees. The footing is a bit treacherous in places, but it offers more cover. From the north we can circle and approach them from behind."

"The old man — you are certain he slept?"

"Unless he snores while awake, quite sure, yes."

"Maco, tell the men we ride now. Send fifty to block the pass and bring fifty to follow us to the north. I'm determined to cut off any escape. Remind them that silence is paramount. Assume the old man is as deadly with a knife as the girl."

"Yes, sire."

They rode in single file under a round moon, up narrow valleys and then down sharp gorges, winding their way behind Risin, who had an uncanny knack for making a path where there was none.

Slowly the peak grew before them. At such a high elevation, the whole world might be seen in daylight. Their horses were unaccustomed to such tall peaks, but they'd been bred and trained for obedience, and freed of the heavy armor that protected their riders in desert conflict. The Throaters had ditched it five days earlier, knowing that many steep climbs awaited them. The armor could be collected on their return.

Near the top, they veered north, through trees that finally ended at a wide meadow. And beyond that meadow, tall boulders.

Risin stopped the column and Jacob pulled his steed abreast. "How far?"

The scout motioned to the south. "The pass is there, ten minutes along the ridge." He nodded ahead. "We cross this meadow, then two miles north along the ridge to the cleft where they sleep."

"By Teeleh's fangs, how did you find them?"

Risin shrugged. "How does water find the sea? It's what I do."

"I was giving you a compliment, Risin, not asking a question. Have you ever actually seen a sea?"

"No, sire."

"Someday, I want you to find a sea and take me there. Lead on."

They broke file and crossed the grassy meadow abreast. Jacob considered the mystery of the woman they had come so far to seize. The 49th. A Mystic whose mind had been wiped. He pondered the way she'd spoken to him while hiding under the cliff, then walked past his men in darkness as if able to see what they could not. The way she'd looked at him before throwing her knife, guiding it wide.

There was an innocence in her voice and her eyes that didn't belong to any warrior so skilled as she.

He understood why Ba'al and his father were so threatened by her — they believed in the prophecy. Perhaps they were right. But the woman he'd encountered didn't strike him as a warrior intent on subjugating the Horde. Or any human, for that matter. Perhaps he could learn something from her. Perhaps they all could.

Risin pulled up hard. Jacob followed the

man's stare and saw shadows where no shadows belonged despite a bright moon. They emerged in a long line along the towering boulders fifty paces directly ahead.

His pulse surged.

"Elyonites," Risin breathed.

Twenty, no more, wrapped in black swaths of clothing from head to foot, save for a thin slit across their eyes. To a man they were mounted on black steeds. If they wore armor, it was hidden beneath their dress.

The last of them emerged from the boulders and pulled alongside the others, where they waited, motionless.

Two questions raced through Jacob's mind, neither involving retreat. Would the sound of battle awaken the woman and give her the time she needed to slip away? What if these warriors had already found her?

"When we engage, you and I will break north with five more. Take us to her quickly! Maco, stay by me."

"The others?" Risin asked.

"The others slaughter these hooded mongrels and wait for our return."

The orders took only seconds to convey. Jacob slowly withdrew his broad blade and palmed a throwing knife.

"Head down, they likely have bows. Don't you worry, boy, you will see your son yet."

Jacob urged his horse to a trot abreast all fifty, straight toward the enemy, who made no effort to move. It occurred to him that they might slip back into the boulders and engage his men piecemeal.

"Breakneck, Maco!" He slapped his mount and plunged toward the waiting line of warriors.

Only when his men were midfield did the line move. Not toward them, but to either side, ten per group spaced out in perfect order as if performing on a stage. They took their mounts to a full gallop, but it was the finesse with which they moved, so evenly in stride, that tugged at Jacob's gut.

The split forced his own men to divide. But the Elyonite warriors showed no intention of engaging. Both lines sped in opposite directions, circling behind.

The first arrows came then, drawn and fired without warning at a full gallop. Each found an exposed neck or head in a stunning display of precision.

"The girl, Risin!" he snapped. "Take me to her!"

Risin veered to the north, followed quickly by Maco and Jacob on his heels with four others, bent low.

Cries filled the meadow, sending alarm down his neck. Rumors of the Elyonite warriors were whispered around campfires, but so were stories of Shataiki and ghosts.

Enraged, Jacob swatted at an arrow streaking for his side. And another, shot from the line of Elyonites circling to his left. A third arrow slammed into the saddle at his back but didn't have the weight to break through.

A glance over his shoulder turned his alarm to dread. At least half of his men were down.

One of the men with him cried out and grabbed at his neck. The warrior toppled off his mount and landed hard.

"Backside!" Jacob cried. "Cut them off! Forward, Risin! Like the wind!"

Ten of the warriors still mounted behind him moved to cut off the line of Elyonites now firing from their flank and rear. The maneuver, however ill-fated for those who obeyed, gave him the cover he needed to reach the boulders with Risin and Maco.

They rounded the towering rock formations at a full gallop, then followed Risin up a narrow gorge, leaving the sounds of dying men behind.

"They were waiting for us!" Maco said. "I've never seen warriors fire with such aim."

"Not now!"

They had to reach the girl and return to

the others before the warriors tracked them. Then get back down the mountain without engaging the enemy. The terrain here was rough, and the path was narrow and would force any pursuit into single file. With luck, his men would buy him the lead he needed.

Risin had said two miles. Under threat of death, the stallions made the treacherous ride in under ten minutes, plunging down ravines and scrambling up steep inclines.

They made no attempt at stealth — there was no time for that now.

"This way." Risin directed his snorting mount to the right of a massive rock, dropped to the ground, and waved Jacob through a narrow gap between two boulders.

Nestled among a grouping of eight rocks lay bare ground, perhaps twenty strides from side to side. At the center of the clearing lay a single form, sleeping on one side. No horses.

"The elder's gone," Risin whispered.

Maco appeared, panting, sword drawn. "We have to hurry."

They did, but the sight of the girl now sleeping so soundly tugged at him. If the Elyonites knew she was here, they would have seized or killed her already. There was no sound of pursuit to their rear.

He glanced up at the boulders. "Maco, keep an eye out. The old man may still be near."

Jacob walked up to the form. Ashes and half-burned sticks from a small fire long dead lay a few feet from her. Her long dark hair was strewn across her face, hiding it from view. A round tattoo on her shoulder glowed white in the moonlight. She'd kicked off the blanket meant to keep her warm, and her tunic was hiked up to expose a bare thigh. She was hugging herself and shivering, yet sleeping still.

Did all Albinos sleep so soundly?

"Sire . . ."

He shut down Risin's whisper with a raised hand. Like all Horde, Jacob found her scent to be off-putting and her smooth skin ugly enough, but not repulsive the way others spoke of such things. If they managed to escape this mountain in one piece, he would treat her with respect and learn more of her ways.

Jacob reached for the rope that Risin held out to him and carefully slipped one end under her head. He was about to close the loop around her neck when she whimpered and flinched in her sleep.

A small hole suddenly appeared on her bare thigh, an injury inflicted with an invisible weapon that jerked her leg. The familiar muted crunch of bone breaking accompanied a soft grunt from her. He jumped back, stunned.

Had he just seen this? Blood was now trickling from the wound and running down her thigh. But none of this awakened her.

"Teeleh help us!" Risin cried. "She's a witch!"

As if in answer to his cry, an arrow slammed into the crown of Risin's head. Jacob heard a grunt and spun. Maco stood ten paces away, eyes wide, a knife lodged in his temple.

Jacob lifted his sight to the boulders and saw them. Five Elyonite warriors wrapped in black, gazing down, bows drawn. One step and he would be dead. He took a calming breath and slowly straightened, hands open and palms out.

"By Elyon, they stink worse dead than alive," one of them muttered.

"This one's mine." A second warrior stepped off the tall boulder, dropped gracefully through the air, and landed on the ground like a cat. He flipped a knife in his hand and stared at Jacob, who stood still, prepared for death. He'd failed Ba'al's mission. His mother would mourn him. This thought more than any other bothered him.

He could try to defend himself, but to what end? Any one of those on the rocks could end his life with an arrow. Better to accept death in peace than make a futile attack that would only betray a baser rage.

He couldn't see the man's face because it was wrapped in black cloth, but his green eyes glinted with resolve. The man had taken one step toward him when one of the others spoke.

"Hold on, what's this?"

Jacob glanced at the man who'd stopped his comrade.

"Her shoulder. She's a Mystic!"

The warrior on the ground looked down at the tattoo on her arm. For a long moment, no one spoke. They'd just stumbled on a great prize, Jacob realized. One they either revered or despised, but one of value nonetheless.

"She's wounded," the warrior across from Jacob said.

"I don't care if she's half dead," the one above snapped. "Put that knife through her temple now."

"No," Jacob said. "You can't."

They looked at him, above and below, taken aback by the tone of his voice.

"Is that so? I suppose we can't kill the infidels at the pass either? And yet we have.

You're the last. Pray tell me, beast, why we should spare a heretic, the only thing in this world worse than the Horde?"

"Because your leaders will demand to question the prophesied one."

The one above spoke. "And what would an animal know about a prophesied one? There is no such thing. These are lies spun by those who undermine Elyon's holy ways."

"I am Jacob, son of Qurong. And the girl you wish to kill is the 49th Mystic."

"Qurong's son . . ." His voice was filled with doubt.

"Yes."

"Then all the more reason you will die."

"I'm only telling you so you don't give your commanders reason to take your heads."

"If it's true," the one above said, "they'll want to torture them for information. There will be gold for these."

The warrior on the ground considered his companion's opinion, then walked up to the woman and shoved the heel of his boot into her wound. She groaned but did not wake.

The man spat to one side. "Filthy heretic. She's already half dead."

"No," Jacob said. "She's only sleeping."

"I say we kill them both now. They stink

of trouble."

"Hold!"

Jacob glanced up and saw that a sixth warrior had appeared, this one with a golden armband that differentiated him from the others.

The warrior nearby dipped his head in respect. "Sire."

The leader dropped to the ground with the grace of a bird of prey. He pulled down the black cloth that covered his face, exposing a jaw chiseled from stone and deep eyes that knew no fear.

He glanced at the 49th, then leveled his gaze at Jacob. "I am Aaron, son of Mosseum, commander of the Elyonite elite. You are Jacob, son of Qurong, you say?"

"I am."

"And you claim this woman is the 49th Mystic?"

"Can you think of any other reason the son of Qurong would find himself so far from his own women? She is no ordinary Albino, I can assure you."

The son of Mosseum studied him for a long moment. He struck Jacob as a man given to few words, confident in his authority and power. From what Jacob had seen on this mountain tonight, the Elyonites more than lived up to the rumors of their fighting prowess. Not that Jacob feared the man — he feared none. Perhaps they would one day test each other on neutral ground. Then he would know what the man was really made of.

Aaron dipped his head. "Consider this woman to have extended your life, son of Qurong. Though I think you will regret it."

He spoke to his men without removing his eyes from Jacob.

"Bind them."

21

I was dreaming, and in that dream, Barth beat my father and shot me. The bullet broke my thigh bone. They dragged me to a cellar, dumped me in a cell, and left me in that dank darkness to contend with throbbing pain. The pain kept me awake for a long time before sleep mercifully put me out of my misery.

That was my dream, and it slowly faded as I returned to consciousness in the real world. The one in which Talya and I had climbed to the pass of the Great Divide, found a small enclave among boulders, and cooked some old corn over a small fire before climbing under blankets to sleep.

Talya had kissed my hand before retiring. "No matter what happens tomorrow," he said, "remember that every encounter is an opportunity for salvation from the storm. What you are tempted to call a problem is only an instrument for awakening so that you can see what is true, as seen Inchristi. As such, it is your gift. Promise me you will remember this."

I was still floating from my experience on the cliff. There I had seen why Yeshua slept through the storm on the sea and asked those with him why they were afraid. There was no reason to be. I had just seen what he had seen, so I wasn't concerned about any coming problems.

"I promise," I said. I'd fallen asleep in the safe place with a smile on my face.

The rocking beneath me pulled me quickly from sleep, and I opened my eyes. Light. Bright light. We were moving!

I jerked up. "Talya?"

Pain shot up my leg and I cried out, grasping at my thigh. Someone had tied a strip of cloth around the wound. The cloth was red with blood.

"Easy . . . Easy, don't move."

A hand rested on my shoulder and I turned, expecting to see Talya. Instead I saw what first appeared to be a monster of sorts, with flaking gray skin and long matted dreadlocks. Horde.

I recoiled, confused and terrified. The wound on my thigh . . . Barth had shot me in my dreams.

"Where's Talya?"

"You're badly wounded. Please try not to move. I did my best to clean and wrap it, but my experience doesn't extend beyond battle dressing. With any luck, these barbarians will have physicians to ease the pain and set your leg. Until then, moving will only cause your bones to grind. Quite painful."

I twisted, searching for Talya. We were in a small horse-drawn cage with filthy straw on the floor. A bald Albino sat in the corner, back to me. We were passing a small wooden house with a green lawn. Ditches lined either side of the dirt road.

Twelve or fourteen warriors dressed from head to foot in black rode tall stallions in two columns, one on each side of us.

"Where are we?"

"Approaching Mosseum," he said. "Capital of the Elyonites."

Slowly, my predicament came into some clarity. Talya had said I would be alone. In no scenario had I imagined I would find myself a captive with a shattered leg.

A young boy was running along the far ditch, jumping up and down, hooting and hollering at the warriors, who paid him no mind. His white tunic was clean and he wore a bandana, green to match his bright eyes.

"We've met," the Scab said. "Twice. Do you remember?"

I looked at him again. "Jacob?"

He lowered his head. "At your service."

"You were pursuing us. Intent on killing me."

"Not true," he said, lifting a finger. "I was to return you to your rightful place in Ba'al's dungeons."

"My rightful place is nowhere near the Horde."

"And yet here you are. I suppose your rightful place is among the Elyonites? They certainly don't think so. If not for me, you would be dead."

"If not for you?"

"Indeed. I told them you were the 49th. So now we find ourselves here, on a delightful ride to their city. A beast, that would be me. A heretic, that would be you. And a mute, that would be him."

The bald man in the corner turned his head and studied me for a moment before returning to stare through the bars.

"I can't get a word out of him," Jacob said, leaning back against the cage with legs folded, chewing on a piece of straw.

"Your men?" I asked him. "Surely you weren't alone."

Darkness settled over his face. "We were

nearly a hundred. The Elyonite warriors, twenty. I alone survived. Maco . . ." He stopped.

Maco. While trapped under the cliff I'd heard him call one of his men that. By his reaction now, I could see they'd been close.

"I'm sorry," I said.

"He was to be a father this week. If I survive, I will see the child wants for nothing."

I didn't know what to do with his comment. How only twenty of the Elyonites had bested a hundred of his men, I couldn't imagine. I'd seen Jacob snatch my blade from the air as if it were a toy.

What did that say about the Elyonite warriors? And what did the remorse written on Jacob's face say about the Horde?

My leg was throbbing and I tried to ease the pain by shifting, but each movement only increased it.

Seeing my struggle, Jacob shifted and tapped his knee. "If you elevate it, the pain will ease."

He was dressed in a thick dark shirt with an open neck and canvas pants tucked into leather boots that hugged his calves. I was dressed in only a long tunic, and my leg was bare. The thought of my skin touching his diseased flesh repulsed me, but his slacks were only cloth, right?

I slowly pushed myself up against the adjacent bars and let him take my exposed ankle, lift my leg, and rest my heel on his knee. The brief contact of his hand on my ankle felt like any human touch. Either way, Talya had said the Horde disease wasn't contagious.

"Better?" he asked.

"Not really, no."

He watched me curiously. "Give it some time."

Two men drove the cart, laughing at something funny that didn't concern us. Beyond our prison, houses rose among wide crop fields and orchards. Corn, wheat, apples, and several other fruit trees. There was no sign of a city, only these rural plots of land.

I was in a strange land without Samuel or Talya, on a mission that now seemed not only impossibly distant but absurd.

Behind the cart, elite warriors rode in aloof supremacy. Inside the cart, the son of Qurong and a silent bald man left me alone with my thoughts, which gave me neither guidance nor comfort. Alone . . . And now captive in both realities.

"What happened?" I asked after a long silence. "At the pass."

"I've been asking myself the same question," Jacob said, looking at my leg. "Your wound . . . It just materialized before my eyes."

While I was dreaming. But I hardly understood how such manifestations could cross between realities, and I had no idea how to make him understand.

"I was shot in another world and it manifested here. But don't ask me how because it won't make sense."

"Another world?"

"Like I said, it won't make much sense."

"Try me."

I wasn't even sure where to begin.

"First, tell me how you found us," I said.

"Us? We found only you."

"Then tell me that."

After a moment, he told me his story, beginning with their pursuit leading up to the Great Divide. How our pace seemed to match theirs, slow or quick. My guide was toying with them. I told him that my guide was no guide, but a Mystic named Talya. And if Talya had wanted to, he could have single-handedly wiped them all out.

"And yet he left you when you needed him most."

"No."

"No?" Jacob scoffed. "He fled."

"The man who toyed with you for seven days fled? The one who stilled the storm only last night? The one who sees no threat from any Horde, any Elyonite, any Albino, just up and fled at the first sight of danger? You don't know Talya. He told me he was leaving."

"You're saying the storm that came and went so quickly was his doing?"

"Yes. He was teaching me to find peace rather than fear in the storm."

"So he conjures a storm to teach the priestess a lesson. Quite a man, this Talya. What did he say of me?"

"Please don't call me a priestess. He told me that you would pose no threat to me."

His brow arched. "Is that so? My father ordered me to kill you if I couldn't take you alive."

"And yet you didn't. Why?"

He thought for a moment before responding. "You're the 49th," he said.

But I saw more in his look than this simple confession. At the very least he was doubtful of his mission and curious about me.

"If Talya knew you would pose no threat to me, he also knew we would be together," I said.

"You put too much faith in an old man."

"Do I? Here we are. Together."

His right brow arched.

"Did you know Samuel of Hunter was also in pursuit?" I asked.

"Samuel? The son of Thomas of Hunter?"

"He was with me at the oasis. Talya said he came after you."

"I see." He stared at the Elyonite warriors filed behind us. "If we had seen him, he would likely be dead."

"Says the man in the cage."

"That would be the doing of the other son," he said. "Aaron, son of Mosseum, ruler of all Elyonites."

"He took us?" I looked at the warriors behind us. "He knows who I am?"

"He does now. And is likely reporting the claim in their courts as we speak."

Three sons of three powerful fathers. Jacob, Samuel, and now Aaron. And me. To what end?

"What else happened at the pass last night?" I asked.

Jacob cleared his throat and told me the rest, sparing no detail. He was right — I would have been killed if not for Jacob's intervention. How could Talya have known it would play out just so? If I ever saw him again, I would have to ask.

"Your satchel," Jacob said, pulling a small leather pouch from inside his cloak. "It was in the cart and I took the liberty of keeping it safe. It appears they took all but the paper and the fruit."

I took the satchel. Talya's, not mine.

"You looked inside?"

"I was looking for something to dress your wound with. I had to settle for a strip of my own undergarment."

I set aside thoughts of his filthy clothing and untied the pouch. Inside I found a strange orange fruit and a sheet of very old paper that had been torn out of a book. Blank on both sides.

The hope that lit my mind was dim, but a spark nonetheless. Talya would never have left these two items without specific intentions. Fruit . . . Not the rhambutan that prevented me from dreaming, but another kind that held another power. What, I didn't yet know. And paper . . . The only thing I could think of was a page from his Book of History. To write on? But there was nothing to write with here.

"What is it?" Jacob asked.

I quickly cinched up the satchel. "It's nothing."

"Really? Because to me it looked like you'd just found a Roush. When a woman says *nothing,* she always means something. Usually something important to her."

"You saw it. It's nothing."

"Fine. Nothing it is. Which means something that I know nothing about."

"Fine, something then. A piece of fruit and a piece of paper. I like to eat and I like to write." I handed the satchel back, and he hid it under his clothing for safekeeping. "Do you write?"

"Does Jacob write? Ask any woman in Qurongi City and she will tell you of the honey that flows from my pen."

A poet. Jacob was nothing if not a contradiction. And yet no more of one than I was.

"It's what your captors said about torture that I would pay attention to," the man in the corner said without turning.

We both looked at him. Followed his stare. The cart had crested a small hill and was heading down a widening road into the valley below. There, in stark contrast to the rural fields we had passed, sprawled a great city.

I was immediately struck by two things. The first was its immensity, not just in size but in structure. A tall, thick wall marked its perimeter. The buildings were made of white stone, each capped with a red roof. Tall structures rose from the city center, the tallest of which was domed and topped with a towering spire. Gold.

The second was the city's cleanliness and order. Every street, every building, every structure had been placed with precision, like a giant spoked wheel with the domed Thrall as its hub.

"Don't let its beauty deceive you," the old man said, turning to us. "They are butchers, eager to aid Elyon by sending all heretics and heathens to an early hell. And if they believe you are the fabled 49th, I fear worse than death for you."

I looked at the man's green eyes. An Albino, but what kind?

"And you are?"

"Cirrus. A heretic like you."

My pulse surged. "You're a Mystic?"

"Heavens no. No, I'm afraid I don't see the material world in the same generous light that your kind do. I see the world for what it is: evil. At the very least, meaningless. We are Gnostics, the fifth kind, servants of Elyon, who made none of what you see. Our only hope is to live in peace until we escape this world. Which for us in this cart will be soon enough."

I looked past him to the city. The farms had given way to a great open expanse of grasslands that pressed up against the city walls.

"What do you mean, the fifth kind?" I asked.

He eyed me curiously. "You're a Mystic. Don't you know?"

"Actually, I've —"

"She was poisoned by our high priest and has lost her memory," Jacob said. "When you say 'fifth kind,' you mean races of human, no?"

"If you will. There are Horde, the diseased ones. There are Albinos, who have been cleansed in the red lakes. And there are Leedhan — Shataiki who have crossbred with Horde. Three races."

Leedhan. My mind skipped to Vlad Smith and I wondered if he was half Shataiki.

"Three races," Jacob said. "And yet you say there are five kinds."

"Because among the Albino race there are three sects: Elyonite, Gnostic, and Mystic. I am of the Gnostics."

"You're forgetting the Circle," I said.

"The who?" the Gnostic asked.

Jacob answered for me. "Albinos on the far side. A few thousand at most, led by Thomas of Hunter."

"Never heard of them," the Gnostic said.

And who are you, Rachelle? Inchristi. *What is known that cannot be named?* Me, I thought. I was Inchristi. But I didn't really

396

know it, or the Second Seal would be on my arm. In fact, I only had one seal. Until I had all five, Talya said, any of them were vulnerable. I carried this truth like a heavy weight.

Cirrus faced the city. "I've only met one Mystic, years ago now, and I was stunned by her power. Yet here I find another who has neither knowledge nor power. Only the mark on her arm."

"Did you not hear me?" Jacob snapped. "She was poisoned by a foul beast who spreads fear and death."

I marveled at Jacob's defense of me. "The Elyonites," I said to the old man, "they're heretics to you. Why?"

Cirrus sighed. "What is a heretic, what is a heretic? Who is to know? The Elyonites have many factions who argue over nuances of ancient Scriptures, which they worship in the same way they worship the red lakes. They've settled on a short list of required beliefs that all must adopt or suffer damnation. Confession of these beliefs makes one an Elyonite, those who claim to be the only true followers of Justin. They are materialists, and they treat the world in the same way they believe Elyon treats them. They say only adherence to certain beliefs can appease Elyon's wrath. Cross those beliefs at your own peril. Need I say more?"

"You know their ruler?" Jacob asked.

"Mosseum. He's an old man, more concerned with maintaining his status than serving Elyon. He's taken the liberty of naming the city after himself. It's the first of seven cities, the largest, but not by much." He paused. "Next you will ask me about their army, so I will tell you. The ones who escort us now are the Court Guard, elite fighters, a hundred thousand strong led by Aaron, a brilliant tactician as you so recently discovered. But the other four hundred thousand are nearly as proficient killers."

He faced Jacob. "I don't know the Horde, but unless you have an army many times the size of theirs, I would stick to your side of the Divide. The Elyonites have spared no expense in amassing an army to protect their beliefs."

Jacob humphed but left it alone. We settled into silence as the cart approached the city.

The main arched gate loomed, and then we were through, into a city with cobblestone streets and manicured lawns — thick carpets of grass with brightly flowered beds. Carts rolled along the streets carrying grain and vegetables and bricks.

Swords and dark brown leathers identified the guards stationed at every corner. All turned to look as we passed, showing respect with their stillness and silence.

Their respect was for the Court Guard. The sight of us garnered spits. I would say no fewer than a hundred residents spat to the side as we passed through their city. I couldn't be sure, but I assumed this was a reaction to Jacob, and I felt myself wanting to tell him not to take it personally.

Instead, I held my tongue, wondering if I was wrong. For all I knew, they were disgusted with me, the Mystic. I could only imagine their reactions if they knew I was also the 49th.

We passed shops and large fields with children playing organized games. Something like field hockey. They had green eyes, as did all Albinos. They wore clean tunics with earth-toned slacks. Sandals. Many wore silver chains with red pendants. Round like red pools, I thought, because Cirrus had told us they worshipped the red lakes.

My fear began to settle. In every way the Elyonites were just people who'd carved out an idyllic life under the rule of law. Surely they would do us no harm.

The city changed as we made our way to its center. Here the buildings were taller and extravagantly appointed with gold and silver trimming. Black flags with the solid red circle at the center swayed in a gentle breeze at every entrance.

The city hub was clearly off-limits to all but a particular class, all dressed in white or black. At the heart stood the massive circular building with a golden dome that I'd seen from the road. We were escorted to a wide wing on its right side.

One of the warriors rode up to the door, spoke briefly with a commander, then turned back and motioned to his men. The door to our cart was unlocked and thrown wide.

"You'd better be worth it," the warrior said to Jacob. "If there's no gold in this for me, I'll find you and drown you myself." He looked at me. "You first." He reached in, grabbed my good leg, and dragged me out of the cart.

Pain screamed up my side and I felt the world start to fade. Jacob was scolding the man and somewhere someone was shouting, but my mind was in a dense fog.

I felt myself thrown over a shoulder. Felt the jostling as they carried me. Heard keys rattling, gates opening and closing. Felt mind-numbing pain when they dumped me on the ground.

"Barbarians!" Jacob shouted.

I cried out as he handled my leg. "Not that!"

"Not what? I have to straighten it!"

"Whatever you're doing, not that."

"Sorry, sorry. But I have to do something."

They'd thrown us in a small cell, maybe four paces per side. The floor was made of stone, and the walls were fashioned with iron bars. There was no sign of the old Gnostic, but Jacob was bent over me, muttering curses.

I looked down and nearly threw up. Whatever had been holding my leg together earlier had clearly given way. My body began to tremble and I closed my eyes, desperate to find some relief.

"I have to —"

"Leave it!" I snapped. "Don't touch me!"

He withdrew, then rushed to the barred door. "By Teeleh's fangs, can we get a physician here!" His voice echoed down an empty corridor.

"Don't say that," I breathed, desperate for relief.

"We need a man of medicine! You can't rot in here like this!"

"Don't invoke Teeleh," I said. "They won't appreciate it." But then I was moaning again, uncaring what he said.

When I opened my eyes, I saw that he was pacing, fists clenched. It had never occurred to me that one such as Jacob would care so much. Of course, he was tasked with returning me to Ba'al. But no . . . it was more.

"This Talya of yours," he said. "What would he say to you now?"

"To look past the pain."

"And can you do this?"

"No."

"But you insist that he intentionally left you, which means he must have known that you would end up here, with me, as you said. So then what provision would he offer for such a time of need? An incantation of some kind. A hex."

"He's not that kind of Mystic."

He withdrew Talya's satchel and quickly untied it. Dumped the contents out.

The page floated to the floor as the orange fruit plopped down by my side. Ignoring the paper, he snatched up the fruit.

"There are rumors the Albinos under Thomas of Hunter use fruit to heal. Do you know what this fruit is?"

Even as he said it, the fog in my mind began to clear. The fruit . . .

"It's not my satchel," I said.

"The wizard's satchel?" He stared at the orange fruit in his hand. "What do you do with it? Eat it?" He dropped to his knees and gently lifted my head. Held the fruit to my lips. "Bite."

I bit deeply. A cool, bitter juice filled my mouth. I chewed on the flesh between my teeth and swallowed.

"Anything?"

"I . . . I don't know. Maybe it takes time."

Jacob raised the fruit to his lips and took a bite. Chewed. Spit out the juice. "It's bitter. A seed, not a fruit."

"Whatever it is, he left it for me. Try the wound."

He looked at my leg, then at the fruit in his hand. A calm began to settle over me as an ancient knowledge of ways long forgotten edged into my instinctive mind.

"Take the wrapping off," I breathed, eyes closed.

I felt his hands on my thigh, unwrapping the bandage he'd applied before my waking.

"Straighten my leg."

"Are you sure?"

"Straighten it."

He maneuvered my leg and I lay still, trying to think beyond the agonizing pain, clinging to consciousness as best I could.

"It's the best I can —"

"Squeeze the juice into the wound."

I wasn't watching but I felt it. Felt the first drop of the fruit's juice make contact with my raw flesh. Felt the tingle erupt there, in the deepest part of my nerves. A soothing heat spread through my bones.

Jacob cried out and jumped back.

The pain was the first to go, replaced by a healing pleasure that rode up my spine and caressed my mind. I could feel my flesh moving, hear my bones popping and scraping as they shifted back into alignment and fused together.

But mostly I felt the warmth of being held by a power far greater than my body. I felt myself being pulled into an endless light, and I trembled with relief and gratitude.

And then I was gone. Swept away in a blissful sleep that plucked me out of that cell, held me in a warm, tender embrace for an eternity, then set me gently down in another cell.

The cell in which I was asleep under the streets of Eden, Utah, two thousand years earlier.

22

Hillary Moses woke from the nightmare in a cold sweat. She'd kicked the covers off the bed in the night, but her skin was clammy and her shirt soaked.

Something was wrong. Terribly, terribly wrong. She knew that like she knew she'd slept late. Late, and if Simon knew, he'd have a word or two to say about it.

Simon . . . Her memories erupted like a volcano and she jerked up in bed. The scene had been seared into her mind in vivid detail, all of it.

She'd awakened in the middle of the night to get a drink — not last night, but the night before that. Simon was either in his chambers at the courthouse or sleeping in the master bedroom where he always slept. She'd been given the fourth bedroom because he didn't want to sleep with her, and that was fine with her. The less she saw of him, the better.

Her hatred of him was so ancient she'd long ago forgotten why she'd ever fallen in love with him in the first place.

Simon, the one who lorded over her with an iron fist.

Simon, the taskmaster who forbade her from making eye contact with any other man.

Simon, the monster who beat her black and blue and then had the gall to tell the others that she'd fallen down the stairs. How many times could a woman fall down the stairs anyway?

She'd always hated him — the whole town knew she hated him — but still she found the strength to be a good wife. Eden depended on her. Humanity's survival required a few sacrifices, and she'd accepted her role as one of those willing to make them. Simon was too important to betray.

That had all changed two nights ago, when Hillary heard the sound of soft laughter on her way to get a glass of water. A woman's laughter.

She'd stopped in the hallway and listened. There it was again, coming from the master bedroom. Stunned, she'd stepped to the door and put her hand on the knob, refusing to consider, much less believe, what a woman's laughter in her husband's room could mean. The sound had to be in her mind.

Which made sense, because her heart had leaped in her chest the moment she'd first seen Vlad Smith in the auditorium. The way he looked at her, the way he put Simon in his place, the way he whispered in her ear . . .

She was hearing the sounds of a woman in Simon's room because she felt guilty for having those thoughts about Vlad. So she opened the door, expecting nothing but a dark room.

The sight that greeted her didn't register at first. Two candles lit. Her husband fully dressed by the window, glass of scotch in his right hand. His other hand was behind a woman's neck, holding her close.

It was Linda Loving, the council member. Their lips were locked in a tender kiss. It was the way they were doing it — so comfortably, like a hand familiar with a well-worn glove — that told Hillary the true story. Simon and Linda's affair was as ancient as Hillary's hatred.

They both noticed her at the same time.

"What are you doing up?" Simon demanded.

"I'm . . ." She was in too much shock to put her words in order. "I'm . . ."

"I'm, I'm . . ." he mocked. "Get back to bed before I beat you deaf and dump you there myself."

She retreated and shut the door, heart crashing into her throat. The rage came then, like a dragon breathing fire. Years of hatred and abuse, breaking through, demanding justice.

Hillary hadn't been able to fall back asleep after seeing what she'd seen, so she'd gotten up in the predawn, dressed, and headed out. To nowhere or anywhere. Then to the hydroelectric plant north of town, thinking she should blow the thing sky-high, just like Vlad had threatened to do.

But no, that would be too risky. Simon would kill her.

Truth was, if she did anything at all that compromised him, he would probably kill her, if for no other reason than to keep his secret a secret.

She'd returned to the house late morning to find Peter in a frantic mess. He told her about the shooting in the sanctuary. Barth had shot Rachelle in the leg and they'd locked her in the cellar.

"Why?"

"Something to do with Vlad," he said. "Something Dad thinks could compromise Eden, but I don't get it."

Neither did Hillary. And at the time she didn't really care — she had her own problems. She retired to her room, where she'd spent the rest of the day, pacing. Simon didn't come home. He was too busy either sucking up to Linda or hunting Vlad.

Now, memories swirling, Hillary threw off the soaked sheet and hurried to the window. The day was overcast. The house was dead quiet. The only course of action that made any sense to her dropped into her mind then. Vlad. He would know what to do.

She had to find Vlad. And now she knew how: Rachelle.

For all she knew she was already too late. She had to hurry.

It took her only a few minutes to throw some clothes on, grab the spare keys, and set her resolve to do this quickly, before anybody knew what was happening. She thought about brushing her teeth and combing her hair, decided not to.

The sky was dark when she stepped outside — way too dark for ten in the morning. A quick scan of the streets and she saw no one. They were all locked down in their homes under the guise of this martial-law nonsense. Someone needed to shove that law down Simon's throat.

Hillary walked quickly, head down,

straight for the back of the courthouse/church/palace for Simon. She'd missed a button and her shirt was crooked. Maybe best to fix that before anyone noticed, but no one was going to notice because she had no intention of being seen.

She stopped ten feet from the back door, noting the cars along First Street for the first time. Dozens of them. The town was in assembly? At ten in the morning?

Images of a full sanctuary skipped through her mind. What if they were putting Rachelle on trial? Why else would they be meeting? Regardless, this was a good thing. It meant everyone would be in the main auditorium. The way to the cellar was down two flights of stairs at the back, to the right of Hillary's office.

She hurried up the steps and opened the back door with a quiver in her hand. Eased inside. No light. The backup battery bank had enough juice to light the sanctuary, but without electricity to recharge them, they'd be dead in a day or two.

Hillary listened for any sound. Nothing. Four walls between her back office and the auditorium.

Barely breathing, she grabbed a flashlight off the counter, eased into the side hall, entered the stairwell, and ran down the steps into the basement, called "the cellar" to distinguish it from any ordinary basement. Other than her, no one outside the council and the security team even knew it existed.

She found Rachelle in the first cell, curled up on the floor beyond the white steel bars. Sleeping. Relief washed over her. Still here, thank God.

With one last glance down the hall, she fumbled with the keys, tried three before landing on the one that opened the lock, and stepped into the cell.

She played the beam of light over Rachelle's body. Saw all the blood around a single hole in her jeans, four inches above her knee. And more blood on her right sleeve. Peter had said something about that. No wound, he'd said. But none of that was Hillary's concern.

"Rachelle?" She pushed on the girl's arm. "Wake up."

I woke with a gasp. "Jacob?"

"It's me, Hillary. Thank God you're alive."

Hillary? Where was I? The light moved and I saw that it was from a flashlight. Eden . . .

Hillary came into view, bent over me. She'd missed a button on her shirt, and sweat plastered her stringy hair to her forehead and cheeks. But it was her frantic eyes that alarmed me.

"What's wrong?" I asked. She was answering, but my mind was on my predicament. I was back in the cellar. From one prison to another. I'd been shot and woken in my dreams with the wound. Then healed when Jacob squeezed the fruit into my wound . . .

I looked down at my leg. Moved it. Then gingerly touched my thigh. No pain. I touched the hole in my jeans and felt my skin. Crusted blood, but no wound.

"Are you listening to me?" Hillary demanded. Her eyes skipped to my leg. "What is it?"

Whatever happened to my body in one dream also happened in the other dream. Present Earth and future Earth.

I clambered to my feet and stared down at my leg.

Hillary looked befuddled. "I thought you were shot."

"I was."

"So what happened?"

"Same thing that happened to my eyes." *Close enough,* I thought.

"Vlad?"

"No, not Vlad. Definitely not Vlad."

Hillary grabbed my arm. She glanced over

412

her shoulder and whispered, "You have to tell me how to find him! They're up there right now, and if he's not with them, that's a problem, so I gotta find him."

"Slow down." I registered her panic no more than I might notice a hand gently tugging on my shirt. Half of me was still swooning from the events in the Elyonite city. "Take a deep breath. Who's up there right now? What's happening?"

"The whole town! I can't take it anymore." She was grabbing her hair with her free hand. "Not a single second."

What had happened to her? What had transformed Hillary Moses from calm to crazed? The town was falling apart. My father . . . They'd taken him to a shed.

That tug of fear was no longer gentle.

"Okay, just take another breath." I had to find my father. "They took my father to a shed. Do you know where that is?"

She absently shook her head, pacing now.

"You hear anything about him?"

Another shake.

I breathed a prayer, hoping Barth hadn't continued to beat him. "What time is it?"

"After ten." She stopped pacing and faced me, eyes wild. "He beats me, Rachelle. He beats me and he's sleeping with that slut on

413

the council. I can't stand by anymore. I just can't."

Beating her? Was it possible? And an affair? I'd always thought of both Simon and Linda as loyal to the bone.

"Which is why you have to tell Vlad that I need him," Hillary begged, reaching for me. "You know how to get to him, right? He healed you. You're special to him, right? I don't know what else to do, please."

She thought Vlad could help her? "You don't understand, Vlad's not who you think he is. And these things you're talking about can't be —"

"Don't tell me what can and can't be!" she cried, recoiling. She shoved a finger at the wall. "I walked in on him! I saw it with my own two eyes! You have the nerve to tell me that each time he beat me these past ten years can't be what it was? You think it's all . . . what, in my mind? How dare you!"

"I'm not saying that. I just think —"

"I don't care what you think!" she snapped, stomping one foot. "You tell me how to find Vlad, you hear me? Or I'm gonna burn this whole town to the ground!"

I took a step back. There would be no reasoning with her in this state of mind. Part of me thought I should run out and lock her in the cell until she cooled down and I could figure out what was going on.

The seal on my shoulder reminded me that there was more to the world than what we saw as problems. *In this world you will have trouble, but have no fear, I have overcome . . .* Yeshua. That could only be good news if we too could overcome, with him. *In the world but not of it.* That state of being beyond polarity was far more powerful than any of us could possibly know in these earthen vessels.

I had to find the Second Seal.

What is known that cannot be named?

I took a calming breath and spoke as evenly as I could. "You say they're meeting upstairs right now?"

"I think so. Yes."

"Then that's the first place to look for him."

"But he'll be there!"

"Who? The Judge?"

"Don't call him that!" she snapped.

"Simon," I corrected. She clearly felt judged and wanted no more of it. "If Simon brought the town together, it's because of him."

"Vlad."

"Yes, Vlad."

"So what do we do?"

"We go up there."

"Now?"

"Right now."

"I don't know if I can take seeing that pig."

The shift in Hillary's demeanor was so radical that I wondered who'd stolen her mind. Planks of judgment and grievance blinded the world, yes, but this? She was hardly the same person.

What was Simon hiding in that room of his?

"I'll be with you," I said. "You can't hide forever. One way or the other, we'll get to the bottom of this, I promise."

"I'm already at the bottom of it. As low as any woman can go."

"Which is why I'm going with you." I stepped up and took her free hand. "I'll be right there with you. Okay?"

Hillary considered my suggestion for a second, then nodded.

"Okay. Okay, good. Just stay close to me. Promise?"

Another nod.

I led her from the cell, down the hall, and into the stairwell. I used echolocation to guide my way up the metal steps because she had the flashlight trained on her feet, two steps behind me. By the time we reached the side door leading into the sanctuary, I'd all but let go of my concern for Hillary.

My thoughts had returned to the seals. And to my father. And to Vlad. And to finding out what was wrong in Eden.

I could hear Hillary's heavy breathing right behind me as I paused at the door and listened.

"Can you hear him?"

Simon's voice spoke over a cacophony of voices, urging calm. Whatever had happened, he was losing control.

I pushed the door open and stepped into the sanctuary.

We were on the east side of the room, to the right of the platform, which was obstructed by the long velvet curtains that hung ceiling to floor on either side of the stage. I couldn't see who was on stage.

What I could see were the other residents. Cindy and Bill. Jarvis, the gardener. William Braxton and his wife closest to me, eyes glued on the stage. All of them.

Half were on their feet and in the aisles, a far cry from the order typically required of Eden's gatherings. A full third of them were talking at once.

"I don't care what the law is!" Cindy was saying. "As far as I'm concerned, until you find Eden's children, there *are* no laws! And if you think you can just shoot me like you

417

shot Miranda, be my guest."

A chill washed down my back. The children? Marcella, Frankie . . . I could see seven or eight younger children from my vantage point. How many were missing?

The room erupted and Simon slammed his gavel down on the block. "Order! For the sake of all that is lawful and godly, *order*!"

"What good is the law if it can't protect our children?" someone shouted.

"We called you here to organize a search." Linda Loving was begging for reason, but her voice was filled with fear. "We can sort out how this happened as soon as we find them. Don't you think I know how you feel? Jordan and Holly are . . ." She burst into tears.

The calm lasted only a few seconds. "So what are we waiting for?" Bill Baxter said from across the auditorium. "I agree with Cindy. We all have a right to search."

"When are you going to get this through your thick skulls?" Barth boomed from the stage. "There's a predator out there. We can't have all of you running through the woods going berserk. Only handpicked members I know I can trust."

He tried to say more but his voice was drowned out by another outburst.

And that outburst was silenced by the loud crack of his gun, fired into the ceiling. I could hear the drywall rain down in the silence following his gunshot. He slapped his gun down on the bench.

"Order means order. You see the gun. One more of you gets out of order and I swear, I put a bullet through your head. Understood?"

I walked into full view then.

Sue, seated next to RG, was the first to see me and her eyes went wide. Then Peter, who glanced at my leg and blinked. Carina, Hillary's seven-year-old daughter, wasn't in the pew next to him . . . She was among the missing children?

Hillary stepped out with me, eyes fixed on the stage. Two, and then a dozen, and then all of them turned to look in our direction.

The sight of me with bloodied shirt and jeans, and Hillary with scrambled hair and crooked shirt, held them in silence. I was watching Barth, whose face had gone white.

"How'd you get out of the prison?"

"I let her out," Hillary said. "Vlad healed her leg."

Barth reached for his gun, but Simon stopped him.

"Leave it, Barth. Just calm down. Everyone just stay calm!"

"What prison?" someone asked.

Then another, "Who shot you?"

The room was a powder keg. Vlad was having his way. They had to understand that I wasn't their enemy. The council was. Vlad was. The whole system was.

I walked across the front, speaking with as strong a voice as I could gather. "It doesn't matter what prison or who shot me. But I can see, can't I? My eyes are healed and my leg is healed. So maybe I'm someone you should listen to."

I could practically see the wheels spinning behind their eyes.

"How many children are missing?"

"Seven," someone said.

"Okay. Seven." I knew there was no way to find them quickly — not if this was Vlad's doing. I would be the key, and the thought of that nauseated me. "And how many of us here? A hundred and fifty? The valley is roughly two square miles, right?"

" 'Bout that," Bill said, nodding at me.

"Frank, Luke," Barth barked. "Grab her by the collar and take her down."

I turned to the stage with the intent of discouraging both Frank and Luke from following his orders, but the sight of Hillary stopped me cold. Barth's glare was on me, otherwise he might have been able to stop her. Using the distraction, Hillary had climbed the steps to the platform, grabbed Barth's gun, and was now marching up to Simon, pistol leveled at his head.

"You sick, lying piece of garbage!"

Simon staggered back, face drawn in shock, both hands raised shoulder high. "Honey . . . What are you doing?"

I realized then that Vlad had somehow modified her memories. Organism was algorithm and he'd changed hers. It was the only explanation.

"No, Hillary!" I yelled. "It's not what you think!"

"This man," she shouted, face beet red, "has been beating me and cheating on me with that whore Linda Loving for years."

"That's not true!" Linda cried.

"As the good judge said, you live by the sword, you die by the sword."

"No, Hillary!" I leaped onto the stage and was halfway to Hillary when the gun discharged with a loud boom. The bullet punched a hole the size of a penny through Simon's forehead and snapped his head back. His huge body crumpled and landed on the platform with a loud thump.

"An eye for an eye," Hillary rasped. "Meet your maker, you sick bastard."

Her action was so unexpected, so ruthless, that it caught even Barth flat-footed.

Peter staggered forward from the first row and slowly sank to his knees. "Dad?"

Jaw set, Hillary tossed the gun on the floor and faced her audience. "If you'd suffered what I have, every single one of you would have done the same," she said.

Peter hung his head and began to softly sob.

A solitary clap from the back of the room cut through the silence. Then another and another.

"Nicely done."

Vlad stood at the back of the sanctuary, grinning, with my father at his side. My father's shirt was torn and bloody, his hair was matted to his scalp, and his eyes were full moons.

"I am so proud of you, my darling," Vlad said. "Finally, a tissue-top with the backbone to stand up to the true monsters in this room."

23

Vlad gave my father a shove. "Join the rest, my friend."

My father stumbled forward, grabbed a pew for support, then stood to the side, looking dazed. But he was alive. And from what I could see, no worse off than when they'd hauled him off to the shed. Vlad had collected him. And done what to him?

"The only problem," Vlad said, shoving a hand into his pocket, "is that dear Simon never did beat Hillary. Not once. Nor did he have this little tryst, though I wouldn't blame him. Linda is a fine-looking tissue-top by any standard."

Hillary tried to say something but could only stammer.

"Shut up and stay put, Hillary." Vlad looked over the residents, wearing that twisted grin. "You see what happens when even one of you disobeys the law?" He was speaking about me. "The only one here who has any sense is Barth. And maybe David."

My father was scowling at Barth. I doubted there were any kind thoughts in his head.

Vlad held up a finger and drilled me with those deep eyes. "I invited one girl to write in the book, but she refused that invitation. God's law, which is now my law, is perfectly clear: accept the invitation or pay the price. So now you all get to pay the price."

Linda Loving stepped up to the bench, face set. "What have you done with my children?"

"I have no idea what happened to your precious little pumpkin rolls, Linda. Ask God. He shares in your problem, surely."

"Stop it with all your crazy talk!" Linda snapped. "God would slaughter a thousand heathens to protect even one of these!" She jabbed her finger at the floor. "Just one of them! Now you tell me where Jordan and Holly are!"

Vlad smiled. "That's a good girl. Feel the problem. Let righteous indignation fuel your fear, in the same way God fears for you."

Talya's voice whispered through my mind. *Against the Fifth Seal there is no defense.* I didn't have the fifth, or the fourth, or the third, or the second. But I did have the First Seal.

"You're wrong," I said, stepping up to the podium. My hands were clammy and my heart was racing. "God doesn't have a problem. You know that as well as I do."

The moment I said it, I knew that he did know.

Vlad lowered his chin. "Is that so?"

I could feel heat from the tattoo on my shoulder. The fog in my mind lifted.

"Neither does Justin. We're just not seeing what he sees."

He went perfectly still at my use of Justin's name, grin affixed to his jaw as if made of plaster. There was a quiver in his fingers. I could see it from all the way across the room.

After a long pause, Vlad lowered his head and stepped to his right.

"Very well, let's go with that. Because the little girl who was blind but can now see is right about one thing. Nothing is what it seems in this world, and that includes Eden." He faced the audience, feet planted wide at the back of the center aisle. "Sit down. All of you. The truth is going to get a little rough."

Half were already seated, and the rest looked around before joining them, including my father, who eased into the last pew. I stayed where I was, facing Vlad squarely.

"You too, Linda," he said. "Barth. Hillary. Sit."

Barth pulled out one of the bench chairs and sat. Hillary too, behind him in one of the side seats.

"Let's start with what year it is. You all think it's June 2018. But you're wrong. The date is actually September 21, 2038."

His words echoed through the auditorium. Not a soul moved. On its face, the claim sounded preposterous, but I wasn't so sure.

Bill Baxter was the first to find a voice. "That's completely absurd. Why are you doing this to us?"

"You mean telling you the truth? Because it now facilitates my own survival. Bill, is it? Bill Baxter. Stand up, Bill."

Bill slowly stood.

"Let me ask you a question, Bill. When was the last time you left this stink hole?"

"You mean Eden?"

"Of course I mean Eden. When?"

Bill hesitated. "Never."

"And why is that?"

"Well . . . it's not permitted."

"Really. How convenient. So no one here has actually ever left the valley, is that right?"

"We've separated ourselves from the world for good reason. There's no reason to leave Eden. Everything we need comes in."

"So you live in a kind of test tube, protected from the world," Vlad said. "And what memory do you have of your life before you came to this valley?"

Bill looked down at Cindy seated beside him. His eyes drifted off her as he tried to recall. "It was a long time ago . . ." He stalled for a second. "It's a bit fuzzy but —"

"Sit down, Bill."

He sat and Vlad nodded at the platform. "Let's try something more recent. Stand up, Hillary. Step up to the bench so we can all see how beautiful you are today."

The pieces were falling into place, but I was too stunned to accept that they were forming the picture I saw. I kept telling myself Vlad was only manipulating us, and by us I meant me. But there was nothing in his tone or demeanor that betrayed the slightest hint of deception.

Hillary was at the bench, shaking.

"How many times did the man you killed beat you, Hillary? Tell them."

She looked as frightened as a mouse. "Hundreds."

"You remember each time like it was yesterday, don't you?"

"Yes."

"And how long have you hated that lying piece of garbage who beat you?"

"I've always hated him."

"Ever call him honey? You know, a term of endearment one might say with a smile to make sure their beloved believes them."

"Honey? I would never call him honey."

Vlad scanned the room. "But the rest of you know that's not true, don't you? Hillary used that particular term of endearment every day, didn't she?"

We all knew that Hillary doted over Simon and that *honey* was what she called him. But she seemed to have no recollection of using the term.

"Memory is a strange thing," Vlad said. "Do you know" — he cocked his head — "that under normal circumstances, a full half of what the average human remembers is radically distorted within a couple of years? Scientific fact."

True. My father had shown me the studies years ago. He wanted me to forget that I was blind. See if my mind could self-correct.

"The only problem is, even knowing this, humans can't bring themselves to doubt their own memories, because it's all they have. For all practical purposes, humans are their memories. You're a mother, a lover, a victim, a writer, a farmer, because you remember being one. But if someone was to figure out how to reformat that hard drive up there" — he tapped the head of the person seated closest to him — "who would you wake up to be? You would have no identity. A human being can't function without an identity, so you cling to the one you remember."

He paced, head lowered.

"But what if someone figured out how to both reformat the hard drive up there *and* reprogram it with a new identity, complete with new memories? Then they would wake up and be someone else, wouldn't they?"

No one spoke.

"Wouldn't they?" he repeated. "You would think good Christians like yourself would know this. Isn't this at least half of what your Jesus fellow taught? Unless you die to the old self, take up the cross, all of that, you can't be who you are in the kingdom. Unless you let go of your attachments to earthly father, children, wife, husband — even your identity of self — you can't be the new you in new wineskin. Let go of the old wineskin. Be transformed by the renewing of your mind, and so on and so forth. Sunday school basics, yes?"

He was using teachings Talya might use, perhaps to confuse me and plant doubt. Even the Shadow of Death knew how the universe worked, because those teachings were true. But the residents of Eden didn't know the meaning of those teachings like I now did, and they were too dumbstruck to respond.

"Has anyone ever wondered why the health of residents in this sinkhole is off-the-charts good? Except for a few poor souls like Betsy and Robert and a handful of others who were tinkered with. Turns out when you take away a person's memory of, say, an allergy, the symptoms stop manifesting. And vice versa. Do you know why?"

"Epigenetics," my father said. "Placebo."

"Exactly. Beliefs affect neural activity. What goes in, comes out. We are all products of our programming. You believe what you were taught to believe, and that expresses itself in your body. That's the way it works in the world of polarity, and by polarity I mean lower nature. Flesh. Form. It's the way the neural synapses in your brains work. Someone please give me a yes, so I don't think you're all idiots."

"It's true."

Vlad jabbed his forefinger at my father. "Thank you, David. And David should know. What David doesn't know is that he, along with everyone not born in this valley, agreed eighteen years ago to have their memories modified. And many of them have had their memories modified again and again since then."

"You're saying . . ." Hillary looked at Simon's body bleeding on the floor. Then back up. "That my memories are wrong?"

Vlad hit an imaginary button in the air. "Bingo! Bingo, bingo! Amazing what a few memories can do. Your turn's up, darling, so please take your seat."

She did, but Betsy was on her feet, glaring. "What do you mean a few poor souls like me were tinkered with?"

"I'm saying all your memories of childhood nastiness are just made up, sweetheart."

She looked dumbfounded. "Why?"

"Why! That's the question of the day. Why did you all agree to be a part of Eden? There's no question that you are, but why? And how?"

He began to pace again like a professor delivering a lecture.

"Was it a carefully planned and executed trial conducted by DARPA? Or was it a matter of human survival? I could tell you almost anything at this point, and you wouldn't know if it was true because you've all had your memories modified."

"I don't buy it," RG said, standing. "It would be way too difficult to pull off. There's no way to hide this valley from the world! What about the sky? It would be impossible to isolate us."

"Impossible? Give me five minutes and I'll heal your delusion. I'm going to give you one story of why and how you're here. You can believe me or not, it really doesn't matter. But one thing you won't deny is that you *are* here, in a bubble, lost to the world and to yourselves."

RG sat back down, unsatisfied, judging by the look on his face.

"Several years before Eden came to be, a splinter group of Isis long thought to have gone underground detonated three nuclear weapons on the same day, one in Moscow, one in Beijing, and one in New York City. I could thrill you with all the details, how those dominoes knocked over a hundred more in the months that followed, but suffice it to say that the fallout soon killed all but twenty-eight million people. Most of those died over the next decade. The day that first nuclear weapon was detonated, DARPA began construction of twelve safe havens, all controlled and monitored from one hub in Salt Lake."

DARPA. Defense Advanced Research Projects Agency. My father and I had often discussed the advancements the governmental agency had made, dating all the way back to the early nineteen hundreds. Though they were best known for advancements like the internet and stealth technology, their greatest achievements were in fringe technologies that slowly made their way into the public sector.

"Like arks, these havens were designed to be completely self-sufficient and self-sustaining. Massive resources went into the project with extensions in Japan, China, Germany, Russia, and Brazil, where another forty-two havens were constructed. Three years later, they populated each haven with between fifty and two hundred carefully screened volunteers. But survival isn't just a matter of biomechanics."

Vlad spread his arms wide.

"And that, my friends, is where you come in. Eden. Because you see, with so much at stake, they had to try more than one approach. It does humanity no good to have the perfect house if the family is always fighting, does it? No. Of some concern to DARPA was that the inhabitants, no matter how well screened, would still bring with them all their psychological baggage. Jealousy, fear, and hopelessness can be just as destructive as nuclear fallout. So they took a rather extreme approach to Eden. Do you see where this is leading us?"

"What about the children?" Linda asked.

"Please keep your mouth shut and let me finish, Linda. I'm almost done."

"But . . ." She glanced around, looking for support, but received none.

I wanted to hear it. All of it.

"Extreme, I say," Vlad continued, "and risky, because DARPA decided to use a relatively new form of genetic engineering — a technology first discovered in 2020 that could isolate and eliminate memories throughout the neural pathways, then imprint the subject's mind with new memories. In this way they could both influence the community and study the effects of memories on a person's behavior and survivability. They chose to do so in Eden based on a strict set of religious laws. Why religious laws? Because there is no fear greater than a religious fear of consequence. Manipulation becomes much easier. Follow?"

"You —"

"Shut up, Linda." He continued without missing a beat. "The residents of Eden would have no memory of any conflict with each other and would think they were living in a paradise of sorts while the rest of the world was sprinting headfirst to a nasty end. They had their hope and would be controlled by the fear of breaking any law that might compromise that hope. This, my friends, is the state in which you have lived for so long."

Now he gave us a pause.

"They needed someone on the inside, naturally. Simon knew everything from the beginning. Eden really was his town. Now it's mine, because I took the liberty of cutting off this valley from the controllers. I have activated explosives that will detonate if anyone tries to enter or exit this valley. You're all stuck here, period. Now . . . Questions."

His mention of the explosives might have caused a ruckus if not for the staggering implications of the rest.

"What about my wife?" my father asked, rising to his feet.

"She was exterminated because her mind wouldn't cooperate with the programming. Neither would your daughter's, but that's another story. Next question."

"You expect me to believe that my memories —"

"Are reformatted and manipulated in a

435

facility just beyond the tunnel. It's a rather complex procedure that takes a good six hours. Technicians from the main control center in Colorado rotate in every six months. Four days ago I took the liberty of killing the last two stationed here, then I rigged the entrance with explosives. No one, including the controllers, can get in; no one, meaning you, can get out. Eden is now cut off from the outside world in every way. I'm quite sure the controllers have been pulling their hair out these last few days."

The claim was too much to grasp, even for me. I tried to imagine being hooked up to electrodes and having my brain reformatted. I knew from my father that erasing and implanting memories had been accomplished in mice and monkeys since 2011 and would be possible with humans one day, but so soon?

Then again, if Vlad was right, it was 2038.

He could clearly see that his assertions weren't penetrating.

"If you still doubt me, just take a good look at Hillary and the slab of meat who used to be Simon. I took her up the mountain in the wee hours yesterday morning, hooked her up, and imprinted her brain with a few memories that suited my purposes. Unfortunately, the controllers have since managed to kill the entire system, so Hillary will be the last."

He eyed me standing at the podium and stayed in the aisle. "Get this through your skulls: beyond the exit tunnel, you'll see nothing but pure hell, a wasteland ravaged by nuclear fallout."

"That can't be right," Maxwell Emerson stammered. "I was on the phone with Salt Lake organizing our holdings just before the terrorists took down the grid —"

"Are you deaf? There *was* no grid failure out there. The terrorist attacks that have you all up in arms were only false information fed to you by the controllers to keep Eden focused. Second to religious fear, there's nothing as effective as an outside threat to create and maintain solidarity among tissue-tops."

"We communicate with the outside world all the time!" Linda objected. "And television . . . Surely you aren't suggesting that none of that is real."

"It's real to you. All external communication functions as part of numerous algorithms and a few controllers who've taken your calls and played their parts. No one in this valley has watched a movie made after 2018 because none have been made. Same for books, music, and news. It's all AI. Every bit and byte of the external world."

My brain hurt. Panic lapped at my mind. The thought that everything I'd believed to be true about this world was only half true felt like a terrible betrayal to me. How could I possibly believe what he was telling us?

"Other than specialized equipment needed, all vehicles and appliances predate 2018, not because Simon had a thing for modest living, but to maintain the illusion. Should I go on?"

"Why hasn't the fallout affected this valley?" my father pressed. "And what about the planes that fly over?"

"The fallout hasn't wiped you out because you live in a protected bubble. As for the planes, no one has ever actually seen a plane fly over, only contrails high above. They're part of a sky that isn't really there."

Vlad scanned the room.

"So hard to swallow, even after watching Hillary's little demonstration. So I've prepared another. Follow me outside. It's time for show-and-tell."

With that Vlad Smith turned and walked out of the church.

The cacophony of a hundred incredulous voices exchanging frantic questions filled the room the moment he was gone. But they hurried from the pews and followed like a herd of sheep after their shepherd.

I was the last to leave. My father waited for me by the pew. His eyes were wide, but the dazed look was gone. He looked at my leg.

"Is this real?" I asked. "It's 2038?"

"I don't know. I . . ." He shook his head.

"But is it possible? I mean, the technology?"

He pushed through the outer door, frowning. "What he said about your mother . . ." He ground his molars. "I always knew there was something wrong."

He wasn't thinking straight. We'd just learned that our whole world was upside down, and he was fixated on an old grievance.

He wasn't done. "Give me one chance and I swear . . ."

I held my hand out and stopped my father on the top step. Vlad stood on the edge of the fountain pool, arms crossed as the town hovered around. I looked at the cliffs, the trees, the sky above us, now overcast and gray, trying to imagine that we were in a haven protected from a world that had been destroyed by the fallout of nuclear detonations.

Where did this leave me? And the seals? He'd said that my mother and I were special. If his only objective was getting me to write in the book, why was he doing this?

"Do you see that sky above you?" Vlad cried out.

We all looked up.

"What do you see?"

Clouds, I thought.

The world suddenly went dark. And I mean pitch-black, because there was no power in Eden and now there was no sky, a fact that drew a chorus of exclamations.

"That is your sky," Vlad's voice rang out. "No? You don't like it? Then how about this?"

The dark sky was replaced by a blue sky with a hot, blazing sun.

"You prefer light? Do you think that ball of fire up there looks like a real sun? It doesn't, in truth, but this is the only sun you know."

The moment I saw that sky, I knew he was telling the truth. I too had seen a real sky, high above the deserts and mountains of Other Earth. I'd assumed the difference in hue was caused by elevation, or distortions in the atmosphere, or perhaps by the shifting of my perceptions from one world to another.

"That's not your sky."

Immediately the darkness above was lit by

a thousand tiny points of light, connected by a grid of long, thin cables or rods of some kind.

"That, my friends, is your real sky. A three-inch thick, three-dimensional matrix of ingenuity stretched over this valley and the three hundred meters beyond. Here is your sky, your surprisingly rare rain and snow — everything but lightning. Its base is constructed of carbyne fibers, a material forty times stronger than diamonds. The electronics above your heads is advanced enough to pop your brains. Impressed?"

Silence.

"What's lightning?" someone asked.

"Something no one in this valley remembers."

The grid above us vanished and the overcast sky was back.

"Better?"

Vlad was holding a device the size of an iPhone between his fingers.

"How do we know what's really out there, past the tunnel?" RG asked.

"You don't. That wasteland awaiting you could be a fabrication. But you'll never know because if you try to leave this valley, you'll pay for it with your life either way. Dare you find out? At least it's safe in here, assuming you play along."

"God help us . . ."

I don't know who said it, but they reflected the sentiment of every last soul in Eden, Utah, in that moment.

"Indeed," Vlad said. "I really am your god. And you, my pathetic tissue-tops, are at my mercy. As of now, the only law that remains in Eden is God's original and only true law: an eye for an eye. If you don't give me an eye for an eye I'm gonna blind all of you. I'm gonna gouge out every single eye in this stink hole and feed your pearls to the swine."

I cringed at his comment about blinding. But if his objective was only to manipulate me, why would such a brilliant adversary continue to mess with the others? He knew there was no way I would ever write him into the book, regardless of what he did.

So then what?

He pointed at the council, who stood together at the perimeter. "Barth!"

The confident bulldog of a man hesitated, mouth parted in shock. "Yeah?"

"Simon is dead. You're in charge. And I want you to execute your charge now. How do you classify murder?"

They were all looking at him. "It's a capital crime."

"Punishable by?"

"Death," Barth said.

"Is that why you killed David's wife? Because she threatened to kill us all?"

Barth blinked. "Yes."

"An eye for an eye?"

"An eye for an eye."

"Good. That's what I told David. Now, please do your duty and kill who needs killing today."

Barth reached down to his ankle, pulled out a gun, turned to Hillary, and shot her in the heart before she could react.

"Good boy," Vlad said. He turned his eyes to me. "Lights out, little girl."

The world went black again. All but one remained in stunned silence. That one was Peter, weeping. I couldn't imagine the pain of losing both mother and father as he had. His sister, Carina, was missing . . . My heart broke for him.

When the sky came back on, Vlad was gone.

But his threat still hung in the air. *Lights out, little girl.*

He was going to blind me.

24

DARPA

Steve Collingsworth's mind tripped back to the administrative meeting earlier that morning.

"I still see waiting as our only reasonable alternative," Bill Hammond, the project leader, had said. His eyes scanned the other six seated around the conference table. "We have to accept the fact that everything we've built could collapse."

Steve had waited for someone else to say what he was thinking — the director perhaps, Theresa Williams, seated at the far end, watching them with hands folded in her lap. But no one did. They'd already stretched ethical boundaries to their breaking point. After so many years, most in the room had long ago set aside their personal convictions for the good of the project. As had he, for the most part.

But this . . .

Steve cleared his throat. "Am I the only one seeing the risks of sitting on this? We've had our share of fortune as it is, but maybe it's time we come clean."

"Our success has nothing to do with fortune," Hammond said, staring him down. "Unless you consider hard-won science from the best minds in the world a matter of mere fortune."

"I'm not talking about the science or the technology. All I'm suggesting is that we reconsider the downside of covering up."

"We've spent the last three days thinking that through and come up empty-handed. Unless you have something new to share with us."

Theresa Williams pushed her chair back, walked to the window, and stared at the desert vista that extended to distant mountains. When she spoke, her words were soft and deliberate.

"As of now, this is still an internal matter. Find a way. I don't care what it takes, find a way to shut him down." She'd faced them all. "Find a way, people, because if he's not bluffing . . . God help us all."

Now, just a few hours later, Steve sat with Walter Hitchman, desperate for a fresh, unbiased view. They'd faced hundreds of technical challenges over the past two decades — untold thousands leading up to the establishment of Eden — but never had they faced the imminent collapse of the entire habitat.

I don't care what it takes, find a way, the director had said. So Steve was, in spite of the protective order that limited details of the incursion to top-level engineers.

"You're sure he's accessed the detonation fail-safe?" Walter asked, leaning back in a swivel chair. "It would take some incredible savvy to break into —"

"And rigged all the exits," Steve interrupted, aware of his sharp tone. "It was the first thing he did. Before severing all lines of communication. And the fact that he was able to operate the memory module before we pulled the plug demonstrates his savvy. This guy's no amateur."

"He knew how to operate the MEP? Who is this guy?"

MEP was a designator for the Memory Editing Protocol used to modify a human brain's memory patterns.

"No one knows, but he's got the administrators running for cover. Hammond's already covering his tracks."

"What about the director?"

"Blindsided. It's not every day mankind's great hope for survival gets thrown under the bus. Even if we figure out how to get out of this mess, heads are gonna roll."

"And all this from one man who found his way in."

Steve shook his head. "He's not just any man. Whoever he is, he knows things he has no business knowing."

"Someone on the inside, then?"

A drop of sweat from Steve's forehead fell and darkened the blueprints he'd spread out on the table. The agency had been locked down for the last three days. Every viable resource had been retasked to finding a solution for Eden.

"It doesn't matter how he got in. The fact is, he's cut us off and taken full control. There has to be another way to get in there without collapsing the seal." Steve slapped the table. "Come on, man. Out of the box. You helped design the thing."

"A thousand engineers helped design it," Walter said.

"Yeah, well, I can't trust a thousand engineers. Most of them didn't even know what they were building."

"Okay," Walter said, spinning in his chair to face a console. An electronic version of the blueprints on the table slowly rotated on his screen, showing the extremities of the sinkhole and its carbyne seal. A few taps on the sensor pad and the architectural drawings shifted to show deeper levels, all the way down to the huge atmospheric conditioners located below the northern cliff.

Walter quickly zoomed back out. "Okay, let's start at the top again. The seal itself is impossible to breach without collapsing the sky — that's what the hatches are for. But you said they're rigged."

"Correct."

"The control facility and all three lower tunnels are also rigged?"

"Everything. We've had a team all over that mountain with sniffers. Explosives everywhere. Forget the entrances. I'm talking about finding a way in that hasn't been conceived of. A way that would escape his notice. Under, through, over . . ."

Steve ran his hand through tangled hair. His brain was fried — twenty-two hours since he'd slept.

"We could haul a digger over there," Walter said. "Low tech. But it would take a week to penetrate the west wall without explosives, and explosives would compromise —"

"No explosives. What about under?"

"Same thing." Walter turned in his chair. "What if we used the purifier vents to release a gas into the valley?"

Steve shook his head. "Unless you can come up with a gas that puts them all out — including Smith — for a week while we tunnel under."

"Blow a hatch before he wakes, then."

"Like I said, blow any of the hatches and we might trigger the emergency protocol."

Walter crossed his arms. "Actually, you didn't say *that.*"

"Well, it's obvious, isn't it? You don't think he would know that? One false move and the whole thing comes down."

Walter leaned forward. "Look, I don't know what you expect me to find that a hundred other engineers haven't, but —"

"You helped figure out how to make this thing, right?" Steve snapped. "So figure out how to unmake it!"

"And if no one can?"

Steve slowly exhaled, eyes on the white wall. For a few long seconds he just stared, mind lost in a thousand dead ends.

"Two more days. If we haven't figured this out by then, I'm going to blow the whistle. The rest of the world has a right to know. Our great white hope is about to go down in flames."

"They'll crucify you."

Steve gave Walter a hard look. "We're dead already."

25

I might say that chaos clawed at the fabric of Eden that morning, when we all learned we lived in a sanctuary created by DARPA in the aftermath of a nuclear war, and our identities had been manipulated through altered memories. All but mine, if Vlad was telling the truth about my brain not taking to the programming. But in truth, he'd started weaving chaos into our fabric the moment he set foot in the hospital with the Book of History days earlier.

All of this to manipulate me. All of it because I was the 49th in another world.

Why?

Lights out, little girl . . .

Within minutes of Vlad's vanishing act, the residents began to unravel. It's hard to explain how the human psyche reacts to the discovery that everything it thought of as true is only a lie. Like a balloon cut free to float away into space, it drifts, lost. In that space, up and down mean nothing, nor do true and false. All bets are off. Familiar laws feel like relative abstractions made up for the benefit of those in power.

Vlad had made it clear: Barth was now the law. Problem was, Barth's tethers to reality had been severed along with ours. Apart from that simple edict, an eye for an eye, I don't think he had any clue how to fulfill his role.

"How do we know he's telling the truth?" Betsy Williamson demanded. "He's saying that my memories of being abandoned as a child are implanted? That all this trauma I've suffered for all these years is based on a lie I believed? My rashes and stomach problems are the result of a false memory?"

The implications of that one question brought a disturbing stillness to the crowd.

RG spoke up. "We shouldn't jump to any conclusions."

"But you saw it! The sky —"

"Yeah, I get it," he snapped. "We live in a bubble as part of an experiment, but that doesn't mean there was a nuclear war or that there aren't people out there right now coming to save us."

"If there were, don't you think they would have come by now?" Barth shot back. "No one's coming because Smith's right."

452

Voices erupted, some with questions, others in protest.

"Okay, shut it down!" Barth stepped up on the wall around the fountain pool, flanked by four of his men, all armed. "Until I figure out what's going on, no one leaves their house. I don't care what you think you need to do — if I see anyone on the streets, they get a bullet. The first will be in your leg. If that doesn't wake you up, the second one goes in your head." He waved his gun about, compensating for his own insecurity. "You hear me?"

"We have to find —"

"Did I give you permission to open your piehole?" he yelled at Martha, who was undoubtedly torn between the news she lived in a nuclear wasteland and the disappearance of her only child, a seven-year-old boy named Buck. "We find the children when I say we find them and not a second sooner."

"Oh please, Barth!" Linda snapped. "If you actually believe that crook, you don't even know who you are! Your brain was wiped as clean as ours! So who are you to tell —"

He fired his gun into the air. "One more word. Just give me an excuse."

Linda glared at him, face red. Apart from

the parents who'd lost their children, and Peter, who'd lost his mother and father, the rest were staring either at Barth or at the sky, still trying to figure out what to believe.

"Now, get!" He motioned with his gun. "Home! All of you!"

Though my father and I started walking in that direction, I had no intention to "get." The moment we cleared the first houses, I grabbed my father's hand and cut west, across the back lawns.

"Where are you going?"

"The tunnel," I said. "We have to see for ourselves."

The moment I suggested it, my father took over, striding ahead of me with purpose, as if he just remembered that going to the tunnel was exactly what he'd planned himself. Together we took the long trek up the road, keeping trees between us and the town center.

My father walked fast, fixated on reaching the tunnel. I asked him what he thought about Vlad's claims, but he shut me down with "not now."

Vlad had said that my mind wouldn't accept their programming, but the idea that DARPA had successfully manipulated the memories of everyone else was scrambling my brain well enough. Even some of the

454

children had been manipulated. Was it true? You'd think that knowing the sky wasn't a real sky would make it obvious, but every time I looked up, I only saw what I'd always seen. The sky.

My thoughts ran in circles, searching for a hopeful course of action, but I couldn't grab any thread of reason that made sense to me, so I recounted what Justin and Talya had told me.

One, I was the 49th Mystic, destined to bring crises that would divide. Truth from untruth. Love from fear. Not only here but far beyond Eden. However crazy that had first sounded, it was now sounding less so.

Two, if I succeeded, the lion would lie down with the lamb. Peace would reign.

Three, I could only succeed by discovering all Five Seals of Truth before the Realm of Mystics was destroyed. I didn't know when that was, but I did know that finding the seals was my personal journey, like ninja training on the job. I couldn't lead the world beyond fear unless I found the way past my own. The thought made my head spin.

Four, if I understood what Talya had said, I would need the first three seals before I could help Eden.

I'd only found one and Eden was falling apart. It all sounded a bit impossible.

What is known that cannot be named? Me, of course. But that wasn't helping. *What is known that cannot be named?* No matter how many times the finger tried to point my thoughts to the answer, no answer came.

It had to be noon by the time we reached the tunnel, but time was now totally relative, because we kept time by the sun, and according to Vlad, the sun wasn't real. For all we knew, it was midnight beyond the valley.

We stood at the entrance and stared into the darkness. Dim light lit the far side a hundred yards ahead, like an eye daring us to come and see what was really there. The tunnel gates were open.

"What do you think we'll find?" I asked.

"Exactly what he said we'd find. Vlad doesn't lie."

I glanced up at my father. Saw his hard glare. Something in him had changed, and I wondered what Vlad had said or done to him in the shed.

I followed him into the dark tunnel. The sound of our feet padding on the asphalt echoed through the chamber. We were past the halfway point when I stopped, taken aback by the sight beyond the open tunnel.

For a moment I thought I was looking into my dreams. The trees that had always been there, beyond our valley, were gone. All I could see now were barren, rocky hills.

"Dad?"

"Keep walking." He marched on, undeterred.

Without so much as a glance at me, he continued out of the tunnel and up to the guardrail, where he stopped, staring at the stark vista.

Pine trees and shrubs extended out for a quarter mile before abruptly ending at a transparent barrier that arched up and over the cliff behind us. Like a dome.

Beyond that dome, the real world lay before us, desolate and dead. Vlad's wastelands.

The asphalt road and guardrail continued another fifty yards before winding to the right and vanishing behind the mountain.

We stood side by side, staring in silence.

"So he was right," I finally said.

Without answering, my father started walking again. I followed him to the bend in the road. Here we could see the road end at a two-story building made of white concrete. No windows, no pitched roof, just a flat, square building built into the transparent dome. At its center, two large steel doors were shut.

Somewhere in that gatehouse was a control room and a facility where memories were wiped clean. If Vlad was right about the sky and the wasteland, he had to be right about everything.

My breaths came in long pulls as I thought of the poisoned air beyond the protective barrier that shielded Eden from the fallout.

Above us: a false sky, now overcast. Ahead: a treed valley that ended at the transparent barrier. Beyond that barrier: desolate death. My palms were wet with sweat.

"I've got two days to kill him," my father said, eyes fixed on the wasteland.

The bitter resolve in his tone surprised me.

"This is it," he continued. "This is the end."

"Kill who?"

"The man who murdered your mother."

Barth. An eye for an eye. But to what end? If my father really meant to find his own justice by murdering the man who'd killed my mother, he would be as guilty as Barth. More, Barth wasn't either stupid or alone. The last thing we needed now was a full-scale civil war.

"You really think that's wise?"

"It's all that matters now," he said, turning back.

"All that matters now is surviving." I hurried to stay with his stride. "You have to hear me out, Dad. Barth isn't the enemy."

"No? And who is? My own mind?"

Yes, I thought. *Yes!* But I knew that wouldn't help him because he was locked in that mind.

"Vlad's the enemy."

My father spun back. "Vlad Smith is the only man in this valley who can save us, don't you see that?"

"Save us? Only DARPA can save us!"

He stepped toward me, jaw set. "The controllers? The controllers, whoever they really are, were working with Simon. Simon, who ordered Barth to kill your mother." He swept his hand at the barren land beyond Eden. "Look at it! Everything we thought was true is half a lie. Everything!"

Yes, but I was thinking about far more than just the town of Eden.

My father continued. "They stole me from me and made me this," he said, stabbing at his head to indicate his brain. "And now *this* is going to fix what they broke, starting with Barth and anyone who gets in my way."

"Nothing gives you the right to murder someone."

"An eye for an eye isn't murder. And as long as Barth's alive, he poses a threat to whatever life we can rebuild on this godforsaken planet."

"That's what Vlad told you when he found you in the shed? He's playing you and Barth against each other, don't you see that?"

He hesitated, then brushed my question aside. "The only way to keep you safe is to end the threats against you. That means ending Barth, not Smith. Smith needs you alive, you said it yourself. Barth, on the other hand, wants us both dead."

Vlad had done something to him — maybe the same thing he'd done to Hillary, even though he'd claimed she was the last. Or maybe he'd used another trick. Or maybe my father's change in disposition was simply a matter of extreme stress. Either way, the man I was looking at wasn't the levelheaded father I'd always known.

I had to tell him what I knew to be the truth.

"Maybe you're right about Vlad," I said, facing the wastelands beyond the barrier. I walked up to the metal railing built to keep cars from falling off the edge. "Where do you think he came from? If it's just a wasteland out there, where's he been all this time?"

"At one of the other havens that failed," he said without missing a beat. "He came the same way the controllers come, protected from the elements."

"And what if he's lying?"

"Does it matter? We're stuck either way. Try to get out, the whole valley blows. Everything, including where we're standing. All of it!"

"It matters because he's stuck here too. He's from another world, and he'll use any form of manipulation possible to force me to write him into that book. Including turning you against me."

I could have slapped him and gotten less of a reaction.

"Is that what you think, honey?" He rushed up to me and pulled me into his arms. "No, no, no. I could never even think . . . How can you say that?" He took my face in his hands, pleading. "We're alone in the world, sweetheart. Even if there is no fallout, we're still stuck." He swept a piece of hair from my face and lowered his hands. "Trust your father, honey. I'm not getting this from dreams."

"My dreams aren't just dreams. Not unless dreams can heal a shattered leg. You have to listen to me."

He glanced down at my leg. "Vlad healed you. Just the way he gave your sight back."

"And how did he do that?"

"By shifting your perception. I don't

know. All I know is that he hasn't hurt a soul since arriving. Or haven't you noticed? Barth and company are set on destroying us all."

"Did Vlad also teach me kung fu? He's lying to us."

"About what? The heavens? The sky?"

"About the power of that book. About healing me. About everything! He's the storm, the Shadow Man, lies that blind. What we're seeing isn't what's really there to be seen."

"No? Then what *is* there to be seen?"

His question triggered vivid memories of my experience with Talya — seeing the darkness in the valley shift with my own perception of that darkness. There are two systems in this plane of existence, he'd said. One bound by polarity, called this world, and one free of polarity, called the kingdom of heaven. Two systems: one bound in fear and control, one flowing with love in which there is no fear, no darkness, no trouble.

Inchristi is all; Inchristi is in all.

If Other Earth mirrored this world, what were we seeing *right now* that was bound in fear rather than love?

Everything.

But none of this would make any sense to my father. It hardly made sense to me. Here in Eden I certainly wasn't knowing it. Experiencing it.

We stood quietly for a minute, he lost in thought, I remembering.

"I'm not trying to undermine your experiences, honey," he finally said. "Before she was murdered . . ." He swallowed his emotion, then continued. "Miranda wondered if you were actually connecting with a higher consciousness. Truth from beyond the world we see." He faced me. "But I can only deal with what my mind offers me right now."

"The shadow of death," I whispered. "An eye for an eye. We're blind, that's all."

"Then the whole world's blind and always has been. There's no changing that today."

"That's not what you told me when I was blind. You told me to believe. That all of what we see in this world is radically limited data coming in through five senses and interpreted by programming in our brains. How many times did you tell me our perception can be re-created so that we see in a whole new way? What if everything we see with these lenses in our heads is only one perception limited by our physical senses? You, of all people, should jump on that."

I could see that he wouldn't. I might as well have told him the world was made of marshmallows.

"We don't have time for that," he said. "I can only live by what I do see today, and what I see is that Barth poses a terrible threat to the survival of this valley. End of story." He turned and strode back toward Eden. "If that costs me my life, so be it, because I know without a shadow of a doubt that if I don't stop him in two days, both you and I will die."

"That's what Vlad told you?" I asked as he walked away. "What happens in two days?"

"The end."

"Of what?"

"Of everything."

26

That exchange formed a terrifying division between myself and my father. We walked through the dark tunnel and returned to the vast basin surrounded by cliffs. I could now deal reasonably well with any threat, I thought. I'd been lost and found, shot and healed, blind and sighted. But the prospect of losing my father threatened me with fresh panic.

Heading into the gloomy valley, I recalled Talya's teaching that fear created more fear. Wrath would only create more wrath. Joining the system of problems by offering it outrage would only produce more of the same.

Wasn't I doing the same thing by worrying for my father? Who would break out of the system if I couldn't?

As we began our descent, it occurred to me that if my father could see what I'd seen in my dreams, he would think very differently about what was happening in Eden. Vlad still had the book, but what if I got it and wrote my father into that reality? The thought swallowed me.

I caught up to him and told him that I wanted to be alone and would come home in a while. He objected, strenuously. Barth would be gunning for me as much as him. But I insisted that I would see anyone coming from that high place. He finally agreed and left me.

I climbed to a small knoll off the road and sat in my own silence for a few hours, contemplating the sky, the town, Vlad, the seals, Talya, Samuel, Jacob, myself . . . All of it.

Down in the town, which I could see clearly from my vantage point, everything looked peaceful. False sky and empty streets, Eden was what it was. Behind closed doors, Linda was undoubtedly pacing and raging. Maybe she'd snuck out and gone looking for the missing children. Barth was either mapping out his new regime or hunting for dissidents. Maxwell Emerson, the town's financier, was probably still trying to figure out how he'd spent so many years hoarding money that didn't exist.

For all I knew, ten more people had been killed. But from where I was sitting, all appeared to be well.

Part of me was desperate to do something. Fix it all. Find the Second Seal. But something Talya had said shut that voice down. *The teaching will appear when the student is ready.* The seal would find me as I surrendered to the journey. I was doing that, right? The seal would come when I was ready.

I was doing everything I knew to do, and that afternoon my path was to sit on the knoll overlooking Eden, because nothing else presented itself to me.

One thought hit me late, as our false sky darkened. That sky was like scales that had blinded us all to truth for many years. If Eden was a lie, maybe my task was simply to undo the lie. Collapse the entire system. Escape Eden.

But that couldn't be. The charges Vlad had planted would kill us all. Even if they didn't, we'd be exposed to the fallout beyond.

I stayed away much longer than I'd planned, so when I returned I was afraid of what I might find. I approached our house from the woods behind and snuck in unseen.

"Dad?" I called out. But the house was empty. He'd left a note on the counter.

> Gone to Linda's. Back soon. Keep the door bolted and stay in your room.

Linda's? I considered going to Linda's house myself but quickly let the notion die. Night was coming and there was nothing I could do without more information. For that I had to dream. Never mind that I would be waking in a prison.

Talya had led me to that prison . . .

I fixed myself some eggs, stripped out of my bloody jeans, showered all the nastiness off, and, since my father still hadn't returned, lay down on my bed. It took me two hours to fall asleep, and then only with the help of two Advil PMs.

The cell in Mosseum City was nearly dark, lit by a single pitch-burning torch at the end of the hall. There were no beds, only the stone floor, one concrete wall, and three other walls formed by iron bars.

Jacob lay with his back to me, snoring softly. How long had I slept?

I checked my thigh. Smooth and whole. Apparently Jacob had taken the liberty of wiping the blood from my leg.

"You're awake?" He twisted, saw me sitting up, and scrambled to his feet. "You're awake! Mother of Teeleh. I thought someone had stolen your mind!"

"How long have I been out?"

"The day and half the night. It will be light soon, though we'll never know it in this coffin. They came."

"Who?"

"One of their overlords, a pompous old croon in a black robe. They called him the prosecutor. It seems they mean to put us on trial at daybreak."

"On what charge?"

"Certainly heresy, and he was utterly curious of you." He waved a hand in disgust. "I'll never understand the way of the Albino, so wrapped up in particular beliefs with which you bless or condemn. It's a wonder any sane soul would want to follow a deity bent upon such punishment."

"And yet you follow Teeleh."

"Teeleh? He's a monster who makes no claim to be good, not a deity who loves with his lips and slays with his hands." He paused. "We should decide on a defense or I'll be dead, and you, worse."

"What could be worse?" His statement alarmed me. "Why do you say that?"

"Terrible suffering in life is worse than death." He looked at me with gentle eyes and lowered his voice. "As the 49th you must know that your enemies do not mean to kill you, but force you into a betrayal of all mysticism. All Mystics. Me, they would kill unless they see a way to leverage my life. But you . . ." His voice trailed off.

"You say this to encourage me?" I demanded.

"Forgive me, I only mean to help."

"So that what? Your Ba'al can torture me again?"

"No." He was quick to respond, and I found surprising comfort in the confidence of his tone. "Never." His eyes shifted to my leg. "Your wound?"

This too gave me comfort. "It's healed," I said. "Completely."

We remained in silence for a few breaths, considering the wonder of it.

Jacob lowered himself to his seat, legs crossed, forearms resting on his knees. "They saw your leg. Your recovery will only support their fear of you as a witch."

"What about the fruit?"

"The guard picked it up with tongs and took it in a box. But I managed to keep this from them." He reached under his shirt and pulled out the page, which he'd folded. "If a piece of fruit shows such power, what can paper do in your hands?"

I took the page from his hand and held it gingerly, half expecting something to happen. Nothing did. I whispered the First Seal. "Origin is Infinite." Nothing. So I repeated it. Still nothing.

"An incantation?"

"No, nothing like that. The First Seal." I recited the finger I'd heard on the cliff. "What is known that cannot be named?"

"How could I know?" he asked. "If it can't be named?"

"I wasn't asking you."

"You're asking the paper?"

"No." Was I? I repeated the question, but to no avail.

"That went well," Jacob said.

"We have to hide it," I said, scrambling to my knees. "It can't fall into their hands."

"Then it has to be on your person. But even so, they might take our clothing to be burned."

"So where?" I looked him over and knew. My hair was too fine to hide a rolled page, but his dreadlocks . . .

It took me ten minutes to tightly roll the page and weave it into the thickets of his locks. Jacob directed me, telling me to be gentle when I jerked too hard.

I learned that hair was a source of great pride for the Horde, nearly sacred in some ways. He recalled the first time he'd allowed a woman to weave his hair — a display of trust and affection.

Despite their traditions in the matters of intimacy, I reminded myself that handling his hair and feeling his head weren't much different from handling my own. Both of our bodies were simply earthen vessels. Even the stench of his skin was a relative preference, noticed by one of five senses — the nose — and interpreted based on cultural programming.

I only had to practice metanoia. New thinking. And the first step in new thinking was to practice letting go of old thinking. Reinterpreting what my senses told me. Envisioning him in the brightest light, if for no reason than to see something in a new way. Had Talya known I would be in a cell with Jacob?

I was nearly finished hiding the page before I realized how profoundly the experience had shifted my perception of him. What was once appalling now knelt with his back to me, a powerful warrior who was like a boy when he set his bravado aside.

And me? What did he think of the woman behind him whose stench was equally offensive to his programming?

Satisfied with my handiwork, I put my hand on his shoulder. For a moment I knelt beside him in silence. This was his earthen vessel. His costume. Could I love this costume?

The thought frightened me and I pulled my hand away. "All done."

He lifted his hand to the back of his hair. "I didn't know Albinos were so adept at weaving hair." He turned and sat facing me.

"Whatever you do, don't leave me," I said.

His brow arched. "So now you trust me?"

"Do I have a choice?"

"You always have a choice. But I have no intention of leaving you, even if I could. It seems our fate is intertwined, like it or not."

I could just barely see his eyes in the darkness.

"Can I ask you a question, Jacob?"

"Any woman can ask me any question she likes. Even an Albino." He caught himself. "Not that I agree with Ba'al that Albinos are diseased demons, mind you. I didn't mean it like that."

"And yet you serve Ba'al as commander of all Throaters."

"Only because I am son of Qurong. And because it wins me favor among the fairer of the sexes."

"What are Albinos to you, then?"

"Another race who've slaughtered my brothers. This was your question?"

"No. My question is why don't you believe

in Elyon, who created this world?"

He shrugged. "Nothing I've heard of Elyon is any different from what I've heard of Teeleh. Both demand to be honored on pain of great suffering. Any deity who manipulates with such a threat is best ignored. Thus, I serve neither."

I found his explanation both insightful and hopeful. His only problem was that he didn't know the same Elyon I knew.

"Now I would ask you a question," he said.

"Of course."

"What are these seals you speak of?"

I thought about it for a second. "They're like markers of my own journey beyond fear," I said. "To understand, you would need to know the whole story. At least to the extent I know it."

"Then tell me. Tell me everything. I must know."

I took a deep breath, leaned back on the bars, and told him everything. Not only about the seals, but about my dreams of Eden, Utah. All of it, more than I had told anyone, including my father and Peter.

He listened with rapt attention, asking questions, often so many that I lost track of where I was. Jacob, son of Qurong, might be a celebrated warrior among his people, but to me he quickly became a curious and insightful seeker.

"My, my," he said quietly when I'd finished. "Your mind makes me dizzy. I can see that I have much to learn."

"That would be me. Only I would say *unlearn.*"

He nodded absently. "Yes, I can see that. Unlearn, then. I have so much to unlearn from you." A pause. "This son of Thomas of Hunter who took you from me —"

"Samuel," I said.

"Yes, Samuel. If your old man —"

"Talya," I interrupted.

"Yes, Talya. If he was right in this mysterious knowing he seems to throw about —"

"With stunning accuracy."

"If he's right, the boy is likely dead by now. You do realize this?"

"Samuel's a man, and I doubt very much he's easy to kill, as you yourself discovered. Even so, he's Albino, neither Mystic nor Gnostic. Why would the Elyonites see any threat from him?"

"He's impetuous and a stranger to Elyonites. Their guard is the kind that kills first and asks later."

The gate to the dungeon squealed.

"They're here," Jacob said, eyes on me. "Be strong. Show no fear. Tell them you know nothing of being the 49th. I said this to save my own life. Blame it on me. You've made no confession yet."

I hadn't considered the option, but I saw his reasoning.

"Tell them nothing of being the 49th," Jacob repeated, putting his hand on mine. "I beg you."

"If I must."

"You must."

I nodded and we rose as four Court Guards approached, boots clacking on the stone floor in cadence. They unlocked the cell and pulled the door wide.

We couldn't see their faces because they were wrapped like the ninjas of ancient Earth. The harsh tone of the leader's voice communicated their demeanor well enough.

"Dress!" He flung two white robes at us. Then a jar of something at Jacob. "Use all of it. The judge will not abide your stench in the courtroom."

We glanced at each other, then retreated to the corners to do as they asked. The scent of a strong perfume filled the room as Jacob wiped their salve over his skin. I could only imagine his humiliation.

I stripped out of my tunic and donned the long white robe without a thought of those who stared at my back.

"This way."

We were led down the corridor, up a flight of stairs, down a very long hallway, and into a vast, ornately appointed chamber with a golden dome. The room was no fewer than a hundred paces across, at least half of which was occupied by a large red pool directly beneath the high ceiling.

Thick velvet ropes ran along the perimeter of the pool, which featured a fountain flowing with blood-red water. A large white statue of a rider on a horse stood at the head of the pool — I immediately recognized Justin.

The walls of the round hall were layered in gold, trimmed with wide silver bands that were inset with rubies and emeralds. Red and purple drapes — silk, I thought — hung in great swaths from the trim.

The chamber was so stunning that I stopped walking. As did Jacob.

"Move."

We moved. Over a polished floor made of emerald marble. Then up one of two sweeping flights of steps that rose to a second level. Across a foyer to a pair of double doors, which were opened by two guards at our approach.

If the hall behind us was lavish, the main courtroom in Mosseum City was extravagant. There were numerous stained-glass images of Justin and red-pool baptisms, thick red carpets, marble benches, exotic black wooden pews, and a throne at the center of the platform.

But none of the room's appointments impressed me. My eyes were glued to the four men on the platform and the seven who sat in what appeared to be a jury box.

The throne was occupied by an older man in white who wore a pointed silk crown. The judge, I thought. To his right by several paces was a second seated man dressed in what I guessed to be ceremonial battle dress — a black jacket with silver buttons, a red collar, and golden arm bands. He was a handsome man with loose curls, his bright eyes trained on Jacob.

"Aaron, son of their ruler," Jacob whispered.

"Which?"

"The one with gold bands."

The guard behind Jacob struck his head. "Silence!"

The son of Qurong didn't take the slightest notice, eyes fixed on the son of Mosseum, archenemy of all Horde. History was being made on account of me.

Two others on the platform were dressed in black robes and stood behind the bench in front of the throne. Their hair was black and slicked back into ponytails. Both had pointed beards and wore heavy chains with the red-pool medallions.

A circular wood floor lay before the raised platform, and on that floor stood Cirrus, the Gnostic heretic from the cart, now dressed in a white robe like ours.

A man I assumed to be the court clerk stood from a desk next to the jurors. "The accused may approach and stand before Mosseum, right arm of Elyon."

Mosseum. The supreme ruler.

Shoves from behind pushed us down the center aisle past empty pews, where we joined Cirrus on the circular floor.

"I present to this court the three accused of heresy for just judgment on this day of reckoning in the purview of Elyon and his son, Justin," the clerk said.

Mosseum flipped a nonchalant hand. "Another day, another heretic. Are we to be overrun by these imbeciles until the sun itself freezes?"

"Your Grace . . ." The clerk seemed surprised. "This is a Gnostic and a beast. And the Mystic of which you were informed."

We stood three abreast in our white robes, facing the judge now fully fixated on us.

479

"So my son tells me." Mosseum, bushy eyebrow cocked, stared at me. "A young Mystic at that. Anyone might claim to be the 49th. She refuses to change her confession?"

"She's made no confession as of yet, Your Grace. It's why we're here. No one has yet spoken to her."

"No? And why not?"

"It is your law, Your Grace. Passed only last week after your third nephew was mistakenly tortured. No one but you may oversee the conviction of heretics."

Mosseum glanced at the court officer. "Yes. Yes, that. A good law."

The clerk bowed. "The truth is for you and you alone to judge, Your Grace."

The ruler slowly pushed himself out of his throne, approached the bench, and peered down at me. I wondered if he might be senile. Either way, he didn't for a moment believe I was the 49th.

"I was under the assumption that the Mystic taken was badly wounded. I see no sign of a wound on this woman."

The court officer had no answer.

"Well, are you wounded?" the ruler asked me.

"No, Your Grace."

One of the men in black to Mosseum's

right gave a slight bow. "If it pleases Your Grace, this is part of the evidence I will present in my arguments." He was the prosecutor, then.

"She's lying to me? She hides her wounds?"

"No, Your Grace. But as I said —"

"Yes, yes, evidence. I heard you." The ruler frowned. "She doesn't look all that threatening to me."

"It is her diabolical philosophy, not her stature, that threatens our way, Your Grace."

Mosseum returned to his throne, sat heavily, and motioned to the man who was to present arguments. "Very well, Jacob. Present the case and be quick about it. What is that ghastly smell, anyway?"

They looked at each other.

"It's the awful perfume you gave Jacob to wear," I said.

One of the jurors gasped. Evidently I was out of order, but the whole scene struck me as deeply offensive. Not that I wasn't sweating under my robe. I was as nervous as I was offended.

"You will not speak until your defense is to be given," the prosecutor snapped. "And to suggest that I wear foul-smelling perfume is a defamation of this court."

"Not you." I nodded at Jacob. "This

Jacob. Did you not know that the Horde have names as well? Your men made him wear the perfume because they didn't like the way he smelled."

The Gnostic Cirrus gave a short, soft chuckle.

"Silence!"

"Forgive her," Jacob began.

"I said silence. Silence! Do heretics not know the meaning of this word?" The prosecutor named Jacob glared at us in turn. "You will obey the law of the church's court or find yourselves in hell. Your appointed defender stands to my right. He will offer all known evidence to save you from judgment. I will present and argue the charges. His Grace will render a verdict and sentence that will be embraced by the jury. The only time you may speak is if asked to speak. Do you understand?"

None of us replied. He accepted our silence as an acknowledgment. Aaron, son of Mosseum, sat still, watching the proceedings with measured curiosity. Of them all, he was the most dangerous, I thought.

It wasn't lost on me that the Elyonites had borrowed some names and traditions from ancient biblical history. Talya said they based much of their doctrine on ancient holy texts found in the Books of History.

"Please, Jacob," Mosseum rasped. "On with it."

"Yes, Your Grace." The prosecutor looked down at an open book. "We have here the rare opportunity to please the court by denouncing the heresies of our three great enemies. We begin with the deluded one who calls himself Gnostic. Step forward."

Cirrus took one pace forward, arms clasped behind his back.

"It is said Gnostics claim that the material world of flesh and substance is evil and of no consequence. Is this your belief?"

Cirrus cleared his throat. "That it is evil, yes."

"Yes, *Your Grace*."

"Yes, Your Grace."

The prosecutor looked at our appointed defender. "Need I say more?"

"I would say so, yes." Our nameless defender had a soft, high-pitched voice for a man.

"If you insist. It is also said that Gnostics, believing all flesh is evil, claim Justin did not live among us in the flesh. Is this your contention?"

"It is."

"There it is, then," the prosecutor said, waving a hand of dismissal.

"Yes, I would say that is enough," our

483

defender said. "Unless he would say something in his own defense."

"Can the word of a heretic be trusted?"

"No."

"Well, then . . ."

"Still, I think his words would be in order, if only for the record. He hasn't been found guilty yet."

The prosecutor glared at his counterpart, then looked back at the Elyonite ruler, who sighed and dipped his head in agreement.

"Very well. Speak, old man."

Again Cirrus cleared his throat. "In your rush to dismiss knowing Elyon beyond the flesh, you deny that the kingdom of heaven is already here, as taught by Justin. Thus you worship the flesh, not Elyon."

"Heresy!" the prosecutor cried. "Anyone with two eyes can see that there is no kingdom of heaven here on earth, you fool. We, Justin's chosen bride, are here to usher it in, and when it comes it will do so with unmistakable signs in the flesh — among those signs, swords dripping with blood. How dare you suggest this is worship of the flesh?"

"Furthermore, you elevate the death of the body to have great meaning, thus you worship death."

"Heresy!"

"You judge a man by his confession. Flesh. And by his deeds. Flesh. And by his adherence to law in the flesh. You build your edifices and tremble at the lakes. Flesh. You wail when your child is ill. Flesh. You do not know Elyon except in the flesh, through rituals and buildings and confessions of loyalty. You have made Elyon in your image of flesh, a father with a beard who paces the sky, wailing with worry and disappointment. And you wait for the kingdom to be ushered in with signs, in the flesh. Thus you worship the flesh."

The courtroom was deadly silent for the space of five breaths. Cirrus was half right, I thought. Talya had quoted Yeshua in saying that the kingdom of heaven wasn't coming with signs but was already among and within us. Also that the death of the body wasn't death but only a shedding of the temporary earthen vessel. But the Gnostic was also half mistaken. The material world was not evil. Justin *had* come in the flesh.

The old man, like the Elyonites, was only following his best convictions, however misguided they were. I wondered if he had a wife or children.

"This is your defense?" the prosecutor demanded. "To insult us all with your lies?"

Cirrus lowered his head. "I only wish to

speak the truth before you take my head."

"Then His Grace, the voice of Justin, will surely send you swiftly to hell." He faced our defender. "Will this suffice?"

"I have nothing to add."

"Good." To Cirrus: "Step back."

The prosecutor looked at Jacob, who stood on my left. Seated on his throne, Mosseum was picking at his mouth with a small ivory toothpick, eyeing me.

"Step forward, Horde," the prosecutor snapped.

Jacob cast me a side glance and a wink, then stepped up. He was trying to embolden me, but he couldn't hide the sweat on his own brow.

"It has come to the attention of this court that you claim to be son of the beast Qurong, sworn enemy of all Albino. Is this true?"

"I am he," Jacob said, dipping his head.

"And you were found protecting a Mystic, the greater enemy. To what end?"

Jacob hesitated. "I was sent by my father as an ambassador to the Elyonites. When it became clear that I would die before completing my mission, I said what needed to be said to spare my life. Nothing more."

He was lying on my behalf as much as his own, determined to persuade them I wasn't the 49th. But I didn't know if I could support that lie. My palms were clammy.

"You're saying it was a fabrication."

"Made for the sake of both our people."

The prosecutor turned to Aaron, who gave him a slight nod.

Back to Jacob: "It is known that the greatest heresy of all is to refuse bathing in the red pools. The disease I see before me is evidence enough that you have refused. As such, you live in denial of Elyon and are subject to death in all ages. Do you deny this charge?"

"I am Horde, if that's what you're asking. And you are right, I cannot serve your deity any more than I can serve Teeleh."

"And yet not to worship Elyon is to worship Teeleh, yes?"

"No," Jacob said.

"No? What kind of answer is that?"

"It is my answer."

"Do you deny that Justin is one with Elyon?"

"I don't know Justin, so I can't say who he is or isn't. I only know what I've heard of him. That he was a loving man who died willingly. I see no more love in this room than I see among my own people. So it would come as a great surprise to me to

487

hear that you serve Justin, who was so loving."

"How dare you blaspheme the name of Justin!" Mosseum thundered, rising from his throne. "What do you know of love? The *law* is love! Ridding this world of all demons like you so followers of Elyon can worship him in peace — that is love. Son of Qurong or not, you are Horde, a devil in disguise. It is my calling to rid the world of every last devil!"

He'd transformed into a monster before our eyes. His son still showed no emotion.

"Are you so blind to your own heresy?" Mosseum demanded.

Jacob blinked.

"Answer me!"

"I am blind, Your Grace. But only to the difference between Elyonites and Horde. My skin is different and I don't follow your deity, but in every other respect, I am just a man who loves women and children and all innocent creatures. Why would I seek a life like yours if it is no different or greater than the one our high priest, Ba'al, offers?"

"To save your putrid self, you utter moron! Do you not wish to live in eternal bliss?"

"Not if it looks anything like you."

His words sent a chill down my back. Was he so eager to meet his death? Or did Jacob, like Cirrus, already know that there was no way to find mercy in this court? He was only stating his truth plainly. My heart surged.

"This is why Elyon despises you," Mosseum said. "You have no . . ." He motioned wildly with his hands, searching for the right word. "Respect! Respect for Elyon. Respect for Justin. Respect for his bride. Only torment awaits your kind."

"Perhaps," Jacob said. "But now you know that I am not afraid to speak my truth. Is it not wiser to sit and discuss these matters over bread than slaughter each other?"

Mosseum glared at him, but Jacob had stalled his attack with diplomacy. My nerves were taut. Whatever he was or wasn't, Jacob, son of Qurong, was a man of profound honor, seeking both to save me and to bridge the gulf between his people and the Elyonites.

The ruler straightened his robe with a tug and slouched back in his throne. "Next!"

The prosecutor, who had retreated from the bench, stepped up. "Back!" He flipped his hand at Jacob. To me: "Forward."

I closed my fingers so they wouldn't shake, and I took one step forward.

"Now to the one that matters, Your Grace. The woman who claims to be the 49th Mystic." He tapped his fingertips on the bench, gathering his words. "You have just heard the beast claim that he lied about your identity to save his skin." He paced to his right. "Is it or is it not true that you were found yesterday by our warriors with a terrible wound in your thigh?"

"It is true, sire," I said.

"And do you have that wound today?"

"No."

"By what means did you come to have no wound?"

"By the means of a fruit invested with Elyon's power. When Jacob applied the juice of that fruit to my wound, I was healed."

"Let the record reflect that in saying 'Jacob' she refers to the Horde by her side," the prosecutor instructed the clerk. "Not me."

Eyes on me. "From the Holy Scriptures all Elyonites know that any power shown of spirit is as likely borne of the Shataiki devils as of any benevolent source. Thus, all meddling in the healing arts is dangerous and deemed witchery." He faced my defender. "Will this suffice for a conviction on the first matter of witchcraft?"

"I would hear her confession," the man said.

"Very well." The prosecutor turned his staunch face back to me. "Do you deny meddling in the healing arts?"

"No."

"And do you not fear that doing so might invite evil upon you?"

Even their truth seeking was bound in fear. And that fear began to press in on me as I stood there. Talya would know what to say, but I wasn't him.

A warm breath suddenly filled my lungs — the same breath I'd felt when first facing down Vlad in Eden's sanctuary. And with it, the same comfort I'd felt on the cliff.

What is known that cannot be named?

I didn't know, but fear fell from me like the shedding of a dead skin when I heard the tender whisper. My fingers tingled and my breathing lightened. There in that deep comfort, I spoke the gentle words that came to me next.

"If I ask my Father for bread, will he give me a stone? If I ask him for a fish, will he give me a snake?[1] No. Then why should I fear deception? Fear only draws to itself that which it fears. And love creates more love. There are only two systems at work, fear and love. You can only serve one master. As for my healing, it was for you more than me. A sign, so that you too might surrender to the only law remaining: the law of grace and love, which knows no fear, because there is no fear of the shadow when you see with love."

The words spilled from my lips.

"The shadow of death gathers to crush this world. Embrace the law of grace and be freed from the law of sin and death that blinds you in this life."

"We are Elyonites!" the prosecutor thundered. "Cleansed in the red waters of Justin!"

"And yet you're still bound by fear. Embrace a love that holds no record of wrong, because without it, all of your other confessions and beliefs are nothing, as Paulus wrote."

"The writings of Paulus embraced in ancient times have been firmly rejected by our council for their repeated claim that man is united with Elyon. They are an abomination!"

"If you don't embrace the love Paulus writes of, you will soon reap a great harvest of suffering, brought upon you by yourself."

Behind him, Mosseum's face had paled. He stared at me, and I felt a rush of compassion for him, for all of them, and for myself as well. Only a moment ago, I too had been bound to the world of trouble.

You are precious to me, dear one.

The gentle words washed over me, and I

nearly burst into tears. The gratitude that filled me was beyond expression.

The prosecutor shoved a finger at me. "The only sign in this courtroom is witchery! You are possessed of Teeleh, the devil of old. The Holy Spirit has filled my heart with its fear in your presence. That fear tells me your doctrine is bound in hell."

"Your fear is only a lack of love," I heard myself saying, "as is all fear. Do you not know that the Spirit of Elyon is infinitely complete and cannot fear or suffer loss? Have you not heard that Justin cannot be bothered, much less be threatened, by Teeleh? If he doesn't fear, why should you?"

He looked shell-shocked. I felt only peace and gratitude.

"Do you not believe that Elyon created this world?" he asked.

"Yes, I do."

"And do you not see all the problems in this world?"

"I do."

"Then you know that Elyon is terribly disturbed by all those problems! He wrings his hands, terribly disappointed by all that has occurred on his watch! He storms the heavens, vowing to rescue his bride, however filthy she might be. He will crush the serpent, Teeleh, and torment all who stand in his way. How can he not fear loss or suffer disappointment? He already suffers, even a child can see that! Are you so blind?"

At his mention of blindness, my nerves began to buzz. But I pressed on, only half hearing Shadow Man's promise to blind me.

"My Father is infinitely complete and cannot feel threatened," I repeated. "There is no fear in love. Is my Father not perfected in love? He never has, nor ever will, fear loss, least of all fear the loss of you, his son."

The prosecutor's hands were shaking. "If Elyon were as you say, there would be no death . . ."

"There is no death, only crumbling jars of clay that are temporal and shift in form — flesh today, dust tomorrow. The struggle called death is finished. You continue your own struggle in vain because you mistake the dust as your true identity."

The man spun to Mosseum. "Your Grace, I have more, but I would spare the church court from further blasphemy in your presence! I move that you issue your verdict now. The evidence is far more than needed."

Mosseum was watching me, jaw firm.

"Your Grace?"

He eased back in his throne. "Continue."

"Your Grace —"

"Finish what you started."

"Yes, Your Grace." The prosecutor looked back down at his ledger and seemed to be searching for his next point. He finally cleared his throat and looked up at me.

"It is further said that Mystics believe in the ancient writings of Paulus and Johnin and Petrus, all of which claim that we participate in the divine nature and are already complete, in union with Elyon.[2] As I've mentioned, these texts have been shown to be heretical. Do you cling to these writings?"

Tell them, dear one. Speak for me.

"Inchristi is all," I said, and I could see the power of the words wash over them like a breeze. "Inchristi is in all. We are the light of the world. The light is divine so we are divine, not as earthen vessels but as we truly are. To deny this is blasphemy. Blasphemy blinds us to who we are as the light."

He stared at me, dumbfounded.

"I see." He walked alongside the bench, running his fingers over the surface. "Furthermore, it is said that Mystics love the Horde as they love themselves. All Elyonites know we cannot love ourselves. In our hearts, we are too wretched to be loved by ourselves. Do you love yourself?"

"Would I not love what my Father loves? Would I not see myself the way Elyon sees me? Would I not give my flesh to see the beauty that Justin sees in me?"

I turned to Jacob, filled with an overwhelming love for him in that moment. The room was still, waiting for my self-incrimination to be confirmed, but none of that concerned me.

I was merely looking into Jacob's gray eyes, wide and misted. I didn't see his flaking skin, nor his long, dirty dreadlocks. These were only his earthen vessel, which meant nothing to me in that moment.

My throat was swollen. "And would I not love all of Elyon's children in the same way he loves me?"

"Enough!" Mosseum rose to his feet, glaring. "I will not hear one more word of this blasphemy!"

"But you must," I said, drilling him with my stare. "I have been delivered to your court to tell you that I am the 49th Mystic, chosen by Justin to bring a great crisis that will divide truth from falsehood and lead all out of fear. Only then will the lion lie down with the lamb."

"You deceiver," Mosseum hissed. "*We* are the lamb of Justin, and we will never yield to the Horde lion. I sentence a beast, a Gnostic, and a Mystic to death by drowning in the black pool this very night."

Aaron rose from his seat, nodded to someone at the back of the auditorium, and approached his father. He spoke too softly to be heard by me, but I could hear the doors behind us opening. Several boots stepped into the room. Guards, I assumed.

Slowly, like a heavy gathering fog, the ruler's sentence sank into my awareness. Death . . .

I closed my eyes, wondering what I had just done. But I had to say what I'd said. My words had come from beyond me.

"It's him," I heard Jacob say quietly. "Be strong, little lamb."

When I opened my eyes, I saw that they'd brought a fourth prisoner into the courthouse. One with long brown hair, arms strapped behind his back, watching me as they tugged him to a halt beside the jury box.

Samuel of Hunter. My heart skipped a beat.

Aaron stood back from his father, who slowly turned to face their new prisoner. Mosseum shifted his eyes to me and held me in a long stare before facing Samuel once more.

"My son tells me that you are Samuel of Hunter, son of the rumored Thomas of Hunter, proselytizer and enemy of the

Horde."

Samuel looked past me to Jacob, eyes hard. "Thomas is my father, if that's what you're asking."

"An Albino who's neither Elyonite nor Mystic, it is said."

"You've heard correctly. We are the Circle."

"And you crossed the Great Divide. Why?"

Samuel faced the ruler. "To save the 49th Mystic from the Horde," he said.

"You know this how?"

"I know what my own intentions are, don't I?"

"I mean the 49th, you fool. How do you know this Mystic is the one?"

Samuel took his time before responding, choosing his words carefully. "Talya, the old man who travels with a lion, told me she was the 49th after I rescued her from the Horde, my sworn enemy."

There could be no more doubt in their minds. Talya had told me that the Elyonites held him in disdain. He was a ghost to them, never available for capture.

Samuel had made it clear that he was enemy of the Horde, not the Elyonites. He'd already spoken to Aaron and was secretly working on a plan to save me, surely. Why Aaron would care, I didn't know.

Mosseum abruptly turned and exited through a door behind his throne.

"Return the Gnostic to his cell to await execution," Aaron ordered. "Take the other three to my library."

"Sire, the law is clear," the prosecutor objected. "No sentence uttered by the supreme ruler may be countermanded under any —"

"Now. Before I sentence you to the same."

27

We stood in Aaron's library, a vast room with hundreds of leather-bound books marked by numbers, not titles. Oil lamps between the tall bookcases supplemented the skylights. Aside from a large desk in the center, a table with six chairs and a couch with burgundy cushions were the only furniture.

Four Court Guards had bound Jacob's and my hands behind our backs and ushered all three of us down a hall and into the room before taking up positions by the door. I was aware of the tension between Jacob and Samuel. Their wary glances spoke clearly enough.

But I was still elevated from the flow of words that had come through me, delivered by a power both beyond me and within. It was as if the light Justin had shown me was flowing through my veins, was one with the Spirit of truth and had spoken.

We stood by the desk, waiting in an awkward silence. But Samuel wasn't one to wait. He positioned himself between me and Jacob, who stood watching. Calm.

"Are you well?" Samuel whispered, urgent.

I looked up into his soft eyes and saw only deep concern. Jacob no doubt thought his pursuit of me was foolish, but I found it heroic. The risks he'd taken, however misguided, humbled me.

I smiled. "Is there no stopping you, Samuel? Talya told you to stay."

"How could I stay, knowing this beast was intent on crushing you? Has he touched you? Harmed you in any way?"

"You mean Jacob. He's shown me nothing but kindness."

Samuel looked baffled, then angry. He cast Jacob a suspicious glare. "Don't mistake his trickery for kindness." Back to me. "I beg you. In your state of amnesia, you may forget what Scabs are capable of, but I don't. Don't believe a word he says. You have to trust me. I'll get you out, I swear it!"

"Coming was a mistake, son of Thomas," Jacob said. "They'll only send you back with your tail between your legs."

"A mistake?" Samuel snarled. "If not for my confirmation that she was the 49th, she would be dead, thanks to you!"

"Is that what you think you did? Save her? How little you know these heathens."

Samuel shifted as if to launch himself at Jacob.

"Stop it, both of you! No one is enemy or heathen here. No one!"

The door opened and Aaron walked in, striding as one who is comfortable in his role as commander. Samuel stepped back, eyes on his new enemy.

Aaron measured each of us curiously, then stepped along the nearest bookcase, hands clasped behind his back. "Do you know what these books contain?" he asked, then answered his own question. "The full history of the Elyonites, copied in meticulous detail by our scribes. Every battle with the Leedhan and the northern Eramites. Every encounter with the southern Horde. The building of every city and the establishment of every social institution and law."

He turned on his heels and faced us.

"But they do not record this." His green eyes drilled me with an even stare. "The day the 49th Mystic stood before the three sons — son of Qurong, son of Thomas, and son of Mosseum — announcing the end of the world as we know it. It is an auspicious day, sure to end in death, wouldn't you say?"

None of us spoke.

"Favorable for one of us, that is. Not all."

"If by one you mean only you," Samuel said, "you don't know who stands before you."

"Be quiet, my boy." Aaron still watched me. "Your time will come."

"I'm not your boy."

"No? And whose boy are you? Thomas of Hunter, fabled commander of the Forest Guard, who defied the Horde before marrying one? Tell me, is that legend true?"

Samuel hesitated. "It is. But the Horde he married was Albino when they wed."

"So then your father agrees with the Elyonite directive of eradicating all Horde."

"I would give my life to see all Horde die," Samuel said.

"I see. And what of Mystics? In particular, this one. The 49th."

Samuel cast me a quick glance. "She presents no threat except to the Horde. Don't you know the prophecy?"

"I do. Which is why you're still alive."

Aaron walked up to me. Looked deeply into my eyes. Slowly lifted his hand and tenderly touched my cheek. It wasn't a cold touch, only inquisitive, like a boy touching a flower for the first time.

"Strange that such a tender one could

strike so much fear in the hearts of the Elyonites. You'll usher in the end of our way of life, they say. I've never heard anyone speak to my father the way you did."

He lowered his hand and sighed.

"Which is why *I* am here," he said, stepping away. "My father is fixed in his old ways, without great regard for strategy. If he had his way, all of you would die today and we would rush to war. But before we execute you, I would consider alternatives that might favor my people."

He studied us again, one by one. "It seems that a day of reckoning is here, ushered in by three sons and a condemned Mystic. I will give each of you one chance to tell me why sparing your life will serve my people. Speak carefully — your life depends on it."

He faced Jacob. "Now, beast. Speak."

Jacob was unflappable. We exchanged a long look before he spoke.

"I have no interest in saving my life for your gain," he said. "Though I will say, my death would crush my mother. But if you're a man of strategy, you should think very carefully about rushing into war. With the Eramites to the north, and all Leedhan, the Horde would present you with an army many times greater than your own. And don't think your victory over my men on the Divide is any indication of weakness. We would wage a ferocious war. Is this what your father wants? Even if you could prevail, how many Elyonites would remain for him to command?"

"As I said, I'm not eager for war. You haven't told me why keeping you alive will serve me."

"And as I said, I'm not interested in saving my life for your gain. I only say that my death would enrage my father and ensure a bitter war." He paused. "Even more, killing Rachelle will end badly for you."

"The 49th," Aaron said.

"Her name is Rachelle."

"She will have her chance to —"

"I speak on her behalf as well," Jacob said, stepping forward. "Her very presence here proves the prophecy is true. Lesser minds might call her a witch, but we've both seen her healing power. Kill her and another 49th will arise in her place, and another and another until the prophecy is fulfilled. Ba'al, priest of my people, assures us on the authority of Teeleh that when the lion lies down with the lamb, all Albino lambs will be subjugated by the Horde lion. The 49th is here, and so it begins."

He was playing Aaron. Talya had said the Horde were terrified of the 49th, thinking it meant the lion would surrender to the lamb and become Albino.

"Assuming the prophecy means what you say," Aaron said. "Some suggest the opposite."

"Perhaps, but I suspect your priests agree with our own. Eventually, Elyonites will surrender to the lion, a terrible problem for you, especially if you make a martyr of the 49th." He took a deep breath. "Unless . . ."

"Go on."

Jacob looked at me. "Unless the 49th betrays her own purpose and opens the way for you to destroy all Mystics. Then raise your army and wage war if you insist. At least your fate will be in your own hands, not in the hands of the Mystics, who toy with you."

I knew he was only working to keep me alive, but the words cut deep. What if I did betray my mission? The thought struck fear into my heart.

"I see," Aaron said. "So your concern is for the Mystic more than yourself."

"My concern is for sound thinking. Kill her or kill me and you will have yourself a war that will end in your subjugation."

Aaron crossed his arms. He dipped his head at Samuel. "And you?"

Samuel looked caught off guard by Jacob's

reasoning. "I wasn't aware that the beasts had the capacity for such sound thinking, but I can see his logic. Albinos must prevail. Killing Rachelle will gain you nothing but trouble. As for him" — he wagged his head in Jacob's direction — "let me take him in chains and kill him on the other side of the Divide. Blame his death on me and spare yourself a war."

"So you too like this Mystic? This . . . Rachelle. It's why you pursued her so far from home?"

Samuel thought carefully before responding. "The son of Qurong was sent to kill her," he said. "I couldn't allow that to happen."

"Why would the Horde want her dead, if they interpret the prophecy to mean the 49th will ensure their own victory?"

"To make a martyr of her and raise holy rage among all Horde. And as I said, I couldn't allow that to happen."

In his own way, Samuel was also playing Aaron. I knew for a fact that he had no such opinion of the prophecy. They were both vying for my life.

"Unlike many, I think the time for war is here," Samuel continued. "But as the beast said, killing her will only keep the prophecy intact and threaten all Albinos, assuming

507

you read the prophecy to foretell their subjugation."

"Which you do as well?"

"We have to assume the worst, wouldn't
you say?"

"Then you agree with Jacob," Aaron said.
"Manipulating the 49th to betray her own
is the only way for Albinos to foil the prophecy."

Samuel looked at me, concerned. "Yes."

"The two sons implore their captor to save
the heretic." He looked at me, amused.
"And you?"

"Me?" My voice sounded thin, stripped of
the power it had held in the courtroom.

"Yes, you." .

No words came. I had nothing to say in
my defense. Nor could I interpret the
prophecy for them. I was only me, seeking
the five seals and bringing division.

But as I looked at Aaron's face, a thought
did come, and I spoke it in a soft voice.

"I see only that all three of you are beautiful and without blame. You just haven't seen
what I have to offer you. One day, if you let
me, I'll show each of you. Nothing you've
seen can compare."

The room went still.

"You're blind, that's all," I said. "But
Justin came to bring sight to the blind."

Aaron looked stunned. I'd just spoken the greatest of all heresies, suggesting that he and his Elyonites — Justin's chosen bride, as they called themselves — were still blind.

I turned to Samuel and saw confusion on his face. But his mind was likely on Jacob. He couldn't fathom my saying that a Scab was beautiful. I wasn't sure I could understand either, I only knew it was how I felt.

Jacob stared at me. Of the three, only he understood, I thought.

"And so it begins," Aaron said. He turned and headed toward the door, mind clearly set. "Sequester Samuel in quarters under house arrest. Take the others to separate cells in the dungeon to await their execution tonight, as ordered."

28

I found myself in a dark cell once more. They'd given me no water and I was thirsty, separated from Jacob, who had the page woven into his hair. But part of me was still preoccupied with the power that had flowed through me in the courtroom.

There was still so much I did not know. Where were my Mystic brothers and sisters? I'd seen the valley with the lake and the colored forest — would I ever see it again? How could the seals find me here, in this dank cell? And what about Eden? It was falling apart at the seams, and what I learned here was supposed to help me there. But how, if I died?

I closed my eyes and set my mind on metanoia, going beyond my thoughts to know the world differently. And in that silent space I trusted that the seals could still find me before the Realm of Mystics could be destroyed. How much time did I have?

Where was the realm? Close, Talya had said, but how close?

I silenced the questions. My only task now was to take the journey with intention and devotion. The words I'd spoken in the courtroom were as much for me as for any of them. If I asked my Father for a fish, would he give me a serpent? If I asked for truth, would he give me a lie?

My earthen vessel didn't know how to seek anything other than information that would reinforce its own programming. My search for the seals, then, would have to rise above this. I would let go of what my brain told me was true as well as the fear that I might be deceived. I would let go of what I thought I knew, so that I could *know* my Father.

These thoughts occupied me as I sat in the corner of the holding cell. But as the hours passed, I began to awaken once more to familiar fears, beginning with my fear of death.

I tried not to think about what drowning would feel like, but once the images filled my mind, I couldn't get them out. It was clear that I'd come to Mosseum to speak plainly to them, yes, but surely my journey wouldn't end here. And what about Jacob? Drowning was the preferred method of execution among the Horde because it caused such pain and dread. Now he would drown because of me.

Unless . . . Unless both Jacob's and Samuel's reasoning had shifted Aaron.

As the hours lengthened, the voices of fear grew. And as they grew, they blinded me further. I knew what was happening as it happened, but I seemed powerless to stop it all. Even knowing that my struggles were simply good teachers, as Talya had said, eased my fear only a little.

I was cold and shivering, condemning myself for not being able to let go of my fear of death, when the soft voice whispered through me once more.

There is no death, dear one. It is a shadow.

With those words, clarity filled my awareness. Tears slipped down my cheeks. I lowered my head onto my knees and shook with gentle sobs. Then I took a deep breath, leaned back against the stone wall, closed my eyes, and waited.

They came for me with heavy footfalls and rattling chains less than an hour later.

A hood blocked my sight, so I couldn't see where they led me or what the preparations looked like, and I think that might have been a good thing. I kept repeating the reassuring words under my breath. *There is no death, dear one. It is a shadow.* Just that, half believing myself, but that half was enough to keep me just beyond the reach of my deepest fears.

The room they took me to was damp and smelled of blood. I could feel the weight of the chains that bound my hands behind my back, the cobblestones under my bare feet, the thick moisture in the air, the goose bumps on my skin when they tore my tunic off.

I could hear the sounds of seven people breathing and walking. By the sound of a grunt, one of them was the old Gnostic. One of them was Jacob, but I knew that by the scent of his skin. The other four were our executioners, who were working at some kind of contraption involving chains and pulleys.

The bag over my head severely limited my echolocation, so this was all I could see.

"Jacob?"

"Yes."

"Silence," one of the guards growled.

I didn't care.

"You are treasured," I said, voice wavering.

"Silence!" A whip's lash bit deeply into my exposed belly.

"As are you, 49th," he returned calmly. "Do not worry, I know my way around death."

Three strikes of a whip cracked through the room.

"By Elyon's wrath, if the old man wasn't already strung up . . ." A guard grunted. "Hurry it up."

There is no death, there is no death . . .

But the fear crept closer now. And when I heard the old man weeping as chains clanked, that fear swallowed me.

I could see it all through my ears. Heavy links of a chain rattling over a pulley as they lowered his suspended body. The splash at his feet as he kicked. The gurgling of water as they plunged his body deep into their black pool of death.

Then silence except for a few bubbles breaking the surface.

The guards in charge of our execution said nothing — three more drownings among a thousand.

A full five minutes passed before the chains ground again, hauling the dead body up. Water splashed and dripped back into the pool; their mechanism creaked. A body landed heavily on the stone floor and was dragged from the room.

Cirrus's earthen vessel was dead.

Rough hands grabbed my arm and steered me around the pool to the far side.

"The shadow, you say?"

"While the other watches. And be quick about it."

The shadow?

I felt clamps being latched to my ankles. My body was now reacting of its own will, trembling as I stood in the cold room, terrified.

"Jacob?"

"Hear Talya, Rachelle! Shift your mind! See light instead of darkness as he taught you!"

A whip cracked, biting into his flesh. My mind was already falling into a deep well of darkness.

They shoved me back onto a table and strapped my arms and legs in place. I'd expected to be chained and lowered into the water. What was happening?

My hood was jerked off, and for the first time I could see the room.

Light from two torches lit the subterranean chamber with rough-hewn walls. Chains and huge hooks hung from the stone. Contraptions of death and torture ran the length of the wall beside me.

The black pool Mosseum had sentenced us to die in was dark as oil. But they'd strapped me to a table far from it. Why?

Fighting panic, I jerked my head around and saw Jacob. He stood bound, chained to the wall ten paces beyond my feet, strong chest rising and falling with deliberate breath. They'd removed his hood and shoved a cloth into his mouth. He was watching me, trying to show me courage, but he couldn't hide the fear in his eyes. Fear for me, I thought, not for himself.

"Jacob . . ."

A fist clubbed my head. "Shut your hole!"

They strapped my forehead and my neck to the table, working quickly. Then an iron grid went over my face, a mask of sorts, one with clamps that bit into my eyebrows and upper cheeks. With a yank my eyelids were spread so that my eyes stayed open, exposed to the air.

It hit me then . . . And when it hit me, nausea flushed through my gut and chest.

"Watch your hands," one of them said, speaking to another. He chuckled. "One cut and you're dead."

They lowered a cage over my head, plunging me into darkness. A hiss sounded above me.

I might have tried to cry out. To thrash against my straps. But I couldn't. Hot waves of terror rolled down my body, paralyzing it.

But the fear didn't stop the voice in my head — the same voice that haunted my nightmares.

I'm going to blind you. And when you see again, I'm going to blind you again. Shadow Man's vow whispered through my mind. *And what happens to you happens to them all. Through you, I'm going to blind them all.*

A black cloth was pulled free from the cage, and my nightmare came to life by the torchlight. A large black snake uncoiled in the cage only inches above me, separated from me by an iron mesh so that it couldn't reach me.

It had a flared hood like a cobra's, and red eyes peering down at me as its forked tongue flickered to taste my scent. This was the serpent they called the shadow.

I could hear Jacob grunting through his gag, struggling against his chains.

My body let go then, and I began to hyperventilate. Once more I was in my nightmare. Once more I could hear Shadow Man chasing me into what I thought had been my safe place. Once more I heard his chuckle behind me.

And then he was there. Shadow Man was there, rushing at me as the black snake above me bared its fangs.

I began to thrash against my restraints, screaming, unable to move my head or close my eyes. The coiled snake struck hard, slamming its fangs into the iron mesh, spraying my spread eyes with its blinding poison.

A terrible pain bit deeply into my eyes as the world darkened. A throbbing ache spread through my head and down my spine.

My mouth was wide, screaming, but my mind was lost in darkness, begging for death because I feared blindness far more. When I died, I would live a new life, one with Elyon. But blind . . . I couldn't live my life blind again!

You think you must die to be one with me, daughter?

The soft voice came from far away, whispering through the darkness. I willed myself to move toward it, desperate to be dead and there. Begging to be dead.

Light exploded in my mind's eye, and suddenly I wasn't there. Not there in the chamber, not on the table. No longer bound.

All I could see was white. All I could hear was the thumping of my heart. So I couldn't be dead, I thought. I instinctively lifted a hand up and stared at it, but I couldn't see it.

I'd long ago learned that contrast is needed for sight. If everything in the world were pure white, without a single shift in hue or a single shadow, no sight would be possible. All would be white, but even that whiteness could not be sight. All of the senses worked on a system of polarity. Without contrast, no human could hear, taste, smell, touch, or see. We wouldn't be able to experience ourselves or the world.

Now you know, daughter. Death is only a shadow.

Meaning erupted in my mind. Without polarity, there could be no experience in the world. My body was as much an experience vessel as an earthen vessel. In the same way shadows allowed the eyes to see, death was playing its part by providing a contrast to life in the world of polarity.

My body was dead, but I wasn't dead, because death was only a shadow experienced while in a body. Life was eternal, before and after the death of the body.

The moment that awareness filled me, wind roared through my ears, and the white world blinked off. I immediately found myself standing on a grassy hill, overlooking a gathering of people — a few hundred —

dressed in ancient clothing. They were from the lowest reaches of society, mostly in tatters. Outcasts, I thought, many of them prostituted and diseased. The worst of offenders, the rejected, the hopeless.

They were seated and looking up at a man with long hair who stood on a boulder, teaching them. His voice carried to me across the valley.

"You are the light of the world," he said. "Do you light a lamp and put it under a basket?"

He was speaking to them, but he was speaking to me, and his meaning was clear. I, like the outcasts he spoke to, was the light of the world, but I was hiding that light in another identity, so it could not be seen by me or by the world.

"The kingdom of heaven is already within you. It does not come from here or there with signs . . ."[1] His voice began to fade away, replaced by the crunching of gravel under feet behind me.

I twisted my head and saw that same teacher walking toward me, only five paces away. I spun around, staring into knowing eyes that seemed to absorb me. Jesus, whom Talya called Yeshua. I knew it by the images from the sanctuary in Eden. The paintings had missed the love and deep knowing in

520

his eyes.

"Always remember," he said, voice gentle, "you have been made complete, a new creature, risen with me. It's not who you think you are as an earthen vessel who lives, but I who live in you, joined as one. I am in you; you are in me. In the same way I am in the world now, so are you. Do you understand these things, daughter?"[2]

I was so stunned that I didn't know what to say, so I said the only thing that came to me in that moment.

"Is . . . Is that the way you really look?"

A glint filled his eye and he smiled. "No. But how else would you recognize me?" A wink.

Then he lifted his hands to the crown of his head and made the motion of one peeling off a costume that was fastened at the top. His flesh fell from him, replaced by a blinding light.

It happened in the space of a single heartbeat, and what had been a man dressed in a long garment was suddenly light that engulfed me with a crackling hum. The light streamed to the right, to the left, high above and far below. I knew immediately that it was infinite. That it had no end.

In that light, I was consumed by an overwhelming love that my body could barely contain. Any more and I knew that my flesh and bone would be scattered to the farthest reaches of the galaxy.

I don't know how long I was in that light, because there was no time in that space. I was in eternal life itself, and that eternal life had no beginning or end, no up or down, no destination, no place. There was no judgment, no darkness, no knowledge of good or evil, no opposites at all.

It was beyond polarity.

Then the light collapsed in on itself, sucked back into a body. I stood gasping for air, stunned.

Only now it wasn't the body called Yeshua who stood before me.

It was Justin, who was Yeshua. And we were no longer in that ancient land, we were on the sands of a white desert. Only Justin and me. His eyes were a bright green and he was smiling like an exuberant child.

"Now," he said with a nod. "You try it."

I blinked. "Me?"

"Is it not written, 'You are glorified'? Show me your glory. Be perfect, as your Father is perfect."[3]

"My glory? But I'm not perfect." And then I spoke my deepest fear — a belief drilled into me by Shadow Man. "I'm wretched."

He dipped his head. "If you insist. But

522

know that how you see yourself doesn't define you. How I see you defines you. How you see yourself only defines your experience in the world. Do you want to know how I see you? Try it."

I hesitated, then tentatively lifted my arms and set my fingers on the crown of my head as if to peel off my body. But the thought of doing so terrified me. More, it felt obscene. Something in me was resisting on a level so fundamental that I could hardly move my fingers. My earthen vessel, I realized. It was clinging to itself, a god of its own making. But that wasn't me.

So I did what he'd done. The moment my fingers entered the crown of my head, my body fell off of me like a loosened garment.

What emerged was a pillar of the exact same light. Not infinite and extending forever, but humming with the same ferocious power. I stood there trembling with love as the light, facing Justin, who smiled and spoke in a voice that reached to the end of the world.

"I am in you and you are in me. One, in the same way I am one with Elyon."

And then I collapsed back into the earthen vessel called Rachelle.

Justin chuckled, face beaming. "You like?"

I was too struck with wonder to form words.

"This is eternal life, to know the Father and the One he sent," Justin said. "Now you see what it means to *know* eternal life while in your earthen vessel. It cannot be adequately explained, only experienced. And in that knowing, there is no darkness. No fear."

My brain was only now coming back to its self-identification. The teachings crystalized for me. I was experiencing myself beyond polarity. I had known the unseen. And in that unseen, I was already complete.

"Are you a part of all?" he asked.

"Yes."

"Inchristi is all," Justin breathed. "Inchristi is in all. You aren't *the* one Inchristi any more than you are *the* Albino or *the* woman. But as you see who you are as Inchristi, as an aspect of Elyon, your experience in the world is full of light and you are saved from darkness. Do you want to be saved?"[4]

What is known that cannot be named?

"To believe in your name," I said, breathless, "is to see myself complete in you, because I'm joined with you. One with you. *Inchristi* means 'one with Christ.' " My words were true, and they shook me to the core. "We are the light."

"Look to the light and you will see me. And when you see me, you will see yourself in me. I am the vine of light and love. Remain in that identity and you will see that there is no problem, because I have overcome the world of problems, as have you, already raised with me. It is finished."

"You are the Light . . ."

"I am."

"You are my Father . . ."

"I am."

"You are the Holy Spirit, like a mother . . ."

"I am."

"You are the Son. Three as One . . ."

"I am."

"Inchristi is me," I said. "And as one, we are *in* my earthen vessel. That's how Inchristi is me *and* in me."

He nodded once, slowly, delighted. His next words were softly spoken, barely more than a whisper, but they shook the universe.

"I am."

With those words, white wiped out the world, and I found myself curled up on a hard surface, breathing hard. I could hear fire crackling. Maybe the light I'd just experienced. But no, this was a flame. Like a torch.

I opened my eyes with a gasp. But it was

still dark. Black. I felt the pain behind my eyes and sat up, gasping.

"Rachelle . . ."

Jacob's voice.

Confusion swarmed me. My eyes were open but it was pitch-dark. Was I still in a dream? Or a near-death experience? But I could feel the cold stone under me and smell Jacob's scent. A torch's flame popped on the wall to my right.

Jacob was by me, arms now pulling me close. "Please forgive me."

"What's happening?" I croaked.

"You don't remember?"

"I . . ."

It came back to me like a flood. The death of Cirrus. The black hooded snake they called the shadow.

They'd blinded me.

29

I started clicking. Immediately the dungeon cell took shape, emerging with the familiar definitions of shapes and density that echolocation offered. The wonder of the world I'd just seen was replaced by the realization of my worst fears.

"I'm blind." My voice was thin, barely a voice at all.

Jacob breathed heavily beside me, one arm around my shoulders. "It's my doing," he said. "You must forgive me, I beg you."

I felt myself tempted to curl up and hide. From myself. From Jacob, who held me, punished by his guilt.

He muttered a curse. "When I see him next, I'll tear his head from his shoulders."

Aaron.

Who are you, dear daughter?

A wretched blind girl who will blind the world, a small part of my mind said. I struggled to keep from sinking into that shadow of shame.

"I am the light," I whispered, but in that darkness I was having a hard time believing it.

"The light?" Jacob said.

"I am complete."

It was a desperate cry of denial from a girl who was far from complete. But I dared not believe that lie, so I recited what I had known.

"For me to live is Justin."

The torch's flame whooshed. My eyes were open, but I could see nothing. And I knew that when I woke in Eden, I would be blind as well. The thought terrified me.

"If Justin lives, I beg him to save his daughter and slay the son who allowed her to fall into such evil hands," Jacob muttered.

"It wasn't your fault," I said, staring blindly at the wall. "If not for you and Samuel, I would probably be dead."

"But blindness . . . For you, it's worse than death."

He knew my story and joined my pain. For this I loved him.

"I thought you were dead," he said. "But you never stopped breathing."

How long had it been? Strange that I hadn't woken in Eden. No, because I had woken in another place. In that light with

Yeshua and Justin, who were greater than me and yet of the same fabric.

"They only just left." His voice was still riddled with anguish.

"Aaron had me blinded because I said he was blind. That's all. So if there is fault, it's mine. And it's only part of my journey." I felt numb. "And yours is to be here with me, not to condemn yourself or feel sorry for me."

I was struggling to believe my own words, though I knew they were true.

"He forced you to watch," I said. "Why didn't they . . ."

"Kill me? Aaron would use me to leverage my father. I'm far more valuable to him alive than dead."

"He's afraid of us."

"How so?"

"Right now they're probably pacing before their priests, terrified that your interpretation of the prophecy confirms their own. That the Horde will crush all Albinos." I felt half dead, slogging through confused emotions.

"You realize I had to play with their minds," Jacob said. "It was the only way —"

"I know, Jacob. It is as it should be."

"And yet . . ."

"And yet I'm blind." I pushed myself up. Clicked. Again the room came into dull view. At least I had that.

"How do my eyes look?" I asked, facing him.

I could feel his breath on my cheek. "Red, but otherwise the same. When the poison clears your eyes will appear normal."

"You know this snake?"

"It's called the shadow because it can blind its prey from three paces. They come from the deep south and live in the red cliffs. One bite will kill even the strongest warrior."

"So Aaron wants me to betray the prophecy, not kill me."

"Yes. Again, please forgive me."

What is known that cannot be named?

Did I know myself? Was I re-cognizing my true self, the one I'd known with Justin?

I had to know that me again. To experience myself seeing beyond the world of polarity. Nothing else mattered anymore, because here I was nothing. I started to rise but dizziness swept over me.

"Easy, you must rest."

"Help me up."

"You're sure?"

"I'm fine, just help me up."

He took my arm and pulled me to my feet.

I stood still until my head cleared. My exchange with Justin returned to my thoughts, and I crossed the cell, clicking, getting my bearings.

"What is this sound you keep making?" he asked.

"Echolocation, remember? It allows me to see in the dark. Shapes mostly. Edges."

"And they don't know you have this skill."

"No." But my mind wasn't on that advantage. It was on the Second Seal.

What is known that cannot be named?

I placed my hand on the wall, feeling the rough, cool stones below the torch. I imagined Yeshua speaking to the crowd of outcasts, people labeled for their perceived flaws. *You are the light of the world.* My breathing thickened.

"Who are you, Jacob?"

"I've been asking the same question all my life."

"And?" I asked, turning my head.

He hesitated. "Jacob. A lover and a warrior in the line of Qurong, whose kingdom I will rule when he passes."

What is known that cannot be named?

"That's only your earthen vessel."

He didn't react.

"Beyond that temporary vessel, *you* are what is known that cannot be named."

"I'm not sure what that could mean," he said.

What is known . . . Experienced.

That cannot be named . . . Reduced to language.

Words were simply symbols of meaning, created by the mind. There were thousands of languages, all with different words that had many definitions. The true Word, as Talya said, wasn't a thing or any book of theology. It was Justin. The light of the world. Inchristi. An aspect of the Creator in form. Incarnate.

Now you know, Justin had said. I had experienced my identity. And what was that identity?

I stepped toward Jacob, drawn like a moth to a flame. "The page in your hair — you still have it?"

"It's safe."

"Give it to me."

He quickly loosened his locks and handed me the tightly rolled page. Heart beating like a tom drum, I dropped to my knees, unrolled it, and spread it on the stone floor. I clicked.

What I saw stilled my breath. The page appeared to me clearly and in color.

I lifted my head and clicked at Jacob. He was only a dimensional shape. But when I clicked again, facing the page, I saw color and words! And I knew those words.

On the page was a new symbol. Like the tattoo on my arm, a white band rimmed the circle, but now a second band lined the white. A brilliant green band.

White: Origin. The Creator, who was infinite.

Green: Life. Me. That aspect of the Creator who was temporarily manifested in the world, in it but not of it. My eternal self was the light of the world. Inchristi is all and in all.

Below the symbol: The words. *What is known that cannot be named?*

Me.

I lifted my head and clicked at Jacob's form, now kneeling before me. "I've known it," I said.

Heart hammering in my chest, I opened my hand and lowered it on the page, over the round symbol.

"I am the Light of the World," I breathed. "Inchristi is me and in me."

At first nothing happened. So I repeated it: "I am the Light of the . . ."

The white circle under my hand began to glow, and I caught my breath. Brilliance like the sun's joined a green hue that streamed up between my fingers.

I heard Jacob grunt as he jerked back.

The glowing circle winked out, and a rush of power surged up my arm, then into my mind, where it exploded like a star. I had been here before, earlier that very night while being blinded.

I gasped, numb to the world around me. My body felt like it might disintegrate, too frail to contain the staggering power flowing through me, even though that power was only a thimbleful in an endless ocean made of light.

My Origin, my God, my Father, who was infinite, had created me in his likeness as the light of the world. What was made in infinite power could not be unmade by any finite power. It could only be hidden by darkness.

And then it was gone, as if someone had pulled the cord that powered it.

But it wasn't gone, was it?

With shaking fingers, I tugged the sleeve of my tunic up over my right arm and stared at the tattoo on my shoulder. This too I could see. A glowing band of emerald green lay inside the white circle.

I released the sleeve, dropped my head, and began to weep.

I had the Second Seal. The green seal.

And that seal was me.

30

I am the light of the World. Inchristi is me and in me. The words kept rolling through my mind as I fell asleep in the cell with Jacob's muscular body pressed against mine for warmth. The torch had long gone out. We'd spoken quietly in the aftermath of my finding the seal — I feeling great humility and wonder, Jacob stunned by what he'd witnessed. Seeing me shiver as the cell grew cold, he'd pulled me close.

I'd never slept in the arms of a man before, at least not that I could remember. The fact that he was Horde seemed completely irrelevant. I accepted his kindness with gratitude, only hoping that my smaller body would offer him as much warmth.

I found myself wondering if I preferred a man like Samuel over a man like Jacob. This was only the programming of my earthen vessel bound to polarity. But in the light, there was no polarity.

It struck me that all conflict was built upon preference for possession. My land, your land. My house, your house. My rights, my food, my child, my religion, my knowledge, my man, my woman, my body . . .

The list of the earthen vessel's attachments to itself was endless. What would happen if a person could let it all go while still in an earthen vessel during this life? It was the question that all the teachings of Yeshua answered. Those who could let go of their slavery to the world's system of protection and fear would sleep through the storm and walk on water, surely.

My mind skipped to Samuel. What a beautiful creature he was. Such a boy at heart, like Jacob. And yet heroic and full of courage. I wondered where they'd put him, and if he was safe. He wasn't an enemy to the Elyonites, nor a heretic in their eyes. In fact, Aaron distrusted him only because of his affection for me.

And what of his father, Thomas? Talya had gone to find him . . . To what end?

My scattered thoughts faded and I slept.

I felt myself being pulled from deep sleep there on my bed in Eden, Utah. *I am the Light of the World. Inchristi is me. Inchristi is also in me.* In me, my earthen vessel. That's who I was. I was Inchristi in an earthen vessel for a brief time. *Rachelle* was only the word used to label that earthen vessel in the world of polarity.

I had the Second Seal. The green seal.

I opened my eyes. And it was only then that I remembered I was blind.

I gasped and sat up as my heart crashed into my throat. I was blind again!

My whole body went rigid and a chill spread over my skin. I clicked and my bedroom came into view just as it had a week ago, before I'd awakened in Other Earth and been healed by Justin.

Was it all just one dream? Had nearly a week really passed?

I threw off the covers and rose shakily to my feet, fighting back waves of fear. No, it couldn't be. The details were too vivid. I'd seen Eden in vibrant color, unlike in any of my previous dreams. I'd been shot in the leg by Barth and been healed. I'd confronted Vlad and found the first two seals.

Eden was in a synthetic bubble created by DARPA . . .

I jerked up my sleeve and looked at my shoulder. Without having to click, I saw the tattoo, clear as day and in full color, a white circle and a green circle, framed by darkness. So it was real. All of it. Including the fact that Shadow Man had blinded me once more.

Including the fact that my father was going off the deep end.

I'd fallen asleep before he came home. And listening now, I could hear only the sound of birds outside. For all I knew, it could be noon.

Clicking quickly, I ran to his room, knocked. When there was no answer, I pushed the door open. Clicked. His bed was made. Alarmed, I hurried to the living room, hoping he'd risen early.

"Dad?"

But he was gone. And I was blind.

I noted the dish I'd used last night still on the counter. My father would have put it in the sink. He hadn't returned at all last night, which meant he was either in trouble or creating it.

I squeezed my hands together and paced. "Get a grip, get a grip." I had to. Vlad was out there somewhere. The fate of Eden was in my hands.

The thought nauseated me. Who was I but a pathetic blind girl? My whole life, Shadow Man had told me this would happen.

For a moment I was in the nightmare again, hearing his low, haunting voice. *I'm going to blind you. And when you see again,*

I'm going to blind you again. And again. His accusation crushed me. *And what happens to you happens to them all. Through you, I'm going to blind them all.*

How could I go from the elation and power of encountering myself as light to such a fragile state? The seals were on my arm, so why this fear?

I felt like I dangled from the face of a cliff, clinging to a vine. Above me, Shadow Man dared me to retreat into my old self. Below me, Shadow Man grinned wickedly, daring me to escape my inevitable future. I knew then that no matter what happened today or tomorrow, my struggle with Shadow Man wasn't over.

Not until I had all five seals.

Rage washed over me, and I screamed at the unfairness of it all. The room returned only silence. It was just me in my living room, a girl born blind so that God's glory could be revealed in her.

Who have you become, dear daughter?

I stilled at the gentle whisper, struck by the truth that sprang from inside of me.

"Nothing different," I whispered. "The same as I was. Your daughter."

Then see yourself as her and be her.

The light of the world. Inchristi. Be that light. In light there is no darkness, only the shadow it creates in the world of polarity.

Shadow Man.

I swallowed and turned my thoughts away from what my eyes did or did not see. My role in this life was the 49th Mystic. I couldn't let physical blindness stop me from trying, one step at a time. I had to do something.

I paced again, thinking through my options. Above all, to the best of my ability, I couldn't let anyone know that I was blind again. Jacob said that my eyes looked normal, apart from a redness that would clear. I needed the town's trust — the fact that I'd been healed gave me at least some respect.

But that meant I couldn't betray my blindness by clicking with my tongue.

Using echolocation, the only way to see is to send out a signal that bounces off of what lies ahead. You click, you read the signals, you move. That's how you walk through the darkness, one step at a time, not knowing what's ahead. Like faith.

I would use a tap or a snap of my fingers if need be. I could still read the returning signals, if not as clearly.

I had to get to Linda's — the note from last night made that clear. But Linda lived on the north side of town. Barth's lookouts would be everywhere. Vlad would be watching.

Vlad . . . I had only two of the seals . . .

But first, I would find my father.

It took me twenty minutes to get ready, only because I moved slowly, going deep into my mind, rehearsing my experiences in Other Earth while I steadied my resolve in this one. To the extent I kept my focus on the light I'd seen as Justin and as me, I could remain in that vine of truth, even if I was blind.

Taking a deep, calming breath, I opened the kitchen door and stepped out into Eden.

I walked around the side of our house and clicked toward the town center. As far as I could tell, the streets were empty.

My first instinct had been to stay out of sight by taking the long way around the town to Linda's house, but I was no longer worried about being discovered. Barth would have come to my house if he wanted me dead.

Gathering courage, trying not to think of my blindness, I walked out on the lawn dressed in jeans, a black shirt, and my Converse tennis shoes. Three rows of houses stood between me and the town square. I walked straight for Third Street, uncaring who saw me.

I had cut through the Botswicks' lawn when I heard John yelling inside the house. John Botswick, butcher by trade, parent of two with his wife, Melanie. They were in their thirties and had married in Eden.

I stopped by the hedge and listened.

Melanie's voice drifted through the wall. "I don't care what you think is best for us! We've lived here this long without any problems, we just have to get back to normal."

"There is no normal anymore!" John roared. "I can't even leave this house without fear of someone putting a bullet in my head. You call that normal?"

"I said we have to get *back* to normal! That's not going to happen if you go out there and cause trouble. That certainly won't happen if you try to break out of the valley into . . . whatever's out there."

"Well, I can tell you one thing," he snapped. "What's in here, what's under this sky they put over us, it has a name: Barth. And as long as Barth has any power, we're all doomed. If you think we have any chance with that lunatic waving his gun around, you're not thinking."

"Oh but you . . . you, John Botswick, you have it all figured out, right? Oh wait, no, that's David. All you have to do is kill Barth

542

and everything will magically fix itself. You think Barth doesn't have half the town cringing behind him? What do you want? War?"

"They have the guns. David said so himself. If it's war . . ."

I didn't hear the rest because I was already walking away, imagining the chaos behind every closed door in Eden. Vlad had gotten to my father, I was sure of it. My father was a scientist not given to impulsiveness. Vlad was manipulating him, sure that I would finally capitulate for fear of his life.

I had to save my father without writing Vlad into the book.

Thinking nothing of my safety, I passed the last house on our block and walked down the middle of Third Street, headed north. There was a large tree on the corner of Second, which ran east-west, and Third, which ran north-south. I could navigate most of the town from memory without echolocation, but I clicked for added comfort anyway. The square came into view as soon as I passed that tree.

The streets surrounding the town square were empty. But the square itself wasn't. I made out three forms, probably Barth's men — two at the entrance to the courthouse, one leaning against the door of Bill's

Hardware, dead ahead. There were knives and axes in that store — and a host of other things that could probably be turned into weapons. Made sense they would guard it.

I kept my eyes directed straight ahead and walked on without missing a beat. None of them called out to stop me. There were no fireworks. It was just me, the blind girl who could now see, walking through the town square.

But that changed when I was within twenty paces of the hardware store. Clicking nonchalantly with my fingers, I saw the form step out to the curb, assault rifle hanging from his right hand.

"That's far enough."

Bill Baxter. He was guarding his store. Was he with Barth now? I could hear the fear in his voice.

I kept walking, eyes fixed past him to the north, my four working senses hyperalert.

"I said stop!"

I didn't stop.

"Take one more step and I swear —"

"You'll what, Bill?" I asked, stopping in the middle of the road, ten feet from where he stood. "Put a bullet in my head? Kill the only thing Vlad Smith wants in this town? Be my guest."

I could hear the soft scrape of his wristwatch on the rifle.

"I didn't know you were a man of violence."

"What do you expect me to do?" His voice was lower now, meant for me alone. "Just roll over and let it all happen?"

"I think you'd be looking for a way to make contact with DARPA."

"We have. Four of us went to the tunnel last night. There's no way out. Even if there was, we'd be dead long before we got anywhere."

So he'd seen what my father and I had seen.

"For the record, I know Barth's turned into a monster and all monsters get what's coming to them," he said. "But he's not the real threat. Vlad Smith is. Way I see it, as long as he's in the picture, we're all doomed. The only way to get to Vlad is by playing his game until we figure out his weakness. We can't even figure out where he keeps disappearing to. So yeah, I'm out here protecting what little I have left in this world, because people are making enemies. And in this town, no one knows what to do with enemies but kill them."

He took a breath. "If people would just shut up and do as they were told, I wouldn't need to be out here. Tell that to your father if you manage to find him."

By the sound of it, my father was fast becoming enemy number one.

"I'm going to find my father, Bill," I said, drilling him with a fake stare. "You're going to let me go because stopping me will only cause you trouble."

I turned back up the street and started to walk.

"Why, for heaven's sake, won't you just write in that freakin' book of his?" he asked.

"Because Vlad's not who you think he is," I said. "And for the record, I'm pretty sure guns won't work with him." The last part was only a guess.

It took me another ten minutes to reach the Loving residence. I encountered four more guards as I walked through the northern half of town. Only one of them tried to stop me, but I ignored him without speaking a single word, and apart from a string of strenuous threats, he let me go. It was as I suspected. Vlad had given Barth the order to leave me alone.

Taking a deep breath, reminding myself to hide my blindness, I rapped on the door. No answer, so I knocked again. And a third time. Surely they could see me through the eyehole.

The door suddenly opened and my father

grabbed my hand. Yanked me in. Slammed the door shut behind me. Rammed home the dead bolt. No one else was in the room.

He spun around. "What are you doing? Do you have any idea what's going on out there?"

"You didn't come home last night."

"I did come home! You were sleeping."

By the strain in his voice, I doubted he'd slept, here or there. I could smell the sweat on his clothes. Probably the same clothes from yesterday.

"Bill tells me you've been busy," I said.

"You talked to Bill? What's gotten into you, wandering around on your own?" A beat. "You okay?"

Could he tell I was blind? My eyes, maybe . . . I said the first thing that came to mind that might throw him off any thought of what was happening to me in this world.

"I was taken captive with Jacob, son of Qurong, and put on trial," I said.

When he answered, his voice was laced with dismissal and pity. "Don't you see, sweetheart? Your mind's programmed with those dreams in there. None of them are real."

"The programming doesn't work on my mind."

"Would you rather have me believe that

547

you're being taken into captivity with some fellow named Jacob? Just try to imagine how that sounds to me."

He had a point.

"Look, Freud would be the first to say your dreams are cathartic," my father said, taking my arm. "Judging by your confidence, he was right. As far as I'm concerned, you just keep on having those dreams. But right now, I have to show you something."

He hadn't mentioned my eyes. And when I tapped my thigh and snapped my fingers as we walked, he didn't seem to notice. That was good. But how long could I keep up the charade?

Someone was making a sandwich in the kitchen, but I didn't notice anyone else on the first floor. My father led the way down the stairs to the basement, me following the sound of his every step, one of the first ways I'd learned to maneuver as a little girl. All council members had similar reinforced basements — bunkers loaded with supplies to supplement the main stores in the event the worst happened.

Like a nuclear war. Even in this detail, DARPA had been deliberate. When the day finally came for the residents of Eden to learn the truth, they would already be primed to accept the stark reality of nuclear war and fallout. It was a part of every psyche in Eden. The whole town had been preparing for what had already happened.

Any other group of people might very well be pulling their hair out. Not the loyal, brainwashed residents of Eden. They were more concerned with the direct threats within the valley. Evidently DARPA hadn't planned for Vlad Smith.

My father pushed through a door at the bottom of the stairs and led me into a huge room lit by hissing kerosene pressure lamps. The town still had no electricity.

I felt beads of sweat on my forehead as I tapped and strained for the view I could manage. No fewer than a dozen forms milled about near one wall and a table in the center of the room. I could smell the sacked grains and tins. Survival stuff.

"What about this section?" Linda's voice. She was standing next to another form, tapping what had to be a map.

"It was too dark. And it's steeper than a steeple there. I doubt anyone could get up there, definitely not kids."

"I don't care how steep it is!" Linda snapped. "Hank, mark section twenty-seven to be searched again as soon as the sun goes down."

"It's pitch-black out there at night —"

"That's what the flashlights are for, Hank."

"No, flashlights are for getting shot at. Searching in conditions like these is absurd."

Linda spun to Hank. "How dare you suggest searching for my children is absurd!" she yelled.

"I didn't say —"

"I don't care what it takes or who gets shot in the process! We're finding them! Get that through your thick skull!"

The room stilled.

My father stepped up to the table. "Take a breath, all of you. The last thing we need is to fight each other. The fastest way to find the children is to take back control of the town. Once we get the guns this afternoon, you'll have all the cover you need to search. We have to get those guns before Barth and his goons have time to react!" He turned to another form. "Any more luck with the recruiting?"

"Anyone else and we run the risk of leaking information to the wrong party." I recognized Scott Wilson's voice.

"Fine. Twenty-four it is. Between the distraction and the assault on the armory, we'll need them all."

I'd tapped nervously as he talked, noting

at least four sleeping on couches, two more along the far wall, maybe in sleeping bags. Half of echolocation is puzzle solving, putting bits of information from all available senses together to make educated guesses. My mind was working furiously to form the best picture possible.

"Any argument?" my father demanded.

"All the guns in the world won't help us if any harm comes to my children before we find them," Linda pressed.

"Which is why we're going this afternoon," my father said, then turned to me. "Rachelle's joining us. She's talked to Bill Baxter. Any chance he'd join us?"

I could feel their eyes on me. All of them. I stepped up to their table and feigned a glance over what I assumed was another map. "What's this?"

"Sniper positions," Scott said. "On rooftops."

My lungs felt heavy. There wasn't enough oxygen in the crowded space. My father had never served in the military, but he seemed to have the mind for it. But it was more than that. Like Linda, my father wasn't thinking clearly. Even if they did get the guns, more guns would only mean more death. I had to find a way to stop them.

"So?" Linda said. "Any chance Bill will

join us?"

"He's with Barth."

"You're sure?"

"He's parked outside the hardware store armed with an assault rifle right now. And they already know something's coming. Try for the guns and it's gonna all go wrong."

"It already has gone wrong," my father said. "We've lived under someone else's thumb for too long — whether that was Simon's, DARPA's, or Barth's hardly matters now. No more. We have Smith behind us, we move now."

"Behind you? He's the real threat here, surely you can see that. Even Bill knows that much."

"Maybe, but not right now," my father said. "Now it's Barth, and Smith won't interfere. We have to take Barth down before he takes us down, or there won't be anyone around to deal with Smith."

"Smith told you he wouldn't stop you?"

"He did."

"So he's playing you against each other, telling Barth to kill anyone who defies his law, then telling you to go after Barth. Don't you see?"

"Be that as it may," Linda said, voice strained, "without Vlad Smith, we all die. We need him, at least for now. But we don't need Barth. As long as he's alive, no one's free in this valley."

Their plan said only one thing to me: more dead bodies.

I wanted to tell them what I knew, everything I'd experienced in Other Earth. But I knew that telling them would accomplish nothing.

I had to *show* them. More to the point, I had to show my father before he ended up dead.

And I knew exactly how I would show him.

"Is there any doubt in this room that when all is said and done, Vlad Smith is the greatest threat to this valley?" I asked them. No one spoke. "You know, Smith . . . the man who coerced Hillary into killing Simon, then ordered Barth to kill Hillary. That Smith."

No one replied.

"And is there any doubt that Vlad seems to have taken an unusual interest in me?"

"As an example," Linda said.

"More than just an example, trust me. I'm his ultimate objective. Even if you don't believe that, it can't hurt to give me one chance to confront him before you do anything crazy that could get half of you killed."

"No," my father objected, turning away. "No one's putting you in harm's way. I won't allow it."

"I just walked past seven of Barth's guards and not one of them stopped me. Why? Because Vlad can't risk me being harmed and he's passed that order on to Barth. I'm the only person in this valley who can confront Vlad."

"What on earth can you accomplish by confronting the man who has his finger on the button that controls this valley?" Linda demanded. "We have children out there, and he may be the only one who can find them!"

"Probably so, because he's the one who took them."

"You know that?"

"Who else?"

"Maybe," she returned immediately. "All the more reason to play by his rules. He wants Barth out of the way, we give him what he wants."

"I *am* giving him what he wants," I said. "Me. All I'm asking is that you wait. What do you have to lose?"

"You!" my father said. "I can't risk that."

"You didn't answer my question," Linda said. "What do you hope to accomplish?"

I hadn't answered because they wouldn't

understand the truth. But I could give them something else.

"To take away his power." I took their silence to be skepticism. "He still wants me to write in the Book of History. If all else fails, I'll do it, but on my own terms. To do that, I have to get to the book. That means calling Vlad out, and I'm the only one he'll come to now."

No one voiced support.

"All I'm asking for is one chance. Like I said, you've got nothing to lose by waiting."

"We have everything to lose!" Linda snapped. "We should be out there right now, ripping Barth's head from his shoulders!"

"Maybe she's onto something," Hank said over by the map. "This all began with her refusing to write in the book. Maybe it's all just a test. Either way, I can't think of a better distraction than her calling Vlad out in the main square. You can bet Barth would be there. And where Barth goes, so do half his men."

The room remained silent except for one of the sleepers, who rolled over and coughed.

"The perfect time to go after the armory," he said.

This wasn't what I had in mind at all. I

555

had to stall them. Expose Vlad. Get my father to see differently before they started a full-fledged civil war.

"Actually, I need you all to be there with me," I said.

Hank ignored me. "Instead of the hydro plant, we create a second distraction south of town, set a house on fire." His voice held fresh enthusiasm. "It would draw Barth south to deal with it. Best chance we'd have of taking the armory, north."

My father wasn't agreeing, but he wasn't rejecting the idea either.

"It has to be tonight," I said, trying to buy time. "You want a distraction, I'll give you one, but only after the sun sets. In the dark."

"We can't wait that long!" Linda said. "Besides, Vlad controls the sun."

"Yes, and it went down last night. There's no reason to think it won't tonight."

"Rachelle's right," my father said. "This could actually work. But I don't think I can show myself around Barth."

"As long as Vlad's there, I think you'll be safe." It was a risk I had to take. "He's after civil war, not just a few shots."

The fact that my father didn't object to the bit about civil war gave me some hope. Maybe he was seeing past his rage.

"Tonight," I reiterated. "You go with me

and stay out of sight until Vlad shows himself."

"And when he does?"

"You come out. I need you to see what I have to show."

He thought about it for a second, then gave me a curt nod. "Fine."

The die was cast. And no one knew that I was blind except me.

31

I stood by the large fountain alone, clicking to see. I'd rolled both of my sleeves up, baring my shoulders. Not that I thought showing Vlad the white and green seals on my arm would undermine him. But I wanted them all to see the luminescent glow of white and green circles. It brought me comfort.

Comfort, because everything I hoped to accomplish depended on my speculation that I'd be able to see the Book of History, just like I'd seen the page in the dungeons with Jacob. There was an energy about it that came with true sight.

I'd spent the day alone in my room, away from anyone who might discover my blindness. Alone and wrestling with a bipolar swing of emotions — one minute resting in the memories of the light, the next settling into deep self-pity that blindness was part of my journey. And I could not shake my terrible fear, knowing that facing Vlad while blind would be no different from entering into my nightmare once again.

It was amazing how quickly I reverted to the world's system of fear and control. Life happened in cycles of forgetting and remembering, Talya said. I knew that intimately now.

My shirt was wet with sweat. I didn't want to be there, standing alone. I hated the fact that I saw no other way.

As Linda and my father had planned, a group of twelve were stealthily setting up for the assault on the armory, adjacent to Barth's house, north. Several of them were armed with guns, the rest with axes and machetes. Another half dozen continued the search for the children with Linda — a compromise she'd demanded and received. The rest were south, preparing to burn Hank's house to the ground. A small sacrifice, he'd said.

I couldn't stop the assault on the armory, but I could stop them from actually using those weapons if they got them.

My father was the key.

And I was the key to him.

He waited behind Bill's Hardware — safe for now and close enough to hear my signal. It was seven o'clock. Had to be.

I swallowed deep, gathered my resolve, and stepped up onto the edge of the fountain pool, exactly where Vlad had stood to show us our false sky only yesterday.

"Vlad!" My voice echoed off the walls of the church. "Vlad Smith! Bring me the book!"

Nothing. But I had no illusions that he would just drop out of the sky. A small part of me thought he wouldn't show at all.

"This is what you wanted!" I cried out, feeling desperation.

I waited with my feet planted on the wide edge, clicking into the darkness around me.

"Vlad!"

I heard the door to the church open and I turned, clicking. A form — one of Barth's guards — stepped out carrying what had to be a machine gun in one hand and a crackling torch in the other. My mind flashed to Other Earth. Why a torch rather than a flashlight?

A second guard came out, carrying another torch. They walked down the steps to the edge of the lawn and planted the torches in the ground. The man on the right faced me.

"I don't know what the deal is with you, but he said you'd be coming. He wanted torches when you arrived, so here you go.

Torches." Then he turned and walked back up the steps. Two more guards with torches had emerged and stood on either side of the door. I had an audience of four.

Then it was eight, because four more emerged, all armed, setting up a perimeter around the landing. Then nine, when a thick form I guessed to be Barth stepped out of the building and stood between his men, hands on his hips like a gunslinger.

Still no sign of Vlad. My palms were greasy.

I heard soft padding of feet as two residents tentatively stepped out of the darkness to my right. Then another, around the corner of the empty bakery.

Barth stepped up — maybe to set the new arrivals straight — when Vlad's voice cut through the still night.

"It's okay, my friend. It'll do them good to watch."

I twisted around, clicking. But I didn't need to click because I could see the slight amber glow around his eyes. I hadn't expected to see more than the book, if he presented it to me. But he, being something other than human from Other Earth, was visible to me.

As was the slight glow from under his jacket. The Book of History.

Vlad was leaning on one of two lamp poles that normally lit the courtyard. His legs were crossed and he looked to be distracted by his hands. Maybe his fingernails, I couldn't tell because that part of him was only a blur.

He spat to one side, unfolded his legs, and lifted his head. A few more residents had braved the night to see what all the yelling was about.

Vlad had his audience. My father had his distraction.

"You're early," Vlad said, stepping closer to the fountain. "Things are just starting to heat up here. I would have figured tomorrow, but here you are. Which means one of two things." He stopped between two torches and stared at me. "Either you're bluffing, in which case you're being rather stupid, or you've learned more than those two seals on your arm have shown you, in which case you're being just as stupid. So which is it?"

Did he know I was blind?

"Now!" I cried. My voice carried, and I was sure my father had heard the simple signal we'd agreed on.

Vlad's head turned toward the corner of the bakery. My father walked forward and stopped forty yards from us.

"I see." Vlad sounded pleased, which concerned me a little. "A family affair, is it?" His head swiveled back to me. "By now you know that the Book of History has more power than any artifact imaginable on this plain. What you still don't know is that you're going to use that power for my gain."

"I know the power of the book, but I also know who you are. And who I am."

"As the Second Seal bears out," he said. "And I cannot deny who I am." He paused. "I've been doing this for five hundred years, my little peach cobbler. Do you think a few circles on the arm of the 49th Mystic will make me quake in my boots?"

A circle of onlookers was forming around us, but I blocked them out, because for all practical purposes, I wasn't there. I was in Other Earth now, confronting what had to be a Shataiki who'd bred with a human to bring his darkness across dimensions.

Regardless of dimension, all darkness was only a shadow. So then I was facing a shadow. Shadows vanished in the light.

"Please," he said, heading slowly toward me. "We're way beyond mincing words. Best to just get it all out in the open. The morons who watch us won't have a clue what to do with the truth. They're too bound up in fear of the Shadow Man. Hmmm? Isn't that what you call me?"

"I call you son of Teeleh."

He stopped with my use of the name. "And I respectfully embrace my oneness with my master. We all have our roles to play. Play your hand, 49th, and I will play mine. At the end, we will see who's standing."

He peeled off his jacket. Folded it and draped it over the stone bench. I could still see the slight glow from the book in the seam pocket.

"You're wondering why I'm not giving you the book," he said. "Do you take me for a fool? Hmmm? I know you didn't come to write what I need you to write. You're leaning on the knowledge found in your dreams, but that won't work here. After all, they're only implanted dreams. None of them are real. Nevertheless, I will speak on your terms."

The bit about my dreams being implanted was a lie for my father's benefit. But I was still preoccupied with the jacket he'd set down. I hadn't considered the possibility that he wouldn't allow me to write.

Did he know that I intended to write my father rather than him into Other Earth? If so, my plan would die on its feet.

"The light you think you can defeat me

with is far too weak," he said. "You're going to need the Third Seal at least, sweet peas. Unfortunately, half the town could be dead by then. They just can't seem to stop themselves, can they?"

I tried to ignore my fear and think of a way to get that book.

"I've had plenty of time to practice waiting for you. And now here you are, playing into my hands."

I faced him, letting the truth of what I had known in Other Earth well up inside of me like a storm.

"Inchristi is all." I said it plainly, as simple fact. "Inchristi is in all." His hands shook as I spoke the truth. "I am Inchristi."

He moved like a striking cobra, crossing the ten paces between us in the space of half a breath. I'd come with no intention to fight — the thought hadn't even crossed my mind. And now he was a yard from my face, roaring with enough ferocity to sweep my hair back and rattle my bones. The pungent scent of dirty socks laced with vanilla filled my nostrils, making me nauseous.

I frantically clicked and ducked instinctively, but not quickly enough to avoid his fist, which clipped the side of my cheek and snapped my head to the side. I staggered back and spun to find footing on the narrow fountain wall, but there was none.

Yielding to my fighting instincts, I dived high, tucked my head under, landed on my right shoulder, and rolled to my feet. I could sense him making adjustments. My momentum was forward, and he would anticipate my trajectory, so I planted my right foot in the grass and threw myself up and backward, over his head as his body rushed under me.

Halfway through my backflip, I twisted sharply to my left and brought both fists around to the side of his head. My club of flesh and bone landed with a crushing impact that threw me wildly off axis. I twisted my body and landed on the ground, both feet firmly planted, facing him as he whirled back to me.

None of the onlookers or guards moved.

If my blow bothered Vlad, he'd fully recovered. He stood ten paces from me, looking amused. "Nice. But as you can see, in the end your pathetic words are powerless."

"Inchristi is all," I said again. "Inchristi is in all."

"That's all you have? I've faced far worse." But his voice was slightly strained.

"Inchristi is all!" Worry nipped at me. "Inchristi is in all."

"You think the power is in a few words?" This time they had no effect on him. "That I dread the path of shamans and faith healers? It's not about words. It's about the heart. Clearly, yours is still as black as mine."

My unease was descending into a full-blown panic.

A soft *whump* filled the air to the south — they'd set fire to the house. But it was too early!

I fisted my hands at my sides and hurled the words at him. "Inchristi is all; Inchristi is in all!" Then again, screaming them now.

"Now you're just wasting my time," I heard Vlad growl. He moved so quickly this time, and I was so distracted by my failure, that I hardly noticed him coming. I only remember a terrible blow to the side of my head.

I dropped like a rock with the cries of "Fire!" and "Rachelle!" echoing through my head. My father was yelling my name.

The world around me was spinning, but I pushed myself to my knees. *The book! Get to the book!*

"Rachelle!" My father, feet pounding.

Fearful for him, I twisted, clicking. He was veering toward Vlad.

"Leave her alone!"

Barth was yelling orders; his guards were sprinting toward the sound of the roaring fire.

Lunging like a sprinter out of the blocks, I shot toward that jacket. Five long strides and I was there.

A terrible thud sounded behind me. My father had unwittingly given me a brief window and would pay a price, but I had singular focus now.

I dropped over the jacket. Dug my hand into the breast pocket. Jerked out the book, fumbling.

With shaking fingers, I flipped it open. The blank page before me glowed. The book had opened to a page with a pen folded into the spine. I grabbed it and scribbled the words as quickly as I could.

My father David into Other Earth.

Vlad reached me and snatched the book from my grasp. He looked at the words I'd written and slowly turned his eyes down to me.

"Welcome to my world," he snarled through a twisted grin.

His fist slammed into my temple and the world winked out.

■ ■ ■ ■

Vlad Smith closed his eyes, groaning with satisfaction. She'd succumbed to his manipulations as planned. And her father, lying on his side, oblivious.

He crossed to the man, ignoring the chaos. None of it mattered now. None but Barth, who had his gun drawn, intent on finishing what he'd started.

"If you even touch him, I will rip your guts out and feed them to the pigs."

Barth stepped back, confused.

"Leave!"

He left. Like a dog with its tail tucked between its legs.

Vlad grabbed David by his collar, dragged him over to the fountain, and plunged his head into the water. Then jerked him out.

The man sputtered and stared as consciousness found him. Blinked, searching for meaning. But that would come later. The 49th clearly knew that David would awaken in the other world the next time he slept here, but did she also know that the book would follow anyone written into that world? It no longer mattered.

Vlad shoved the Book of History into the man's armpit, held him steady for a beat, and hammered the top of his head. Like a bull hit by an iron wedge, the man sagged, unconscious in this world, alive in another.

The book under his arm shimmered for a brief moment, then vanished.

"Sweet dreams, Tissue-top."

32

Darkness. The kind of darkness that one could call a reduction of black itself. But only for a breath before David's mind entered the state called dreaming. Not just any dream, but a lucid dream in which he knew he was dreaming.

In reality, he'd just made the mistake of crossing Vlad Smith, who'd crushed him with a single blow. Note to self: never cross Vlad. But he was slowly waking now, knowing he would make it right by doing what needed to be done.

David opened his eyes, expecting to see the courtyard and the fountain. A synthetic black sky overhead. Instead, the sky above him was made of stone.

He sat up and looked around a room, perhaps twenty by twenty, lit by flaming sconces, two to a wall. Between two of the torches, a large blackened sculpture of a winged cobra with red rubies for eyes stared at him.

He shivered. The serpent was not unlike the one Rachelle had described from her nightmares.

To his right: a golden bowl, filled with a foul-smelling liquid. Daggers with jeweled handles and other medieval utensils that looked good only for prying and cutting hung on the wall to his left.

His heart hammered. Where was he?

In a dream. A nightmare, but it didn't need to be a nightmare. He couldn't remember the last time he'd felt true fear in his dreams, in part because he rarely remembered his dreams, in part because he'd studied them at great length for Rachelle's benefit and in doing so learned how to disassociate himself from those fabrications of the mind.

I've made a mistake with Vlad, and as a result, I'm terrified. Now my mind is creating a scenario that will allow me to work through that fear of him safely. Dream researchers had long ago argued that nightmares provided the mind with this remarkable gift.

I don't have to feel fear, but if I do, that's okay too. Same thing he'd told Rachelle a hundred times.

He lowered his eyes to the cold surface on

which he'd awakened. A gray stone table. One darkened by stains. Bloodstains. He was naked except for a loincloth.

He knew he was dreaming, but this particular dream was so lifelike that he was having a hard time distinguishing it from reality. Only logic told him as much. It was precisely these kinds of dreams that had afflicted Rachelle for so many years.

He twisted, saw a velvet curtain in a doorway, and was sweeping his feet off the table when his hand bumped an object on the stone surface at his side.

The book. Vlad's book. He'd brought the journal with him. Naturally. His mind was dipping itself into this fabricated reality through the power of both Rachelle's and Smith's persuasions. Even awake, the mind could sink deep into hypnotic suggestion.

Something Rachelle had said at the tunnel tripped through his thoughts. What if the whole human race was seeing the material world through distorted perception? Just like he was now, in this dream. It was the teaching of ancient mystics. And of quantum physics. Though it made no sense to any scientist, one hundred years of experiments had shown over and over, without fail, that in some impossible way the world was being created in its current state by the consciousness of the observer.

They called it the observer problem, because it conflicted with all logic. Nearly all of modern electronics were soundly based on quantum principles, even though no one knew why they worked. There would be no cell phones without quantum physics. In this way, cutting-edge science was perhaps even more mystical than religion. In fact, it supported what many religions denied, namely, that humans had the power to change the world through thought and belief alone. He'd drilled these ideas into Rachelle her whole life.

But this . . . this was a dream. He had to hold on to that simple truth.

Motion to his right caught his attention and he turned. A scrawny man in a white robe stood in front of the doorway, staring at him. His skin was light gray and his hair long, knitted in dreadlocks. Around his neck hung a medallion of the same winged serpent that seemed to be the focus of this room.

This was a priest. David was in a room reserved for sacrifices of some kind.

It's a nightmare, David. Only a nightmare. A good part of his mind seemed to know that, but his heart was pounding, oblivious to logic.

The man snapped his fingers without taking his eyes off David. Two others much larger than the priest stepped through the curtain and took up positions on either side of the table. They were dressed in black with sheathed swords slung on their waists.

"How did an Albino find its way into our holy place?" the thin priest asked.

David cleared his throat. "I —"

"I wasn't asking you!" the priest snapped. "But since you seem so eager to tell me, answer."

David wasn't sure how to answer the man. He had no memory of being anywhere but here, at least in this dream. "I'm dreaming," he finally said.

The priest slowly stepped around the table and was halfway around when his eyes fell on the book. He studied David with renewed interest.

"So you are an Albino, but one who dreams of another world."

David's mind was fabricating a world taken from Rachelle's descriptions of her own dream world. In that dream world, she too was an Albino. And these must be the Horde. This one in particular was called Ba'al.

David knew it was all a fabrication, but his mind was quickly being swallowed by its own illusions. The fear he felt was undeniable.

"This is the dream. I'm dreaming you because my daughter, Rachelle, is having nightmares, and now my mind's re-creating those nightmares. None of this even exists."

The priest's fascination grew. "I see. And this daughter, who is she?"

"My daughter."

"Who is your daughter? In her nightmares, I mean. Who does she claim to be?"

"She's haunted by the Shadow Man. But like I said —"

"And tell me, do you know where your daughter is in this dream of hers?"

A pinprick of concern for Rachelle nipped at his mind. But none of it was real. He, if not Rachelle, had to remain tethered to reality.

He shrugged, aware of the sweat snaking past his temples. "That I can't tell you, except to say that she's dreaming she was taken captive with one of your own. I can't remember the name."

"Perhaps I can help you. My name —"

"Is Ba'al," David said. "I do remember that. Servant of Teeleh. So you see, I can name these fears of hers. But I have no intention of making them my own."

The priest had gone rigid. When he spoke

576

again his voice came slow and low, barely above a whisper.

"No, of course you don't. And the name of the one who took her captive — was it by chance Jacob, son of Qurong?"

"Jacob. Yes. They were taken together."

The priest blinked. "By the Elyonites?"

"Yes. Yes, Elyonites. But this —"

"Send for Qurong!" the priest snapped.

"Yes, my lord." The voice came from a third man who'd entered without David's awareness.

"Tell him I have urgent news of the 49th!"

"Yes, my lord." The guard dipped past the curtain and was gone.

A dream, David. A dream, a dream. All illusion is as powerful in its effect on the mind as the truth. The mind can't distinguish truth from illusion using the five senses.

But he was in a lucid dream, knowing it was only that — a dream. He had to cling to that knowledge. If he could work through this nightmare, maybe he could better help Rachelle work through hers.

The priest approached him, long robe swaying about his ankles, deeply attentive. "You are correct in saying that this is only a dream. So tell me . . . what exists in reality?"

"A world gone mad that you'd know nothing about."

577

"Mad how? By whose hand?"

"Our own hand. Nuclear fallout. DARPA."

Ba'al reached for the book, took it in his long, crooked fingers, and set it down on a long bench next to a line of four daggers.

"Tell me, in these dreams of yours, is this Shadow Man who haunts your daughter one named Vlad van Valerik?"

David hesitated. "Vlad Smith, you mean. But that's not the dream. This is."

"Bind him to the table," Ba'al ordered. "Do not harm him yet." He walked for the exit.

Without hesitation the two warriors in black robes strode toward him.

"Hold on . . ."

The guard on the right slugged his temple and David grunted. They muscled him back down onto the table despite his frantic objections.

In short order, they clasped his wrists and ankles in chains attached to iron rings at each corner of the stone table. Then they returned to their former positions.

He now lay on his back, spread-eagle, iron clasps digging into his wrists and ankles. Chained to a stone table used for sacrifice. His body was shaking.

A nightmare, David. It's a dream, just a dream.

He closed his eyes and lay as still as he could, begging himself to wake up.

33

I woke in the Elyonites' dungeon with a start, my confrontation with Vlad in the courtyard still crashing through my mind. The face-off left me with conflicting emotions. On the one hand, I'd successfully written my father into Other Earth so he could see through Vlad's lies. Or at least I assumed I had successfully written him in — I'd never actually seen it work before.

On the other hand, my father had been attacked by Vlad, and I didn't know how he fared.

Was he here?

I jerked up and clicked, searching the cell. A form, Jacob by his shape, lay beside me, soundly sleeping. I twisted around, half expecting to see my father. But there was only Jacob.

Where was my father then? I'd awakened in the desert, where the Roush had found me . . . I wondered if they were talking to him now. The thought that he might have ended up with the Horde crossed my mind, but I let it go with a shiver. Surely not. I was the one who'd written him in, after all.

Me, the 49th, who was bringing a sword to divide and searching for the five seals so I could lead them all from blindness.

I looked down at my arm, where I could see the two circles in full color. I still had to find the Third Seal, but I had no clue how. No finger to point the way. Would all five seals be preceded by a finger? I hadn't thought to ask Talya while I had the chance.

I lay back down and stared into the darkness. The previous day had been filled with the wonder of finding the Second Seal. Jacob had been as deeply affected as I was, questioning nonstop like a child on the cusp of finding a great treasure in the forest. But now, what good would it do me if I couldn't find the third? I needed the first three to save Eden, Talya had said.

I could still hear the thud of my father being struck by Vlad. Imagined him falling in a heap. What if he'd been killed by that blow? No. If Vlad wanted him dead, he would have done it long ago.

I swallowed and turned on my side, lost in a sea of concern. And it was then, as I stared at the dark cell, that I saw the faint glow on the wall. At first I thought I was imagining it, because I was blind.

Blind to all but the circles on my . . .

I shoved myself up on one arm, straining for view.

Behind me, Jacob grunted and jerked awake. "What is it?"

His concern hardly registered. I was fixated on the wall because I was now certain that the luminescence was real. Thin markings were etched into the stone.

Scrambling to my feet, I rushed to the wall, pulse pounding.

"What is it?" Jacob demanded. "It's pitch-dark."

You can't see it? I meant to say, but the words didn't come out. I could make out the faint marks, and as I reached my hand toward them, they glowed brighter.

I withdrew, stunned.

Jacob was at my back, breathing over my shoulder. "Words . . ." He stepped up, seeing what I saw. "Does it never end with you?"

I blinked and stepped closer. There, etched into the stone surface, words that had somehow manifested as we slept.

What is Lost
That can never be Lost?

For the moment, concerns over what had happened to my father vanished. Thoughts of my encounter with the green seal the previous night flooded my mind. Wonder filled me, as it would a child first seeing the ocean.

"It's the third finger," I whispered.

"Pointing to the Third Seal."

"Yes."

"This is always how it happens? You find one seal and the finger pointing to the next simply manifests?"

"I don't find the seals," I murmured. "They find me when I'm ready, as do the fingers."

What is lost that can never be lost?

I heard Jacob reach for the wall and push it with his hand, as if expecting it to give way.

"It's a clue," I said. "Not a doorway."

"So it seems. But nothing that *seems* to be true is true with you." He paused. "It's like there are two of you — the 49th Mystic and Rachelle. So ask her what this means. Ask her if this is a lost doorway or just a riddle."

He was referring to our first encounter in the canyons, when he'd communicated to me through his man.

"This isn't a game."

583

"No, not a game." I heard him cross his arms. "Still, put your hand on the wall and ask the 49th what she should do now."

"The wall isn't the 49th. I am."

"Understood. But you are far beyond the comings and goings of any mortal I know. What do you have to lose? What if we have been given a way out of this dungeon?"

"I can't just speak to a rock," I said. "It feels . . . I don't know . . . flippant."

"True. Far too flippant. Still . . ."

If only to amuse him, I lifted my hand and pressed my palm flat against the words, thinking to ask it his question, but I didn't get that far. The moment my palm touched that cold stone surface, the words brightened, shimmering with light.

I gasped and jerked my hand away as power flowed into my arm. Jacob stepped back.

"By the fangs of Teeleh . . . Is there no end to your power?"

"It's not my power."

And with that acknowledgment, the writing on the wall faded and winked out.

"It's gone."

"It's not gone," I said. "I have it. I have the third finger. What is lost that can never be lost?"

"So when you have the answer to this

riddle, you will find the Third Seal."

"Not quite. When I know it, when I experience the truth this finger points to, the Third Seal will come to me."

We stood in the darkness, silent for several long beats.

"How long?"

"As long as it takes."

"We don't have that long. Aaron will try to break you. We have to get you out before he can do that." He sighed. "I've been thinking . . . If Talya knew I would be with you, perhaps he also knew that I would save you."

"Save me how?"

"The Albinos are clever and skilled, I'll give them that much. But they aren't as powerful as Horde. I know I could take down three, maybe four, before —"

"No!" I spun in his direction, clicked, and grabbed his arm. "No, Jacob. Not that way, it's way too dangerous! We have to trust the seals."

"The seals are for your mind! It doesn't mean there's no place for the sword."

"I'm the sword!" I snapped.

"So you've said. And you've cut them deep. If Talya led you here, into this hell — if he knew I'd be with you — he must have also known that I could help you. And not with my mind! What's lost but never lost? You. You're lost, but with your power and my strength, you can be found where you belong."

Among my people . . .

"My power doesn't work like that," I said. "There are way too many guards above our heads, regardless."

"You can see in the dark, they can't."

"I'm only a Mystic, not a warrior!"

"You're forgetting, I've seen you move. And you're forgetting who I am. The only reason they took me was because I was distracted by you. If we take them off guard —"

"No."

As if on cue, the outer dungeon gate squealed, and we both turned to the sound of boots. Many boots.

"Torches," he whispered. "Are you sure? If the opportunity —"

"I'm sure. Not like this."

The boots grew louder.

"I fear they'll separate us. It's what I would do. Aaron's accomplished his objective in forcing me to see his resolve."

The thought hadn't occurred to me, and the moment Jacob said it, his fear became mine. I couldn't bear the thought of being without him. He had to be wrong!

Surely . . .

Keys rattled. The door was thrown wide. Several quick clicks told me there were eight of them, two torches. So many?

"Out!"

"To where?" Jacob demanded.

The guard spat. "Not you. The Mystic."

Jacob stepped forward, pushing me back with his arm. "To where? She's with me."

One of them chuckled. "I didn't know Horde mated with Albino heretics in the —"

"Shut it, Borland!" To Jacob: "If you suffer any delusion that she's with you, Scabs are denser than I thought. You're both with Aaron, to do with as he pleases. You stay. She goes. Don't make me say it again."

I stepped forward, easing his arm down. "It's okay, Jacob. I'll go."

"Rachelle, I beg you . . ."

"We're their guests. And so we honor them. There's nothing else we can do," I said bravely. But I wasn't so brave. And there *was* something I could do. Something I had to do.

I turned and put my arms around his muscled body and pressed my face against his chest. "Stay strong, son of Qurong. Remember everything I've told you. Remember my heart for you."

He held me awkwardly. "And mine for you," he whispered.

"Are you deaf?" the guard snarled.

"I swear, if you harm one more hair on her body," Jacob growled, "I will appeal to the fangs of Teeleh himself and unleash terrible suffering on all that is Elyonite!"

"No, Jacob," I said, lifting my face and touching his with my hand. "Not like that."

"Don't let them break you." His voice was urgent. "Never give up hope. I'll come."

He said it as if he knew more than I about what might happen to me. Did he?

"Of course," I said. "Never."

I said it with as much courage as I could manage, but my breath was coming hard as I turned from Jacob and surrendered myself to my captors. My heart was pounding as they slammed the cage shut and led me down the corridor. My skin was clammy as we descended a long flight of steps deeper into the bowels of their dungeon.

And when they shoved me into a ten-by-ten hole far beneath their city, my mind began to go numb.

They left me on the muddy ground to contend with a silence so deep that I could hardly hear, much less see. I was cast out like refuse.

Blind. And utterly alone.

34

An hour passed before the priest returned, an eternity in those endless moments of trying to wake from the nightmare. David kept reminding himself of the truth, and his mind seemed to accept that truth, but his emotions stubbornly followed the evidence fed to them by his five senses. His eyes saw the room, his nose smelled the stench of death, his ears heard the crackling of torches' burning wicks, his skin felt the biting iron, his tongue tasted bitter sweat on his upper lip.

But these had to be illusions.

The dream swallowed him whole, and for the first time, David actually knew what his daughter had suffered her whole life.

He heard them before he saw them because the entrance was behind his head, out of sight without a painful twisting of his body.

"You are sure?" a deep voice demanded.

"There can be no mistake, Lord Qurong," Ba'al answered. "He's opened the gateway between the worlds."

"The Leedhan."

"Yes. Vlad. But there is more. This one claims his daughter was taken by the Elyonites." A brief pause. "With Jacob."

The one named Qurong was silent.

"I cannot stress the urgency of our situation enough, my lord. We must bring Vlad through at all —"

"I don't care about this Vlad of yours! You're sure my son is in their hands?"

"Are you so blind?" Ba'al rasped. "The very fate of all Horde now rests in the hands of Vlad, Shadow of Death, instrument of Teeleh!"

For a few moments no one spoke, and David lay still, hoping that he would wake *now,* before they did whatever they planned on doing.

Heavy boots rounded the table, and a large man wearing leather chest armor came into view. Like a Viking warrior, David thought. Gray eyes, though not as light as Ba'al's. A heavy beard and long, thick dreadlocks.

The commander's jaw clenched. "He looks like any other Albino to me," Qurong said. "How do you know you can trust him?"

"How could any Albino know that Jacob pursues the 49th unless they have access to hidden knowledge?"

"This whole business of the 49th is madness! If any harm comes to my son, I swear by the name of Teeleh that I will drown you myself."

"That madness will be your undoing. Choose your words carefully. We now have no choice but to —"

"Do not tell me what choice I have!" Qurong snarled, jerking his head to the priest. "I have no desire for a war with the Elyonites."

"No, of course not, my lord. And yet they have her."

Qurong returned his glare to David. "What else has he confessed?"

"We haven't questioned him yet."

Nausea rose in David's gut. Qurong stepped up, grasped David's cheeks between his thumb and forefinger, and squeezed.

"What else do you know about my son? Tell me!"

David tried to shake his head, but the man's grip prevented even that much. The fingers released him.

"Nothing, I swear. I . . ." He considered making something up, if only to appease the man. Or recant his statement about

Jacob being taken — anything to avoid the various sharp instruments in the room. "I'll tell you anything you want to know if you release me from these chains."

"You'll tell me what I want to know now or you'll die in these chains!"

"I have said everything!" David shouted, furious at his predicament. "This is a dream, for heaven's sake!"

"Tell me what you know."

"That my daughter is dreaming of being taken by a group of fanatics that call themselves Elyonites. That she's with a warrior named Jacob, who was also taken. That's all I know."

"How could you know this?" the commander demanded.

"I *don't* know this! It's a dream. She told me her dream and that's all."

"The shadow Leedhan sent him," Ba'al said, stepping up. "As I said, he calls himself Vlad Smith."

Qurong crossed to the book and picked it up, flipped through its pages, and studied something written.

"So the book is real," he said.

"But of course, my lord. As is the other world. And above all, Vlad, who will save us."

The commander slapped the book down.

"Then prove it. Work your magic. Bring Vlad. Save my son."

"I can't use the book. Its power is available only to the 49th and any humans who've crossed."

"You're human!"

"Yes, but I haven't crossed."

"So then this Vlad can use it if he crosses —"

"No. Vlad isn't human. But he can save your son and prevent our subjugation to the Albino lamb if this one will bring him through." He gestured to David. "This human has the power to use the book."

They glared at each other, and David thought Qurong might confront the priest with more than just a stare and harsh words.

Instead, the commander turned abruptly and walked toward the exit.

"Begging your pardon, my lord, but where are you going? We've only just —"

"To hear sense from my warlords rather than witchcraft from you!" Qurong interrupted, turning back. "To wage a holy war of all wars against the Albinos on both sides of the Divide if I must! Isn't that what you've always longed for, priest?"

"My desire is only to follow Teeleh's desires. And his is to ensure his supremacy through the failure of the 49th. Only then can we rid the world of all Albinos."

Qurong spat to one side. "Then do what you must. Use your knives. Bring Vlad from this other world. But know this: if any harm comes to my son, I will slaughter you and your priests with the same sword that I bloody in holy war."

35

A gunshot woke me. One fired in the distance, but not so far away that it didn't give me a start. I jerked my head and opened my eyes. Darkness . . . I clicked and saw that I was still on the ground beside the fountain where Vlad had knocked me out.

In Other Earth, I was destitute and alone.

In Eden, I was waking to a nightmare.

I pushed myself to one knee and quickly scanned my surroundings with soft clicks. There was no sign of my father. No sign of anyone that I could see. But the occasional popping of gunfire north of town was all the sign I needed.

No smoke that I could smell — enough time had passed for the house fire to burn itself out. The distant chirping of birds told me it was morning.

A chill swept through the valley. My heart was in my throat. Today was the day that my father had assured me would be the end.

The end to what?

To everything, he said.

What is lost that cannot be lost?

I didn't know. Nor did I know what had happened to my father. I had to find out if he'd crossed over, and if so, where he was. What he'd learned. If he was safe, here and there.

I had to find him!

Claws of urgency bit deep into my mind as I launched myself into a run, headed north, clicking. Within three strides I was at a full sprint, headed straight toward the gunfire. I'd start my search there.

There could only be two reasons my father had left me on the ground through the night. Either he was now so far gone that other concerns took precedence over me, or he was incapacitated.

Why had Shadow Man left me alive? Why not just kill me after I'd written my father into Other Earth with the book? But I already knew . . . His objectives extended far beyond Eden, and he needed me, the 49th, to finish what he'd started here.

You're blind, Rachelle. Only a blind girl. He's doing what he promised to do. You've failed already.

The gunfire was coming from the north-east, the direction of the hospital. And beyond that, the hydroelectric plant. But Linda's house was my first objective and I flew like the wind, trusting my instincts and sharpened senses. Right up Third Street and then left on Wooded Lane, up the alleyway to the corner of a storehouse across the street from Linda's house, where I pulled up, breathing hard through my nose.

I would have expected the church to be Barth's primary headquarters, but I hadn't encountered a soul. Many residents would have holed up at the first sound of gunfire, but no guards?

And my clicks showed me none near Linda's house.

I crossed the street in a fast walk and tried the door. Locked.

A bullet smashed into the wood frame by my hand, and I jerked back with a cry of alarm. Ducking to my right, I threw myself flat behind the hedge that surrounded the house.

I wasn't the only one who'd sought refuge behind the bushes. I landed on a body. I tried to scramble off of it, but another bullet crashed through the window above me, pinning me down.

Breathe, Rachelle. Calm. Trust your instincts.

The cold body under me had a rifle, I

could feel it with my right hand. How many more had been killed?

Staying low, I yanked the rifle from the man's death grip, leaned back, and swung the gun's stock at the window above me with enough force to shatter the glass. I felt for the trigger, shoved the rifle above the hedge, and fired two quick shots in the general direction of the gunfire aimed at me.

Without hesitation, I released the rifle, dived through the opening I'd created, tucked my body so I would land on my arms, and rolled to my feet inside Linda's living room, clicking madly. Two shots tore holes in the far wall.

"Dad!"

Nothing. The basement.

I reached the stairwell in five long strides and ducked inside.

"Linda!"

Still nothing. I didn't hear their soft, urgent voices until I was halfway down and around the first landing. Ten more strides and I was there, throwing the door open, clicking without concern of being found blind.

I startled a dozen forms, several snatching up their weapons. I lifted my hands.

"It's me!"

"Rachelle?" I spun to the sound of Linda's voice. "You're . . . Why are you clicking?"

Whatever attempt they'd made on the armory had clearly succeeded. Everyone in the room seemed to be armed.

"Where's my father?"

"You don't know?" She sounded confused.

"Know what?"

"Where he is?" She turned to the others. "We thought he was with you." She closed the distance between us, seeming like she wanted to offer me comfort, but I raised my hand to stop her.

"I haven't seen him since last night. Tell me what you know."

"Why are you clicking? You're blind again?"

"We're all blind, Linda. Just tell me what you know."

"We haven't seen him either, not since he left to create the distraction at the courthouse. What happened?"

"None of you were there? At the fire?"

"No. Craig and Randall . . . None of them made it. The rest took the armory. We got the guns."

"Where's Vlad?"

"We don't know."

"And Barth?"

"He's holed up at the hospital with his guys."

The hospital? A bell went off somewhere in my mind.

"Why the hospital?"

"Thick walls, open ground . . ." She sounded like she might break down and begin crying.

"Barth's house is a fortress with open lawns," I said. "When did they move to the hospital?"

"We killed four of them," someone said. Bill Baxter, by his voice. He'd switched sides.

"When?"

"Most last night —"

"No, when did Barth move his men to the hospital?"

"Last night. After we got the guns."

Again, why the hospital? What did the hospital have that Barth's fortress didn't? My father? Vlad, with my father. Sedating him . . .

A wave of panic rode my bones. What if Vlad had wanted me to write my father into Other Earth and was using him?

"Listen to me carefully," I snapped. "No one leaves this house. For any reason. I don't know about your little war, but something much worse is coming down. Don't

600

ask me how I know that, just know that your life depends on believing me. Forget Barth, forget the guns, forget everything you think you know. Just stay here and pray."

"We're all gonna die in this valley," someone said, voice breaking. "There's no way out."

Maybe he was right. But I had to find my father.

I walked up to the table, clicking. Grabbed a handgun.

"How do you use this?"

No one moved; no one spoke.

"How?"

"Safety's off." I recognized the butcher's voice. "Just point it and pull the trigger. It's a nine millimeter semiauto."

"Show me the safety." I could make out the gun's form but not the finer details. "Put my thumb on it."

He set his weapon down, took my hand, and showed me. The room had gone perfectly still. Any lingering doubt about the state of my sight was put to rest.

"You sure about this?" he asked.

I turned and strode from the room, leaving them in a mild state of shock. Linda called out for me when I was halfway up the stairs, but I didn't respond.

I can't say that I had much of a plan as I

let myself out the back door and sprinted for the corner of the next house. Nor that I was afraid for my life. I was past that, maybe because the adrenaline now pumping through my veins had altered my mind so that I could apply acute focus to the challenge at hand. I'm sure that was part of it, but the larger part was my desperation to get to my father.

It took me ten minutes to reach the back side of the hospital, echolocating on the run through the trees the long way around. The rear door would be locked and the windows likely guarded. But I wasn't going for either the door or the windows.

I had to get up the corner escape ladder to the roof. Following my mother's death, my father had taken up smoking for a year. He told me he'd often taken breaks up there, hidden from prying eyes. He'd also locked himself out once and decided to hide a key under one of the air conditioners. It was still there, he said — you never knew when you might want to get out for a break.

I didn't want to get out. I wanted in. I hadn't decided what I'd do when I got there.

One step at a time was all I knew to do now. Like echolocation, not seeing too far ahead. Faith. I would act and then react to whatever presented itself to me. There was no time for a plan.

The ladder was on the northeast corner of the two-story building. Its precise location wouldn't come into view until I was much closer, but I was sure it was there, forty paces ahead. At night, I would have an advantage over anyone else. Now, only my speed and agility could compensate for my blindness.

With one last deep breath, I left the trees, bent over, sprinting for the northeast corner.

Five steps before I reached it the shot came, snapping over my head. Still at a full run, I dived into a roll, palmed the gun at my waist, and came up firing in the direction of the gunshot.

The bullet wasn't on any target, but I didn't stop to consider my bad aim — I was already sprinting to my right, angling for the corner, searching for that ladder with a string of rapid clicks.

Its shape came into view when I was ten paces out, and I hurled my gun up on the roof, still at a full sprint.

They might have seen me running, but unless they were hanging out the window, they couldn't see me taking to the ladder. Blood pumping through my veins, I launched myself into the air and landed on the ladder a third of the way up.

Then I was up, surprised by my speed under the influence of adrenaline and Other Earth agility.

I rolled onto the roof, out of sight, hoping they thought I'd ducked around the side of the hospital.

Palming the gun with a prayer that it would still function, I crossed to the air conditioner closest to the stairwell door and felt along the bottom edge until my fingers found the hidden key. Relief washed over me. Without the key, I would only be stranded.

Ten seconds later I unlocked the dead bolt, let myself into the upper stairwell, and shut myself in.

Silence. No hum of light bulbs. Without power, the hospital would be dark where there were no windows. They would be as blind as me.

But I could see in the dark.

What is lost that can never be lost, Rachelle?

The question whispered through my mind, and I paused in the darkness on that top step. The world seemed to still around me, and for a moment I felt disoriented. Like the stairwell I was in didn't really exist. Like I was just dreaming all of this.

It did exist, of course, but I felt momentarily dislocated from it, suspended in time. Raw stillness.

What is lost that can never be lost?

I lifted my sleeve and stared at the glow of the white and green bands tattooed deep into my arm. These I could see, blind or not. My breathing thickened.

What is lost that can never be lost? Me, I thought, but *Me* was the Second Seal.

And then time crashed back into my awareness, more acutely than before. Strange how my experiences in Other Earth didn't align as easily with my perceptions in this world. Which was a problem, because Talya had said that the key to saving Eden was the Third Seal, and it was now the sixth day and I still had no clue where to find the Third Seal.

One step at a time. Baby steps.

I clicked and followed the shapes and shadows down the stairs and around one corner to the first-floor hall entrance. I didn't hesitate at the door. Nor when my clicks showed me two guards running down the hall toward me, knowing the sound of their gunfire would bring others.

I sprinted directly for them, closing the twenty paces with quickness I didn't know I had. They both jumped back, guns rising.

But I changed my course before they

could fire. Leaped high to my left, took two long strides on the wall, and flew toward them from an angle that required them to adjust their weapons.

Then I was there, silent as an arrow in the night, leading with my left foot as I brought it around. It was my speed, not my weight, that gave my blow its force. My heel snapped the first guard's head back before slamming into the face of the second. They dropped like two sacks of grain.

I landed like a cat beside them, heart slamming.

Only then, crouched in that silent hallway, did it occur to me that the safest place to keep someone alive in a building that was receiving gunfire would be the basement. Underground, where few ventured. The basement where, for all we knew, Vlad Smith had been holed up for the last week.

I hurried back to the stairwell and slipped in, breathless. Moving on the tips of my toes, I flew down the metal stairs to the lower level. There were no windows in the basement. It would be pitch-black.

I hesitated at the entrance to the basement hallway, then pulled the door open. I clicked as softly as I could. The hall was empty.

My mind spun. If Vlad was down here, he

might hear my clicking. I held my breath and eased down the corridor, acutely aware of the slightest sounds.

But it was my fine-tuned sense of smell that stopped me halfway down the hall. I could pick out the familiar smell of bleach and disinfectant mingled with a general medicinal scent I'd come to associate with the hospital. But now another scent hung in the air, however faint. Dirty socks. A hint of vanilla.

Vlad was here.

Ignoring the warning bells that told me to run, I gathered my resolve, touched the wall to guide me, and crept forward, keenly aware of the scent, stronger now. I dared not click, but I didn't need echolocation to find the three doors in that hall. Two on my left, down and across the corridor.

One directly ahead. And as I moved toward it, that scent grew stronger. Imagined or not, it didn't matter. I could only follow what senses were available to me, trailing my hand along the wall.

My fingers touched the door frame and I froze.

Still no sound from inside. Could I hear the faint flickering of flame? No, but I could smell his scent. And if I could smell him, would he soon smell me?

607

I found the doorknob with my left hand and the gun in my waistband with my right. Before I could lose courage, I yanked the door wide, clicking like an insect.

He was seated on a chair not ten feet from the door, feet propped up on the counter, reading something by the light of a lantern. I knew it was him because of his glowing eyes and now the faint tinge of red at his fingertips as well. And I knew that the form on the gurney to my right had to be my father, hooked up to an IV.

Even before Vlad looked up, I knew that he'd mistaken my approach for someone else. And when he did look up, he didn't have time to react because I pulled the trigger and sent a bullet into his chest.

Then another. And a third, jerking the trigger in rapid succession.

Now he reacted, first with shock. Then with a soft chuckle. "Touché." The word died with a final wheeze as his lungs shut down.

Relief flooded my body. I'd killed him?

But his reaction made it clear that death wasn't something he feared. I wasn't even sure bullets could kill him in this world. We had to move quickly.

I spun to my father, who hadn't moved. A dozen thoughts collided in my mind, the loudest being that Shadow Man was keeping him sedated. Asleep in this world.

Awake in Other Earth.

And with that single, isolated thought, I was sure that Vlad had manipulated me into writing my father into the book. Having crossed, my father could now use the book. Vlad had been a step ahead of me all along!

But my father was still sedated, which meant he was in Other Earth right now, under the influence of someone who was working with Vlad to open the gateway for him to cross.

The Book of History had crossed with my father?

Dread washed over me. I had to wake him before he used the book!

I rushed to my father's side, knocking over a tray in my hurry. "Dad?" I shook his face. "Wake up!"

He was out cold, veins flowing with narcotics. I ripped out the IV and shook him again. "Dad!"

I knew sedatives well enough — following my mother's death, my father had studied them thoroughly, desperate to learn how she could have died. I also knew that only time or another drug, like an adrenaline injection, could wake a person from anesthesia.

Vlad would have taken no chances, surely. He might need to wake my father as well, if only to apply his own forms of manipulation. I could only hope . . .

I searched the counter next to Vlad's slumped form with a string of clicks. Two syringes. One small, maybe Propofol or some similar drug. One larger, self-contained. My heart leaped.

I snatched up the large plastic syringe and fumbled with the seal. A thump startled me. I half expected Vlad to be rising. He wasn't. His hand had fallen from the chair's arm and struck the side of the counter.

Shooting the drug into my father's thigh would slow the effect by a good thirty seconds and bring him out slowly — time I didn't have. I ripped the plastic sleeve off the syringe, frantically searched his inner arm for the bulge of his vein, the prick from the IV I'd just pulled out. I lined up the needle with the pinprick on his arm, slipped it in, hoping I'd hit the vein, and injected a small amount of adrenaline into his bloodstream.

Nothing happened. So I gave him more.

When nothing still happened, I shot half the contents into his arm.

He came up with a snort like an electrocuted bull, and I jumped back.

"Oh, God!" he bellowed.

"It's me. Rachelle. Try to keep quiet."

"Oh, God!" He clutched at his chest. "Oh, God!" Gasping.

Silence no longer mattered. We had to get out, that was all.

"I just injected you with adrenaline," I said, speaking quickly. "We have to get you out of here. You have to climb the stairs. Down the fire escape. Can you do that?"

He was panting. I could only imagine what kind of horror I'd just pulled him from.

I grabbed for his hand. "You've had a nightmare, I know. But right now . . ."

My words died in my throat when I felt his two bloodied fingers in my hand. Two fingernails were missing. He was being tortured in Other Earth.

Revulsion rose from my gut, and for a second I thought I might throw up. His fate was in my hands. I had to keep him awake. We had to move!

"Okay, listen to me. I need you to focus now. We have to get out of here and keep you awake. If you go back under, you go back into that same nightmare. You understand?"

"I . . . It's real . . ."

I pulled his legs from the gurney and

grabbed his hand. "Stand up." But he wasn't moving. "Stand up!" I tugged his arm.

This time he stood, shaking from the shot of adrenaline, but more than fully aware. Why was he hesitating?

Something else was bothering him.

"Dad, you have to trust me, please. We have to get out!"

"Okay." He followed but with some reluctance, I thought.

I felt like a child leading a Saint Bernard on a leash, but we managed, first to the dark hall, then to the stairwell, where he twisted back.

"What is it?"

"I have to kill Barth," he said.

"Have you lost your mind?" Poor choice of words. "This isn't about killing anymore. It's about saving Eden!"

"You don't understand! He's got the whole valley rigged with explosives. If I don't kill Barth by noon, we'll all die."

My father's desperation to kill Barth and kill him quickly suddenly made sense. Vlad had played everyone, knowing that if my father went after Barth under duress, Barth would return the favor. Fearing for my father's life, I would eventually write him into the book if only to pull him out of his madness. Talya had said Vlad wasn't permitted to take life with his own hands, but blindness and deception were far more effective than guns. They were the Shadow's weapons.

"No one's going to die," I said. "Not Barth, not you, not me. He can't blow up this valley until he has what he wants. He still needs both of us, but we have to go."

Where to, I didn't yet know. Baby steps.

"What are you going to do?" he croaked.

What is lost that can never be lost?

"I'm going to find the Third Seal. Hurry!"

36

Ba'al stood over the sacrificial table, infuriated. The Albino lay spread-eagle on the stone surface, head tilted to one side, unresponsive.

The priest Nastros, his most experienced interrogator, was frantically checking the man's eyes, pulling up the lids to expose them to the torchlight. What he'd anticipated being a rather straightforward exercise in persuasion had taken far too long already.

He had here, on his table, the father of the 49th Mystic in the other world. So then, Vlad had come to their aid from that dimension, as Teeleh had foreseen. The leverage this father might provide them could not be underestimated.

Thus, the man must remain alive. Plied but alive. At least until he used the book to open the gateway for Vlad himself. Only then could Vlad force the 49th to betray herself and all Mystics in both dimensions.

"He's dead to the world," Nastros said. "I don't understand it. He seemed to faint for no reason."

"No man faints without reason," Ba'al snapped.

"But you saw it yourself. I had numbed his pain so that he took up the quill."

Ba'al took the ink pen from the Albino's fingers and set it beside the open book. Learning that the man wrote with his right hand, they'd applied pain to the left. Why the man had resisted writing for as long as he did was a mystery. He'd convinced himself that he was in a dream and yet remained stubborn, concerned about his daughter.

That changed when they extracted the fingernails. He'd already put the pen to the page when he inexplicably collapsed. Could the book do this to a man?

Ba'al lifted both hands above his head and slammed his fists down on the man's chest. "Wake!"

"My lord, we've tried the potions . . ."

Like a man possessed, Ba'al beat on the Albino's chest with as much strength as he could gather in his frail form. "Wake!" Then three times, robes fluttering about his flying arms. "Wake, wake, wake!"

But the man did not stir.

A terrible fear seeped into Ba'al's veins.

"You will wake him or you will take his place," he rasped. "You will wake him and encourage him to write the words of his own will before he has drawn ten breaths. Do you understand?"

The priest dipped his head. "He will wake, I swear it. And he will write."

Using echolocation without thought, I moved quickly through the trees, praying my father wouldn't go after Barth. I had to keep him awake and trusting.

What is lost that can never be lost?

The finger kept trying to point my thoughts to the Third Seal, and each time the world seemed to quiet momentarily. I recalled Talya's words: *Remember, set your eyes on what is unseen, not on the finger itself. It only points. If you focus your attention on the finger alone, it will block your sight of that to which it points.*

But that didn't seem to help.

We were well south of the hospital before I pulled up. I hadn't heard any more gunfire. An eerie silence had settled over the valley. Above us, the clouded sky seemed to press down, sealing us in as much as protecting us from the wasteland beyond.

"Rachelle . . ." My father held his bloodied

fingers gingerly. "You're clicking again. Is it back?"

My blindness. For a few seconds a terrible self-pity gripped me. A rage at having seen so clearly, then losing that gift. But I didn't have time to let it crush me right now.

"Yes," was all I said.

"I'm sorry . . . I . . ."

I turned and wrapped my arms around him. For a moment I was just his daughter again, and I wanted it to stay that way.

"This is all my fault, not yours," I said through the knot in my throat. "I'm so sorry, I had no idea that you would end up where you did."

"It's okay, it's . . ." He rubbed my back. "So the dreams are real?" Still struggling to believe. "Ba'al is real?"

He was in Ba'al's Thrall. *Dear God, help him.* I pulled back and gently lifted his wounded hand. "If they weren't real, Vlad wouldn't need you to write him into the book, into Other Earth. Whatever you do, tell me you won't."

"I won't."

"Promise me."

"I promise. But I can't go back there. I thought I could handle it, just a nightmare. But if you're saying . . ."

"Nightmare or not, it doesn't matter. Like

any storm, to the extent you put your faith in it, it masters you." A bell went off deep in my mind and I hesitated, feeling oddly separated from my words. "Just don't write."

What had I said that struck that bell? *To the extent you put your faith in it, it masters you.* Like the disciples in the storm. *Why are you afraid? Oh you of little faith.*

What is lost that can never be lost? Faith? It made no sense.

". . . are we going?" I heard my father ask.

I tilted my head up to him, reminded of his frailty. He was like all the residents of Eden, fractured in every conceivable way, no longer knowing what to believe after learning they had lived for so long in an illusion.

But wasn't that also true of the whole world?

Lift your eyes and see what is unseen. Change your perception.

"What time is it?" I asked.

"Late morning, I guess."

"And you're sure the explosives will go off at noon?"

"I don't know what I think anymore, but I believed it when he said it to me in the shed. Noon on the sixth day if I didn't kill Barth. And it makes sense, doesn't it? Assuming you're right, if he doesn't get what he wants, it would be like him to bring the whole town down with him."

"Maybe. His objective goes way beyond Eden and he still needs me, so I doubt he'll let me die. But everyone else . . ." I didn't need to finish.

"Then no matter what we do, Eden will end up under a pile of rubble. Anyone who survives the explosives will be exposed to the fallout when the sky collapses."

My pulse spiked.

"With any luck, Vlad's dead," I said. "If not, he still needs you as much as he needs me. So we need to put you where no one can get to you."

"Where?"

I took his hand and headed toward the center of town. "The prison below the church."

"Lock ourselves inside?"

"Only you. It's you they need now, not me."

A beat passed as he wrestled with this thought. We'd reversed roles. I was now his protector and he was beginning to accept it, at least for now.

"What are you going to do?"

Baby steps. Just one at a time, like clicking through a dark labyrinth. I began to run with my father close on my heels.

"I'm going to try to save Eden."

I said that, but I don't know if I believed it because as far as I could see, I was out of options. What was I supposed to do, find all the explosives and figure out which wires to snip? Gather a divided town and convince them all to hide in bunkers? The best I could do was hope that Vlad had lied about the explosives, though I was sure he hadn't.

What is lost that can never be lost?

Or I could find the Third Seal.

That strange calm came again, and this time it lingered. With the other two seals, their truth had been suggested to me before I experienced them, so I assumed I'd already been given the answer to the third riddle. But what? The seals weren't information or dogma. I had to *know* them. Experience them intimately.

We jogged to the edge of town and were crossing the greenbelt behind Bill's Hardware when my father grabbed my arm, gasping. "No . . ."

"What is it?"

"The sky just went dark except . . . his face . . . Vlad's face is on it, covering the whole thing. It's him . . ." His voice broke. "He's grinning down at us. At the whole town."

The Shadow of Death bore down on

Eden, mocking us all. Vlad was alive. Reminding us that we lived in a bubble that he alone controlled.

What is lost that can never be lost?

A slight vibration ran up my spine and sent a faint buzz through my skull. Distant voices were shouting; somewhere far away a gun fired. But it all sounded detached to me. My mind was doing something other than listening to sounds here.

Vlad was alive. But that wasn't entirely true. *I* was the one who was alive.

In one fell swoop, my first encounter with Justin filled my awareness. Me, holding a stone that was my life, my mission, all that I would experience. My veins filled with light, because I was the light of the world, like him.

My dad was talking, but he sounded far away. I lowered my eyes and looked at my arms. Immediately I could see them, the real them. Once again my skin was translucent; once more I could see my veins, flowing with light beneath my skin.

I glanced up but was still blind. My father was pointing, talking frantically. He couldn't see the light. I looked down again . . . . But I could see. The light was right there, flowing through my veins, casting an ethereal glow through my arms and body.

The ancient mystic Paulus had seen this light when the scales fell from his eyes. Talya's words on the cliff returned to me: *Let the scales fall from your eyes.*

Though I walk through the valley of the shadow of death, I will fear no evil. Because that shadow is nothing to fear but fear itself. You can't defeat a shadow. You need only turn to the light, ignoring the shadow cast by the earthen vessel.

Polarity. Light and dark. And I was the light as well.

I didn't need to defeat Vlad, I just needed to bring down the illusion created by his shadow. To collapse that view of the world so that we could see another world already present. The solution was to remove the scales that blinded me to true sight.

What blinded Eden to the world beyond this valley? The sky . . . The bubble . . . Any thought of its crumbling brought fear. And for good reason. Even if there was a way to bring down the sky, doing so would leave us in the wasteland.

A distant and low chuckle reverberated through the valley, as if originating from the image on the dome above us, but I couldn't be sure because it seemed to come from everywhere at once.

From me, I thought. From my own mind.

I looked up at my father and spoke with an authority that surprised even me. "Get to the courthouse as quickly as you can. Find your way to the basement — there's a key by the door in Hillary's office. Flashlight's in the basket. Get down to the cells and lock yourself in."

"What?"

"He needs you. He's coming for you."

"What about you?"

"Go. Run!"

He ran.

37

I walked straight for the fountain in the town square, but I didn't feel like I was walking on the soles of my own feet. Of her feet. I wasn't walking on the soles of Rachelle's feet, because Rachelle was only the label of my earthen vessel. My true identity wasn't that temporal flesh, that avatar, that jar of clay. I had only joined with it for a very short time called "this life," which ended almost as soon as it began.

Beyond her was me. The eternal me who was the light of the world because I was Inchristi.

And as Inchristi, there was no problem, because it was finished — death was no more. Like my true Father, who could not be threatened or compromised in any way, I too was safe. Fear was caused by the shadow of death only to the extent I aligned with it rather than to the light that I was.

Rachelle the earthen vessel saw a problem,

but that problem wasn't shared by the me who was the light.

What is lost that can never be lost, daughter of Elyon? The question whispered through me, gentle and inviting.

My skin was tingling. Simon Moses had once preached a story about a man called Stephen who had seen a great light and stood in perfect peace as he was stoned to death. That light was the law, Simon declared.

Simon had the wrong law. The light wasn't the law of death. It was the law of grace.

Whether I saw it or not, I was the light of the world. I stood by the fountain and felt like Stephen, embraced by a light that also filled me. Inchristi is me.

"After all you've been through . . . You didn't really think a bullet or two would solve your problems, surely not."

I stopped five feet from the fountain and turned to the voice, clicking. Vlad stood in front of the door to the church, arms crossed, chewing on something, maybe a toothpick. His eyes glowed red and were as plain to me as the tattoo on my shoulder.

Shadow Man. The accuser. Had he seen my father? Worry gnawed at my mind. My earthen vessel mind.

"You still don't understand who you're

dealing with, do you?" he said, lowering his arms, descending the stone steps. "It's only you and me now, so let's be boringly plain, shall we? You think the shadow isn't real? How absurd. Just look around you, sweet pea. I see a very big problem. And in" — he pulled something from his pocket — "fifty-seven minutes, every last soul in this stink hole you call Eden is going to feel that very big problem. At least for a few minutes. Then they won't feel anything because they'll be dead."

"There is no death," I said.

"Of course not. But that doesn't make it not real. Real is what your mind thinks it is. And I'm just getting started with you."

Keep your eyes on me, dear one. Don't be afraid of the shadow. A slight tremor shook my lower jaw and I breathed deep, settling into the voice of my Comforter.

"An illusion is an illusion because people see it as real," I said. "And that illusion has as much effect on any human as the truth. Like you say, our tissue-tops can only process what our algorithms know based on a system of logic and beliefs. But there's a way beyond that illusion. A way to see Inchristi, and in that sight I know you cannot harm the true me."

"No? Well, as it turns out, I'm about to

introduce you to a whole new form of harm."

"To my earthen vessel," I said. "Not to me."

He stopped, ten paces away now, staring at me, toying with that toothpick between his teeth. He chuckled.

"My, my, we've been a busy girl in yonder place. Learning more than the mind can hold, are we? We have the white seal and the green seal and we are quite proud of our progress."

He spit the toothpick out.

"You've caught on to the fact that religion's fear is like this synthetic sky over our heads, protecting all the frightened little fearmongers inside from a threat that keeps them on the straight and narrow but is utterly powerless in this life. The 49th does so well. But you still have two very significant problems."

"Do I?"

"You're blind again. And if you think I'm done blinding you, you underestimate me. Again and again, isn't that what I promised? The whole world will hate you. And I mean all of it, not just this stink hole. Through you, I'm going to blind them. Keep them powerless."

Fear pulled at me. The unfairness of my

blindness . . .

The story from the Gospel of John tripped through my mind. Why was this one born blind? Whose sin caused it? Neither her sin, nor the sin of any other, but so that God's glory would be revealed in her. That was my story.[1]

It was the story of everyone. I, the 49th Mystic, represented all of humanity. The experience of finding light in the darkness was somehow worth all of that darkness. The very point of it.

"And that's the other problem," he said. "You still feel fear."

But that wasn't me. It was her, my earthen vessel. Shadow Man's only purpose was to blind the earthen vessel, but even being blind, either physically or spiritually, didn't change who I was as the daughter of Elyon. It only changed the experience I had of this life.

"Yes," I said. "She does."

He slowly paced to my right. "She?"

"Rachelle," I said, lifting my eyes to the sky. *Lift your eyes and you will see the harvest is ripe . . .* "My earthen vessel." My voice sounded distant to my own ears.

"Your earthen vessel *is* who you are!" he snarled. Fear laced his tone. I was chipping away at his confidence. "I'm going to help you know that."

He was accusing me, but I didn't care. My face was turned up, and I imagined his face grinning down at me from the sky. So easy to believe it was real. The law. Simon Moses's law. Fear-based religion. Protecting us from what? The wrath that would crush us if we didn't follow that law?

Meaning fell into my mind and I blinked.

"The fallout . . ." It was all I said because he was coming for me, a black wraith with red eyes.

My instincts took over and I shifted to my right. It's all I did, just a simple shift. But flowing with such power, my movement was blindingly quick and I sidestepped him easily.

His lower body slammed into the concrete pool, shattering the wall; his head struck the fountain top, smashing it into a hundred pieces.

Let go, daughter.

The words breathed through me and the world stilled. It was true — focused on protecting myself from Vlad, my mind was distracted by its fight-or-flight programming. I had to let go of that part of my mind.

Tell me, what is lost that can never be lost?

The Third Seal was the only hope for

629

Eden, and I could feel it pulling at me.

I looked up at the sky again, even as Vlad snarled and rushed me like a battering ram. This time his arm struck my shoulder, but I was turning with the impact and the blow only spun me from my feet. I landed on my back, staring at the synthetic sky, and half of me was already rolling to my feet to evade another blow.

Turn to the light, dear one.

But the other half was breathing the voice.

I let my muscles relax and I lay still, ignoring the alarm bells clanging in my mind.

Don't be afraid of the shadow light creates.

Then that shadow was over me, twisted with darkness. He grabbed my waistband, plucked me from the ground, took two long steps, and slammed me down on the broken fountain. The blow to my back knocked the wind from me.

I knew that no amount of effort would free me from the powerful grip pinning me to the concrete.

"That's better," he said. The darkness faded from his face and he gave me a wink. "Much, much better."

He lifted his head.

"Who is the father of this child under my fist?" he roared. "I'll give you to the count of three to present yourself, or I'll rip her

630

throat out. And don't think I need her, because I don't. I need you!"

It was a lie, he did need me, but my father would believe him. Fear sank its teeth deep into my mind again. The fact that I was feeling it so strongly generated its own fear, because it meant I was slipping. Then spiraling.

I began to panic and my mouth responded, beginning a cry of objection that was cut short when he slugged me in the solar plexus.

"One!"

Tears stung my eyes. I tried to speak, but my lungs refused to work.

"Two!"

"I'm here!" I heard my father running down the church's stone steps. "Let her go. Please . . . Just don't . . ."

Vlad released me and was on him before he could finish the sentence. I don't know where he struck my father, only that the crunching blow rendered him unconscious before he hit the ground. By the time I had twisted my head, fearing the worst, I saw that it had already happened.

My father lay in a heap with one leg folded awkwardly under his body.

David blinked once, then opened his eyes.

A charred stone ceiling shifted in shadows cast by wavering torchlight. He was back. Rachelle . . .

He jerked up, felt the restraints bite deeply into his wrists, and collapsed back onto their stone table.

"He's awake!"

It was his tormentor — the priest who had worked on his fingers. But his fingers no longer concerned him. Only two thoughts did.

Vlad had Rachelle.

He no longer needed her alive.

David had spent his whole life protecting his daughter. Every waking moment helping her cope with her blindness in the cruel world of darkness. Nothing but his daughter's safety mattered to him. There was now only one way to save her.

The one called Ba'al walked up to the table, gray eyes bloodshot.

"You're awake."

Tears filled David's eyes and spilled past his temples.

"It doesn't have to be painful," Ba'al said. "The choice is yours. But I will help you make the right choice if you insist. In this way, pain can be your friend."

"If I . . ." David's voice hitched and he

cleared his throat. "What happens if I write?"

"You don't know? You will return Vlad to us."

"Here, in this dream?"

Ba'al hesitated, then dipped his head. "Yes. To this dream."

"Away from my daughter?"

Another hesitation. "Yes. Away from your daughter."

"Then I'll write," he breathed.

"You'll write?"

"Yes. I'll write."

"A wise choice." To the other priest: "Give me the book."

How can you describe the connection between a loving father and a daughter who has depended on him for guidance and love her whole life? How can you fathom the fear she might feel at the prospect of losing him?

I can't describe the connection. I can only describe the momentary terror that washed through me as I lay on my back, facing the sky. I couldn't bear to look at my father, crumpled on the ground.

Everything that I thought protected me in this life teetered on a razor's edge. If not for the words I heard next, I might have died there.

What is lost that can never be lost? Look beyond the finger. See what it points to, daughter.

It wasn't the meaning of the words that calmed me. It was the sweet, soft, caring, and yet utterly unconcerned way in which I heard those words that flooded me with warmth and eased my panic.

So why should the evidence this valley presented fill me with fear?

I closed my eyes. I wanted to see another world. I *had* to see the unseen. The realm that was here and now and flowing with light. The one I'd seen with Talya.

That's good. Trust me. Look past the evidence that blinds you. See the light.

Tears burst into my eyes. "Elyon," I croaked, barely audible.

Tell me who I am.

You are infinite. You are love. You are the light. Nothing can threaten you.

And who are you?

I'm your daughter, made in your likeness, the light of the world. I'm Inchristi. Nothing can threaten me either.

Never. Now tell me, what is lost that can never be lost?

My perception, I thought. Even when I don't see the truth, I'm still seeing. Sight can be lost, but it's never really lost. It's

634

only seeing something else.

The moment I thought it, heat spread through my extremities and warmed my fingers. But there was more to the Third Seal. What is lost? What is not lost?

A journey.

Even when I was lost in the journey of life, I was still going somewhere. Right then, feeling so lost, I was still on a journey of some kind.

What journey?

The journey of perception. Of learning to see.

Open your eyes, daughter.

The heat had spread up to my face, burning hot now. I opened my eyes and saw the air was flowing with wisps of colored light, sprinkled with a thousand tiny stars, like fireflies twinkling on and off, not only above me but all around me.

I was seeing what normal eyes could not see.

And there was more. The sky . . . The image of the seals on my arm now filled the entire sky. A white band, glowing like a polished pearl. *Origin is Infinite.* Inlaid with a green band, me in the world of creation. *I am the Light of the World.* And now a deep black core that shone like polished onyx. Perception . . . Blindness was and always had been my only challenge.

My pulse pounded — no other sound now. Just the crashing of a heart on the verge of uncovering a hidden treasure. The sky . . . like scales that blinded. *Let the scales fall from your eyes.*

The sky was blinding us, I thought. It was blinding the whole world to the sight of the unseen. The light. My journey in this life was to see the light. I knew this already, but now I was experiencing it on my own. *Knowing* it.

Barely able to breathe for the anticipation coursing through me, I slowly lifted my hand so my palm faced the sky, spread my fingers wide, and spoke the words that filled my mind.

"Seeing the Light in Darkness," I breathed, "is my Journey."

My body was that of a girl, laid out on her back, helpless. But in the next moment, white light erupted from my body and shot to the sky with a ferocious hum. It pierced the core of the black circle, then spread to the outer white band.

The moment it made contact with the outer ring, the sky detonated with a blinding, silent flash, brighter than any sun.

It's all I saw for a few seconds, because I reflexively clamped my eyes shut. But it's not all I experienced. I felt the light collapse back into my chest, my body trembling with raw pleasure. My mind was soaring on the wings of numbing wonder. My right shoulder felt as though it was on fire.

I was being branded.

I had found the Third Seal.

And then, just like twice before, the power was gone, leaving me there on the fountain, limp, tingling in the afterglow.

But the light wasn't entirely gone. I could see it through my eyelids the way you see the sun with your eyes shut. Red and hot.

My eyes snapped wide. The clouds were gone. A blazing sun stood high above in an amazingly blue sky. My sight was back!

Something was falling, like a mist or ash, slowly drifting down from high above the valley.

The scales had fallen. I'd collapsed the synthetic sky.

38

I lay stunned by my fully restored sight, trying to make sense of what my eyes were seeing. I had collapsed the barrier that protected Eden from radiation poisoning.

I reached for my right sleeve and jerked it
up. A black circle, shiny like onyx, filled in
the center of the white and green bands,
still glowing. Black showed that although I
was often blind to the truth that I was the
light, I could learn to see. Three of five seals.

White: *Origin is Infinite.*

Green: *I am the Light of the World.*

Black: *Seeing the Light in Darkness is my
Journey.*

The scales had fallen from my eyes. I was
seeing the light in darkness.

And then I remembered Vlad and the
explosives.

I twisted and rolled off the fountain, ignoring the pain that flashed down my spine.
There was no sign of Vlad. He'd vanished,

but his threat against Eden remained. He'd rigged the valley to blow — of that I was quite sure.

As to his threat regarding the fallout? I doubted it.

My father lay where he'd fallen, still oblivious. But that's not what froze me. It was the light glowing around him. Coming from him. I blinked as if to correct my sight, but the light remained.

I slowly turned my head and saw two residents, Abel and Susan, standing dumbstruck, staring up at the sky. They too glowed slightly. This was the same light I'd seen in my veins with Justin, only now I was seeing it more plainly. My perception of the world had changed.

New creatures. All things new. The light of the world. I was seeing who they really were, but were they seeing it?

No, I thought as two more people stumbled into the open. They were, however, seeing the falling sky.

I stepped down from the pool and crossed the lawn just as the first flecks of ash from our vaporized sky reached the ground. Like snowflakes, only lighter, floating down in silence, landing on my face and arms, the grass, blanketing the entire town.

Walking toward my father's limp form, I

felt as free as those flakes. As brilliant as the light coming from my father.

I knelt on one knee and shook him, then patted his face. "Dad! Dad, wake up!"

Only a half hour had passed since I'd shot him full of adrenaline, and he needed no more encouragement to regain consciousness. His eyes fluttered open and he stared up into my face, still lost between worlds.

"Listen carefully," I said, still taken aback by the light emanating from him. "I'll explain everything later, but right now we need to clear the valley. We have forty-five minutes before this whole valley blows."

He saw the falling ash and jerked up. "What happened?"

"The sky fell," I said. "It's okay, it's a good thing. But it won't matter if we can't get everyone out." I hesitated. "Can you see anything strange? Like light?"

"The sky?"

My father couldn't see the light I was seeing.

He twisted, looking frantically around. "Where is he?"

Vlad.

"Gone," I said.

Our eyes met and I knew immediately that he'd written Vlad into Other Earth. Not by the look in his eyes, but by a thought that entered my mind. His thought. I dismissed it as my mind playing tricks.

"Don't worry about Vlad right now," I said. "All of it's part of our journey."

His eyes filled with tears. "She was right."

"Who was?"

"Miranda. She wondered if you were an oracle, going beyond and bringing back the keys to truth. That through you we were experiencing one of the most extraordinary events in all of human history. She was right. I'm so sorry . . . I . . ." Emotion choked him off.

I pulled his head close and kissed his forehead. "Thank you for saving me."

He hadn't really saved me, but he'd tried with all he knew to do, and that was all that mattered to me. He was still in Ba'al's Thrall — Elyon only knew what he would endure while he waited for me to save him.

And what if I couldn't? I was in a deep hole below the Elyonite city, all alone, dead to that world as I slept there, dreaming this. Vlad was now there somewhere, sure he would blind me again. And through my blindness, he would blind the world. It was what the Shadow of Death did.

But not in Eden. Not today.

I put my hands on my father's shoulders. "Forget about all that now. Right now we have to clear this valley. Get everyone to the tunnel." I glanced up and saw seven or eight people walking tentatively down Third Street, led by a shell-shocked Linda, who held her hand out, watching the flakes alighting on her palm. All of them had that same light.

"How many are we now?" I asked.

My father pushed himself to his feet, staring at the sky, finally coming to himself. "What about the fallout?"

"I'm not sure," I said, speaking with more urgency now. "But that won't matter either if we can't clear this valley. How many? A hundred forty?"

"I don't know." He looked at Linda, grappling with memories of last night. "It depends."

"The fewer cars the better. The tunnel isn't big enough. Get the vans and trucks. Use a bullhorn. Do whatever you need to do, just get everyone up into that tunnel in the next thirty minutes."

"What about you?"

I stood. "I need to find out what's waiting for us up there."

Boots pounded on the pavement and Barth tore around the church, then pulled up sharply, glowing with the same light coming from my father. He stared at the sky, Linda, my father, and me. At least a dozen more residents had emerged from hiding to see the new sky filled with ash. All of them, the light of the world and not knowing it.

The light faded and winked out. But not exactly. I just wasn't seeing the world as clearly as I had a moment ago.

"What's happening?" Barth stammered.

"Vlad's happening," I said, walking toward him. Then loudly, turning so they could all hear me, I said, "He rigged the whole town to blow in forty-five minutes. Follow my father and Barth. Get everyone to the tunnel. Everyone!" Then to Barth: "I need a car."

He hesitated, still in shock. Dug into his pocket and pulled out a set of keys. "The blue truck." Behind him, parked on First Street. "It's an automatic."

I closed the distance between us and put my fingers on the keys, but I lingered there, eyeing him closely.

"It's over, Barth. Vlad's gone. Help my father."

He hesitated, then gave me a short nod.

"No more guns," I pressed. "Promise me."

Another nod. I took the keys and headed for Linda.

"You heard her, everyone!" Barth

snapped. "Let's move it!"

They moved, hesitant for a moment, then with something close to panic as the threat of explosions settled in.

Bill was yelling, "The town's gonna blow!" at the top of his lungs, running for his hardware store. Cindy Jarvis was shouting something about the buses. My father was trying to urge calm, shouting for Bill to grab three bullhorns.

Barth turned and ran north in the direction of his house, maybe unconcerned about the fate of the rest, maybe just to get to his wife and children.

The fact that seven children were still missing sat like a stone in my gut, but I had a notion — the only hope for them, really.

"You can drive, right, Linda?"

The moment her eyes met mine, I knew her fear. Knew it in the same way I had known my father's thoughts only a minute earlier.

"Yes, but what —"

"I need someone to drive me to the tunnel," I interrupted, hurrying for the blue pickup truck. "And I need you with me."

"What for?"

"To find the children."

I dared not give Linda any false hope as she

sped up the blacktop, taking the switchbacks at a speed that had me clinging to the center console. "If they're not where I think they are, then we'll make another sweep," I said.

"Where do you think they are?"

"It's just a hunch."

"What hunch?"

"You'll see."

"Why can't you tell me?"

She overdrove a corner and overcorrected at the last minute, sending us careening toward the ditch before jerking back on course, though on the wrong side now.

"Getting us there in one piece would be helpful," I said.

"Sorry."

"Just focus."

She gripped the wheel in both hands and bore down, face white.

It took us less than ten minutes to reach the exit. The gated fence on our side of the cliff was open, as was the tunnel. But there was no light coming through from the other side, which could only mean that the exit doors on the tunnel were closed.

If Vlad had locked them, we'd have to find a way through. Short of that, we'd hunker down in the tunnel and hope the walls were thick enough to protect us from any blasts.

Linda pulled to a screeching stop at the

tunnel entrance. We stared into the long darkness, silent for a few breaths.

"Now what?" she asked.

I opened my door. "Wait here."

"No way. I'm coming."

I set my mind on the far end of the tunnel and walked up the yellow dashes in the middle of the road, leaving Linda to follow. The darkness didn't bother me. I could see well enough with my blind sight, one foot in front of the other, like walking through any dark valley.

Halfway through, I began to jog. Linda needed no encouragement. The slapping of our shoes on the pavement sounded like two tap drums out of sync.

A paper-thin thread of light ran down the center seam of the twin doors, and I kept my eyes on it, only it. Then I was there, grasping the large vertical handle, tugging. There was no lock that I could see.

Linda crashed into the door, breathing heavily.

"Pull!" I said.

She pulled.

The large doors grated as the metal wheels on which they rode squealed stubbornly.

"Pull!" she cried.

I pulled.

The door gained some momentum and

suddenly rolled freely, coasting wide to reveal the world beyond Eden.

Linda and I stood side by side, panting, gazing at majestic green mountains as far as we could see. Towering red boulders framed pine and aspen in a valley that descended to a huge lake twenty or thirty miles distant. My heart soared.

"How . . ." Linda took a step forward, shaking her head. "This isn't right. What about the fallout?"

"There never was any fallout," I said, walking past her. "He lied to us."

"Why?"

"He wanted us totally unraveled and divided. He pitted my father against Barth, knowing I would try to save my father. If not for the threat of fallout, we might have banded together, desperate to get out. Smart."

A wide band of ash several hundred yards down the valley marked the perimeter of the collapsed dome. The last time I'd stood here looking out, the green trees had ended there, at the edge of a wasteland. But that wasteland had been only an image on a screen, like the synthetic sky inside.

A thumping sound reached me, and for a second I thought it might be the detonations inside Eden. Then I saw the black helicopter circling wide.

"So we aren't in a safe haven?" Linda asked.

"No. None of that was true. But we are in a bubble, isolated from the rest of the world. We were, that is."

She turned to me, stupefied. "So then why, if there was no nuclear war?"

"I don't know yet."

The sound of beating rotors grew louder as the helicopter spotted us and sharply turned down. Tires screeched behind us at the mouth of the tunnel as the first of Eden's residents arrived.

"You mean the rest of the world still exists? There was no war?"

"That's what I mean. The synthetic sky was real enough, but the story about the fallout was Vlad turning the screws. And it worked. Nothing like a nuclear holocaust to terrify the tissue-tops."

"What about my children? You think . . ."

"I'm hoping whoever's in the helicopter can tell us where they are. But I don't know, Linda. I really don't."

The helicopter angled in toward us, blowing up dust and debris as it feathered its blades for a landing on the turnaround up the road. Feet slapped the pavement behind us. Dozens of them. Then slowed to a walk as the scene before them came into view.

The black helicopter settled to the ground.

"Let's go," I said to Linda.

A tall, slim man in a navy suit dropped from the helicopter's open door, took one long look around, and walked toward us as the engine wound down. We met halfway.

His eyes were bleary and red, his face drawn tight. He nodded and looked past us to the open tunnel.

"I need to speak to Simon Moses."

I hesitated, not sure how I should address him. So I just said it: "Vlad Smith had him executed."

His face paled. "Who's in charge?"

"She is," Linda said, stepping forward and pointing at me. "We . . . Can you tell us where the missing children are?"

The man eyed her, then me, mired in deep fear. And in that fear, I knew his thoughts. Not the words of those thoughts, necessarily. Just the meaning of them before they became my own thoughts and words. It was the third time I'd been able to perceive what someone else was thinking when they were under duress.

The Third Seal had expanded my perceptions. I knew some things about this man, starting with his name, which was Steve.

"What children?" Steve asked.

"My children!" Linda looked at me, eyes frantic. Then at him, angry. "You don't know where they are?"

"I . . . You have missing children?"

"Are you deaf?"

A car door slammed near the tunnel behind us. The faint voice of a young boy reached me over the helicopter's dying rotors. "Can I see my mommy now?"

I twisted back and saw Barth's black Suburban, doors open. Jordan, Linda's boy, stood next to Barth, hand in his. Several others were climbing out behind them. The missing children.

"Jordan?" Linda sobbed. She took off, tearing for them.

By the look of shame on Barth's face, I knew . . . He'd taken them on Vlad's orders. More chaos. I felt pity for the man. He'd only acted out of his programming from the start. The whole town had. Just like the whole world.

Linda swept her boy off the ground and grabbed her daughter, weeping tears of joy that filled my throat with a knot. Other cars had pulled up, bringing other residents. All emerged staring at the world beyond the bubble — a world they'd never seen.

I saw little Carina among them, blonde curls tangled but otherwise no sign of harm.

I wondered if she knew that both her father and mother were dead. I wanted to rush to her and hug her and tell her how beautiful she was.

But if we didn't deal with the explosives, she wouldn't be the only child without a mother or father. My pulse surged, like a clock wound too tight. Time was running out.

"We would have come in days ago," Steve was saying behind me. "But we knew he'd detonate the explosives we'd set as a safeguard when we built the town. And the ones he rigged at all the entrances. We have no clue how he hacked the system." He was talking in a rush, spilling all of his secrets, seeking absolution as he paced, one hand in his hair. "You have to understand, I —"

"It's okay, slow down." I decided to cut to the chase for his sake as much as ours. "Your name is Steve and you're from the Defense Advanced Research Projects Agency," I said. "DARPA. You helped create Eden and it's all gone wrong so you're afraid. But you know that you were only doing what you were told. It's going to be okay, but we have to get everyone out."

He stared at me, at a loss. "How did you know my name?"

"The same way I brought the sky down,"

I said. "But I don't think you'd understand."
I refocused. "What year is it?"

"2038. You brought the seal down?"

"Who's the president?"

"Calvin Johnson." He swallowed. "I'm so
sorry. I . . . What's your name?"

Inchristi, I thought.

"Rachelle," I said.

"Rachelle Matthews? The programming
didn't work with you. I thought you were
blind."

"I was."

"And . . . You really brought it down?"

"What's Project Eden?"

"A controlled experiment in epigenetics
and quantum consciousness. Its purpose
was to study the effects of both physical and
cognitive perception to better understand to
what extent we create our reality based on
agreed-upon beliefs. It was a noble concept,
you understand, dedicated to the survival of
our species."

"Are there other towns like this?"

"No. Just Eden." Steve buried his face in
his hands. "I'm so sorry. I'm so sorry. We're
gonna pay a price for this. The whole
world's gonna crucify us. All of the initial
residents volunteered. They knew we'd wipe
their memories . . . But they're gonna say
we should have known."

"Then maybe it's best if the world doesn't know. Right now we have to —"

"They already do! This place will be crawling with media within the hour — I made the call as soon as the seal collapsed." Seal. Evidently DARPA's official term for our sky. "There are two choppers on the way as we speak. We couldn't get in, you realize. Not without blowing the whole sky. You can't cut through it." He eyed me, unbelieving. "You're sure you took it down? How? It's made from carbyne fibers." A beat. "What else can you do?"

I wasn't sure even I knew. But I was sure they would want to know. The whole world would.

"How far out? The helicopters."

"Maybe ten minutes."

My mind spun. "Vlad said the whole town would blow. We have maybe twenty-five minutes. You said you planted the explosives as a safeguard, I'm assuming to cover your tracks in the event of a meltdown. He found access to whatever triggers those explosives, right?"

His face went white. "It's on a countdown? Where's Smith?"

"He's gone. Can you defuse the explosives?"

"What do you mean, gone?"

"He vanished when I brought the sky down. Can you defuse them?"

He shook his head. "No. Half of them are buried under the town. The triggers are —"

"Is there a way off the mountain?" I looked at the building that blocked the main road to our right. The only way in or out by road. "Through the control center? Three helicopters can't carry a hundred and forty people."

"The control center's rigged, and if we could defuse the explosives we would have done it last week." He faced me. "A hundred and forty? Should be 152 without Simon."

"He wasn't the only one who died." I had to get him focused. "And if this whole mountain comes down —"

"There's no chance of that. The cliffs and town, yes, but not the tunnel or the mountain. It's solid rock, ninety-four feet at its thinnest, right through. No one was ever going to find or compromise this place — even from the sky it looked just like it always looked, a sinkhole. The seal both camouflaged and protected it from above. It took us two years —"

"We're running out of time." I couldn't see Peter among the gathering residents. He was still in the valley. "You're sure we're safe this side of the tunnel?"

"Sorry. Yes." He paced. "Without question."

"Then take me back in," I said, stepping past him. "We have to find the rest. All of them."

The next twenty-five minutes brought a flurry of activity.

Steve had regained a measure of command and worked methodically, doing his best to put a dent in an overwhelming guilt that had been building for days. He instructed Walter, the only other man besides the pilot who'd come with him, to group Eden's residents at the turnaround, clear of the tunnel in case there was any blowback.

The moment we were airborne, he radioed the inbound police and gave them specific instructions. They would have fifteen minutes to clear stragglers and any dead bodies they could find.

My purpose for being there was only to offer my voice. Not all in the town were as strong-willed as Barth and Linda. Many had hidden themselves, struggling to cope with minds fractured by the discovery that their lives were a lie. Hearing a strange voice bellowing out instructions over a bullhorn might not persuade the most damaged.

But if they heard my voice over the helicopter's PA system, they would believe. I was the girl who'd stood up to Vlad. The blind one who could now see.

On our first pass, we picked up Jerome Clement, a farmer who'd hidden his two children, Smitty and Cassandra, in a grain silo east of town. Then Old Man Butterworth on the same pass. He'd taken his rifle and was hunkered down in a large pile of hay bales, a hundred yards past the silo.

Peter still wasn't among those who'd made it out, and my urgency grew.

"Peter! We have to find him!"

"Simon's son?"

"He lost his mother and father both. We have to find him."

What if he'd gone deep, overwhelmed by the deaths of his parents?

Trucks and cars spilling over with residents snaked up the switchbacks as we made that first pass. My father still raced through the town, leaning out the window of his red Toyota truck, shouting his warning over a bullhorn. He'd loaded several dead bodies in the bed, Simon and Hillary among them.

The large black helicopters arrived and started making their rounds while we were on our second pass. By then the vehicles snaking up the blacktop had thinned to a dozen at most. We found three more stragglers, among them Betsy and her poodle, Puddle.

Betsy, who always had some form of eczema on her arms and neck. Today, only two days after learning that all her memories of childhood trauma had been implanted, the rash was gone, leaving her aged skin clear.

How many others had experienced spontaneous remissions of various conditions since learning they'd only been believing their programming? Most were probably still clinging to various forms of fear. Not Betsy. Betsy was smiling.

But there was still no sign of Peter.

By our third pass, my father's red truck was the only vehicle to be seen heading up the road. There were still horses and cows, chickens, goats, and maybe a pet or two, though I doubted the latter — their owners would have taken them as part of their family. But the livestock were in the fields, and Steve assured me that there wasn't enough rock in the cliffs to cover all the fields. At least some would survive.

I prayed he was right. But Peter was still missing and we were running out of time.

"We have to find him!"

"We're cutting it close."

"Go in again."

I used the bullhorn, calling Peter's name for the whole valley to hear, but he still didn't show himself. I could only hope that he'd gotten out some other way, but I worried that he had no intention of leaving the valley.

On that fourth and final pass, we picked up my father just beyond the tunnel.

"Still no sign of Peter?"

My father shook his head.

I didn't know what to think.

"Everyone else made it?"

"I've asked the group twice — no one else is missing anyone." He turned heavy eyes and stared at the gathering, some still dazed, others animated and talking. "Barth said he buried Miranda in a hole by the hydro. I don't think we have enough time to retrieve her body."

I wondered if Barth would be prosecuted for murder. Most of me hoped not. Innocent by reason of insanity, just like the whole world, I thought. Every last human on earth was acting out of their programming, however lost. *Forgive them, for they know not what they do.*

Either way, the real fallout of Eden would soon shake the world. They would all hear about the blind girl who could see — the one who'd brought down the synthetic sky. And then what?

And then the 49th Mystic would bring a sword to divide. *Elyon, help me . . .*

"One more pass," I said.

"We're out of time," Steve said. Radio chatter squawked on the speakers. The two helicopters were pulling out, heading back to refuel before returning with others to begin the evacuation to Salt Lake.

"I want to see it from the sky," I said.

Steve nodded. "Take her up, Jake. Give us a view of the valley, but stay clear."

From our view a thousand feet above the town, Eden looked like a perfectly peaceful piece of heaven dropped into the center of a lush green bowl with red walls. White and beige houses lined squared streets around the large church. Not a structure was out of place by even a foot. The perfect picture of law.

It was the first time my father had seen Eden from the air. He gripped my hand and stared down, unblinking. There was little to say now. Either Vlad had initiated a detonation countdown or he hadn't.

Regardless, it no longer mattered to the residents. They would be picking up the pieces of their lives for years to come, and those pieces would form a whole new way of thinking. They would experience their own metanoia, taking them beyond the imprinting of the world.

As Ralph Waldo Emerson once wrote, "The mind, once stretched by a new idea, never returns to its original dimensions." Many in Eden wouldn't simply recover; they would soar and lead others to rise above the confines of society's programming. Some might sink into despair and never recover — time would tell.

My heart broke for Peter, but there was nothing I could do now. Was this his journey? I would ask Talya if I ever got out of the Elyonite dungeon.

My father turned his head from the window and leaned forward to Steve, who was seated next to the pilot. "How much time . . ."

A soft rumble cut him off and he turned his head back.

Billowing dust came first as tons of explosives let loose their ferocious energy under the town and in the cliffs. I prayed no one had been left behind.

The blast's concussion hit the helicopter — a gentle jolt at our altitude. Then secondary explosions erupted from the billowing clouds of dust. The cliffs were collapsing like waterfalls of stone, caving in on all sides.

I'd never seen a demolition on television for the simple reason that I'd been blind until five days ago, but I imagined this one would be considered a work of art by those who made tearing down the old to make room for the new their life's work.

Wasn't that everyone's life work? You could not put new wine in an old wineskin, Talya said. The old mind in the valley of the law was the old wineskin. And now it was no more.

My father pulled away from the window and dropped his head back on the headrest, eyes closed. Tears ran down his face. I leaned over, drew my legs up on the bench seat, and rested my head on his thigh. It was over.

But I knew that wasn't true. If not for me, Project Eden would still be intact and unaware. Lost. Now they were free. Was I, the 49th Mystic, really expected to do the same thing for the rest of the world? I couldn't imagine how. Nor wanting to.

And yet the white, the green, and the black seals were on my arm. I was the 49th Mystic. Two more seals awaited me. Against the Fifth Seal there is no defense, Talya had said. I had to find the Fourth and Fifth Seal before the Realm of Mystics was destroyed, or all would be lost.

I closed my eyes and let the beating rotor drown out my thoughts. It was over for Eden.

It was just beginning for the rest of both worlds.

39

Vlad Smith was his name. Here they had called him Marsuuv. Leedhan. A shape-shifter spun from the shadow of death.

It was good to be home.

He stood in Ba'al's Thrall, patiently awaiting the ruler's arrival, gazing at all the instruments that struck fear in minds bound by polarity. The priest stood to his right, silent as ordered, still in shock at his arrival.

David lay on the table next to the Book of History in which he'd written, awake in the world of Eden, all but dead here. Actually, Eden was now a pile of rubble. A nice thought. But it no longer concerned him. He, not being human, had vanished from that place when written into the book, unlike David, who existed in both worlds now.

The door crashed open and a man with heavy dreadlocks strode into the room. "What's the meaning of this?" Qurong, supreme ruler of all living Horde. He took one look at Vlad's naked body and stopped short.

"Qurong, is it? So good to finally meet you."

"And who in Teeleh's name are you?"

Vlad smiled, and with that smile shifted from human to his natural form. Leedhan, with translucent skin the color of the full moon, one eye blue, one amber.

"Who am I? The law, the yin of the yang, the darkness that hides the light, the fear that betrays peace, the illusion that masquerades as reality, the Shadow of Death." He raised his brow. "Should I go on?"

Qurong glared at him but was visibly unnerved all the same. Such was the disposition of all great warriors facing those whose power vastly exceeded their own. At least he had the good sense to know it.

"He is Marsuuv," Ba'al rasped, finally finding his voice. "The one from Teeleh who has come to crush the Mystic."

"Yes," Vlad said. "That one. The one who's waited for centuries in an ancient reality for this day to come. But it isn't I who'll crush the Realm of Mystics. It is you. Unless, of course, you want the lamb called Albino to force the lion Horde into submission." He let the man drink in his words. "Do you?"

Qurong's self-assurance drained from his face as he surrendered to Vlad's power. He slowly dipped his head.

"Is that a yes, you want to be forced into slavery, or a no, you don't?"

"No."

"Good. Then you'll do exactly what I order. Say yes."

Qurong glanced at Ba'al.

"Not to him, to me. Say yes."

"Yes," the ruler said.

"Good. Then I'll be direct. You will take your full army east to the Great Divide. Not in a month, not in a week, but now. In war, you will crush all Albinos. Beyond the city of Mosseum, you will be led to the Realm of Mystics, and you will destroy it. Not a single Mystic must live to spread Justin's lies. Do you understand?"

Qurong hesitated, then nodded.

"If you will, sire," Ba'al dared to venture. "I was to understand that the 49th must betray her way and —"

"She will!" Vlad interrupted, walking to the table. He picked up the Book of History and studied David's unconscious form. "And to that end I will need your prisoner." He strode toward the door. "Have him ready to travel in an hour. I need a bath and respectable clothing."

"Of course. Where will you take him?"

Vlad turned at the door. "To the 49th Mystic, naturally. My work has only just begun."

40

The sun was high over Talya's head when he crested a barren hill and looked down at a vast network of canyons carved into a broad plateau. The Natalga Gap. He brought his mount to a halt with a simple thought, then settled in his saddle. The lion Judah stood under a scraggly shade tree, eyes fixed on the empty lands ahead.

Empty but for a solitary figure mounted on a pale stallion half a mile distant, staring his way.

So . . . Thomas of Hunter still paid attention to his dreams — not of the other world, but in this world. Talya had summoned him here in one.

He'd heard countless tales of Thomas of Hunter's exploits, some of them surely fabricated by his enemies. Depending on who was telling the tale, he was a ghost, a wraith, a god, a coward, or simply a mighty warrior against which no one could prevail.

In the end, they all pointed to one seemingly indisputable fact: the whole earth had been shaped by this one man from another world.

And would be again.

Without Thomas of Hunter, there would be no bridge between the worlds. No 49th Mystic, even though Thomas knew nothing of the way of the Mystics.

Now, the 49th needed him. Even more, Thomas and his Circle needed her.

Talya looked over at Judah, who sensed his gaze and turned his big head, seemingly aware of the gravity of the moment.

"The legend lives," Talya muttered. He faced that legend and nodded. "Come what may."

He took his mount down the slope to the Natalga Gap.

To the fate awaiting them all.

To Thomas.

The Story Continues
Rise of the Mystics
October 2018

TALYA'S JOURNAL:
ON THE FORGOTTEN WAY

Key excerpts from the journal of Talya, who herein did transcribe those teachings of Yeshua, Paulus, Johnin, and Petrus as written in the ancient Books of History called Scriptures. (Talya's personal notes in parentheses.)
Organized by Rachelle, the 49th Mystic

Relating to Chapter 14

1) <u>There is no fear in love</u>; but perfect love casts out fear, because fear involves punishment, and <u>the one who fears is not perfected in love</u>. (God cannot fear loss, for God is perfected in love. Indeed, God is love.)

First Book of Johnin 4:18

2) From that time Jesus began to preach and say, "<u>Repent</u> (metanoia, change your cognitive perception, go beyond your knowledge), <u>for the kingdom of heaven is at hand</u>" (already here and in your very being).

Book of Matthew 4:17

Do not conform to the pattern of this world (polarity), but be transformed by the renewing of your mind.

Paulus to Rome 12:2 NIV

3) Love is patient, love is kind. Love does not envy, is not boastful, is not conceited, does not act improperly, is not selfish, is not provoked. (Some translators have inserted the word *easily* before *provoked*, though Paulus didn't write it.)

[Love] does not keep a record of wrongs. (*Does not keep a record* or *keeps no record* is a legal term meaning "does not take into account" or "makes no accounting of." Paulus's word for *wrong* is singular, the same word he and Yeshua used for *evil*, and so was translated as "takes no account of evil" by many scribes. Other scribes have felt compelled to insert extra words of their own, such as *deeds* or *thoughts* following the word *evil*, but again, these words are not in Paulus's writings, penned in Greek.)

Paulus's First Letter to
Corinth 13:4–5 HCSB

4) If I . . . know all mysteries and all knowledge (doctrine and confessions); and if I have all faith, so as to remove mountains, but do not have love, I am nothing. And if I give all my possessions to feed the poor, and if I surrender my body to be burned (service and loyalty to beliefs), but do not have love (true love,

which does not take into account wrong), it profits me nothing.

Paulus's First Letter to Corinth 13:2–3

By this everyone will know that you are my disciples, if you <u>love</u> one another. (Love that holds no record of wrong is the true evidence of Christ. Good doctrine or confession in itself is not the evidence of Christ but the evidence of intelligence alone.)

Book of Johnin 13:35 NIV

5) I am the vine, you are the branches; <u>he who abides in Me and I in him, he bears much fruit</u> (love), <u>for apart from Me you can do nothing</u> (all is vanity in the earthen vessel alone) . . . My Father is glorified by this, that you bear much fruit, and so prove to be My disciples. Just as the Father has loved Me, I have also loved you; <u>abide in My love</u>. (True love is the greatest of all fruit, the evidence of Christ.)

Book of Johnin 15:5, 8–9

6) No one pours new wine into <u>old wine-skins</u> (old identity in polarity, law). Otherwise, the new wine will burst the skins; the wine will run out and the wineskins

673

will be ruined. No, <u>new wine must be poured into new wineskins</u> (new identity beyond polarity, law).

Book of Luke 5:37–38 NIV

Wherefore <u>the law was our schoolmaster</u> to bring us unto Christ, that we might be justified by faith. But after that faith is come (Inchristi), we are <u>no longer under a schoolmaster</u>.

Paulus to Galatia 3:24–25 KJV

The former regulation (the law of Moses) is set aside because it was <u>weak and useless</u> . . . and a better hope is introduced (the law of grace), by which we draw near to God (know him intimately).

Paulus to Hebrews 7:18–19 NIV

<u>The Law came in so that the transgression would increase</u> (the more you try to fulfill the demands of polarity/law, the more failure it brings); but where sin increased, <u>grace abounded all the more</u>, so that, as sin reigned in death, even so grace would reign through righteousness (state of our being) to eternal life through

Jesus Christ our Lord (who we are, right now).

Paulus to Rome 5:20–21

Since you died with Christ to the elemental spiritual forces of this world (polarity), why, as though you still belonged to the world, do you submit to its rules: "Do not handle! Do not taste! Do not touch!"? These rules, which have to do with things that are all destined to perish with use (the law), are based on merely human commands and teachings. (The law is weak and useless — old wineskin — yet still embraced by man.)

Paulus to Colossae 2:20–22 NIV

For what the Law could not do, <u>weak as it was</u> through the flesh, God did . . . so that the requirement of the Law <u>might be fulfilled in us</u>. (The requirement of the law is to bring wholeness, but it cannot, and is fulfilled only by a grace that holds no record of wrong, which is also God's love.)

Paulus to Rome 8:3–4

Do not think that I have come to abolish the Law or the Prophets; I have not come to abolish them but to fulfill them. (The law is fulfilled in us as it fails and thus leads us to the love of Christ in us.)

Book of Matthew 5:17 NIV

7) Therefore, there is now <u>no condemnation</u> for those who are in Christ Jesus, because through Christ Jesus the law of the Spirit who gives life (true love) <u>has set you free from the law of sin and death</u>. (Condemnation and fear. Sin is a state of blindness. Whatever is not done in faith is sin or darkness. Most live in sin or darkness most of the time.)

Paulus to Rome 8:1–2 NIV

<u>The Father judges no one</u>, but has given all judgment to the Son . . . Do not think that I will accuse you to the Father. (Neither does the Son accuse us.) There is <u>one who accuses you: Moses</u> (the law, polarity), on whom you have set your hope.

Talya's note: If one puts their trust in law — polarity — they are condemned by it, not by the Father or the Christ. In any given moment, one reaps the effects of whatever system they put their faith in. Most live in blindness to grace and true love, clinging to the law of polarity, holding record of wrong, and thus are mastered by polarity.

Book of Johnin 5:22, 45 ESV

8) Do not suppose that I have come to bring peace to the earth. I did not come to bring peace, <u>but a sword</u>. (The old mind will always resist the truth, which is like a sword of true love, holding no record of wrong. Thus those clinging to the old mind will feel deeply divided by that sword and will cry "heresy" to protect their investment in ideologies dependent on fear and control.)

Book of Matthew 10:34 NIV

9) Say not ye, There are yet four months, and then cometh harvest? behold, I say unto you, <u>Lift up your eyes, and look</u> (change your perception, metanoia) on the fields; for they are white <u>already</u> to harvest. (The kingdom is beyond time and cause and effect. This is the basis for all that is miraculous, seen in spirit.)

Book of Johnin 4:35 KJV

The harvest is plentiful (already ripe) but the workers are few. (Few see this.) Ask the Lord of the harvest, therefore, to send out workers into his harvest field. (Yeshua's invitation to be one who sees the harvest now, the kingdom that is now present.)

Book of Matthew 9:37–38 NIV

Now having been questioned by the Pharisees as to when the kingdom of God was coming, He answered them and said, "The kingdom of God is not coming with signs to be observed (it is now, not later); nor will they say, 'Look, here it is!' or, 'There it is!' (It is beyond our dimension of space, neither above nor below, not seen with earthly eyes.) For behold, the kingdom of God is in your midst" (already within your very being).

Book of Luke 17:20–21

10) The eye (singular, perception) is the lamp (shows you) of the body (our earthly experience); so then if your eye is clear, your whole body will be full of light. (Proper perception sees light and beauty.) But if your eye is bad, your whole body will be full of darkness. (The state of most, most of the time.) If then the light that is in you (the light is already in us) is darkness, how great is the darkness (suffering in this life)!

Book of Matthew 6:22–23

How can you say to your brother, "Brother, let me take the speck out of your eye," when you yourself fail to see the plank in your own eye? (Judgment of others.) You hypocrite, <u>first take the plank out of your eye, and then you will see clearly</u> to remove the speck from your brother's eye. (Unless you see clearly, you will walk in judgment rather than love.)

Book of Luke 6:42 NIV

If your right eye causes you to <u>stumble</u> (stumbling is spiritual blindness), pluck it out and cast it from you (after all, it is only part of the earthen vessel). For it is better for you that one of your members should perish and not that your whole body (experience in this life) should be cast into Gehenna. (Gehenna: the place of suffering.)

Book of Matthew 5:29 BLB

11) This is why I speak to them in parables: "Though seeing (with earthly eyes), they do not see (with spiritual eyes); though hearing (with the natural mind), they do not hear or understand" (its true meaning, because true meaning comes from beyond the logical mind — this is revelation).

Book of Matthew 13:13 NIV

12) The kingdom of heaven is like treasure hidden in a field. When a man found it, he hid it again, and then in his joy went and sold all he had and bought that field. (Only as we are willing to part with all that we think defines us are we able to possess the hidden treasure that truly defines us.)

Book of Matthew 13:44 NIV

13) And this is eternal life: to know you (present tense: to know is to have intimate experience with), the only true God, and the one whom you sent — Jesus the Messiah. (The only direct definition of Eternal Life, spoken by Yeshua.)

Book of Johnin 17:3 ISV

The glory which You have given Me I have given to them, that they may be one, just as (in the same way) We are one; I in them and You in Me, that they may be perfected in unity, so that the world may know that You sent Me, and loved them, even as (in the same way) You have loved Me. (The power of knowing that glory is a staggering love that holds no record of wrong. Only then will the world know they are loved.)

Book of Johnin 17:22–23

Relating to Chapter 17

1) Truly I tell you, unless you change and become like little children, you will never enter the kingdom of heaven. (To enter is to experience that dimension now in our midst. *Childlike* — full of wonder and belief. *Childish* — selfish clinging.)

Book of Matthew 18:3 NIV

At that time Jesus said, "I praise You, Father, Lord of heaven and earth, that You have hidden these things from the wise and intelligent (human logic and systematic theology based on reason in the human construct) and have revealed them to infants."

Talya's note: Intelligence is not required, and this always frustrates the intelligent mind. Infants trust without human logic. Metanoia is a return to this spiritual state, the process of becoming or being reborn like an infant. As also said by Yeshua: unless one is born again (becoming like an infant) they cannot <u>see</u> (perceive) the kingdom (which is already here and everywhere). This re-birthing process is the process also called transformation, awakening, alignment, purification, and sancti-

fication.
Book of Matthew 11:25

Jesus looked at them and said, "With man this is impossible, but <u>with God all things are possible</u>." (God is beyond space and time, as is our identity in him. Miraculous manifestation in space and time is possible in that identity.)
Book of Matthew 19:26 NIV

2) Truly, truly, I say to you, he who believes in Me (to believe in is to identify with), the works that I do, he will do also; and greater works than these he will do; because I go to the Father. Whatever you ask in My name, that will I do (most who claim to follow him do not ask in his identity but in their own, separate from him), so that the Father may be glorified in the Son.
Book of Johnin 14:12–13

3) For God, who said, "Light shall shine out of darkness," is the One who <u>has shone in our hearts to give the Light</u> of the knowledge of the glory of God in the face of Christ. (We are that light Inchristi.) But we have this treasure <u>in earthen vessels</u> (dust to dust), so that the surpassing greatness of the power will be of God and

not from ourselves (the earthen vessel self).

Paulus's Second Letter to
Corinth 4:6–7

So we fix our eyes (perception) not on what is seen (earthen vessel self and all polarity), but on what is unseen, since what is seen is temporary (dust to dust), but what is unseen is eternal (true spiritual self — eternal, beyond time and space).

Paulus's Second Letter to
Corinth 4:18 NIV

Before I formed you in the womb I knew you. (Not *knew about* you, but *knew* you. To know is to have intimate relationship with. Even so, a thought of the infinite is no less real than its manifestation in form.)

Prophet Jeremiah 1:5 NIV

For we know that if the tent that is our earthly home (earthen vessel) is destroyed, we have a building from God, a house not made with hands, eternal in the heavens. (The heavens — that "building from God" — is a dimension here and now and within, beyond polarity.)

Paulus's Second Letter to
Corinth 5:1 ESV

Therefore from now on <u>we recognize no one according to the flesh</u> (earthen vessel, including our own body); even though we have known Christ according to the flesh (when he was in an earthen vessel like ours), yet now <u>we know Him in this way no longer</u>. (We recognize ourselves in spirit and truth, not according to the flesh.)

Talya's note: The Gnostics erroneously claim that the body is evil or of no consequence, and so claim Christ could not have come in the flesh or rise in body. In truth, Christ did rise in body — yet one very different from our current bodies limited by physics. Paulus called this the glorified body, one that is not subject to the laws of physics nor the physical limitations we have in earthen vessels.

Paulus's Second Letter to Corinth 5:16

4) <u>There is no fear in love</u>; but perfect love casts out fear, because fear involves punishment, and the one who fears is not perfected in love. (One cannot love God and fear him at the same time. Fear of punishment is only a failure to grasp God's love.)

First Book of Johnin 4:18

This is the message we have heard from Him and announce to you, that <u>God is Light, and in Him there is no darkness at all</u>. If we say that we have fellowship with Him and yet walk in the darkness, we lie and do not practice the truth.(Love that holds no record of wrong is light. Most walk in darkness most of the time not because they are not the light, but because they are blind to that light.)

First Book of Johnin 1:5–6

When he had received the drink, Jesus said, "<u>It is finished</u>." With that, he bowed his head and gave up his spirit (transcended his body).

Talya's note: On that cross Yeshua quotes both the first and last line of Psalm 22, the great lament of all humanity, beginning with David's fear of being forsaken: "My God, my God, why have you forsaken me?" The psalmist then corrects this fallacy in writing: "For he has <u>not</u> . . . hidden his face from [the afflicted one]." God wouldn't, couldn't, turn his face from his Son, nor us. David ends as Yeshua did: "He has done it!" or "It is finished." Death is no more. It is only then that David writes the next Psalm: "Even though I walk through the valley of the shadow of death (the world of polarity), I fear no evil." Why? Because death is only a shadow in that valley. It is finished! *Selah.*

Book of Johnin 19:30 NIV;
Psalm 22:1, 24, 31 NIV; Psalm 23:4

5) Since, then, you <u>have been raised with Christ</u> (already), set your hearts on things above (the spiritual dimension in our very being), where Christ is, seated at the right hand of God (with you, established in union). Set your minds on <u>things above</u> (<u>dimension of the kingdom within</u>), not on <u>earthly things</u> (world of polarity — two kingdoms: things above and earthly things). For you died, and your life is <u>now hidden with Christ in God</u> (in union with: our true state of being right now).

Paulus to Colossae 3:1–3 NIV

But God, being rich in mercy, because of His great love with which He loved us, even when we were dead in our transgressions (before we knew we were in darkness), made us alive together with Christ . . . and <u>raised us up with Him (already), and seated us with Him in the heavenly places</u> in Christ Jesus (established in union with Christ).

Paulus to Ephesus 2:4–6

Therefore if any man be in Christ, he is <u>a new creature</u>: old things (polarity) are passed away; behold, <u>all things are become new</u>. (Perception of the world changes in that awareness.)

Paulus's Second Letter to Corinth 5:17 KJV

See to it that no one takes you captive through philosophy and empty deception, according to the tradition of men (including religious tradition), according to the <u>elementary principles of the world</u> (the world of polarity), rather than according to Christ (who is beyond polarity). For in Him (in our union with him) all the fullness of Deity dwells in bodily form (he dwells in our earthen vessels), and in Him you <u>have been made complete</u> (already perfect), and He is the head over all rule and authority. (We are who he, as the final authority, says we are: complete, not who we think we are as earthen vessels. The old self identifies as an earthen vessel flesh self and thus denies who we truly are, one with the divine.)

Talya's note: Paulus, writing to the Philippians, explained that his earthly experience of his true identity was not yet perfected, thus he continued to press on. As do we all.

Paulus to Colossae 2:8–10

No one can serve two masters (two systems), for either he will hate the one and love the other; or else he will be devoted to one and despise the other. You cannot serve (align yourself with) both God and Mammon. (Mammon: the system of the world, polarity, symbolized by money. Christ is not subject to polarity. Neither are we as we align to our union with him.)

Book of Matthew 6:24 NHEB

6) [You] have put on the new self (a new way of being in the world) who is being renewed (metanoia, transforming of the mind) to a true knowledge according to the image of the One who created him — a renewal (awakening) in which there is no distinction between Greek and Jew, circumcised and uncircumcised, barbarian, Scythian (seen as the worst of the worst in his day), slave and freeman, but Christ is all, and in all. (We are one with Christ, and that One, our true identity,

lives in our earthen vessel. Inchristi is all; Inchristi is in all.)

Paulus to Colossae 3:10–11

7) He (Yeshua) said to them, "<u>Why are you afraid</u>, you men of little faith?" Then He got up and rebuked the winds and the sea, and it became perfectly calm. (Yeshua was asleep, undisturbed by the storms of life. We are afraid when we do not see as he sees, beyond the storms of this life. His sight is seeing the unseen, the kingdom of heaven now present in our midst.)

Book of Matthew 8:26

8) And immediately something like scales fell from his [Paulus's] eyes, and he regained his sight. Then he rose and was baptized. (Symbolizing his new sight in Spirit, followed by baptism, which signified his drowning to find new life. Paulus was then sent by Christ "to open their eyes, so that they may turn from darkness to light.")

Book of Acts 9:18; 26:18 ESV

9) For Scripture says, The two will become one flesh. But anyone joined to the Lord <u>is one spirit with Him</u>. (Not in flesh but as spirit. Our true identity, not in temporal

earthen vessel flesh but as spirit.)

Paulus's First Letter to
Corinth 6:16–17 HCSB

And they two shall be <u>one</u> flesh. This is <u>a</u>
<u>great mystery</u>: but I speak concerning
Christ and the church. (How we can be
one with Christ is the great mystery,
incomprehensible to Paulus's intellect and
ours, thus mysticism.)

Paulus to Ephesus 5:31–32 KJV

10) The Father . . . <u>will give you another</u>
<u>Helper</u> . . . that is the Spirit of truth . . .
In that day you will know that <u>I am in My</u>
<u>Father, and you in Me, and I in you</u>. (We
will know that we are one with Christ.
Knowing our union with our Creator is
the primary function of the Spirit. Only
then can we bear the Spirit's fruit of love,
joy, and peace in this life.)

Book of Johnin 14:16–17, 20

<u>The glory which You have given Me I have</u>
<u>given to them</u> (same glory), that they may
be one, just as (in the same way) <u>We are</u>
<u>one</u>; I in them and You in Me, that they
may be perfected in unity (now), so that
the world may know that You sent Me
(now), and loved them (now), even as You

have loved Me. (The power of knowing our union Inchristi is a true love that holds no record of wrong. It always flows like living water from those who now know who they are Inchristi. Only then will the world know they are loved.)

Book of Johnin 17:22–23

11) <u>You are the light of the world</u>. A city set on a hill cannot be hidden; nor does anyone light a lamp and put it <u>under a basket</u>, but on the lampstand, and it gives light to all. (Yeshua declared this to the outcast and destitute of his day. The good news.)

Book of Matthew 5:14–15

12) He has made us competent as ministers of a new covenant — not of the letter but of the Spirit; <u>for the letter kills, but the Spirit gives life</u>. (Written words are not the Word. The Word is Christ in us, Inchristi.)

Paulus's Second Letter to
Corinth 3:6 NIV

Relating to Chapter 26

1) <u>Ask and it will be given to you</u>; seek and you will find; knock and the door will be opened to you . . . Which of you, <u>if your</u>

691

son asks for bread, will give him a stone? Or if he asks for a fish, will give him a snake? . . . How much more will your Father in heaven give good gifts to those who ask him! (No need to fear.)

Book of Matthew 7:7, 9–11 NIV

2) Through these he has given us his very great and precious promises, so that through them you may participate in the divine nature. (Participate in divinity, joined as one with Christ. Our true identity is the light divine, already risen, dwelling temporarily in earthen vessels.)

Second Book of Petrus 1:4 NIV

The glory which You have given Me I have given to them (the same glory) that they may be one, just as (in the same way) We are one; I in them and You in Me, that they may be perfected in unity (experience that union), so that the world may know that You sent Me, and loved them, even as (in the same way) You have loved Me. (A love that holds no record of wrong is the natural fruit of our awakening to union with Christ. Only this love will show the world Christ. This love is our testimony of the good news. Gospel.)

Book of Johnin 17:22–23

In that day (the coming of the Spirit of Truth) you will know that <u>I am in My Father, and you in Me, and I in you</u>. (Yeshua's powerful statement of union.)

Book of Johnin 14:20

I have been crucified with Christ; and <u>it is no longer I who live</u> (old self is a lie), but Christ lives in me (true identity Inchristi); and the life which I now live in the flesh (in the earthen vessel) I live by faith in the Son of God, who loved me and gave Himself up for me.

Paulus to Galatia 2:20

For you have died and your life is hidden with Christ in God (true identity).

Paulus to Colossae 3:3

For to me, to live <u>is Christ</u> and to die is gain. (When our bodies die, we gain by fully realizing who we already were before our bodies died. Inchristi.)

Paulus to Philippi 1:21

Relating to Chapter 28

1) Now having been questioned by the Pharisees as to when the kingdom of God was coming, He answered them and said, "<u>The kingdom of God is not coming with</u>

signs to be observed (not a future event that signs will show us); <u>nor will they say, 'Look, here it is!' or, 'There it is!'</u> (It is not seen with eyes, above or below, nor is it a destination.) For behold, the kingdom of God is in your midst." (It is everywhere now and within. A dimension now present.)

Book of Luke 17:20–21

2) But God, being rich in mercy, because of His great love with which He loved us, even when we were dead in our transgressions, made us alive together with Christ (in the same way Christ lives today, so do we — as spirit), <u>and raised us up with Him, and seated us with Him in the heavenly places</u> in Christ Jesus. (We are already raised, spirit rather than flesh.)

Paulus to Ephesus 2:4–6

Therefore if anyone is (since a person is) in Christ, he is a new creature (not who he thought he was); the old things passed away; behold, new things have come. (When one awakens to the truth, their old view of reality is replaced by a new one.)

Paulus's Second Letter to
Corinth 5:17

For in Him all the fullness of Deity dwells in bodily form (Christ dwells in our earthen vessels), and in (union with) Him <u>you have been made complete</u> (Greek word means "perfect"), and He is the head over all rule and authority.

Paulus to Colossae 2:9–10

I have been crucified with Christ; and <u>it is no longer I who live, but Christ lives in me</u>; and the life which I now live in the flesh I live by faith in the Son of God, who loved me and gave Himself up for me.

Paulus to Galatia 2:20

The Father . . . <u>will give you another Helper</u> . . . that is the Spirit of truth . . . In that day you will know that <u>I am in the Father, and you in Me, and I in you</u> (joined as one).

Book of Johnin 14:16–17, 20

If <u>you have died with Christ</u> to the elementary principles of the world (polarity), why, as if you were living in the world, do you submit yourself to decrees . . . ?

Paulus to Colossae 2:20

<u>As He is, so also are we in this world.</u> (How is Christ right now? That is who we

are, right now. He in us, we in him, one in the Father. <u>Inchristi is all; Inchristi is in all.</u>)

First Book of Johnin 4:17

3) And those whom he <u>foreknew</u> (all his children, before the foundations of the universe), he also fashioned in the likeness of the image of his Son, that he would be The Firstborn of many brethren (brothers; Christ is our elder brother). And those whom he pre-fashioned (all of his children), he called, and those whom he called, he made righteous, and those whom he made righteous, <u>he glorified</u>. (Past tense. Our true state of being right now. All who were known in the mind of God before creation are now glorified, however blind to their glory.)

Paulus to Rome 8:29–30 ABPE

The <u>glory</u> which You (God) have given Me (Yeshua) I <u>have given</u> to them (us) that they may be one, just as (in the same way) <u>We are one; I in them and You in Me.</u> (We have the same glory that Christ has, right now, not as infinite beings, but as an aspect of the Infinite, one with him.)

Book of Johnin 17:22–23

Be perfect (be, not become, perfect), as your heavenly Father is perfect. (We are complete Inchristi, thus we are invited to act as we truly are, complete.)

Book of Matthew 5:48

4) But Christ is all, and in all. (Christ is me, and joined as one, we are in my earthen vessel. Both is and in. Paulus's most direct statement of many on our union with Christ. Inchristi.)

Paulus to Colossae 3:11

For many will come in My name, saying, "I am the Christ," and will mislead many. (No other is the Christ in exclusion any more than they are the Albino or the Christian. Christ is all and in all, the great mystery. Nor can any earthen vessel claim they are Christ, for Christ is Spirit, not earthen vessel.)

Book of Matthew 24:5

But God, being rich in mercy, because of His great love with which He loved us, even when we were dead in our transgressions, made us alive together with Christ . . . and raised us up with Him, and seated us with Him in the heavenly places in Christ Jesus. (Only blindness prevents us from seeing what is true of who we are, resurrected in Christ.)

Paulus to Ephesus 2:4–6

That I may know Him and the power of His resurrection (to know the great power of our resurrection with Christ) and the fellowship of His sufferings, being conformed to His death (by counting our earthen vessel as dead).

Paulus to Philippi 3:10

Therefore from now on we recognize no one according to the flesh (earthen vessel), even though we have known Christ according to the flesh (when he was in an earthen vessel), yet now we know Him in this way no longer.

Paulus's Second Letter to Corinth 5:16

Referring to Chapter 37

1) As He [Jesus] passed by, He saw a man blind from birth. And His disciples asked Him, "Rabbi, who sinned, this man or his parents, that he would be born blind?" Jesus answered, "It was neither that this man sinned, nor his parents; but it was so that the works (glory) of God might be displayed in him." (As in us all.)

Book of Johnin 9:1–3

Of note to all who read the letters of Paulus

Paulus's letters written later in his life (Colossians, Ephesians, and so on) were more mystical than earlier letters and focused on our true identity as one with Christ while we yet live in these earthen vessels, which return to dust. He called our being one with Christ "the great mystery" (letter to Ephesus 5:32).

Thus, we call ourselves Mystics.

This is the essence of our mysticism: aligning to our union with the infinite One who cannot be fathomed by intellect alone. By doing so, we find ourselves in the world but not of it, flowing with peace, power, and above all, a love that holds no record of wrong, the truest evidence of our awakening, without which all other evidence is nothing. Only this kind of love will awaken the world to the glory of Christ made manifest on earth.

AUTHOR'S NOTE

You've just finished the first book in the two-book saga Beyond the Circle. Two worlds hang in the balance of the final two seals. Rachelle will surely go from the frying pan into the fire, Vlad is only just beginning, and Thomas Hunter's world will be turned inside out. There is no defense against the Fifth Seal, but getting to it will cost everything.

We are all on the same journey of discovering ourselves in this world, just like Rachelle. It's the journey from fear to love, from darkness to light, from blindness to sight.

If the journey draws you in any way, please visit The49thMystic.com. There you will find much more: additional content, behind-the-scenes interviews, and more of Yeshua's teaching in *The Forgotten Way,* including a daily guide that will assist you in taking the same journey Rachelle is taking to find and

know the truth of who you are in this reality we call the world. Dive deep.

Ted Dekker

ADDITIONAL COPYRIGHT INFORMATION

Unless otherwise indicated, Scripture quotations are from the New American Standard Bible®, copyright © 1960, 1962, 1963, 1968, 1971, 1972, 1973, 1975, 1977, 1995 by The Lockman Foundation. Used by permission. (www.Lockman.org)

Scripture quotations labeled ABPE are from The Original Aramaic New Testament in Plain English — with Psalms & Proverbs. Copyright © 2007; 8th edition Copyright © 2013. All rights reserved. Used by permission.

Scripture quotations labeled BLB are from The Holy Bible, Berean Literal Bible, BLB. Copyright © 2016 by Bible Hub. Used by permission. All rights reserved worldwide.

Scripture quotations labeled ESV are from The Holy Bible, English Standard Version®

ABOUT THE AUTHOR

Ted Dekker is the award-winning and *New York Times* bestselling author of more than forty novels, with over ten million copies sold worldwide. Born in the jungles of Indonesia to missionary parents, he lived among cannibals. His upbringing as a stranger in a fascinating and sometimes frightening culture fueled his imagination, and it was during the lonely times as a child that he became a storyteller.

Dekker's passion is simple — to explore truth through mind-bending stories that invite readers to see the world through a different lens. His fiction has been honored with numerous awards, including two Christy Awards, two Inspy Awards, an RT Reviewers' Choice Award, and an ECPA Gold Medallion. In 2013, NPR readers nationwide put him in the Top 50 Thriller Authors of All Time.

Dekker lives in Nashville, Tennessee, with

his wife, Lee Ann, and their four children, Rachelle, JT, Kara, and Chelise.